A TORCH IN HIS HEART

Also by Anna Belfrage

The Graham Saga
A Rip in the Veil
Like Chaff in the Wind
The Prodigal Son
A Newfound Land
Serpents in the Garden
Revenge and Retribution
Whither Thou Goest
To Catch a Falling Star
There is Always a Tomorrow

The King's Greatest Enemy
In the Shadow of the Storm
Days of Sun and Glory
Under the Approaching Dark
The Cold Light of Dawn

Praise for *The Graham Saga*

"A brilliantly enjoyable read"
HNS Reviews

"This is a series that will take both your heart and your head to places both light and dark, disheartening and uplifting, fantastic and frightening, but all utterly unforgettable"
WTF are you reading

"Anna writes deep, emotional historical novels, adding the fantastical element of the time slip and a "what if?" scenario, and creates for us a world in which to be lost in on rainy days and weekend reading fests."
Oh for the Hook of a Book

"It seems Belfrage cannot put a foot wrong. Long may she continue to give us installments in this truly wonderful series."
Kincavel's Korner

"An admirably ambitious series"
The Bookseller

Further to excellent reviews, The Graham Saga has been awarded multiple B.R.A.G. Medallions, won a bronze and a silver medallion in the annual Reader's Favorite Awards, has five HNS Editor's Choice, has been shortlisted for the HNS Indie Book of the Year in 2014, and the sixth book in the series won the HNS Indie Book of the Year in 2015.

Praise for *The King's Greatest Enemy*

"The writing itself is a huge success from every angle – great and memorable characters, marvellous descriptions, lively dialogue, a complex and intriguing plot, and large-scale conflict."
Readers' Favorite

"There is something rather wonderful about this exciting historical series which, with every successive story, grows in depth and complexity, and which offers a fascinating glimpse into life at one of the most controversial royal courts."
Jaffareadstoo

"Anna Belfrage is a born storyteller, and she obviously has done exceptional research, adding to the credibility of the facts (...) this is commendable, highly recommended historical fiction."
Historical Novel Society

"You need this book. You won't regret it. If you're an historical fiction lover, you will fall into this book like no other. If you're not an historical fiction lover? You're about to be."
Pursuing Stacie

Further to lovely reviews, The King's Greatest Enemy has been awarded four B.R.A.G. Medallions, an IPPY award, been nominated as a Reader's Favourite Finalist and Runner Up in Historical Fiction. Two of the books have also been named HNS Editor's Choice.

ANNA BELFRAGE

A TORCH IN HIS HEART

Matador
9 Priory Business Park,
Wistow Road, Kibworth Beauchamp,
Leicestershire. LE8 0RX
Tel: 0116 279 2299
Email: books@troubador.co.uk
Web: www.troubador.co.uk/matador
Twitter: @matadorbooks

ISBN 978 1789015 737

British Library Cataloguing in Publication Data.
A catalogue record for this book is available from the British Library.

Typeset in 11pt Bembo by Troubador Publishing Ltd, Leicester, UK

Matador is an imprint of Troubador Publishing Ltd

For my Heathcliff, my very own eternal torchbearer.

Chapter 1

His eyes snapped open. She was here! Jason Morris lay without breathing, without moving, his heart racing in his chest. Yes. She was here, he was sure of it. He took a deep breath, a ragged sound that tore through the silent darkness of the large bedroom. Finally, after all these years, he had found her.

He closed his eyes, and in his head a myriad of memory fragments danced, slivers of long ago days and events, small bursting images—all of them of her. Her hair; a heavy braid that fell down her back to graze the upper slopes of her buttocks, her eyes like the Bosporus under a setting sun.

He sat up, hunted about for his mobile phone. Three a.m., and the darkness of the night was no longer absolute. He lay back down, submerged himself in more memories. Juniper; she always smelled of juniper...and rosemary and sun-warmed mint. And when he'd undressed her, the linen of her shift had been coarse under his fingers. He recalled the brooch that decorated her long linen tunic and the necklace she always wore, a gift from him.

He licked his lips, thinking that he wasn't sure, not anymore, if the images he conserved in his head had anything at all to do with the reality of her, his lost woman. So many centuries ago, so many lives in between—of course she would be different from the laughing girl he remembered. He raised his hand and splayed his fingers, smiling as the ghost girl in his head braided her fingers with his. She was here, somewhere close. His woman, his love...Well, he couldn't go back to sleep now so he rolled out of bed, making his way to the bathroom without switching on the light.

Jason drank from the tap, splashed his face and dragged his wet hands through his hair. On purpose he'd let it grow out to fall almost to his shoulders, a weak attempt to recreate himself as he was then all those years ago. He wondered if

1

she'd recognise him, if when he called her name she'd know immediately who he was. He wiped at his face. Maybe she would remember all of it and stare at him before turning on her toes to flee. He hoped not.

"Helle," he said to the night, "my Helle."

And in a bed, in a room several streets away, a young woman twisted in her sleep.

* * *

Helle Madsen was nervous. An unfamiliar sensation, she admitted to herself as she rode the elevator—oops, the *lift*—up to the tenth-floor offices of Woolf & Partners. She tightened her hold on her laptop bag and tried out various smiles in the mirror, trying to find one that would make her look cool and relaxed rather than uptight. Not much luck there…

With a deep breath, she pushed the glass door open and headed towards the receptionist, a young woman with the most amazing hairdo, a welter of blonde and reddish curls piled on top of her head and held in place by what looked like lacquered chopsticks—were lacquered chopsticks.

"Hi," Helle said. "Helle Madsen to see Mr Sam Woolf."

"Helen?" The receptionist frowned at her screen.

"No, Helle—like Helen but without the 'n'."

The receptionist gave her a nice, if uninterested, smile and invited her to sit, assuring her Mr Woolf would see her shortly.

Helle took a seat by the windows, peering down at the traffic below. London. She had to pinch herself not to break out in a goofy grin. She was in London, and if she played her cards right, she might even be invited to stay beyond the six-month secondment. A woman tapped by on high heels, and Helle glanced her way, taking in her strict business attire before studying her black pants. Maybe she should have worn a skirt. Yes, she should probably have worn a skirt, she corrected herself, as two more women came marching by, legs encased in shimmering pantyhose. Shit.

"Miss Madsen?" The soft voice came from somewhere to her right, and Helle lurched to her feet. A suave blonde gave her a slight smile before indicating Helle should follow her. They walked down a long corridor, turned to the left, where the blonde ushered Helle into a huge corner office.

"Your visitor, Mr Woolf," she said before retiring, closing the door in her wake. Helle remained where she was, uncertain what to do as long as the man kept his back to her. He was standing at the other side of the desk, staring out through the floor-to-ceiling windows. In dark pants, with a white tailored shirt that clung to impressively broad shoulders, the man before her radiated power, in everything from his casual stance to the way he was talking to whoever was on the opposite end of the telephone line.

"No," he said calmly. "You'll do it my way or pay the consequences. Surely you know that by now, Simon." He was watching her blurred reflection in the window and Helle shifted on her feet, considering whether to leave and allow him his privacy. She took a couple of steps towards the door, but he raised his hand. He flicked it and pointed his index finger to a chair. She sat down, he gave her a thumbs up. "Tomorrow. Ten sharp. And don't fail me this time. If you do…" The threat in his dark voice made Helle shiver and feel quite sorry for this unknown Simon.

Mr Woolf finished his call and didn't even glance at her before picking up a paper from his desk and reading it. Typical intimidating tactic. Helle willed herself to remain still and relaxed.

"Helle," he said. "Now that is a name I haven't heard in a very, very long time." He raised his head and looked at her properly. A shocked exclamation escaped him, blood draining so fast out of his face that Helle worried he was about to faint. And then she wasn't worrying about him anymore, she was worrying about herself, quailing under the look he gave her.

Black, black eyes bored into hers. For a moment, Helle's vision fragmented, and the man standing in front of her was not wearing a shirt and a designer tie, he was in a mantle embroidered with gold, but the look on his face was just as angry, just as dangerous. She was already out of her chair, backing towards the door. *Flee! Run!* Her brain screeched warnings, perspiration broke out along her spine, and Helle bit back on a whimper.

"Damn!" Woolf's voice cut through her panic. "My apologies," he continued, coming towards her, and when Helle dared look at him he was back to looking normal, the intensity in his eyes no longer threatening. "For a moment there, you reminded me of someone I used to know—a long, long time ago." He regarded her avidly, as if waiting for a reaction.

"Oh." A person whose guts he obviously hated. There went her opportunity of extending her secondment, and all because of an unfortunate resemblance to an unknown woman.

"Please," he gestured towards the chair. "Sit down." Once she'd complied, he sat down as well—a bit too close. He gave her a brilliant smile, and Helle could almost convince herself she'd imagined the menace oozing from him some moments earlier. Almost. She gave him a guarded look and gripped her laptop bag. If he tried anything, she could always use it to defend herself with. Or run. She was a very, very fast runner.

Sam Woolf was studying her in silence, cataloguing every inch of her. It made her itch, somehow, and she had to ignore the urge to button up her suit jacket as his eyes drifted over her breasts. She decided to give as good as she got, taking in his thick, black hair, the long legs, the hands lying open and relaxed on his lap. She allowed her eyes to linger on his broad chest and on his sculpted mouth. Finally, she met his eyes. His mouth quirked into a smile, but his eyes were as flat and cold as obsidian.

"I beg your pardon," he said. "I was staring too openly, but it is a rare thing indeed to have an attractive number-cruncher in my office."

Helle's skin heated. Jerk. She should get up and leave—*yes, yes*, her subconscious agreed—but she wanted this job, and she knew for a fact that she was good at it, attractive or not. To her relief, Woolf reverted to being a pure professional and over the coming hour he walked her through her résumé, asking a number of detailed questions about everything from deal-structures to the finer aspects of merge accounting.

4

By noon, Helle had a desk, a phone and a laptop—she wasn't allowed to use her own to access the company's various files and data-rooms. Come evening, she had been assigned to three different teams, and her calendar was full for the coming month. Throughout the day, there'd been moments when she'd felt Sam Woolf's eyes resting on her, but whenever she'd turned, he'd averted his gaze. What was the matter with him? And why did the weight of his eyes make her entire body scream in warning?

"Sam Woolf?" Alison gurgled with laughter. "And you're feeling intimidated by him? Welcome to the club, honey." Helle gave Alison an irritated look. Her best friend and flatmate had been in London all of three months more than Helle, so she didn't need to sound as if she knew everything, did she? "We frequent the same clubs," Alison explained with a shrug. "He's hot—very hot, in fact."

"He is?" Helle tried to assess her new boss objectively. No, she couldn't quite define him as hot—predatory, yes, and handsome, with those very dark eyes and the matching dark hair. From what she'd seen of him, he was in good shape despite being at least ten years older than she was, and she supposed it helped that he was loaded—according to her mother, Woolf had enough money to buy a Central American state should he want to, although Mum was hard put to come up with a reason why anyone would want to do that.

"I think so," Alison said. "But then I like dark and dangerous, while you prefer milksops."

"I do not!" Helle threw a cushion at her.

Alison held up one finger. "Will." She held up the second finger. "Carlos."

"He was dark."

"And about as dangerous as a tame slug."

"Alison!"

"I'm just telling the truth." Alison ducked to avoid the next cushion. "Admit it, your guys have been…uhh… unexciting."

"To you perhaps."

"And to you." Alison's voice gentled. "You've never really been in love, have you?"

Helle rolled her eyes. Alison's psychologist training meant she could be a pain in the butt at times. Unfortunately, she was right.

"I guess not." Not like Alison, who went through romances like other people went through sheets.

Alison moved closer. "They're not all jerks."

"But Dad was." Helle picked at the tassels of the closest cushion. "He broke Mum's heart."

"I don't think Ben meant to. He just fell in love with someone else."

"Yeah: with Barbie." Helle frowned, recalling far too many months in which her mother's weeping woke her at night, just because her dad had followed his dick to pretty, busty Janine. She cleared her throat. "Anyway, you want Sam Woolf, you can have him—I'm going nowhere near him."

Alison's responding laugh rang false. "I don't think things work like that with him. In Sam Woolf's world, he does the choosing, and I don't think I'm his type." Petite, curvy and with a mane of dark hair that contrasted nicely with her green eyes, Alison was a veritable guy magnet—but with a tendency to fall hard for those who did not drool at her feet.

As luck would have it, Helle arrived at the same time as Mr Woolf the next morning. He motioned for her to enter the lift first. His arm brushed hers. Her nape prickled. She pretended concentration on her phone but was acutely aware he was watching her intently. Maybe he was thinking of the woman Helle resembled, but whatever the case, it unnerved her, even more when he didn't stand aside to let her out, forcing her to squeeze by him.

"Helle?" His voice called her back. She turned. "I hope you'll like it here," he said. "And don't mind me. I can be moody at times." Helle gave him a tentative smile and hurried off, shoulders relaxing. They'd got off to a bad start, that was all, and Helle wondered vaguely what her unknown double could possibly have done to Sam Woolf to leave him with a permanent aversion for women with short blonde curls. She shrugged: none of her business, was it?

From what she gathered over the coming hours, Sam Woolf was a respected boss—liked, even, and especially by the female staff who all seemed to think the sun shone out of his well-defined ass. A nice ass, Helle concluded after a discreet look in that direction, no matter how intimidating the man was.

Over the following days, she participated in a couple of meetings with Woolf. He was unfailingly polite and impressively knowledgeable, that dazzling smile of his lighting up the room. But rarely did the smile touch his eyes, and far too often Helle caught him staring at her, an assessing, dark expression flitting over his face. Despite all this, by Friday, Helle could almost laugh at her reactions on Monday. It was as simple as Sam Woolf having had a bad day when they met—of course it was.

The next few weeks passed in a buzz. Woolf & Partners was a highly rated acquisitions broker and at present the company was running several projects, two of which were divestments. Helle's desk overflowed with drafted contracts, with complex Excel sheets and PowerPoint presentations.

Other than Sam Woolf, the day-to-day was managed by his junior partner, a round and cheerful person named Percy Wilkinson who had a preference for pinstripe suits and very colourful ties. Behind his jovial exterior, Percy had the mentality of a shark and razor-sharp analytical skills, repeatedly calling Helle out on her conclusions. Had he not been as quick to praise as he was to criticize, he'd have been a major pain in the butt, but as it was Helle enjoyed working with him.

The days flew by, and quite often Helle would stay well into the evenings. Sometimes, she was the last person there — bar Sam Woolf, who seemed to live in his corner office.

"More tea?" he asked one evening, making Helle jump. She nodded, pouring water from the kettle over the teabag. "How quaint. An American with English habits."

"Blame my Mum," Helle replied. "She's as English as they come." Which was why Miriam Cohen had always insisted

Helle call her Mum and not Mom, turning a persistent deaf ear otherwise.

"Ah. That explains why you're such a nice mid-Atlantic blend."

Was he coming on to her? Helle pretended great interest in her tea, even more so when he sauntered over to stand beside her. Too close. She could smell his cologne, a distinctive blend of sandalwood and spices, could hear the rustle of the fabric of his pants, but most of all she could feel his eyes on her. Her heartbeat picked up.

"Look at me," he commanded. Helle met those blazing black eyes that had so frightened her on her first day. "I don't like it when my staff ignores me."

"I wasn't ignoring you. I was making tea," she retorted, leaning away from him. His eyes. She couldn't get away from them. They seemed to be drilling into her brain, and she was no longer in the narrow kitchenette of Woolf & Partners, she was somewhere else entirely. There was grit in her mouth, she was bleeding from her nose, and the man looming over her was hurting her. Woolf. Not Sam Woolf, of course, not him. But it *was* Woolf, eyes narrowed in anger, hair long and curly.

The teacup shattered on the marble floor, the sound recalling Helle to the present. Woolf was still looking at her, but now with an amused expression, his full mouth curling into a satisfied smile. Bastard! What was his game? Helle crouched to pick up the pieces of china. For what seemed an eternity, he remained where he was, looking down at her. Then abruptly he left.

"He did what?" Mum's voice was sharp with anger.

"Well, that's the point, isn't it? He didn't actually do anything. He just told me to look at him, and when I did..." She couldn't quite describe the resulting sensation of vertigo, of being sucked into a dark vortex. And all those images... Helle squeezed her eyes shut in a feeble attempt to block out black, black eyes and a face contorted with anger.

"But he frightened you," Mum said drily.

"Yeah." Helle gnawed at her lip. "I'm just being silly, right?"

"I don't know, darling." Her mother sounded hesitant. "Your gut rarely lies."

"It's just six months." Helle traced a six on the table, gripping her phone harder. "It will look great on my résumé."

Miriam chuckled. "Now where do you get that ambitious streak from, huh?"

Helle rolled her eyes. "You."

"Ha!" Mum laughed again, and for the next few minutes regaled Helle with a detailed description of her recent trip to Asia.

"You be careful," her mother said, just as they were about to hang up. "And if that man continues to pull stunts like that, walk out. No CV is worth being humiliated."

Helle promised Mum that she would. But she promised herself she was going to stay the distance. She hadn't come all this way to be run off like a frightened dog by a man with eyes the colour of pitch.

Late next afternoon, Woolf found her in one of the conference rooms.

"I just want to apologise for yesterday." He frowned. "Not that I know what for, but I seemed to have frightened you." Helle chose not to meet his gaze. Instead, she said something about not being quite sure what had happened.

"Ah." He leaned back against the wall and shoved his hands into his pockets—hands that fisted and unclenched, causing the fine wool of his pants to shift with his movement. "So what do you think of Thrimble?"

"Thrimble?"

"The company you're currently analysing," he explained, sounding annoyed. With relief, Helle plunged into a detailed discussion regarding the over-leveraged company and its potential valuation.

It was well past seven by the time Woolf decided they were done. Helle sat back and pressed her hand to her forehead. A headache was building just behind her left eye.

"Tired?" Sam sounded anything but. He came round to her side and sat down on the table, close enough that his leg brushed her hand. Helle scooted backwards

"A little."

"I can help." Without asking permission, he cupped her face, tilting it upwards so that her eyes met his. His hands clamped the sides of her head. If she moved, she was sure she'd snap her neck. Slowly, his thumbs massaged her temples. A loud whooshing filled her head. *Dangerous*, her brain shrieked, *very, very dangerous*. Helle was trapped by his eyes, pools of darkness that filled her vision, while in her head his voice resonated, deep and silky as it repeated her name, wound itself around the pain.

When he let her go, the headache was gone. She shuddered, slightly nauseous. And not a little scared. "What was that?"

"That? Oh, that's an old healing technique my grandmother taught me." He smiled. "Dinner?"

"Now?"

"Absolutely now." He stood, his muscled thighs outlined against the cloth of his pants.

"I'm not sure—"

"Now." He took her by the arm, helped her to her feet, and steered her to the door.

She hadn't expected something as rustic as this, but the food at the little Greek restaurant just off Lancaster Gate more than made up for its dilapidated exterior.

Woolf knew everyone and at some point he even seemed to be talking Greek, but when she asked he laughed and said that it was Turkish. "A very antiquated form of Turkish. You see, quite a few Greek people have Turkish roots," he said, and went on to regale her with an abbreviated history of Greek and Turkish interaction just as the Ottoman Empire was crumbling into non-existence. "And are you one of those Turkish Greeks?" she asked, fascinated by his story.

"Me?" Something dark fluttered over his face. "Oh no, not me. I am of ancient Turkish blood. Very ancient." He gave her a long look. "So ancient, in fact, that to me the Greeks are nothing but greedy colonists who came to steal our land." Sam leaned forward. "Like three thousand years ago." He watched her intently, as if expecting some sort of reaction.

"Your family must be good at holding grudges," she said

weakly. Sam Woolf sat back, picked up his wine glass and regarded her over the rim.

"Oh yes," he said softly. Helle shivered and returned her attention to her food.

There was no repeat of the dinner. Helle was mostly relieved but somewhat insulted—as if Woolf had taken it upon himself to take her out for a dry run and decided she wasn't worth it. But there were still moments when she'd catch him watching her, those dark eyes of his narrowed into an inscrutable expression. Sometimes he would enter the room she was working in, and the moment he did, her skin prickled. Very unsettling, so all in all, Helle was more than happy when her workload doubled, burying her in numbers and spreadsheets.

The Thrimble deal went through, Woolf whizzed in and out of the office concluding one deal after the other. September somehow became October before he returned from his latest trip with a satisfied expression and several new projects to work with. Most of these new projects ended up on Helle's desk and she could feel the daggered looks some of the other consultants threw her as yet again Sam Woolf called her into his office to discuss a new divestment project.

"Lunch?" he suggested one day, his tone indicating it was not an offer but an order.

"I don't know," Helle hedged. "I have so much to do, and—"

"Lunch." He took hold of her elbow and steered her towards the exit. "You have to eat." Every woman they passed scowled at Helle. She scowled back.

Over the coming week, he took her out to lunch every day, long meals in which he mostly spoke about work, now and then about her and never about himself. His fingers would, as if by chance, brush her arm. At times, he'd sit beside her rather than opposite her and every time he did, Helle had to make an effort not to shrink away, her heart rate picking up when he casually draped his arm along the backrest. It seemed to amuse him, this instinctive recoil.

Helle had never felt so confused in her life: Sam Woolf was good-looking, intense and knowledgeable about everything from the demise of Troy to the present situation in the Middle East. He was good company, polite and interested, so why did every instinct tell her to flee when he sat too close, what was it that made her scalp tingle whenever his hand brushed hers?

"Love?" Alison suggested when Helle shared this with her.

"Love?" Helle just raised her brows. No way. This was a constant disquiet, an uncomfortable prickling along her spine whenever he was close.

"Lust, then," Alison amended. She cocked her head. "He is hot, Helle. Even you must give him that."

Objectively, Alison was right. From how the muscles in his arms and torso shifted under the cotton of his shirt as he stretched across the table for a pen to the way he moved, with the grace of a huge cat, Woolf was very much an alpha male, and the girls in the office drooled. Unfortunately, he ignored them, instead scrutinising Helle as if she were a fly and he a hungry gecko.

Lunches, private meetings, long evenings sitting side by side as they worked through yet another of their projects—all this proximity kept Helle's pulse at a constant high. No matter that his behaviour was unfailingly correct, she always emerged with the sensation that he was studying her, as avidly as a lepidopterist might study a rare butterfly, as if she were an object to acquire for his collection. It made her shiver.

"Doing anything this weekend?" he asked one Friday afternoon, sitting back in his chair.

"Umm…" Helle shrugged. "Alison and I are going out."

"Alison?" He sat forward.

"My flatmate." Helle brushed an annoying curl off her face. "My best friend."

"Ah." He tapped at his mouth with his fountain-pen. "So, no boys in your life?"

"Boys?" Helle tried to avoid his gaze. "I am too old for boys, Mr Woolf."

"Yes, I suppose you are," he said, and his eyes heated, burning into hers. "But are you old enough to take on a man?"

Helle had no idea what to reply—or how to break eye contact, as frozen as a doe in the glare of headlights. Woolf sucked on his pen, not saying anything, and yet his voice slithered through her brain, low and silky, as it described the things he would do to her. Things she would want him to do, the voice told her, things she would beg him to do, trapped in the borderland between pleasure and pain. Pain? Helle shuddered.

"Are you all right?" Woolf's beautiful mouth curled into an amused smile.

Helle rose, amazed that her knees didn't fold. "I must go."

"By all means." He stood up as well and accompanied her to the door. "Have a nice weekend, Helle," he said, standing so that his breath tickled her cheek.

"You too," she managed to say, before escaping his presence.

Helle sagged against the wall, trying to regain some composure. She should look for another job. Like now, she thought, but an hour or so later she was engrossed in yet another company's business profile, turning it inside out as she analysed its numbers. Besides, Woolf & Partners was the shit, as they said, and working here would help her land another job in London—assuming she stuck it out for four more months.

He knew the big man facing them was a king—his mother had told him so, going on to say he was descended from Helios himself—but Jason was disappointed, having expected someone swathed in the finest of fabrics and with an imposing head-dress, not this huge bear of a man whose blue eyes crinkled at the corners at the sight of Jason's mother.

"Nefirie!" The large man moved forward, arms open as if to embrace his mother. Jason's lips twitched into a smile when Nefirie stepped out of reach, pressed the palms of her hands together, and offered the man a stately bow instead. Jason listened with half an ear to the adults, his eyes on the little girl standing to the side. The king's daughter, he guessed, studying her clothes. An embroidered tunic covered a linen garment that fell almost to her sandaled feet. Jason brushed his hand over his own serviceable tunic, an indeterminate

shade of grey. He'd never seen a girl with hair the colour of the sun. It was pulled back into a tight, thick braid, but miniature curls danced around her hairline and escaped from the bright red ribbon that held the plait in place.

She met his eyes and Jason's lungs contracted, leaving him without air. Blue, blue eyes, streaked with green. Huge eyes, fringed by thick lashes. Jason inhaled. As a moth drawn to an uncovered flame, he moved towards her. She was younger than him, her head not quite reaching his shoulder. But when she held out her hand, he took it, her small fingers interlacing with his. And just like that, this unknown girl walked straight into Jason's heart.

Chapter 2

"Hmm?" Jason Morris made an effort and returned his attention to Steve Darrow. His Mergers & Acquisitions manager gave him an irritated look, flipping his overlong hair out of his face.

"You're not listening."

"Yes I was," Jason lied. He'd been miles away, his mind preoccupied with other matters. He bit into a pickle. "You were telling me why we should buy that little utility company."

Steve's cheeks went quite pink with enthusiasm. "It's a great outfit! It—"

"Does high-margin service work, I know. But that's not what I'm interested in."

"It's a bargain, you know it is."

"Not for me."

Steve launched into a monologue about why it made sense to purchase the company and Jason stopped listening. Instead, he took advantage of the opportunity to return to the matter that was constantly gnawing at him. Helle.

For weeks now, he'd felt her presence everywhere. At first, he'd tried to tell himself he was imagining things, but with every day he became more and more convinced that she was here, very close, and he vacillated between utter euphoria and the darkest of fears. What if he found her too late? Last time he'd felt her this close, he'd only seen her as a floating corpse. No, not this time. Fate would not be that cruel, not again. Three goddamn millennia searching for her, and never had he felt her presence as strongly as he did right now.

Steve elbowed him. Jason grunted.

"Sorry." Steve didn't look sorry. "You were miles off again. Are you sick or something? I've never seen you this distracted."

Jason merely smiled. 'Sick' did not quite cover his affliction. But Steve was right, this constant preoccupation with Helle left him unfocussed and irascible. It hadn't helped that he'd

15

quarrelled with Juliet about it when she insisted it was time he stopped this futile, idiotic search for a woman he'd known and loved so many lives ago. As if he could. And Juliet knew, damn it, she was the only person in his life—or should that be lives?—who knew that once he regained the memories of his distant first life, he had had but one objective:find Helle. No effing choice; throughout his endless lives there'd been no choice—ever.

Jason twirled his empty glass around. Not only Juliet knew, he reminded himself. If Helle was anywhere close, chances were Samion was too. Jason's body-hair bristled, a recollection of intense pain making his pulse race. Not this time, he vowed. This time, Samion would not kill him—or Helle.

"Here." Steve set down a fresh half pint. "I think you need it."

"Thanks." He rarely drank during the day, but Steve was right. Jason made an effort and directed his attention to his companion. "Any news on the Turkish company?" Now this was something much more in line with Jason's interests, a small high-tech company that desperately needed an investor to fund the next phase in their development.

"They've confirmed next week." Steve dug out his phone – something of an effort given the tight cut of his trousers. Steve believed in slim fit and in ridiculously expensive tailored shirts. "Somewhere called Kadiköy."

"Eastern Istanbul." Normally, Jason would be over the moon to be heading for Istanbul to visit a potential acquisition. At present, it was an imposition, a drain on time he should be spending looking for her. Her. These last few weeks, every time he saw a woman with golden curls, his heart raced. Every time he saw a female jogger take off at speed, he narrowed his eyes, hoping this would be her, his Helle. No such luck.

They finished their beers in relative silence. Steve was busy with his phone, Jason was yet again lost in memories. He smiled to himself. She'd been a child the first time he saw her, all that wild hair tamed into a neat, thick braid.

They pushed their way out of the pub, now and then stopping to nod at acquaintances—well, Steve did, his background in one of the more well-known Private Equity firms ensuring he knew more or less everyone and their dog. Jason was not much of a networker, preferring to keep the low profile that allowed him to do his thing without garnering too much attention. But he smiled and shook hands, all the while making for the door and the faint patch of October sun outside.

Jason blinked at the sun, taking a moment to savour the light in his face. He could hear Steve, still inside the pub, laughing at something. Jason adjusted his waistcoat and shrugged on his jacket, tugging the cuffs into place. A tall man in a navy suit, one among the many in the City of London, except that he chose to wear his hair longer than most and refused to take off the little diamond ear-stud that adorned one of his ears. After all, a man had to stick out somehow.

He leaned back against the wall, watching the people around him. Pub patrons spilled out on the pavement, little groups of mostly men discussing the markets while sipping at their beer. On the opposite side of the street was a sandwich shop, an Italian place that did excellent business, to judge from the number of people going in and out. One of those people was blonde. One of those people stepped out into the sun holding a paper bag. One of those people was her. Jason's stomach contracted so fast the beer he'd recently drunk came hurtling back up.

"Shit!" He steadied himself against the wall, swallowing repeatedly to rid his mouth of the sour taste of beer and bile. There, on the other side of the street, was Helle. For the first time in eons, she was within touching distance, and it made his vision blur, his breathing catch. His Helle—close enough to hail. She was standing in a patch of light, looking up and down the street as if undecided where to go. Sun gilded her curls, brushed her cheek, and when she turned her head, he caught a glimpse of her profile. The line of her jaw, the elegance of her neck, the contours of her breasts, pressing against the fabric of her shirt—she looked remarkably the same and yet totally different.

He debated whether to run across the street, make himself known to her, but resisted, his stomach lurching. Detachedly, he analysed his trembling hands, the sudden outbreak of cold sweat along his spine. He was scared—shit scared, to be correct. After all these years, he'd finally found her, and now he couldn't quite work up the nerve to go to her. Jason licked his lips, watching her stride down the street. She still moved with that feline grace he remembered—back straight, legs gliding over the ground—and with every step her hips swayed, a gentle shifting from side to side that left him breathless and hot.

Steve appeared beside him. "Ready? We've got that phone conference in fifteen minutes and—"

"You can handle it." Jason cut him off, eyes on Helle's back. "I'll be back as soon as I can." With that he was off, walking as fast as he could to keep her in sight.

"Jason!" Steve called after him. In response, Jason lifted his arm and waved. Not now.

She came to a halt by one of the more modern buildings on Cannon Street. A revolving sign proclaimed this to be the headquarters of Woolf & Partners. He frowned. He'd never had any dealings with that company but recognised the name as one of the more innovative brokers around, with a reputation for being able to dress up any corporate corpse into something resembling a blushing bride. A lucrative business, to judge from their offices.

He returned his attention to her, noting how she slowed her pace as she approached the entrance, as if she was in two minds about entering. She half-turned, and her eyes were just as blue as he remembered them, her brows as dark and elegant. He staggered back, took a couple of breaths in an effort to calm his racing pulse and stepped towards her. Too late; she was almost at the door, that head of bright curls clearly visible among the suits. Very softly, he called her name. She turned on her heel, brows pulled together as she scanned the teeming pavement. Jason squared his shoulders, but before he could call out her name again, she was gone, disappearing into the dark foyer.

He stood staring at the building, willing her to reappear. His Helle, at last, and he was amazed that she should at the same time be so familiar and yet so different—but this Helle was an adult, albeit a young one, while his Helle, well...

"Helle," he whispered. Just saying her name made him break out in a smile. She was here, and all he had to do was work up the courage to walk up to her, hoping she'd recognise him as the man who'd loved her all those years ago. Jason rubbed at his wrists. A gift: yes, he'd give her something to nudge her dormant memories alive, a talisman to keep her safe. Safe? Jason's scalp itched with sudden premonition. If Helle was here, it was but a matter of time before Samion showed. Jason gritted his teeth. This time, he'd keep her safe. Of course he would.

One Tuesday, there was a box on Helle's desk. A little cardboard box, with her name on it.

"Marigold?" Helle held the box up. "What's this?"

"I have no idea," Marigold replied, fiddling with one of her chopsticks. Sometimes, she used one of them to scratch her back, at others to poke around in her ear, and returning it to its position in her hair was always a precarious operation. "It came this morning. Special delivery."

"For me?"

"Seeing as it has your name on it." Marigold went back to her chopstick efforts.

The little package rattled when Helle turned it this way and that, and once she'd managed to saw her way through multiple layers of tape, a necklace fell out.

Helle traced a finger over the braided leather and for some odd reason just touching it made her feel warm all over. She picked it up, and the familiarity of how it felt and smelled made her smile. She remembered... Stop! Helle shook her head to clear it of images of a young boy, half-naked and with windblown hair. A boy who held out his hand, a braided leather necklace dangling from it. A vague memory stirred, a jumbled collection of remembered sensations, of heat and dust, of an endless sea that sparkled a deep blue under the sun, of sandals and linen tunics that chafed along the seams.

"Hallucinations," she muttered to herself. Too much work, too little sleep, and on top of it this new non-sugar diet—no wonder she felt light-headed, which was probably why she was convinced she'd heard someone call her name yesterday.

The necklace consisted of one length of braided leather to go round the neck, another length of leather that hung from it, decorated with one blue marble painted so as to resemble an eye, and three carved wooden images. Even before she'd studied them, Helle knew one was a lion, one was a ram and the third was a boat.

"Argo," she smiled, touching the miniature ship. And the ram was the one that had carried mythological Phrixus and his sister Helle all the way to Kolchis, except that Helle had been so entranced by the mermaids she'd let go and dropped to her death—or subsequent aquatic life—in the Hellespont. That particular myth she'd heard repeatedly when she was a child, her father laughing when he called her his own little wannabe mermaid.

And as to the lion…she squinted as she studied it, fingers running over the beautifully carved feline shape. She stroked the lioness along her back, and the room filled with the scents of resin and pines in Mediterranean heat. Low, whitewashed buildings, goats, women with spindles and looms, and someone calling for her, shouting her name. Helle closed her eyes, suffused with an inexplicable sensation of grief. What was the matter with her?

She considered stuffing the necklace back into its box, but instead she fastened it round her neck. The amulets nestled between her breasts, feeling as if they'd always been there, and for the rest of the morning Helle would now and then pause what she was doing just to touch the carved figures. And every time she did, it was as if someone caressed her cheek, light fingers resting for an instant against her skin.

"You're sure there was no card?" Helle asked Marigold at lunch.

"Huh?" Marigold gave her a vacant look.

"With the box."

"Nope, no card." Marigold tilted her head to the side. "Secret boyfriend?"

"Very secret—so secret even I don't know he exists."
But Helle smiled, cupping her hand over the little figurines.
Whoever had given her this liked her.

The day after, she squeezed herself into one of her new
skirts—a reward for several weeks without chocolate and cake,
combined with longer morning runs—and was rather pleased
at the reaction she caused in the office. When Woolf yelled
for her to come into his office, her heels click-clacked over
the polished floor, and being three inches taller than normal
imbued her with courage as she stepped into his room. He
threw her a glance, half-froze and looked at her again before
giving an approving nod and beckoning her inside.

She had just spread out her Excel sheets on Woolf's desk
for yet another review when he took hold of her chin.

"What's this?" he demanded, nudging at the amulets of her
necklace, visible due to the v-neck of her cashmere jumper.
He retracted his finger as if burnt and uttered a vicious curse.

"A necklace," she replied, attempting to wrest free from his
hold. The little blue marble hummed with heat.

"Where did you get it?"

"A friend gave it to me." Well, she assumed it was a friendly
person. Why else send her a gift?

"Who?" His eyes bored into hers, dark wells that sucked
her in.

"I don't think that is any of your business, Mr Woolf."
Helle yanked herself free.

"Who?" he repeated, leaning over the desk so that his face
was uncomfortably close to hers. "Who?" He slammed his
hand down on the table, making Helle jump. This time, she
listened to the shrieking little voice in her head that told her
to run and bolted out of her chair. Before he could stop her,
she fled the room, half-running to the rest room.

He was waiting for her when she finally came out. Leaning
against the opposite wall, hands in his pockets, he looked calm
and unruffled. Her knees went weak.

"I was out of order." He gestured at her neck. "It's just
that I don't like seeing you wearing rubbish like that." Helle

blinked. Was he jealous? No, possessive, she amended, and cold ripples travelled up and down her spine.

"It's not rubbish to me." She closed her hand protectively over the necklace. "Someone made it for me." And saying it, she knew it was true. Someone had carved these specific little figures for her. Only for her. It made her smile, and she caressed the leather necklace—until she recalled Woolf's presence.

"Fucking Wanderer," he muttered. "I'll give you gold, not some stinky leather." He tilted his head. "Something to mark you as mine."

"Excuse me?" Helle was confused.

"You heard." With a curt nod, he left.

"He thinks you're hot," Alison summarised later that same day. She grimaced at Helle's plate, filled with broccoli and chicken. "Obviously, your diet is paying off."

"I don't want him to think me hot!" Helle speared a piece of broccoli. "I just find him...scary, I guess." She chewed slowly. "He's too intense."

"Men like that don't share," Alison said.

"Men like that aren't my type." Just thinking of him touching her made Helle's skin pucker. Sam Woolf was too domineering, too demanding, too dangerous. For reassurance, she touched her necklace, rubbing her fingers over the little ship.

"I bet he's generous." Alison waggled her brows. "Jewellery, clothes, fancy holidays..."

"Yeah—as long as one does as he says."

"What? You think he's into collars and whips?" Alison chortled. "Seriously?" There was an avid look on her face, her tongue darting out to wet her lips.

Helle frowned at her friend. "I don't think he needs them." No, because Woolf had eyes that left you incoherent and trembling, and hands that could...Helle swallowed and changed the subject by asking Alison if she wanted tea or coffee.

Every day, Woolf would at some point or another look at her neck. At the sight of her necklace, his brows pulled together, but he didn't ask any more questions, nor did he in any way refer to his odd comment outside the rest-room. Now and then, she'd catch him looking at her in a way that had warning bells ringing in her head, but she had no time to analyse any of this, not when Woolf retreated into a frenzied work mode, barking at her that they had an upcoming deadline next Wednesday.

Helle spent the entire weekend attempting to keep up with his demands. According to Alison, this was merely a tactic, ensuring she spent all her waking time with Woolf. If anything, that made Helle cringe inside, and yet again she decided to look for a new job, but when would she find the time to do so?

"You're good at this," Woolf said on the Tuesday evening, having just flipped through her presentation. "I bet you spent your first years as a consultant only doing PowerPoint."

"Doesn't everyone?"

"Not me. I went straight for the deals."

Of course he did, Helle thought snidely, he owned the company. "Was it your father who started the company?" she asked—just to signal she knew he hadn't had to make much of an effort to become a partner.

"My father?" He laughed and got to his feet. "Mr Woolf senior was a cautious man. He never had the vision to create something like this." He gestured at the glass windows, the sleek furniture. "He merely gave me my name." He beckoned her over so that she was standing by the windows, staring down at the street far below, seeing a collection of moving headlights, no more. His arm brushed hers and it sent a jolt through her.

"I like my name," he said.

"Yeah, it suits you," she muttered.

"Excuse me?" He shifted that much closer, and Helle's pulse began to thud. Her amulets buzzed in warning. Suddenly he was standing behind her, one arm on either side of her. She pretended to study the traffic below, trying to ignore the patches of heat blooming all over her torso at his proximity.

"The presentation," she said. "We need to get it done."

He laughed softly but stepped back, and all of her slumped with relief. "I've already prepared the file we'll be sending out."

"You have?" She was confused. She'd done the file.

"Here." He handed her a print-out, sat back to watch her as she read it.

Helle had an excellent memory when it came to numbers. She flipped from page to page.

"These aren't my numbers," she said, throwing the document onto the table.

"No?" Woolf chuckled. "Well, now they are."

Helle shook her head. "They've been tweaked, tampered with."

"Really?" He wagged a finger at her. "Now, that's not something an honest financial analyst would do, is it?"

"I'm telling you, they're not mine! With these sales numbers…" Based on these numbers, the value of the company doubled.

"You were saying?" Woolf asked in a derisive voice.

"You're cooking the books!"

"Me? I think you'll find it's you that's done the cooking. Every single schedule in this presentation comes from your spreadsheets, files only you have touched."

"I would never…" Helle spluttered.

"But you have." He produced a list of computer logs from one of his drawers. "See? And look at these files for the Thrimble deal—all of them prepared by you, all of them, how should we put it, adjusted."

"I…" She stood. His hand came down on her wrist.

"No, no," he said. "You're not going anywhere. Not until you're fully clear as to what applies." He leaned towards her. "Sit. Now," he continued once she'd complied, "let's get some things straight. You work for me. I tell you to jump, you do so."

"I'll resign." She lifted her chin, meeting his eyes. Big, big mistake. His black eyes bored into her, and she quailed under the weight of his stare, overwhelmed with a need to please him, because otherwise…oh yes, a silky voice whispered in her head, otherwise it would hurt. She flinched when his hand began to stroke her arm, fingers drawing patterns across her skin. But she didn't snatch her arm out of reach; the voice in her head simply wouldn't let her.

"You're such an ambitious young woman, aren't you?" he murmured. "So young, and already with quite the impressive track record." His fingers stopped circling. Instead, he encircled her wrist, hard enough to make her take a sharp breath. It made him smile. "You came here planning on icing the cake, but instead…" He sneered. "You resign, and I'll issue a memo explaining we were forced to let you go after having found you tampering with various files. Various. And before you say anything, I have all the evidence I need, plus, if required, there will be a bank account in your name with some rather dubious deposits in it."

"But I haven't…" she began. He increased the pressure of his fingers and she gasped.

"Protest your innocence all you want. No one will believe you, not when I can produce all those files." He released her arm. "Your career will be over before it began—no one wants a financial analyst with the integrity of a street whore."

"Why?" she asked, massaging her burning skin.

"Why? Call it collateral. You're a good number-cruncher, and I'll be able to put you to good use. Besides, I like having you under my thumb." He studied her, a slow insulting look that lingered far too long on her breasts. "In fact, I'm looking forward to having all of you under me."

"In your dreams," she croaked, which only made him laugh.

"Open your laptop," he ordered. She didn't want to, but obeyed anyway, incapable of breaking eye-contact. She couldn't move aside when he sauntered over to sit beside her, his thigh pressing against hers. This close, he dominated her physically, no matter that his eyes were no longer eating into her soul. She was distinctly aware of the coiled power in his arms, of his expensive cologne, of that invasive voice, now far too close to her ear.

"You're going to send an e-mail," he explained. "To the prospective buyers." He flashed her a smile. "With the presentation."

He watched her as a hawk as she typed out names, as she attached the file she found listed under her own documents.

Not her file, because he had her open it, laughing at her obvious distress when all those falsified numbers rolled by.

"Send it."

Her finger shook, but she did as he told her to.

"Good girl." He brushed at her hair. "See? That wasn't hard, was it? Welcome to the world of financial crime." His hand dropped to her thigh, travelled up under her skirt.

"Stop!" She shoved his hand aside.

"Why?" His fingers were back.

"This is sexual harassment," she managed to say, slapping away his inquisitive digits.

"And who will believe you? They've seen you hovering around me, begging for my attention."

"Hovering? You've had me working project after project with you."

"There's not a girl in this office who doesn't know what you're up to." He smirked. "And it helps, of course, that I've let drop the odd comment about how eager you are." His fingers brushed at her breast. "Best get used to it, Ms Madsen. I own you. From now on, I call and you come running."

She shook her head. Never.

"No?" His breath tickled her ear. "Well, it's either doing as I tell you, or ending up in prison." With the grace of a panther he rose and strolled towards the door. "Don't forget to turn off the lights when you leave."

Helle had no idea quite how she made it home. Alison was away on night duty, and it was a relief not to have to confront her, not now, when Woolf had torn her integrity apart. Those files…She gulped. She had no doubt he'd hang her out to dry if she left, but if she stayed…That hand on her thigh, the way his fingers touched where they had no right to touch—he'd take what he wanted if she stayed, and when those black eyes bored into her, she was incapable of defending herself, wanting only to obey. Shit.

Helle sank down to sit on the tile floor of the shower. Scalding water poured over her and she scrubbed and scrubbed, but it didn't help. He'd soiled her—and even worse, she'd let him.

Nefirie bent to dip her hand in the water. She shouldn't have come, she shouldn't have brought him here. And now that he had seen that golden-haired child, her son was trapped. Jason's eyes had fused with Helle's, strands of fate forever twisted together... It made her shiver. It was wrong; it wasn't meant to be, but the Mother seemed to have other plans. She raised her eyes to the evening star, as yet the merest shimmer against the twilight sky. It wouldn't end well and it was all her fault.

"Mother?" Nefirie started at Jason's voice. He sat down by her feet and leaned his head against her legs. They didn't speak, but sat quiet as the summer sky darkened and the stars began to twinkle high above.

"I saw a shooting star last night," Jason said suddenly.

"And what did you wish for?" Nefire smiled, stroking his long, dark red hair.

"I can't tell you that," he teased, "you're not supposed to tell." He picked a pebble from the ground and tossed it out to sea. "Will it matter?"

"What?"

"Will it matter that I'm a Wanderer and not a king?"

"Yes son, I'm afraid it will. Some things aren't meant to be, and royal girls are wedded to their equals, not itinerant healers such as us." And he was meant for other things, for a Wanderer wife and a Wanderer life.

Jason shook his head mulishly and threw another stone into the water. "Helle is mine," he said. "She always will be."

Nefirie didn't reply. She just stroked his cheek and stared out across the sea. He was far too young, she raged, and this was not supposed to be.

Chapter 3

The next morning was hell on earth. Helle considered staying at home and calling in sick, but a terse text demanding her presence at an upcoming meeting killed that option. Besides, hiding at home wouldn't sort out her problem—not that she had any idea how to sort it. So she dressed in her most elegant power suit, hid herself behind a mask of make-up and straightened her spine, chin held high.

By the time she reached the office, she'd made two decisions: never look Woolf in the eyes again and do whatever she had to do to leave with her professional reputation intact.

Woolf was all business. Hours of reviewing numbers and options, of discussing just how to attract the right buyers, had Helle relaxing, submerging herself in work. Woolf barked at Helle, he yelled at Marigold for more coffee, and as the day wore on, he discarded jacket and vest, undid his tie and rolled up the sleeves of his shirt, throwing the elegant gold cufflinks to rattle on the table.

It was well past eight when Woolf decided to call it a day.

"Food?" he asked the room at large.

Percy shook his head. "I have to get home. Ella is teething, and—"

"Yes, yes." Woolf waved his hand at him.

"I—" Helle got to her feet.

"Stay." His command had her sinking back down. "Chinese? Japanese?"

"I want to go home," Helle muttered.

"Japanese it is," Woolf decided, ignoring her comment. "You want some, Winston?"

Their latest hire lit up and nodded eagerly. Helle drew in a relieved breath. Not alone.

It was a stilted meal. Helle shoved the sushi about on her plate. She was too aware of Woolf's eyes, of the smile that played on his lips. He was enjoying this little power game of his, having peppered the day with sly insinuations as to how quickly a budding career could be destroyed. Helle squared her shoulders: all she had to do was get into his computer system and erase the files. Ha! How was she to do that? Helle speared the sushi with her chopstick. She was trapped.

Winston left. Helle made a half-hearted attempt to leave with him, but Woolf just raised a brow and she sat down, her insides knotting. Once Winston was gone, he strolled over to stand in front of her. She ducked her head.

"No," he commanded. "Look at me."

No way. With the speed of a striking cobra he gripped her arm and lifted her to her feet. Once again, she was trapped by his gaze. Yet again, his voice seemed to glide through her brain, laughing mockingly as it presented one image after the other of her, with him. In some of the images she was so young, hair tumbling almost to her waist. Impossible. She'd never had hair that long. Most certainly possible, his voice told her. Very, very possible.

Helle didn't understand, but was brutally recalled to the here and now when he took hold of the necklace and yanked. She fell against his chest. His hand knotted itself in her hair, holding her immobile as he kissed her. Forceful and invasive, it was a kiss that made her want to gag. When he released her mouth, she shoved him, taking him by surprise. He stumbled and cursed, while she fled to the other side of the table.

Woolf's mouth widened into a smile. "You're only postponing the inevitable."

"I'm resigning. Now." She swept her papers together, eyes on anything but him.

"You do that and I'll have you eviscerated." He sounded mildly amused. "The moment you walk out that door, I'll press 'send' on my computer, and come tomorrow you'll be in jail."

"I haven't done anything! I'll—"

"Tut-tut." His fingers danced over the table top. "And who sent out that e-mail yesterday?" His eyes gleamed. "Get used to it, Helle. You belong to me." He stretched languidly. "We can continue this discussion tomorrow." His face hardened. "And if you don't show…" He dragged a finger over his neck for emphasis.

Somehow, she made it through the next day. Woolf was nowhere in sight but had left instructions that Helle was to populate the data room with files related to their latest divestment candidate. The tampered files. Well, she wasn't going to do it. She locked herself into an office and submerged herself in a world of spreadsheets and financial info, reconstructing her original files.

She scurried outside for an early lunch. She'd spent most of the morning jumping at any sound that could potentially mean Woolf was close and had almost keeled over when Winston had knocked on her door. A patch of sunlight, a Starbucks Latte and two Mars bars—just what she needed to calm her frayed nerves, no-sugar diet or not. There had to be a way out. Helle pulled out her phone and considered calling her mother for advice. It almost made her laugh to imagine her enraged mother storming through the office to take on Woolf. She shivered; something told her he wouldn't care less. Deflated, she unwrapped a third Mars bar.

"Mr Woolf was looking for you," Marigold informed her when Helle returned to the office. "Maybe he had hoped for yet another cosy little lunch."

"I'm sure he found someone else to go with," Helle snapped. Marigold looked at her from under her false lashes.

"Oooo, what got into you?" She leaned closer. "We all know what you're doing."

"Doing?" Helle was taken aback by Marigold's bitchy tone.

Marigold snorted. "He is out of your league. And frankly, it's disgusting to watch you constantly making eyes at him."

"Me? I'm not doing anything! It's him—"

"Yes, yes." Marigold waved her hand. "Tell it to someone who cares."

Right; she had to resign. Shit; she couldn't—not until she'd sorted these damned files.

It was past midnight when she was done, her corrected files uploaded into the data room, a copy saved on the cloud. Helle felt vindicated, somehow. Any prospective buyer who did their homework would quickly conclude the original presentation was wrong. Now all she had to do was to find and delete all those other files he supposedly had, and seeing as the office was empty, what better time than now?

It was by mere chance she found the picture. Among all the other Excel documents, the few jpegs stood out, and she'd casually opened one after the other, most of them from some Christmas do. And then there was this one, and Helle didn't quite know what do with it, staring at the poor woman in the foreground, the other two in the background. The woman with her face to the camera was crying. She was naked, covered with bruises, and there was Woolf, and…

Woolf crashed her door open. Helle jerked, closing the file.

"Do you take me for a fool?" Muffled treads on the carpet and he was looming over her, white crisp shirt sufficiently unbuttoned for her to see some of his chest hair. She gulped, scooting backwards. He gripped the armrests of her chair and pulled her towards him. "I told you to upload the files. Not rework them!"

"I'm not a criminal," she retorted, eyes firmly on his nose rather than his eyes.

"You little idiot! Have you any idea how much money I've got riding on this deal?" He had hold of her shoulders and shook her.

"Let me go!" She kicked him. Hard. He released her, sitting down on her desk instead. Too close, in Helle's opinion, his powerful thighs straddling hers.

"You're not leaving until you fix this," he said, now back to his normal calm voice. But his jaw worked, his usually so impeccable hair falling forward in a mess of black curls.

"I can't. I've deleted all the falsified files." She patted herself on her back for that foresight.

Woolf's brows rose. "How fortunate I have backups." He closed his thighs round hers, pinning her to the chair, and leaned forward. This close, she couldn't avoid his eyes, and his beautiful mouth twisted into a pleased smile when she sagged in the chair. "Now," he said softly, "be a good girl and do as I say. I wouldn't want to have to punish you."

But he would. Her head filled with broken images of her on her knees, and him... Oh, God! He nodded. "That's just the start," he said, brushing his knuckles gently down her cheek. "But you will come to accept it as your destiny."

She wanted very much to protest, but he had her mesmerised, and when his hands slid down the column of her throat, tightening ever so slightly before continuing down to her blouse, she was incapable of as much as batting an eyelid. The buttons popped open. His fingers traced the lacy edge of her bra.

"Soon," he said in a husky voice. "You and I, Helle. Forever."

Never, she wanted to yell. But couldn't. Instead, she sat paralysed when he produced his phone and snapped a couple of pictures of her.

"Nice." His fingers lingered over the swell of her breasts. "But first, we sort the matter of your disobedience," he said, shifting to the side so that she could access her keyboard. "Go on," he urged, and she had to move even closer to him to reach. She made as if to button her shirt, but his eyes stopped her. Instead, he had her accessing a folder on the network, blocking her view as he typed the password. There were all the files she'd just deleted—plus dozens more.

He remained sitting beside her until she'd uploaded every single one. Afterwards, he adjusted her clothes, patted her cheek and disappeared in the direction of the video conference room. Helle sat stunned. Only when she heard him talk, a loud conversation in Portuguese, did she find the courage to leave.

Jason stopped breathing. "Who's this?" he asked in as casual a tone as he could muster. He knew, of course. Samion, Prince of Kolchis, was for various reasons engraved forever in his memory, but that man had worn his oiled hair long, mantles in the richest of colours swirling as he strode across the courtyard of his sun-drenched palace.

"That?" Nigel Hawkins leaned across the desk. "That's Sam Woolf, President and main shareholder of Woolf & Partners."

Jason's stomach churned. "Shit." Damn! If he'd known Helle was working for Samion, he'd never have gone to Turkey, deal or no deal. Known? He should have checked, protected her. Anger and panic had his pulse racing, fingers tightening on the pen he was holding.

Nigel frowned. "Are you all right? You look as if you've seen a ghost."

"Worse. I've seen him." He wanted to spit at his screen.

"What? You don't like him?"

"I…" Jason broke off. Explaining to his best friend about Woolf, meant explaining to him about a lot of other things. "I know him under a different name, and let's just say the man has a finger in every putrid business pie around," he said, having no idea, but being quite sure all the same. Samion was one of nature's predators, always feathering his own nest at the expense of others.

"Go to the police," Nigel suggested, but his eyes gleamed, his narrow face barely containing his grin.

"Without anything to show?" Jason's fingers flew over his keyboard. "Best take a look first."

"Need my help?"

"You know I do." While Jason was more than adept at finding his way through the virtual world of computer networks, Nigel was by far the better hacker—the best, actually.

"What are we looking for?" Nigel asked.

"I don't know. Something, anything."

Entering Woolf & Partners' general set-up was not an issue. A number of servers, a traditional structure of replicated files, each employee storing their work under a folder in their own name. Jason found Helle's documents. A series of spreadsheets, with a very odd history of deleting and uploading a number of large files. Strange. He browsed the data-rooms—once again, files had been uploaded, deleted and replaced by what seemed as identical files, but weren't, size-wise.

Accessing Woolf's private server was much more of a challenge. With Nigel's help, he finally managed to bypass security, scanning a neat list of folders. Two stuck out. One was named *Helle*, the other was named *Stuff*.

"You need me anymore?" Nigel asked, all of him jangling as he stood. Jason shook his head, throwing his friend but a cursory look. By now, he'd grown accustomed to Nigel walking about with so many bangles and necklaces he jingled as he walked.

Interesting. The *Helle* folder contained several of those Excel files that had been uploaded into the data-room. Jason frowned. Some sort of blackmail? He opened the files. How odd: all of them created within the last week. He dug further. Definitely some sort of blackmail, as whoever had created these and modified them was not the person named as the author. Helle Madsen's name appeared everywhere, but from what Jason could see, the files had originated with her but been worked on by someone else, someone skilled enough to delete almost all traces of himself. Almost.

The folder also contained a number of pictures. Pictures taken on the sly, some of them in the rest-room. Woolf must have installed a camera behind the mirrors, Jason concluded, staring at a sequence of pictures. In the first, Helle was adjusting her stockings, skirt hiked to reveal lacy knickers. The second, she was putting on lipstick. The third, she was braced against the wash-stand, one hand clutching the little amulets Jason had given her. In the next, she was entirely naked, holding on to the sink while Woolf fucked her from behind. Rage clouded Jason's brain, made him curse out loud, until he realised the picture had been shopped, Helle's face on another woman's body.

There was a sequence of such pictures, each one more lurid than the last. Sick bastard, Jason thought. The last pictures to be added were recent, from the day before. Helle, eyes wide with apprehension. Helle, her shirt unbuttoned to reveal a lacy bra. Had it not been for the stunned look on her face, the picture would have been sensual. As it was, all he could see was the panic in Helle's eyes. Jason's closed his hands into tight fists.

He continued digging. Some hours later, he'd discovered Woolf had bought a sizeable share in the company he was presently divesting—very much under the table. Not the first time he'd done that, Jason concluded, frowning at the fine print on his screen. And as to the other things he'd found in the aptly named folder *Stuff*… Clearly, Sam Woolf in this modern reincarnation was no better than in his previous lives—but the documents were circumstantial at best. Unfortunately.

Next morning, Jason took up position outside Woolf & Partners. It was gone nine before Helle appeared. Rounded back, downcast eyes—this was not the woman he'd seen less than a fortnight ago. She dragged her feet, slowing her pace the closer she got to Woolf & Partners. If anything, she reminded him of a prisoner walking the last few yards to the waiting gallows—and God alone knew he'd seen that happen more than once. For some moments she stood perfectly still, studying her toes.

He had to do something—the question was what. The obvious answer was to make himself known to her, but just the thought of doing so had his stomach fluttering, his windpipe shrivelling. He couldn't quite find the courage to face her, to risk seeing her recoil and flee.

"Coward," he muttered, and was just about to take that first step towards her when she squared her shoulders. With a firm grip on the strap of her laptop bag she marched towards the entrance.

"Helle!" he called, but he'd left it too late. She was swallowed into the darkness beyond. Shit. Jason fiddled with one of the buttons on his cashmere overcoat. Well, one thing he could do—had to do. Oh, yes: that file marked *Helle* was about to disappear.

She could swear she'd heard someone call her name. A familiar voice, and Helle wheeled on her toes, trying to locate the person through the tinted glass of the foyer walls. Too many people on the pavement outside, and although she had an impression of a tall man in a dark blue coat staring intently in her direction, he was gone before she could properly see him.

Woolf was nowhere around, so Helle spent the morning trying to access his files. Didn't work. To be honest, she had no idea how to, but the fact that there was a folder named *Helle* in there had her trying everything she could think of, even going as far as googling 'hacking', but coming up with zero useful stuff. Damn!

Think, think, think, she urged herself, but came up with nothing new. Either she resigned and risked Woolf would be vindictive enough to ruin her career, or she stayed and subjected herself to being at his beck and call. No: that was not an option. Helle groaned and threw herself backwards in her chair just as her phone rang.

"Mum?" Helle had to swallow a couple of times to keep her voice steady.

"Darling? Are you all right?" Her mother had the instincts of a bloodhound at times.

"Er…"

"Helle?" Her mother's voice dropped an octave or two, softening into a caress.

"Oh, Mum," Helle said, and she began to cry.

She couldn't tell her everything—she didn't want to tell her. But she could tell her enough to make Mum understand her dilemma, and once she was done she fell silent.

"Shit," Mum said, her voice shaking with rage. She cleared her throat. "Well, you can't stay there."

"But—" Helle said.

"No buts." Her mother was firm. "It's not as if you'll starve, is it?"

"No, generally they feed prison inmates."

Mum snorted. "He's bluffing! He doesn't want that sort of publicity. At most, he can make you *persona non grata* in the Private Equity industry."

"But my job, my career!"

"For God's sake, Helle, who cares? You'll sort that out." She sounded brisk. "If nothing else, I can fix you a job. You'd make a good business controller."

Helle grimaced but made a noncommittal sound. Mum laughed. "I know. A fate worse than death."

"More or less."

"Huh." Her mother snorted. "I have to go, darling. But I'll call tomorrow, to make sure you're safely out of there, okay?"

"I can take care of myself," Helle protested.

"Of course you can." With that and a series of loud kisses, Mum hung up.

Resign—potentially be accused of criminal activities. Stay on—be forced to participate in said activities. Neither of the alternatives sounded all that attractive. Even worse, Woolf had other plans for her, plans that made her stomach tighten. Helle's head ached with all this thinking. One hour, two hours. She sensed Woolf at the door, but didn't turn his way, and before he entered, Percy called for him. Helle tucked her hands under her thighs to stop them from trembling.

Her mail pinged. A new mail from an unknown sender, labelled as '*your friend*'. Well, she could do with a friend right now, so she opened it.

He no longer has the files. Helle had to read that over and over again. *They're all gone. All of them. Get out while you can.* Someone knew! She slumped over her desk. Deleted… She read the message yet again. She stood, took a turn around her desk, sat down, read the message again, stood, and did it all again. She glanced at her watch. Three o'clock.

Get out while you can. Yes, good advice. But there was something she had to do first. Half an hour later, her original files were back in the data-room. Helle stuffed her laptop in her bag, grabbed her coat and made for the door.

She was halfway across the foyer, when she heard Woolf's voice. Ignore it. She kept on walking.

"Helle!" he barked. Moments later, he was beside her. "Who gave you permission to leave?" he hissed, his voice a velvet whip that had her subconscious cringing.

"I did." She avoided direct eye contact. She wanted to tell him she was resigning, but the words swelled in her mouth, impossible to enunciate.

"What?" He laughed. "I don't think so." He blocked her way.

"Step aside, or I'll scream. I mean it," she added, proud of how confident she sounded.

Woolf seemed to grow. His voice invaded her, his scent had her choking. He placed a hand on her arm, fingers sinking into her flesh with such force it made her gasp.

"You will pay for this," he said almost inaudibly. Helle's knees wobbled. Woolf stepped aside. Helle didn't wait for the lift. She ran all the way down the stairs.

Helle wasn't quite sure how to explain things to Alison. Instead, she muttered something about being tired.

"I left early," she finished. "After all, it's Friday."

"So we go partying," Alison suggested, brightening at the thought.

"Umm…" Helle was looking forward to an evening at home, hours in which to decide what to do and how to do it.

"Oh come on," Alison said. She plunked herself down beside Helle. "It's him, isn't it?"

"Him?"

"Sammie the hottie."

Helle shrugged. "I don't like him." Major, major understatement.

Alison gave her a penetrating look. "What has he done to you?"

"Nothing," Helle lied.

"Hmm." Alison sounded unconvinced. "Did he hurt you? Because if he did—"

Helle's stomach cramped. Woolf would eat Alison for lunch. "Just leave it, okay?"

"But—"

"Alison! I don't want to talk about it—at all."

"Okay, okay. Keep your hair on." Alison sounded hurt. Helle pulled up her knees and hugged her legs close.

"He's…dangerous. Too much to handle." She rested her cheek on her knees. Alison looked on the verge of saying something. Helle decided to avert the impending inquisition by asking her what they should wear for their evening out.

"You're right" Alison said later. They were jostling their way up to Covent Garden, surrounded by hordes of people. "You've been working way too much." She gave Helle an appraising look. "And I'm not entirely sure that no sugar diet of yours is doing you any good—you look wasted."

"I needed to lose a couple of pounds." Helle pinched at her waist, making Alison roll her eyes and mutter something about feeling insulted. "And as to work, we've had so much to do with this new project."

Alison slipped her arm through Helle's. "Well, we're going to have fun tonight, right?"

Helle gave her a bright, if false, smile. "Absolutely."

How they ended up at the club, Helle had no idea. It was several hours past midnight, and Alison had consumed so many shots she should have been comatose, but instead her friend was gyrating on the dance floor, accompanied by a good-looking Dutch dude who was doing more ogling than dancing.

Helle ordered some more wine, shook her head in a no when someone asked her to dance and retired to sit to the side. Her shoes were killing her and her skirt kept riding up, revealing the lacy border of her hold-ups.

"Dance?" The voice came from her right.

"No, thanks." Helle didn't even look up. A hand closed round hers, and Helle recognised the ring embossed with a wolf's head, the gold-plated Rolex. She was pulled to her feet.

"Dance," Woolf said, steering her into the mass of moving people.

"I don't want to!" Helle tried to pull free.

"But I do."

He was a good dancer—which he knew. When the music changed, he pulled Helle into his arms. He plastered her to him, crooning along with the music, and anyone watching them would think him totally infatuated with her.

"How?" he asked.

"How what?"

"You hacked my system, deleted my files."

"I did not." No, her unknown white knight had done that.

"But you knew they were gone." He ground his hips against her. "That's why you challenged me today, left without my permission."

"I don't need your permission." She placed her hands on his chest and tried to dislodge him from her.

"That's where you're wrong." He tilted her face up, his eyes met hers, and the room started spinning. Not again. Please not here! He stared down at her, and in the depths of his eyes she saw herself—but another self, an unknown younger self, a girl with long blonde curls, dressed in the sheerest of linen that tumbled in embroidered lengths to her sandaled feet. A girl who was brutally disrobed by the man with black eyes, who was pushed down on her back in an ornate tent, the canvas walls too thin to muffle her sobs of pain. A girl child promised to Prince Samion as his bride, but who gave her heart to another and was punished for it.

Helle blinked, trying to rid herself of these confusing visions. He smiled. She tried to pull back, but he wouldn't let her. Those eyes. They ate into her brain, they commanded her to allow him to do as he pleased. His hand slid under her skirt, and she didn't want him to touch her like that, but his eyes had her immobilised, as incapable of breaking free from him as a hypnotised mouse would be of stopping the serpent from swallowing it.

"Trying to keep your distance from me?" He laughed. "It doesn't work that way. You're mine," Woolf said, and his voice came from a distance, echoing in her head. "This time, you will be mine. Forever." He touched her face, fingers running gently over her cheek. "You were meant for me," he murmured, "but he stole you." His hand slid down her arm, closed on her wrist.

Stole her? Who? Not that she cared, because she could feel his erection pressing into her, and all of her shrivelled at the thought of what he wanted to do to her—she could see it in his eyes—but she had no choice. Once, she had defied him. This time, he would not allow it. This time, he would hurt her. The pressure on her wrist increased. He laughed, and she heard something snapping into place, something cold and hard encircling her wrist. He took her hand and led her off the dance floor. She followed mutely. *Obey*, her brain thudded, *obey, obey, obey*.

Someone crashed into them. Woolf cursed. Helle was suddenly free of his hold. She didn't stop to think. She shoved through the dancers, making for the safety of the rest-room. There, she pushed through the queue and huddled down by the washstands, as far away from the door as possible.

"Helle?" Alison gripped her arms and Helle stumbled to her feet. The rest-room was dark, and she had no idea where she was. She swayed. "You're drunk as a skunk," Alison said, steadying Helle. "What are you doing here? I've been looking all over for you."

"I don't know," Helle mumbled. Her head hurt, and she was so dizzy she almost believed Alison when she repeated that Helle was drunk. Except that she knew she'd not had more than a couple of glasses of wine, and she felt as if she'd drunk an entire vodka bottle on her own.

"What's this?" Alison held up Helle's hand.

Helle couldn't reply, staring at the polished steel bracelet adorned with diamonds that now encircled her right wrist. A manacle, reminding her just who she belonged to.

Chapter 4

All Saturday, she spent in a haze, incapable of more than monosyllabic responses to Alison's concerned questions. If it hadn't been for that drunk dancer…No, don't go there, she tried to tell herself, but that didn't help. Fact was, if Woolf hadn't lost his hold on her, she'd have gone with him, allowed him to do whatever he wanted, and it filled her with shame—and fear—that she should be so weak. Alternatively, he had slipped her something. Yes, that was it: he'd drugged her, although for the life of her, she couldn't see how he could have done it.

Sometime well after midnight on Sunday, she fell asleep. Not the deep, dreamless sleep she craved, no, this was a restless tossing, dreams blooming in her brain of lions and golden days, of bubbling laughter and singing voices. She dreamed of meadows and pine groves, of mountains that tumbled to the sea and of dusty, sun-baked afternoons. She dreamed of black eyes, of a dark voice that rang in her head as her lungs collapsed in pain.

But mostly she dreamed of a golden-eyed man—her man. She felt his lips on her skin and his hands in her hair, and she heard him promise to love her today and all the coming tomorrows.

In the bleached hours just before dawn she kicked off the sweaty tangle of sheets and sat up.

"Jason," she said out loud and saw the fading image of the dream man nod and smile, "you're my Jason." A ghost from a long-lost life…

"You're going nuts," she muttered. Yup, all of this was crazy, but all the same she hugged her pillow and stared at the wall, knowing she would never hold her Jason in her arms again. She didn't know how to bear it, feeling her heart freeze and shatter into thousands of glittering, ice-cold shards.

Come morning, the dreams had receded to be nothing but vague recollections—except for the faded image of a boy with amber eyes that made her smile. Jason, his name was Jason.

It took her forever to work up the nerve to go to the office on the Monday. She was going to give him the resignation and then leave. Easy peasy, and she'd tell him that she never wanted to see him again. Ever. And then she'd demand that he remove the damned bracelet, because no matter her efforts she couldn't get it off. It consisted of various segments, but try as she might, Helle could find no clasp, no opening mechanism. It seemed to her it weighed a ton, branding her his property.

Through the heavy door to the foyer, to the lift, and Helle had to hug herself. Her cuff kept on riding up, displaying the bracelet to the world, and she felt as conspicuous as she walked through the reception as if she'd been naked. His. Helle wanted to throw up. Resign. She drew in a deep breath. He had no hold over her, she reminded herself. But she knew that if he snapped his fingers, she'd jump, so scared was she of displeasing him, of seeing those dark eyes blaze.

The office was half-empty, and when she peeked, she noted that Woolf's office was dark. Helle leaned against the wall and drew in gulps of air. He wasn't here, she wouldn't have to face him.

"Is Mr Woolf out for the day?" she asked Marigold.

"How would I know?" Marigold replied.

"Well, seeing as you're the receptionist," Helle said.

Marigold's eyes drifted down to Helle's wrist and the shiny bracelet. "Nice. He gave you that?"

Helle tugged at her sleeve. "I don't want it," she began, "but—"

"Spare me the details." Marigold sneered. "You must have made him very happy."

"Happy?" Helle's cheeks grew hot.

"He didn't give you that because you're good at PowerPoint, did he?" Marigold sniffed, before turning her back on Helle.

Wow! Branded the office whore by air-headed Marigold. Helle considered defending herself, but decided there was no point—or need, as she wasn't planning on staying. Now that Woolf was out, she could resign to Percy, his second-in-command, instead. Her shoulders dropped from their previously so tense position. Percy she could handle—any day of the week.

She marched into Percy's office.

"Do you have a moment?" she asked.

He held up his hand to indicate she should wait, and continued writing. "Sorry, I just have to get this down." Moments later, he sat back. "So, what can I help you with? Lost sight of Sam, have you?"

She cringed at his tone. "I'm resigning." She shoved the letter across the table. Percy just looked at it before sneering at her.

"What, too much of a coward to tell him to his face? I'm not doing it for you."

"I can't stay!" She pressed her hands to her thighs to stop them from trembling. "I just have to—"

"Blah, blah, blah." Percy exaggerated a yawn. "Do you think you're the first gold digger to come after him?" He snorted. "Let me tell you, there's been a progression of them, young women who offer themselves to him and then collapse like bloody soufflés when they realise he isn't about to marry them—ever."

"I haven't—"

"No? When you first started here, you wore trousers every day. Now look at you, all high heels and tight little skirts." He leaned forward. "Shit, Helle, you bend over and very little is left to the imagination, if you see what I mean."

"I don't bend over."

"Not for me you don't, but for him…" He tapped his nose. "Anyway, if you want to leave, I'm not stopping you, but if you walk out today, leaving us high and dry, I'll make sure every partner of every Private Equity firm—both here and in New York—knows just what a hot little tart you are." He gave her the letter and waved her out of his room.

It felt like the walk of shame. Out of Percy's room, down the passage, across the foyer and all the way to her desk, Helle was aware of eyes and hushed comments, the odd snicker.

"Sod it," she muttered to herself. She couldn't stay. She

couldn't leave! Trapped. The bracelet on her wrist seemed to tighten into an unbearable vice.

"Percy Wilkinson will see us at noon." Steve said. "Are you seriously considering doing business with them?"

He'd rather submerge himself in a vat of battery acid, but Jason managed a nod. "I might be interested in one of the companies they're presently divesting." A lie. This was just a way to get inside Woolf's offices and ascertain Helle was no longer there. Something told him that might not be the case, a constant niggle of unease gnawing on his brain.

"Everything they have for sale is overpriced," Steve said.

Undoubtedly—and after having studied those files he'd found in Woolf's computer, he knew why.

"We're meeting them, no more." Jason shrugged on his jacket. "If nothing else, it gives us a chance to size up the competition."

"Competition?" Steve laughed. "Sorry, Jason, but that's like comparing a gnat to an elephant." He shoved the file he was holding into his briefcase. "They could buy your company with what they have in petty cash."

"How fortunate it is not for sale," Jason retorted. "Get Will into a suit, will you?"

"What? He's coming with us?"

"Why not? Enhances our image, don't you think?" Besides, there was a comfort in numbers when breaching the wolf's den.

"Will?" Steve snorted. "Only if you tell him to shut up. He's a great IT guy but wouldn't know a balance sheet if it bit him."

"Not many do," Jason said, leading the way to the door. "And don't forget the ties." Steve groaned, making Jason smile. His fashion-conscious M&A manager detested wearing the red company ties, suggesting it was time Morris & Son updated their apparel. Not happening, as the patterned red silk had been designed by Jason's mother.

Woolf came just before lunch. Helle heard him, laughing in the reception. This was it. She had to do this—had to leave before she burst apart. And as to her career… She blew out her cheeks. Mum was right. She'd survive, somehow.

Helle packed her rucksack, shrugged on her coat and marched out into the reception, arriving just as a group of men emerged from the lift. Marigold rushed to meet them, three men in suits with matching red ties. Pathetic, Helle thought, grinning despite her mounting panic. Woolf was no longer in the reception, and the thought of entering his office had her pulse accelerating. She stood there, holding her resignation letter, when her gaze fell on one of the visitors. Every single atom of oxygen fled her body.

"Jason?" she croaked, taking a half-step in his direction. Jason? She'd never clapped eyes on him before—well, apart from in her recent dreams. The man named Jason inclined his head. Eyes the colour of amber met hers, and Helle couldn't stop herself from smiling, blinking furiously at the tears that were springing to her eyes.

He raked a hand through his mahogany coloured hair. Helle recognised the mannerism—he always dragged his fingers through his hair when he was stressed about something. But his hair used to be so much longer, and Helle had never seen him in a shirt and tie—hang on! She'd never seen him, full stop. And yet she knew exactly what his mouth would feel like on hers, just as she knew he had a mole the size of a thumbnail just above his right hip, and that the pinkie on his left hand was crooked.

"You! What are you doing here?" Woolf's voice heaved with anger and Helle cringed. His footsteps echoed on the marble floor. Helle kept her eyes on Jason, the small hairs along her nape bristling when Woolf ended up standing right behind her.

"You know why I'm here," Jason said. "I'm here for her." He smiled at Helle.

"You know this man?" Percy barked, appearing from one of the conference rooms.

"Know him?" Helle's fingers went to the little ship adorning her necklace. Argo, Jason's ship. She shared a look with unknown Jason, received the slightest of smiles in return. "Yes, I think I do." Dark brows over those eagle eyes, a straight nose, high cheekbones, a square chin—his face radiated determination.

"I knew you'd show up at some point," Woolf spat. "But this time you're too late, Wanderer."

Wanderer? Helle suppressed an urge to laugh. Whatever this Jason might be, he was definitely not a Traveller. His tailored three-piece suit, the handmade shoes and the bespoke cufflinks spoke of wealth, not of a childhood in a draughty caravan somewhere.

"Too late?" Jason crossed his arms over his chest. "We'll see about that." Where Woolf's voice was dark, Jason's was just as deep, but there was a hoarseness to it that made him sound older than he looked. From under her lashes, Helle studied him, this oh, so familiar unknown man. Around thirty, she'd guess, tallish and well-built, if nowhere close to Woolf's powerful build.

He smiled at her and her heart did somersaults. How she'd missed that glorious smile! Get a grip, she admonished herself, you're hallucinating or something—you don't know this man from Adam. But she did, she most definitely did, from the way his hair grew in a whorl at his nape to the smooth curve of his buttocks. Helle shook her head. These last few days of disrupted sleep and heightened tension were playing havoc with her senses.

Woolf and Jason faced off, two men in suits fighting a deadly duel with their eyes. Those two had history, Helle concluded—plenty of it. After some moments, Woolf snorted.

"You'll have to leave empty-handed this time." He gripped Helle by the arm. "And you're coming with me." Her skin shrank together at his touch, but she stumbled after him, incapable of disobeying him when he was standing so close. Jason met her eyes, and somehow that gave her the energy required to wrench free.

"Don't touch me," she said in a low voice, taking several steps to the side.

"Do as I say," Woolf snarled, and the bracelet tightened round her wrist.

"No." Helle found her voice. "I'm resigning."

"What?" Woolf turned dark eyes her way, the intensity in them making her reel back.

"You heard me. Here." She held out her letter. He refused to take it. The bracelet was like a vice round her arm.

"Are you all right?" Jason sounded concerned, stepping between her and Woolf. He leaned towards her. "Don't look him in the eyes," he whispered. "Ever." Duh. She'd worked that one out on her own, thank you very much.

"Get out!" Woolf shoved at Jason, almost sending him sprawling. Jason righted himself slowly, while Percy blubbered apologies.

"It's not your fault," Jason cut him off. He looked at Helle again. "Coming?"

She nodded, placing her letter on the reception counter.

Woolf blocked her. "Look at me."

Nope. This time, Helle kept her eyes on the floor, on her hands—on anything but him and his mesmerising eyes. Jason opened the door, gesturing for her to come. Helle squeezed past Woolf and ran.

"Helle!" Woolf's voice echoed through the reception. "Stay, damn it. Don't—" She didn't hear the rest, already hurtling down the stairs.

She exited onto the street in a welter of arms and legs, clutching her rucksack as if it were a lifeline. Bending, she braced herself against her knees and took a couple of deep breaths.

"Helle."

She didn't need to raise her head to know who the speaker was. Jason. She licked her lips and straightened up, trying out a shy smile. His companions were walking down the street in the general direction of the river.

"Sorry about taking off like that. I just had to get out."

"Can't blame you. Obnoxious air in there." He was standing just in front of her, still in his immaculate suit, still with those cufflinks that caught the sun. But now she noted the stud in his ear, just visible below the heavy sweep of his hair.

"You used to wear it longer." Helle touched his hair. "It used to be long enough to braid." Now where did that come from? Her hand trembled as she lowered it.

"And you used to braid it, remember?"

No of course she didn't! She'd never met him before, except that she was swamped by an image of him sitting in front of her, and she working her way through his hair. It was hot and dusty, in the distance she could see the dark blue of the sea, and… I'm going crazy, she thought, stumbling to a nearby bench. She just had to sit down before she fainted or something.

"Are you okay?" He sounded concerned, crouching before her. She met his eyes. This close, they were extraordinary, a light brown that glowed golden closest to the pupil, darkening to a bright copper at the edges. Fringed with dark lashes, they smiled at her. Helle extended a hand and placed it on his cheek.

"Jason." Her voice caressed his name. "You're my Jason." He nodded and covered her hand with his own. Just as she'd expected, his touch was very warm.

"Jason," she repeated, and then she swung at him, her eyes filling with angry tears. "What took you so long?" She almost cried with surprising rage. "And where the bloody hell have you been?"

He didn't reply, grabbing first one, then the other wrist and pulling her close enough to wrap his arms tight around her. They overbalanced, him landing on his backside with Helle in his lap.

"Helle," he whispered in her hair and she slipped her arms round this totally unknown man, buried her face against his shoulder and wept. God, how she had missed him!

"I—" she snivelled. "I don't know who you are," she whispered, "and yet I know you, don't I?"

"Yes, you most certainly do. We go a long way back, you and I." When she made as if to rise, he tightened his grip. "No. Let me hold you a little while longer." Helle pressed her cheek against his chest, her lungs filling with his familiar scent, of citrus and sunlit seas, of ripening wheat and olive oil.

Helle scooted across the bench. Nefirie glanced her way and the girl smiled tentatively. Nefirie did not smile back.

"Child," she said in greeting, before going back to her work, the air filling with the sharp scents of rosemary and sage. Nefirie brought the pestle down in long steady strokes, her thoughts elsewhere.

"You were here when Mama left." The child's voice broke the restful silence. Nefirie looked at her before staring through the open door at the courtyard beyond, at present a glare of bright light. Summer noon and the heat was such that only the insane ventured outside, the grove of pine trees on the further side drenching the air with the heavy scent of resin.

Nefirie nodded. "Yes, I was passing by, and Elessa asked me to help."

"You smiled at me," whispered the child. Nefirie didn't reply.

"Where's Jason?" Nefirie asked instead, biting back a smile at the answering scowl.

"He's with his friends, and I'm not allowed, because I'm a girl. That's so unfair, don't you think?" The words came in a rush. "I can't help being a girl, I would much rather be a boy, like Jason." She obviously wanted to say more, but snapped her mouth closed.

Nefirie sighed. She would also have preferred it if this wayward child had been a boy, if nothing else for her son's sake. In time, she thought, the fact that you are a girl will be what keeps him at your side, forever. She studied the girl with a flare of resentment.

"Is it difficult to be a Wanderer?" the child asked.

"It's not a choice, it's a birthright," Nefirie said. "Those of us that are born to it cannot think of having another life. So I don't know if it's more difficult than any other life."

Helle shook her head impatiently. "Not that. You know so much. Isn't it difficult to learn all that?"

"Yes, it is, and yet it isn't. We are born already predisposed to this life. We heal, and we go where we're needed. It's really quite simple, we do what we do best."

The child's eyes looked at her intently. She had Kantor's eyes, the blue irises splintered by bright turquoise flecks.

"Will Jason be a Wanderer when he grows up?" she asked, and Nefirie smiled outright. This was what she really wanted to know.

"Why do you ask?"

Helle squirmed. "I don't think my father will like it if he's a

Wanderer," she said, far more knowing than a nine-year-old girl should be.

"No, he probably won't," Nefirie agreed, feeling a sudden surge of hope. Kantor would wed his daughter elsewhere and her son would be free to go. Heartbroken but safe.

Chapter 5

"You're kidding me!" Alison sat back and stared. "What? You meet a complete stranger and you know his name?" She'd been quiet for most of Helle's recent monologue, making adequate commiserating noises when Helle told her she'd resigned.

Helle settled herself even deeper in the armchair. She liked this little café with its eclectic collection of furniture and its dark interior. "I know," Helle said, looking longingly at Alison's muffin. "Weird, huh?" For the first time in a fortnight, she felt as if she could breathe, bubbles of elation whizzing through her. No more Woolf—ever. And Jason…she hugged herself, trying to suppress the grin that tugged at her mouth.

"Weird? Here, you need it." Alison shoved the muffin in Helle's direction. "There must be some sort of rational explanation."

"Mmm…mmm" Helle said through her full mouth. As of now, the no sugar diet was a thing of the past. "I'm all ears," she said, once she'd swallowed.

"You've met him before, obviously."

"Duh. Except I don't remember ever having done so."

"You knew his name—you must have met him. Or maybe he's super-famous and you've seen him all over billboards or something."

"Yeah, that makes sense. He's super-famous and gorgeous and no one else in the office as much as bats an eyelid."

"Gorgeous?" Alison teased.

"I guess." Tall, nice broad shoulders, long legs, those startling light eyes and that soft lower lip—yes, all in all, Jason Morris was not bad, not bad at all. She was overwhelmed by an image of him laughing as she straddled him, and as far as she could see they were both naked and… Stop it! She grabbed at her tea and drank, scalding her tongue in the process.

"So now what?" Alison asked.

"I'm meeting him," Helle said. "Tomorrow." It made her want to leap about with anticipation. Her and Jason, together again after all these years. All these years? Yet again an image flooded into her, this time of what looked like a whitewashed compound, a collection of small buildings set against a verdant hill. There were hens and goats, it was hot and under a gnarled olive sat an old woman, her arms held out… The image faded as quickly as it had come. "Holy shit."

"What?" Alison leaned forward and took hold of her hand. "Are you okay?"

"I don't know. I keep on seeing these strange pictures in my head." She gave Alison a wobbly smile. "It's probably because I've been sleeping so badly lately."

"You have?"

"I told you, remember? How I've been having these… dreams."

"Nightmares?"

"No, dreams—I think." Helle gnawed at her lip. "Always the same."

"Like you had before?" Alison asked.

"Sort of." Helle threw Alison a cautious look. "But that was ages ago." When they were little kids who spent their time in Alison's backyard building treehouses.

"And still…" Alison shrugged. "It scared your mother, it frightened your dad, and you definitely scared me!" She laughed. "You were sleeping at my place, and suddenly you're running all over the room, screaming that your lions weren't there." She grew serious. "Lions this time as well?"

Helle nodded. "All the time. And then there's this man…" She gave her best friend a bright smile. "Listen to me, any moment I'll whip out the Tarot cards and tell your fortune. It's probably all due to stress—or that stupid diet."

"Told you so: life is too short to abstain from the good stuff." Alison grinned and decided they both needed a slice of Red Velvet cake to round things off.

As they made to leave, Alison took hold of Helle's arm. "I'm coming with you tomorrow."

"No way!" Helle glowered at her.

Alison stared straight back. "I just want to meet him—and make sure he meets me."

"Why?"

"So that he knows you're not alone." Alison frowned. "I don't like this, okay? There's something odd about it."

"Tell me about it," Helle muttered.

He'd not been this nervous in ages. Like for three thousand years, give or take. Jason muffled a laugh, wiped his hands up and down his jeans and went back to scanning the street for her. For Helle. She was here. He'd seen her again, held her again—and she even recognised him, however vaguely. Jason tapped his fingers against the table. Unfortunately, Samion was here too. That scene yesterday could have escalated into something nasty, but all in all, Jason was glad he'd taken the decision to go in after her when he'd seen her arrive at the office, looking as if she hadn't slept all night.

"Accursed," he muttered, "you should be rotting in permanent purgatory." Sam Woolf was a dangerous bastard. Jason knew that from personal experience, and it sufficed for him to touch his hands to recall the cold of the iron manacles, the sweat running down his back as the Wizard Prince of Kolchis rewarded his temerity with pain.

Jason shook his head. This was all in the past, and in the here and now he and Woolf were more evenly matched than they'd been back then. He chewed his lip, considering just how explicitly he should warn Helle about Woolf. He smiled crookedly; a moot point by now. He'd seen how she'd recoiled at his touch, all of her cringing under the weight of his eyes. Jason laughed darkly: it was one thing to be affected by Prince Samion, another entirely to attempt to fight him off. And unless Helle knew what he could do, how effortlessly he could invade your brain, she'd never stand a chance.

His thoughts were interrupted by Helle herself, walking arm in arm with a young woman. If he squinted, he could pretend she was in a linen tunic, a fine woollen mantle covering her shoulders. As it was, the sight of her legs in her tight jeans was more than compensation, and he couldn't quite tear his eyes away from her body, from the swing of her hips and her neat waist.

She was wearing a white shirt under her open jacket. It strained somewhat over her chest, and Jason wondered what it would be like to undo those buttons. Enough. Not now. And why had she brought someone else along?

He pretended to be engrossed in his tablet when they entered the café, and only when she coughed did he raise his face. She gave him a hesitant smile. He rose and took her hand—he just had to. Her eyes met his, the turquoise flecks that bordered the pupil as bright as he remembered them—as were her blonde curls, even if her hair was short, not a heavy braid the colour of ripe corn. Her braid. His throat tightened. Her braid, brutally chopped off and thrown on his bed. Jason made an effort to collect himself. She'll think you're crazy, he warned himself, and belatedly turned to greet Helle's friend. Two narrowed green eyes regarded him.

"So how come you know each other?" this unknown woman asked, eyeing their clasped hands.

"Alison!" Helle hissed.

"Nice to meet you too," Jason replied, giving Alison a wide smile.

"You think?" Alison sat down. "You don't know me yet." She tossed her long, smooth hair over her shoulder and gave him a challenging look. "So how? I've known Helle all her life, and let me tell you she would never have kept someone like you secret from me." She looked him over, waves of suspicion emanating from her.

"Maybe you don't know her as well as you think," Jason said, drawing Helle down to sit beside him.

Alison raised perfect dark brows. "Seriously? A hunk like you? Helle would have talked holes in my ears."

"Thanks a million," Helle said. "And it's not as if we live joined at the hip, do we? You were here while I was working in Chicago."

"But you didn't meet him there, did you?" Alison demanded.

Helle slumped. "No." She glanced at Jason.

"Which neatly brings us back to my first question: how do you know each other?"

Jason cleared his throat. "We go back three thousand years or so," he declaimed, rolling his eyes. "A simple case of reincarnated souls."

"Reincarnated souls?" Alison spluttered. "Don't be an idiot."

"I'm pulling your leg." No he wasn't, but sometimes the truth was so impossible it made for a nice diversion. He racked his brain. "I'm not sure when Helle first noticed me, but I know for a fact I ran into her at a financial do in Frankfurt, and since then I've seen her a couple of times more. Wasn't it in Atlanta last time?" he asked, turning to Helle. Her mouth twitched and under the table she kicked him.

"Atlanta?" She creased her brows. "Oh yes! We were at that boring conference about global mergers."

Alison looked from one to the other. "I'm not buying that."

Jason made a helpless gesture. Beside him, Helle mirrored his expression. Alison scowled. Scowled some more.

"Fine! Have it your way." She stood up. "But you be careful," she said to Helle, "and you," she added, turning to Jason, "you hurt her and I'll come after you." Jason was wise enough not to grin. Moments later, Alison was gone.

"Atlanta?" Helle asked.

Jason studied his hand, still clutching hers. "Never been there in my life." Not this life, at any rate.

"And I've never been to Frankfurt." Eyes the deep blue of the Sea of Marmara met his, making it difficult for him to breathe.

"Horrible liars the both of us." Jason threaded his fingers through hers. He could have sat for hours playing with her hand. The skin was lightly tanned and freckled, the nails too short. "You still bite your nails?" he teased.

"Still?" Her voice shook. "I don't understand."

"You will." He didn't want to explain—not today.

"This is all really weird, isn't it?" she said, tracing a pattern on the table.

"Very." He covered her hand with his. "But we don't need to talk about it yet. We can just decide we did, in fact, meet in Frankfurt."

She smiled. "Or Atlanta."

They sat in silence. She felt no need to talk, all she wanted to do was to sit like this and look at him while holding hands. He had nice hands, strong and long-fingered, the nails neatly cut. A faint scar ringed his right wrist, another his left, and she ran a light finger over them, feeling him tremble at her touch. Manacles. The word popped unbidden into her head—as did a graphic image of a naked and emaciated Jason, hanging from chains.

Helle released his wrists.

"Hey," he said softly. He leaned towards her and that glorious hair fell forward, heavy strands of dark mahogany covering his face. She couldn't help herself. She leaned forward and dug into all that hair, finger-combing it off his face. It felt just as she knew it would, but the smell was different. Discreetly she sniffed, picking up the scent of a branded shampoo rather than the vaguely remembered perfume of chamomile and mint she had expected.

He took hold of her hands again. Eyes the colour of sunlit mists met hers. She studied his mouth, and she couldn't stop herself from wetting her lips. He had a beautiful mouth, the lower lip soft and kissable. He smiled, and her breath caught. Without quite knowing how, she leaned forward, placing her lips over his.

Jason pulled away, looking flushed.

"I'm sorry," she stuttered, feeling every kind of fool. What was she doing, kissing a virtual stranger? She tried to disengage her hands, but he wouldn't let her.

"Don't be sorry. I was just surprised—but pleased." He licked his lip, and everything in Helle's belly tightened. She needed him. Wanted him. Now! A sense of urgency flared through her, her brain telling her time was short, too short to waste. Look at what had happened last time… Last time? With an effort, she waved these disturbing and confusing thoughts aside. She tightened her hold on his hands. A long finger caressed her inner wrist, and Helle pressed her legs together in a vain effort to relieve the sudden ache that bloomed between her thighs.

"How can I be so attracted to you?" Helle gave him a heated look. "I don't know you, and all I can think of is that I need you to hold me, that I want to press my cheek to your chest and hear your heart beat."

"I feel the same." He squeezed her hand. "But I'm not sure we should go there yet."

"No?" She was disappointed.

"Not yet." He raised a hand to her hot cheek. "But soon." Helle leaned into his touch. Those fingers... she knew they would leave trails of fire down her skin, they would ignite her like a bonfire, leave her drained and exultant.

"Who are you?" she groaned. "And who am I?"

"Later." He kissed her fingers. "Later, Helle."

He walked her home, a slow desultory stroll through the autumnal London parks. They sat for some time on a bench in Green Park, took the long way round through Kensington Gardens, and emerged into the eastern part of Notting Hill. Or maybe Bayswater would be more correct, but Alison preferred to say they lived in Notting Hill.

"You live here?" He surveyed the low buildings lining the Queen's Mews, old stable-blocks converted into living accommodations, most of them worth a minor fortune.

"I wish." Helle threw a longing look at the dark red door of one the houses. Whoever lived there was a budding botanist, at least to judge from the display of potted plants that surrounded the door. She led the way, taking a right into Salem Street. A brick house stood right at the corner. "This is it. Alison and I share."

"Oh." He threw her a look. "Pricy part of town."

Helle shrugged. "We can afford it." Well, to be quite precise, Helle could afford it, one of the benefits of having a generous and guilt-ridden father. "And you? Where do you live?"

Jason smiled. "Where I can afford to."

"And where is that?" she asked.

Jason shuffled on his feet. "Kensington. I inherited a house." He grinned. "I'm loaded." No kidding. She could see it in his lightweight cashmere sweater, in the Omega watch on his wrist. His shirt was exclusive cotton. She'd bet her pay-check—except she didn't have one anymore—on his shoes being handmade. "Major difference from last time round," he added in a low voice. Helle pretended she hadn't heard.

They were at her street when Helle's phone rang. She glanced at it and rejected the call with a shaking hand.

"What?" Jason drew her to a halt.

"It's him," she croaked. "Sam Woolf." The steel bracelet began to pulse, and she clutched it.

"He gave you that?" Jason asked, and there was a hint of disapproval in his voice.

"Gave? He just put it on, and now it won't come off." She banged the bracelet at a nearby lamp-post.

"Hey!" Jason grabbed at her arm. "Careful, you'll hurt yourself."

"I hate it!" She yanked at the bracelet. For some reason, Jason looked relieved. He traced the leather band of her necklace.

"And this, do you hate this?"

"No." She brushed at a wayward lock of hair. "But that's because you gave it to me. You did, didn't you?"

"I did. I made it for you." He took her hand and frowned down at the steel cuff. Try as she might, Helle had not been able to find the clasp. Jason set a finger to it. Heat surged through her. He put two fingers on it and closed his eyes, slowly moving his fingers up and down the polished metal.

"Aha," he said, increasing the pressure. With a clunk the bracelet fell open. "A puzzle," he said with a smile. "Takes brains, not violence to open it."

"Thanks a lot." She held the bracelet gingerly. It was still throbbing, a steady drumming that tickled her palm.

He heaved himself out of the water, watching her approach. She was swimming slowly now that the race was lost, and he knew exactly how angry she was at losing yet again. He grinned. She would never best him in the water. Her hands gripped the cliff edge and she straightened up, lifting her upper body out of the water, a mere arm's length from him.

"I hate it when you do that," she grumbled, "I don't need a head start."

He wasn't listening, his eyes drawn to her chest and the softly budding mounds, each crowned with a pink-brown nipple. A wave of desire swept through him, and he instinctively moved away, before his hand reached out to touch. She watched him, confused, following his gaze. He blushed, and turned his head, staring intently out to sea.

"Jason?" She sounded hesitant. "What's the matter?" She put a hand on his back. Jason stood up.

"I don't think we should do this anymore," he said, his voice thick. "I don't think your father would approve."

Chapter 6

The night had been plagued by phone calls. At some point, Helle had switched the damn thing off, but in the chilly light of the November dawn she restarted it, blinking as she counted the number of missed calls. Thirty-two, all of them from Woolf. As many messages, and a number of texts. She listened to the first few, but after the third time of hearing him threaten her with hell's fires if she didn't get herself together and return to him, she deleted the rest.

"You look awful," Alison said in lieu of greeting when Helle stumbled out into the kitchen.

"I feel awful." Helle downed a glass of orange juice and hunted about for the peanut butter. First all those phone calls, and then some hours of vivid dreams, most of them starring Jason and her. Very explicit dreams, and she felt a flush rising up her face as she considered some of the more intimate aspects of them.

"Because of him?"

"Which him?" Helle stuck a spoon of peanut butter in her mouth.

"That's so gross," Alison scolded. "And what sort of breakfast is that anyway?"

"Comfort breakfast." Helle scowled at the rain-spattered windows. "I need a run."

"No one is stopping you." Alison blew on her tea. "Things went bad with Jason?"

"No." Helle wasn't sure she wanted to talk about Jason—not yet.

"So it's Sam Woolf," Alison's voice caressed the name.

"He's been calling all night." Helle decided she needed some more peanut butter.

"He's in love with you," Alison offered.

"In love?" Helle snorted with hollow laughter. "Woolf

61

doesn't do love." She chewed her lip. "He collects possessions."

Alison rolled her eyes. "Sometimes you're so dramatic. You make him sound like some sort of Bluebeard."

"Good likeness," Helle muttered.

"What did he do to you?" Concerned green eyes watched her intently.

"He…" Helle swallowed. Shit. "He ripped my dignity to shreds." Alison's eyes widened. "And no, I do not want to talk about it."

"Did he hurt you?"

"Physically?" Helle shook her head. Alison opened her mouth, but Helle held up her hand. "Don't."

"Okay, fine, I get it." Alison stood. "And anyway, I'm late." She dumped her dishes in the sink. "What are you doing today?"

"I'm seeing Jason."

"Oh? In my opinion, he's the really freaky one."

"Fortunately, in this case your opinion doesn't count." Helle stuck her tongue out to mitigate the reprimand.

"Huh." Alison wagged her finger at her before sweeping from the room.

"Shouldn't you be at work?" Helle asked Jason when he came by just before noon. A long run followed by a hot shower had her feeling much better—and things were further improved by seeing him on her doorstep. Jason was in a three-piece suit, dark blue with a faint pinstripe that picked up the muted pink of his shirt. Pink and white stylised peonies flowered against the dark blue background of his tie, his tousled hair long enough to brush his collar.

"Benefits of owning my own company," he said with a shrug. "Besides, I've been at it since six—phone conference with my Japanese partner."

"Do you dress up like that for a phone conference?"

Jason laughed. "No. But it does impress the ladies—in my office and elsewhere."

"Oh." Something green and toothy snarled in the pit of her stomach. She didn't want him impressing ladies.

"So, you ready?" Jason leaned against the door jamb. "I recall promising you lunch."

Helle grabbed her coat, stuffed her phone and keys into her pockets and skipped down the stairs.

He grinned. "That eager for my company, Miss Madsen?"

"I'm starving," she retorted.

"Ah." He extended his hand, his warm fingers closing round hers. "Well, we can't have that, can we?"

She came to a standstill at the kerb. "That's yours?"

"It is." He opened the passenger door. "Do you like it?"

"I love it." She studied the green Aston Martin DB5. "Where did you find it? This is like what, fifty years old?"

"My father had it. I've just renovated it." He smiled. "And upgraded the engine somewhat."

The car purred like a happy tiger. Helle ran her hand over the leather of her seat, fingered the walnut inlays in the dashboard. "You did all this yourself?"

"Most of it." He glanced at her. "Iranian or Turkish?"

"Whatever."

His lips curved. "McDonald's?"

"I'm not a food snob."

"Well, I am."

It took a long time to drive all the way to the East End, but Jason assured her it would be worth it, taking her by the hand as he led her into a small restaurant that essentially consisted of one long narrow passage with six tables on one side. In a matter of moments, mezes and a basket of warm bread had landed on the table, Jason conversing effortlessly with the owner. Helle frowned. He spoke Turkish too?

"Where did you learn Turkish?"

"In Turkey." He ripped off a piece of bread and dipped it in one of the sauces.

"What, you've lived there?"

"I have." He sounded curt.

"Woolf speaks Turkish too." Helle shoved an olive back and forth across her plate. "Is that where you met?"

"Met?" Jason frowned.

"Well, you must have met before, right? You know each other."

63

Jason sighed, and dragged a hand through his hair. Such magnificent hair was really wasted on a man, shifting from the darkest of reds to something akin to purple. Like the colour of a very good wine—a heavy rioja or a zinfandel. She just had to…Her hand rose of itself to smooth his hair. He froze, eyes the colour of gold locked with hers. He had a dark ring round the iris, increasing the intensity of his gaze.

"Look, Helle, I—" He took hold of her hand.

"This is beyond weird, isn't it?" Helle linked her fingers with his. "And you know much more than I do."

"I do."

She nodded, toyed some more with her food.

"Do you have any memories of me?" he asked softly. Memories? She gave him a quizzical look.

"Not as such. I only see you in my dreams." In response, he tightened his hold on her hand.

"Nothing else?"

"Nothing," she replied, ignoring the sudden picture in her brain of a teenaged Jason grinning at her as he lifted himself out of a deep blue sea. She blinked it away in surprise.

"Well then," he said. "I suppose I will have to tell you myself." He sounded as if he was considering volunteering for a beheading.

"You don't have to." She leaned towards him. "We met in Frankfurt, remember?" Even as she said it, she knew it wouldn't work, but for now she wanted to pretend.

Jason gave her a crooked smile. "I thought it was Atlanta." He brushed at her cheek. "At some point I will have to tell you, but it would be nice if it could wait a while. I'd like us to get to know each other a bit before I share." He grimaced, and Helle couldn't help but wonder what it was about all this that made him look so uneasy.

"Hey, if it's that bad just don't tell me."

"I have to." He managed a smile, picked up her olive with his free hand and popped it into her mouth. "But first of all, we eat."

The lunch took forever, a collection of dishes ranging from finely chopped salads to barbequed miniature skewers of meat and fried vegetables. When he dropped her off back home he leaned towards her and planted a soft kiss on her cheek. It made her tingle all over, so she turned to face him, inviting him to kiss her properly. All he did was kiss her sedately on the mouth, but he looked very pleased as he drove off.

Come Saturday. Alison was doing double shifts at the hospital and Helle was looking forward to a day of loitering about in the apartment before her afternoon date with Jason. She was doing some much needed cleaning with the radio at full volume when someone banged at her door.

"Oops." She turned the volume down. Mrs Simmons downstairs was no fan of loud music.

She opened the door, already apologising. "I'm so sorry, Mrs..." Her voice tailed off. There was Woolf, leaning back against the opposite wall. Helle's windpipe shrunk into something the size of a drinking straw. He looked amused, but Helle could feel the contained rage emanating from him, all the way from his black curls to his polished footwear.

"Aren't you going to invite me in?" he asked, that dark voice of his caressing her ears. Helle shook her head. "Oh, but I think you are, Helle." He was at the door, advancing into her home. Helle retreated, her every nerve shrieking in alarm. Woolf kicked the door closed and leaned back against it. "Alone at last."

He spoke again, but Helle couldn't hear him. The little blue bead was buzzing so loudly it drowned out his voice. Her hand closed on the bottle of cleaning solution. If he came too close, she'd spray him in the face.

Woolf sauntered over to the sofa and sat down, crossing one leg over the other. He adjusted the creases on his dark pants. "Come here."

No way. Helle remained where she was. She glanced at her phone, lying on the kitchen counter. Too far away. Shit. Her legs dipped, sweat broke out along her spine, under her breasts. The bottle slipped in her hands.

He frowned. "I don't like disobedient women. I'll punish you if you don't come here this instant."

"No," Helle managed to say.

Woolf regarded her intently, but Helle had learnt her lesson, making sure she didn't meet his eyes full on. It irked him, she could see, and after some tense minutes he stood. His eyes locked onto her wrist.

"What have you done with the bracelet?"

"I took it off."

"You?" His voice was full of derision. "It was the Wanderer, wasn't it?" He took two long strides in her direction. "I forbid you to see him," he snarled. "How dare he try to poach what's mine—again!" He took a deep breath, closed his eyes. When he opened them again, he looked calmer. "I can give you anything he can, in fact, I can give you more—of everything." He wet his lips. "I can give you what you need, I can keep you safe." His voice was a seductive murmur, weaving a spell round her brain. "You should be with me—that was how things were supposed to be." There was a tinge of regret in his voice, eyes soft and warm. He took yet another step towards her.

"Don't come any closer," she warned, holding up the bottle of cleaning fluid, finger on the spray trigger.

Woolf laughed. "You think that will stop me?" He held up his hands. "I don't mean you any harm—as long as you do as I say."

"Then leave—now."

"I want you back in the office on Monday."

"I've resigned." She was never going back. The moment she stepped into his territory, she'd be lost.

"And I'm telling you I want you back there anyway." He looked irritated. "You're our best analyst, and your quitting like that leaves us high and dry."

"That's what you get when you coerce people into doing stuff they don't want to do." She breathed in. "And harass them sexually."

"What?" His eyes smouldered. "When were you sexually harassed?"

"You know when." She licked her lips.

His brows rose, that beautiful mouth of his curving into a smile. "Some mild flirting, Ms Madsen. And I can't recall you saying no the other night when I undid your shirt."

She didn't reply.

He laughed. "Oh yes, that's right: you never did, did you?" He took a step towards her. "You can never say no to me, Helle. We both know you're mine, don't we?"

Helle shook her head. She lifted the bottle, her arms trembling wildly. He came to a halt.

"Put it down before I lose my temper," he said, and Helle's knees wobbled at the threat in his voice. Woolf reached for the bottle. His fingers were almost touching it, a small smile lurking at the corner of his mouth, when Helle somehow found the strength to squirt. He howled when the liquid hit his neck and face.

"Get out!" Helle yelled—no, shrieked. She found the courage to push him. He swore, swinging blindly in her direction.

"Bitch!" He made a grab for her. Helle screamed again. And again, when his fingers tangled with her hair.

"Helle?" Mrs Simmons' nasal voice came from somewhere down the stairs.

"Help!" Helle yelled. "Help, me, he's…" A violent shove sent her crashing against the wall. She curled together in a ball, eyes squished shut. Any moment now, he'd grab her. She screamed. And screamed.

"Helle, dearie." Mrs Simmons patted her back. "What on earth is the matter?"

"He…" she stuttered, turning to point at Woolf. Except that there was no Woolf. Other than Mrs Simmons and Helle, the apartment was empty.

The policeman looked bored. After ascertaining that Mrs Simmons had seen no one, met no one on the stairs, he studied Helle dispassionately.

"So he just disappeared into thin air?" She could hear the amusement in his voice.

"Of course not." Helle was nursing a cup of builder's tea, courtesy of Mrs Simmons. "He must have climbed out of a window or something."

"Ah." The policeman strolled about, inspecting each

window. "They're all closed." He opened one and stuck his head out. "And he'd have to be a monkey to climb down from here."

"Or he climbed upwards," Jason said, appearing in the door. Clearly, men in cashmere overcoats and silk scarves made a stronger impression on the policeman than distraught young women in sweats. The officer didn't dismiss Jason's statement out of hand, but stuck his head out again.

"Maybe," he said after his little inspection. "But I hold it unlikely." He studied the room. "Very odd, sir," he added, and Helle could hear he didn't believe a word of it. With a muttered goodbye he left.

"Are you all right?" Jason crouched beside her. "I came as soon as I could."

"I…" She drew in a shaky breath. "He was here, Jason, here!"

"I believe you." He put an arm round her shoulder and pulled her close enough that she could rest her head against him.

"He'll not hurt you," Jason said. "I won't let him." His warm hand ran up and down her arm.

Somehow, Helle wasn't entirely convinced.

Elessa sank the comb roughly into Helle's hair. "I told you to be back in time," she nagged, tugging her way through the wayward curls.

Helle shrugged. "I forgot." She smiled secretively, lashes coming down to shield those bright blue eyes of hers.

Elessa snorted. Forgot while she was out with Jason! "You're nearly twelve," she scolded. "You should behave with more modesty. You must stop running around with Jason. People talk."

Helle turned around. "Why do they talk?" she asked, tearing off a piece of her thumbnail.

Elessa sighed. "You're of royal birth, and soon, your father will choose a husband for you. It's unseemly that you spend so much time with that boy. What will your future husband think?"

Helle was staring at her. "I will not wed anyone but Jason," Helle stated, her brows puckering.

"That's not your choice, child," Elessa said, pulling the comb

through Helle's hair until it hung like a golden mantle to her waist. Helle took hold of her wrist.

"I'll never wed anyone but Jason," she repeated. "That's the way it will be. Jason or no one."

Chapter 7

To Helle's relief, Woolf made no further attempt to contact her. Instead, the following week was refreshingly normal. Helle caught up with her dad and her brothers, a long Skype session with three little boys as blond and curly-haired as she was. She loved them all, but she didn't know them as well as she'd have liked, feeling disloyal to Mum when she went to visit with Dad and Janine or when she spent hours on Skype with Dad's new family. Well, what Mum didn't know wouldn't hurt her, and Helle was too fond of Callum, Kim and Eric—and Dad—to give up on these weekly sessions.

Other than managing her private life, Helle fell into a routine, taking long runs in the morning and meeting Jason most evenings after his work. Well, 'normal' might be stretching it a bit. At every meeting with Jason, she experienced unsettling déjà-vus and some of this spilled over to her nights, a jumble of recurring dreams lining up to disturb her sleep.

Most of these dreams were about Jason, dreams in which he touched and kissed her the way she desperately wished he would every time she clapped eyes on him. So far, all he had done was hold her hand or kiss her chastely, elegantly avoiding her attempts at more serious making out. At one level Helle supposed he was right, while at the other she screamed at his rejection, but in her dreams he was everything she wanted and more, a man who took and gave, who made her soar.

And then there were the dreams of other things; a graceful red-haired woman, her eyes the piercing yellow of a bird of prey; dappled afternoons in a warm courtyard, soft voices laughing as skeins of wool were rolled into balls of yarn; women in long tunics dancing complicated dances around burning flames, cheering as they jumped each of the seven fires, laughing as they swung the children high above the glowing embers.

Sometimes the dreams became familiar nightmares, the colourful images paling away into the dawning sky as her mind filled with that dark, threatening man and his hard hands. Helle would wake to wet cheeks and a thundering heart, sitting up for hours to stop herself from falling asleep again.

"This won't work," she told Jason on the Friday, relaxing in his arms. They were in her living room, sprawled on the sofa as they watched some inane action series starring a modern day Robin Hood.

"Hmm?"

Helle struggled up to sit. "I can't do the 'let's pretend we met in Frankfurt' anymore. I need some answers. Since we met…well, it's as if my brain has gone into overdrive, frantically trying to make sense of all this." And as to her body, it screamed at her to love him, to make the most of what time they might have together.

Jason leaned back with his eyes closed. His jaws clenched and unclenched rhythmically. "You're not going to believe me."

"But I need to know."

He was silent for a while. "Yes," he finally said. "I suppose you do." He took her hand and kissed her knuckles. "Can we do it tomorrow?"

"Tomorrow."

Helle woke the next morning feeling apprehensive. Jason had looked so nervous when he promised her some answers she'd gone to bed feeling like a wreck after hours of attempting to analyse his reaction. What could possibly be so bad as to have him breaking out in a sweat? After all, she already knew that something was seriously weird.

He had insisted they talk outdoors, so Helle bundled herself into jeans and her down-vest, a gigantic scarf wrapped umpteen times around her neck, before she braved the nippy cold. Not that nippy, she concluded as she walked briskly through Kensington Gardens. In fact the day showed promise of sun.

Jason was sitting on a bench, legs extended before him. She could see he was tense, the hollows under his eyes bruised with lack of sleep.

"Hi," she said. "Didn't you sleep well?"

"Not really," Jason's mouth twisted into a rueful smile. "I had a lot on my mind."

Helle nodded and caressed his cheek. "It shows. You look pretty awful."

"Why thank you," he replied sarcastically, leaning away from her touch. It made her feel like a fool, and he saw that, shaking his head ever so slightly. "It's just that I'm a bit nervous." He patted the bench beside him, and she sank down to sit, turned so she could see his face.

The wind rustled through the high grasses that bordered the path. Right in front of them a couple of women were walking the sum total of five dogs, all of them unleashed, all of them yapping happily as they barged through the carpet of leaves that covered the ground. Sycamores raised their bare branches to the sky and an inquisitive squirrel hopped by, halting for a moment to regard them expectantly before going along. Jason did not seem to register any of this, eyes lost in the distance.

"How long have you known me?" Jason asked, breaking the silence.

"Err…two weeks?" At most.

He smiled very crookedly. "Really?" He took her hand, and their fingers braided tight, tight.

"That I know of," she told him, squinting against the sun. "I see you when I dream, but I'm not sure that counts."

"How long have you dreamed of me?"

"I'm not really sure. When I was a kid, I used to dream a lot about me and a bunch of lions, and I think you were in those dreams as well." She felt embarrassed admitting this, recalling faded images of a laughing boy, his teeth flashing in the setting sun, his long dark hair whipping in the wind.

"And now?" Jason asked.

"Now I dream of you like you are, more or less. And we… umm…well, you know."

He laughed and squeezed her hand. "I don't. Won't you describe things for me?"

"No." She dreamed of him in intimate situations and she

wasn't about to give him a blow by blow description of that. "Besides, you know exactly what I'm referring to." She raised her free hand to touch his mouth, his cheek.

"I do." He gave her a serious look. "Those lions, Helle. Three golden beasts that ran with you through the darkening dusk."

What? She felt her mouth slackening into a disbelieving and unflattering 'o'. He grimaced, looking at her apprehensively.

"For real?" she squawked.

"Yes, very much for real."

Oh, boy. Helle quelled a sudden impulse to laugh. Hysterically.

"To me it's still so recent. I only have to close my eyes and see us as we were, the two of us running through the sunset with the lions at our heels. Can you see it?" he asked tweaking her cheek. Helle trawled through her mind, chasing vague memories of even vaguer dreams

"Very little; the cliffs falling off towards the sea, the pine trees... And you, laughing like crazy."

"Well, it was rather exhilarating. As far as I know it's not something many people get to do."

No. In actual fact, Helle had never heard of anyone running around with a bunch of lions. Mowgli and the wolves, yes, but lions? She wanted to dismiss it out of hand, but when she closed her eyes, she saw the red dust that rose beneath her feet, the heaving flanks of the beasts that accompanied them, their yellow eyes intent when they turned to stare at her.

"But how?" Helle tensed her thighs, quivering with a sudden desire to run, to revel in her speed.

"Later," he promised. "So, no other dreams? Apart from the ones where we're..." He raised his eyebrows in an articulate insinuation, smiling at the responding rush of blood up her face.

"Odd bits and pieces, but I'm not really sure what they are."

He nodded and looked away, and then he lifted their braided hands to his mouth and kissed her fingers. He didn't say anything for a while, chewing at his lip.

"Please hear me out, Helle," he finally said. "That's all I can ask, but please stay and listen."

She promised she would, made nervous by his obvious unease.

He took a big breath, scanning her face warily.

"You and I came into this world for our first lives a long time ago, when the fall of Troy was still a faded memory, not yet a myth. We lived in a small country—well, more of a village—on the south-eastern shore of the Black Sea. It was called Tarokyie, a place where the summers were hot, and the winters covered the mountains in blankets of snow and shrouded the shores with fog."

She sat quiet. It was difficult to talk when her lower jaw was hovering somewhere at her waist level. He grimaced at her expression but ploughed on.

"I was the son of the healer, and you were the daughter of the king, supposedly descended in a straight line from Phrixos. That's where you get your name from."

Helle laughed shakily. That was ridiculous. The story of Phrixos and Helle was a myth, a bedtime story her father used to tell her. But she could smell the wafting scents of sun-warmed rosemary and thyme, of drying shrubs and homemade bread, of resin and trampled grapes.

"I was named Helle after my Danish great-grandmother," she told him sternly, trying to ignore her olfactory hallucinations. She often wished her parents had given her a different name, tired as she was of explaining that no, she wasn't called Helen, she was Helle. Jason smiled at her, running his thumb over the back of her hand.

"No you weren't. You were named after Phrixos' sister, grandchild of the sun." He tweaked at her hair. "That, according to your father, was why you had hair the colour of sunlight."

She didn't know what to say. On the one hand, it was so easy to dismiss all of it as bullshit, thereby branding this gorgeous man a potential delusional danger and herself as a crazy insomniac burdened with weird dreams. On the other hand... but no, it was totally impossible. So why was she seeing squat houses clambering up a verdant mountain slope? And who was the old woman who held out her arms to Helle, her brown braids laced with silver? How could she possibly know that the old woman would smell of honey and fresh cheese, or that her fingertips had calluses after a lifetime spinning wool into yarn?

Helle cleared her throat. "And I suppose you're called Jason after the Greek myth guy, right?"

"Yes, I was, and your father wasn't too thrilled by that, seeing as your House never forgave Jason for stealing the Golden Fleece. I think my mother did it on purpose. She sometimes considered your father a pompous arse, always harping on about his bloodline and all that." He chuckled quietly, a faraway look in his eyes.

Right, she had to leave. This was just too much, to sit and listen to this man talk of stuff that belonged in fairy tales as if it was the truth. Seriously, the Golden Fleece? She made a half-hearted attempt to stand up. Jason just held on to her hand.

"You promised," he said, and in his eyes she saw apprehension.

"I did." She settled back down.

"We walked the coastline, my mother and I. She was a Wanderer, a healer of such renown people would walk for days for her counsel." He threw her a quick look. Helle nodded to show she understood. Like an itinerant doctor. An image threw itself across her brain; long red hair, pale white hands and eyes as golden as his. It didn't even surprise her when the image inclined her head gravely in greeting, instead she found herself nodding back, which the red-haired lady obviously found very amusing to judge from the look on her fading face.

"What about the lions?" she asked.

He smiled down at her. "A hunter killed the lioness and brought the cubs as a gift to your father. You smuggled them into your bed, slept with them, fed them. By the time they were grown, they'd adopted you. Where you went, there they went."

Absolutely incredible. Who had ever heard of a kid playing with lions and not ending up on the menu? Poor guy, he was definitely mentally ill, in need of the closest insanity ward.

Alternatively, he was telling the truth. Yup, Helle's gut told her. *No way*, her rational mind shrieked, whacking angrily at the inside of her head. Helle stood up abruptly, yanking her hand free.

"You're just making this up, right? Tell me you're just inventing this."

He looked at her, shaking his head slowly, and she backed away a few steps, furiously trying to clear her head of the strange images whizzing through it. Pictures of another place, a place where the heat bounced off the ground and people lolled in the shade. A place where the scent of juniper perfumed sleepy, sun-drenched hollows, where rosebushes clambered over a courtyard wall. Helle squirmed: mental fantasies.

"This is totally unbelievable."

"I know," he agreed, "but it could've been worse. I could've shown up in a tunic and mantle."

She muffled a laugh and took a step closer. "If you had, I'd have taken you for some weirdo and kept my distance."

"No you wouldn't. You'd have fallen into my arms even if I'd been stark naked."

"How would you know?" she asked, trying to ignore the pleasing but distracting image of a nude Jason.

"Because there's no choice," he said. "Not for me, at least."

"I still think it was smart of you to look normal," she insisted.

"I am normal," he replied drily, ignoring her disbelieving headshake, "very, very normal."

"Of course," she said sarcastically. "Everyone knows it's the norm to be reborn."

"Happens much more often than you think," he bit back. "You'd be surprised to know how many old souls wander the earth."

"Oh, and you'd know? You just look at someone and can tell?"

"It takes one to know one." He extended his hand to her. "Please come and sit."

She allowed him to take her hand, but sat down with some distance between them.

"Sam Woolf," she said, and her gut clenched in warning. "Is he also from that past life?"

"He is." Jason licked his lips. "But I don't want to talk about him—not now, not yet."

The way he said it had Helle's scalp tingling. Woolf's voice rang in her head; loud and clear it promised pain and retribution if she didn't do as he said. Woolf's voice chuckled, became as smooth and soft as silk, repeating that she belonged to him, not to some upstart Wanderer.

"Helle?" Jason shook her. "Are you all right?"

"My head. Sometimes—" She bit off.

"You hear him, don't you?" Jason said bitterly. "He whispers and cajoles, he threatens and promises." His eyes hardened. "I know how manipulative he can be," he muttered, more to himself than to her. "Woolf is dangerous, Helle. Powerful beyond your comprehension, he is a man who stops at nothing to get what he wants."

"And that is?" she asked, even though she already knew, a heavy weight settling in the pit of her stomach.

"You." He traced a light line over her forehead. "But I won't let him take you—not this time." He gripped her nape, holding her still as he bent his head to kiss her. Close-lipped at first, his tongue flitting across her lips until she opened her mouth to him. And it was just like in Helle's dreams, a strong demanding kiss that made the world around her spin, blood racing madly through her veins.

"Not fair," she protested feebly, when they came up for air. "You're making it very difficult for me to think rationally by doing this."

He laughed softly and kissed her again. "Don't you like it?"

"My point exactly," she gasped as he nuzzled her throat, "I like it too much."

"Good. I've waited a very long time to do this again."

And he kissed her some more, which was perfectly fine with Helle, because no matter how potentially crazy this man was, he was a formidable kisser.

Jason sat back abruptly. "I'd almost given up hope that I'd ever see you again. The odds were definitely not in favour, but there seemed to be no point to all these endless lives if I wouldn't someday find you again."

"Endless lives?" she stuttered. "Like more than two?"

"Many, many more. Life after life after life…"

Helle didn't even try to wrap her head around that one. It sounded awful, a sentence of continued existences, an endless trudging through time. Assuming, of course, that he was telling the truth. A quick peek revealed he was frowning, jaw clenched so tight she suspected his teeth must be hurting.

"I was so glad to see you," he said, looking up to meet her eyes. "There you were, in the flesh. Not a figment of my imagination, not a dream…" He broke off and gave her an unsteady smile. "And you even knew my name."

"I did. I'd missed you so much, but I didn't even know it was you I was missing." She'd been so happy to see him, but afraid and angry as well. Angry because he had been gone too long, afraid because he really shouldn't exist. Shit. She felt borderline insane, sitting here discussing long gone lives as if they were facts. *Impossible*, her brain scoffed. Maybe. Or maybe not, because he was here, very much alive, thereby proving that sometimes impossible things did happen.

Jason was sitting with his head bowed and she tentatively raised a hand to his head, smoothing a strand of hair off his face. She sank her fingers into that glorious mane. So soft, she smiled, digging deeper until she felt the bone structure beneath, hearing him groan at her touch. Mine, her hands told her: this man was hers and had been hers since time began, and she would kill whoever tried to take him from her. She leaped up, crossing her arms to stop her heart from permanently damaging her ribs with its pounding.

"What?" Jason gave her a worried look, but Helle just shook her head. She didn't know this man—not really. And still she knew everything that mattered about him and all she wanted to do was to take his hand and never let him walk away from her again.

"Come here," Jason's voice broke through the fogs of her internal debate and she sat down, her hand slipping automatically into his. He draped an arm over her shoulders and held her close, his lips buried in her hair.

"Can you recall all your lives?" she asked after a while, working hard to sound as if it was commonplace to run into people who claimed to have been reincarnated over the eons.

"No, not everything, bits and pieces mostly. It can come in quite handy to have a degree in medicine from a previous existence."

"Yeah, as long as it isn't from the thirteenth century. Leeches and mustard poultices would be somewhat outdated today."

He laughed out loud. "1960s, Harvard."

Boy that must have been a short life, Helle thought sadly, having done the math.

"Forty-five," he said with a hitch to his voice, "I was forty-five when I died."

Helle sat back against the bench and studied him. His pulse thudded in the hollow of his throat, and she had to suppress a sudden desire to lean in and kiss him there—he used to like that. He flushed under her scrutiny.

"So, was I wrong to tell you?" A shadow flew across his face, making the hollows under his eyes darker than before.

"No, I asked you to. Besides, I was getting pretty worried about those dreams, thinking that maybe I was crazy." Now she knew she was—or at least borderline abnormal. She shivered and felt his arm tightening round her in response. "But it's difficult to believe—and it scares me."

"Scare you enough to make you walk away from me?"

Helle cradled his face. "What an incredibly stupid question. You already know I won't." But she should, her subconscious hollered. She should up and leave, ASAP.

"I hoped you wouldn't," he corrected, "but I didn't know."

Helle's phone beeped. She glanced at the display. "Oh, shit. Alison is going to kill me."

"I hope not. That would require me killing her in revenge."

"We're going shopping," Helle explained, standing up. Alison was an avid shopper, the kind of girl who would turn a shoe store upside down as she tried on twenty pairs before deciding none of them fit.

Jason stood up gracefully and kissed her brow before stepping back. "So, see you later?"

"Not tonight. Alison and I are meeting up with some of her friends."

He scowled.

"Girl friends," Helle clarified. "We're going to that Argentinian steak house, just off Piccadilly."

"Ah. Tomorrow?"

"Tomorrow." She took his hand as they walked towards the closest park exit. Just as he was about to leave, she called him back. "Jason?"

"Yes?"

"It's only the good dreams that are memories, right?"

His face shuttered, his eyes inscrutable. "What do you mean?"

Helle twisted, uncomfortable with discussing dreams as being potentially true.

"It's just that sometimes I dream a pretty scary dream, and it always ends with me dying."

Jason put the back of his hand against her face. "You did die, Helle. Back then. You must've died several times since then."

"I must?" She sounded absurdly surprised and laughed at herself. "Yeah, I must have, I suppose."

"Otherwise you'd be a ghost or a very, very old crone, and I mean incredibly old, with skin like a crocodile and no teeth. Rather unappealing, not my type at all." He dipped his head and kissed her, a full open-mouthed kiss that left her hot and breathless.

"I guess I am your type," she said, making him chuckle.

"Definitely." One more kiss and he was off.

"Happy birthday," Jason mumbled and gave her a small package, tightly wrapped in a piece of cloth.

"My birthday was more than a week ago."

Jason nodded. "I know. But I wasn't here, was I?" He tugged at her braid. "But if you want me to, I can take it back."

She didn't. She carefully unwrapped the little package and shook out a long, bright blue ribbon.

"I thought it would look good with your eyes," he muttered, clearly embarrassed.

"Thank you." She stepped closer to him, and put her hand on his sleeve. "Will you help me braid it into my plait?"

His hands trembled as he undid her hair, spilling it down her back. She sat perfectly still, feeling his warm breath on her neck. His deft hands braided her hair, threading the blue ribbon through. When he was done, he rested his hands on her shoulder. She stared straight ahead, her heart thudding loudly. She could hear her pulse and wondered if he could as well. He leaned forward and pressed his lips to her throat, sending a shiver of delight through her. She lifted one hand to his face, gently caressing his smooth cheek.

Chapter 8

That same evening, Woolf reappeared in Helle's life.

"You knew he would be here?" Helle demanded, wheeling to scowl at Alison. After spending Saturday afternoon shopping, they were now standing in a dark and very modern bar, all black and white with stainless steel touches. The ideal environment for a man like Woolf, at present lounging against the counter further in.

"He just wants to see you." Alison fluffed at her hair. "He says you're overreacting to stuff. A drink before dinner, no more."

"What, you talked to him? When? Where?"

In response, Alison held up her phone. "This morning."

"You had no right!" She had to get out. Now. As yet, Woolf hadn't registered her presence, but any second now he'd glance at the door. Without as much as a look at Alison, Helle made for the exit.

It was cold outside. She pulled her coat closed and began walking briskly in the direction of home. Her phone rang. Alison. Helle rejected the call. It rang again. Helle clicked the reject button. Again. With an irritated sound, Helle answered.

"Running from me?" Woolf's voice almost had Helle's legs folding. She hung up, kicked off her shoes and ran.

The main door stood ajar when she reached home. Helle sneaked up the stairs. The door to the apartment was closed, but there was a faint line of light spilling from beneath it, and when she rested her ear against the door she heard music. Plus she smelled food, and with a sob of relief she pushed the door open.

"Mum?"

"Helle!" Her mother held out her arms, and Helle fell into them, glad that her mother was stout enough—and strong enough—to handle it. "Ouff," her mother said, disengaging herself. She studied Helle, eyes sweeping up and down her body. "You all right?"

"Sort of." Helle wandered over to the stove. Miriam always cooked when she came over, and the lamb and aubergine casserole presently in the pot smelled divine.

"Why sort of?" Her mother opened a bottle of wine, poured them both a glass.

"How come you're here?" Helle asked instead. She just had to hug her again.

"Oh, you know me. Always off to some distant corner of the world or other." Her mother hugged her back—hard.

"London isn't exactly the back of beyond."

"I'm only here for the weekend. I fly to Mumbai on Monday." Mum sipped at her wine. "I should probably have called ahead, but this was a spur of the moment thing and I wanted to surprise you."

Helle raised her brows. Her mother never did spur of the moment. Ever since Dad walked out of the door, she had retreated into a life of structure and work, everything organised, no room for the unexpected.

"I was worried," Mum said shortly. "All that stuff with your former boss…" She made a face. "You really should sue him, you know."

"But I won't." Helle dropped her eyes to her feet, dirty and wet in her thin nylons. Her mother followed her gaze.

"What—"

"The shoes pinched." Helle wasn't about to admit galloping through the streets of London just to get away from Woolf.

"Ah." Mum looked unconvinced. She leaned back against the counter and crossed her arms. God knows what she would have said next, but whatever it was, the sound of someone knocking interrupted her. Helle's mouth dried up. Woolf? She tried to concentrate, attempting to discern who might be on the other side of the door.

"Helle?" Jason's voice had her expelling her breath. "You okay?"

Helle opened the door wide. "Hi," she murmured. She brushed her fingers over his hand. "My mother is here."

"Oh." He looked uncertain, all of a sudden.

"Who's that?" Mum nudged at Helle, wanting to see.

"This is Jason." Helle stood aside to let him in.

This was not what he had expected. Jason tried out a smile on the rather formidable lady who was studying him over the rims of her glasses. Didn't work. She pursed her lips and looked him up and down.

"Jason?" She turned to Helle. "What a coincidence, right?"

"Eh?" Helle looked confused. Her mother lowered her voice, more or less whispering in Helle's ear. Jason, however, had excellent hearing, and he made out his own name combined with recurring dreams and lions. No wonder the lady regarded him with apprehension.

Jason took the opportunity to study Helle's mother, a woman of approximately Helle's height but with none of Helle's curves. Brown, straight hair, a strong chin—only in the shape of their brows and the colour of their eyes did mother and daughter share any common features.

After their brief whispered conference, Helle's mother stuck out her hand.

"I'm Miriam. Miriam Cohen." Piercing blue eyes studied him intently.

"Jason Morris, pleased to meet you." Not Madsen? He glanced at Helle, who just looked straight back at him.

"My parents are divorced," she said, as if in reply to an unvoiced question.

"Better for him, better for me." Miriam grinned, the smile not reaching her eyes.

"Ah." He could sense an ocean of hurt here. "So you don't see your father that often?" he asked Helle.

"Not really." She sounded dismissive. "He's got his hands full—you know, young wife, young kids."

Yet another ocean of hurt. Jason decided to change the subject by asking Miriam what brought her to London.

"Work," she replied. "And I thought I'd drop in on Helle and make sure she's okay." She met his eyes, he stared back. A protective mother, making sure he knew it. Mentally, he tipped his hat at her—parents should look out for their children. In this particular case, he doubted Miriam Cohen could do anything at all to protect her offspring from Samion. Just thinking of the former Prince of Kolchis had the skin between his shoulder blades prickling, and he carefully clasped his hands together in an effort to control the sudden rush of heat.

"Mum, you make me sound like a ten-year-old."

"Not that far off. You should have left Woolf & Partners the moment he started harassing you."

Helle blushed. "It's in the past, okay?"

"Hmph!" Miriam sounded less than convinced. "Have you eaten?" she asked, turning to Jason. A very abrupt change of subject—and one everyone was grateful for, he reflected.

"No," he said.

"So join us."

"I shouldn't intrude," he tried.

"You're not." Helle smiled shyly at him. "I'd like you to stay—and Mum's cooking is to die for."

Yes, the scents were mouth-watering, and he made out thyme and sage, limes and tomatoes.

"Lamb?" he asked. "And pancetta?"

"My, my." Miriam laughed. "A budding chef?"

"Not so budding," Jason said with a grin. "I'm not bad in a kitchen." He sauntered over to where the food was bubbling. Moments later, he and Miriam were in a deep discussion as to the merits of frying the aubergine before adding it to casseroles. He smiled to himself; the way to a man's heart went through his stomach, they said. The way to a woman's heart could very often be through her cooking.

While they were setting the table, he took the opportunity to lean forward and kiss the little birthmark just to the left of Helle's mouth. It reminded him of Mariette, the young girl he'd wooed in late 18th century France. She'd had a *mouche* just there and a general resemblance to Helle, as had all his women—with the notable exception of Juliet.

He shifted on his feet. At some point he would have to tell her about Juliet, if nothing else because there was a very real possibility they would meet.

"What?" she asked.

"Hmm?"

"You zoned out." She handed him the glasses and a salad bowl.

"I did?" He brushed at a wayward curl. "Are you all right? You looked as if you'd seen a ghost when..." He broke off, realising just how that sounded.

"You were following me?" she asked.

"I can't help myself. Now that you're back in my life, I just have to be close to you."

"You do? Like a benevolent stalker, huh?" A smile tugged at her mouth.

"Benevolent at any rate." He threw a look at Miriam, presently frowning down at her gnocchi. "I saw you come out of the bar and I was just about to call your name when you took off." He tapped her nose. "You're fast." Not that it surprised him—he'd seen her run for hours in that distant past.

"Woolf was there." Helle lowered her voice to a whisper. "He'd asked Alison to set it up—like a surprise date."

"Alison?" Jason decided then and there that he didn't like the green-eyed minx all that much.

"It's impolite to whisper," Miriam said, without turning around.

"Sorry, Mum." Helle took his hand. "We'll talk later," she murmured.

Dinner was relaxed, with most of the conversation centring on the heady world of business. They had a heated debate about globalisation, went on to discuss the current inertia of the European economy, and ended up speculating about the potential consequences of China's present policy in Africa. After coffee and tea, Miriam stood up. "I have to get going."

"Going?" Helle frowned. "I thought you were staying here."

"Here?" Miriam laughed. "A bit too crowded, darling."

"So where are you staying?" Helle got to her feet. "We can walk you there."

"I'll take a cab." She sounded evasive. Jason studied her with interest, noting the slight blush on her cheeks.

"I'll call you one." There was a devilish glint in Helle's eyes. "Just tell me where you're going."

"No need." Miriam sounded triumphant. "I use Uber."

"You're not staying at a hotel, are you?" Helle narrowed her eyes. "You're staying with Phil." She crowed out loud when Miriam scowled. "Ha! I told you, Mum." She waltzed over to hug Miriam. "I'm so glad for you," she said, in a softer tone.

Miriam hugged her back. "It's just a night, Helle. Not exactly a lifetime commitment."

"We all have to start somewhere."

The apartment felt strangely quiet once Miriam had left. Jason led Helle over to the sofa and sat down, pulling her down on his lap. She curled up, her arms round his neck, and they just sat like that, watching the candles flicker and flare.

He shifted beneath her.

"Am I too heavy?" she asked. Never. He could sit like this until the planet stopped turning, holding her to his heart. But all this close proximity was doing things to him, and he could feel his erection swell and grow. She, apparently, felt it too, settling her bottom all that much closer to his groin. He ran his hand down her back. She raised her face from his chest and they kissed, a slow dance that grew in intensity, him holding her still as his tongue explored her mouth.

She fell backwards onto the sofa, pulling him with her, and his hands were on her breasts, in her hair, his mouth still glued to hers. Helle. His Helle. He groaned out loud and disengaged himself, pulling back.

"What?" she asked, sitting up as well. He ran his hands up and down her thighs. His pulse was loud in his head, and in his jeans his erection strained painfully against the cloth. God, how he wanted her, and to judge from her wet mouth and wide eyes, she wanted him too.

"I must go," he said, stumbling to his feet.

"Why?" She grabbed hold of him. "Why don't you stay? Please."

"I..." He wanted nothing more, but didn't trust himself to be as gentle as she needed. He wanted to possess her, claim her, rather than make love to her. Besides, he owed it to her to reveal all his secrets before he took her to bed. The thought sent a jolt of fear through him. "I think it's too soon," he said, wincing at how hurt she looked.

"Fine." She rose. "Well go on! You know your way out, right?" Her eyes brimmed with unshed tears, and all he wanted to do was kiss them.

"Don't be like that." He stood close enough to feel her body warmth. "I want to stay." He stooped to kiss her brow. "I just don't think I should—not yet."

"Just go," she said, turning her back on him.

"See you tomorrow?"

"Maybe."

Jason sighed. "I'm not doing this to hurt you."

"But you are." She dashed a hand over her eyes.

"Helle," he groaned, and tried to pull her into his arms. She was having none of it, brusquely pulling free.

"Go."

"Not until you promise we'll meet tomorrow."

"What's the point? So that you can spout some more impossible stuff about how we are meant for each other only to pull back the moment things heat up?"

"I just think we should take it slow." He hated talking to her back, so he took hold of her shoulders and whirled her round. "We have a lifetime before us, Helle."

"How do you know that?" She tilted her head back to meet his eyes. "I get the feeling things went really, really bad last time round. What's to say they won't this time as well?"

"They won't." He had to believe that was true, despite the presence of that accursed Samion.

"Please don't leave," she said, hanging her head. "Please."

Jason caved. "Okay, I'll stay. But I'll sleep on the sofa."

They were still awake, cuddled together on the sofa, when the door banged open. Alison stepped inside.

"There you are," she said, when Helle stuck her head up

88

over the sofa-back. "Sam and I have been so worried, and—"

"Sam?" Jason sat up beside Helle.

"What's he doing here?" Alison asked, glowering at Jason. She pulled off her knee-high boots, slammed the door shut and padded over towards them. "Sam says—"

"I don't care what Woolf says," Helle interrupted. "And why had you told him where we'd be?"

"He just wants to talk to you," Alison said. "Clear things up."

Jason made a derisive sound. "Sure."

Alison ignored him. "The poor man is beside himself. Doesn't he deserve the chance to explain himself?"

"No." Helle loaded her voice with ice. "I never want to see him or talk to him again. Ever."

Alison squirmed. "Sorry, it's just—"

"Yeah, I know. He's a persuasive kind of guy."

Alison's mouth softened into a little pout. "Very."

Jason stood abruptly. "I'm going home." He touched Helle's cheek. "You okay with that?" he asked quietly. She felt a sting of disappointment but managed to give him a smile.

"Of course."

His mouth tipped into a faint smile. "You're a terrible liar. I just feel three's a crowd, okay?" He kissed her nose. "Tomorrow?"

"Tomorrow." But she hugged herself when he left, wishing he had stayed the night to hold her close.

"Did I interrupt something?" Alison asked, coming over to plunk herself down beside Helle.

"Not really." Helle shifted to the side.

"Helle." Alison rolled her eyes. "I'm sorry, okay?" She pulled her legs up. "So, how serious is this Jason thing?"

"Pretty serious, I guess." Leaving aside the fact that the stupid man was leaving her hot, bothered and sexually frustrated.

"Promise me you'll be careful." Alison's brow puckered. "Sam says—" She broke off. "You've just met him, so don't go rushing headlong into a relationship with someone you don't know."

"Oh, I know a lot of stuff about him." Much more than you would ever believe, she added silently.

"Whatever." Alison pummelled one of the decorative cushions and stuck it behind her head. "Boy, I'm tired." She closed her eyes, a smile hovering over her mouth.

"What?" Helle asked.

"Nothing." Alison's smile converted into a huge grin. "I just had a great time."

Helle laughed as she ran off, throwing teasing looks at him.

"You can never catch me," she called, weaving in and out between the trees. Her tunic lay discarded by the water, her sheer linen undergarment clinging to her damp skin. He growled and pretended to pounce, making her laugh all the more as she darted further away beneath the trees.

Of course Jason caught her. She wanted him to. When he finally tackled her to the ground she no longer laughed. She lay in his arms and shivered with surprising, unfamiliar pleasure. And pain, as his hand closed around her wrist, suddenly very hot.

Afterwards, she studied the blisters and smiled softly to herself. She made him burn. He made her his.

Chapter 9

On the Monday, there was a curt knock on the door. Two men stood outside, requesting that Helle accompany them to Woolf & Partners, as there were suspicions of data theft.

"Who, me?" Helle didn't like the look of them—big and bulky, with shoulders that strained the matching black of their suit jackets.

"You're requested to cooperate, Ms Madsen."

Helle shook her head. "I'm not going back there. We can go to a nearby police station instead."

"That," the older of the two men said, "is not your call, Ms Madsen." He nodded at his colleague. "We are authorised to bring you along—we hope to do so without resorting to force."

"I want to see your papers," Helle said, backing away. The younger man held up something that looked like a badge. Did English policemen have badges? Helle wasn't sure, but her every instinct was telling her these men were not here as representatives of the law. They had Sam Woolf stamped all over them.

"We're waiting."

"In case you haven't noticed, I'm not dressed. I guess you'll have to wait some more." She evaded the hands of the older of the two and managed to slip into her bedroom, banging the door closed behind her. Her phone. She stuffed it into her sweats, just as the door flew open.

"We've been instructed not to leave you alone."

"I'm going to the bathroom. Want to join me while I pee?"

Helle texted Jason while she was in the toilet. He responded, promising he would do what he could. There was a demanding knock on the door. Moments later, Helle was shepherded towards a waiting car. One of the goons carried her bag, containing her laptop.

To the obvious surprise of Helle's escort, a lawyer stood waiting in the foyer of Woolf & Partners. Not exactly your everyday lawyer, the man who introduced himself as Curtis Crew was well over six feet tall. Broad shoulders tapered off to narrow hips, and when he came towards them, his body moved with the grace of an athlete.

"She doesn't need a solicitor," the younger of the men said.

"In which case she isn't accompanying you any further." Curtis blocked their way. "And I want to see your ID—now." Yet again, papers were produced, the two men sharing looks when Curtis produced a phone and photographed the documents. "Data theft?" He snorted. "Isn't that what Woolf & Partners do for a living—albeit somewhat legally?"

Neither of the men replied. At Curtis' curt command, Helle's bag was returned to her. He placed a hand at her back and steered her towards the lifts. Her steps faltered. She gripped the strap of her bag for reassurance and glanced at the giant beside her. A deep breath, two, and she preceded Curtis into the lift.

There was a whole delegation waiting. Percy was hovering in the background, but it was to Woolf Helle's eyes flew. He was standing by the reception desk. No suit: instead he was in jeans and a tight-fitting green cable-knit sweater, which clung to his powerful torso and highlighted his intense colouring.

"Why are you doing this?" Having Curtis at her back gave Helle courage. Woolf just looked at her, eyes travelling up and down her body, lingering for an instant on her face. "Why?" she repeated. "Isn't it enough that you threaten me in my home?"

"Threaten?" He sounded hoarse. "I am trying to make you understand what's good for you." He straightened up, and Helle backed straight into Curtis' comforting bulk.

"My own good? And as part of that you're accusing me of data theft?"

"Whatever it takes to get you back here," he said softly. "Anything to have you with me, Helle."

"We have been compromised," Percy interrupted. "Someone has breached our security. Naturally, we have to follow up." In response, Helle managed a snort, cradling her laptop bag to her chest.

"What exactly is my client doing here?" Curtis asked once they were seated in one of the conference rooms. Woolf had not accompanied them, and without him in the room, Helle's pulse was reverting to a more normal level. Percy shifted in his seat.

"There are concerns," he said. "Our LAN has been broken into. Things have been deleted."

"Really?" Curtis drawled. He flipped open his iPad and started taking notes. "And why would this implicate my client?"

"Why? Because it happened just before she left," Percy snapped. "Files have disappeared."

"Not me," Helle said. But she had a pretty good idea who.

"Which we will easily verify by going through your laptop," Percy replied.

"Her private laptop?" Curtis raised a brow. "And is there a search warrant in place for this invasion of Ms Madsen's privacy?"

Percy blustered. "If she's innocent, why would she have a problem with us going through it?"

"If you've got reasonable cause for suspicion, why haven't you arranged for a warrant?" Curtis adjusted his cuffs—pristine white linen that contrasted with his dark skin.

Helle glanced upwards. There was a small camera mounted in one corner, trained directly on the chair she was sitting in. Was Woolf watching her at this precise moment? Dark laughter invaded her head. Like tendrils of fine silk, his voice seemed to seep into every wrinkle in her brain. Helle pressed her hands to her temples, trying to will it away, to stop herself from hearing what he was saying. Her breathing became uncomfortably shallow, and in her head he laughed at her.

"Helle? Are you all right?" Curtis' face was very close.

"Not really." She had to get out of here. She half rose. The two men at the door automatically stood to block the exit. Curtis was saying something, his hand at her elbow. Shaking, Helle pulled out her laptop. "Here, go ahead and check it."

Curtis frowned. "What? You have no reason to—"

"Just let them do it," Helle interrupted. "I have nothing to hide." The moment the two men disappeared with her laptop, the voice in her head disappeared. She hid her face in her hands and tried to stop her legs from trembling.

"What's wrong?" Curtis asked.

"I don't know." She gave him a wobbly smile. "A dizzy spell, I think. I never had time for breakfast this morning."

"Have some water." Percy looked genuinely concerned.

"Thanks."

A half hour later, the laptop was returned to her. "Nothing," one of the so-called investigators told her.

"I know." She stood. "Can I leave now?"

"I will escort you from the premises," Curtis said, standing as well. He moved towards the door, like an icebreaker preparing the way, and Helle hurried after him. Endless minutes waiting for the lift—yet another camera registering them—endless minutes going down, and then they were back outside. Never had November drizzle felt quite as wonderful, never had the sound of traffic been so welcome. On the opposite side of Cannon Street, Jason's Aston Martin was idling. The window slid down, revealing Jason with his phone pressed to his ear.

"I'll be off." Curtis shook her hand. "Will you be all right?"

Helle gestured in the direction of the car. "Sure."

She was halfway to the car, when someone grabbed her from behind.

"Mr Woolf has some further questions."

"Let me go!" She kicked and flailed, but with her arm wrenched up behind her back she was being forced back towards the building. The door to the Aston Martin flew open. Jason came sprinting towards her.

"Take your hands off her," Jason snarled.

"Make me."

Helle groaned out loud when the man increased the pressure on her arm. Jason's hand shot out, closing on the man's forearm. There was a sizzling sound, a strange smell filled the air, and the man shrieked, letting go of Helle. His sleeve was burned away, his forearm covered in blisters, the visible skin a sickening pink hue.

"My arm," the man moaned. "Fucking hell, my arm!"

"Come." Jason made as if to take Helle's hand.

"What…" She took a step back from him. "How…" She stared at his hands. The fingers were bright red. "Sweetest Jesus," she muttered and fled.

Jason caught up with her at the street corner. "Don't run from me, Helle. Don't—" His face twisted together in anguish. "I couldn't bear it if you did."

"What are you?" she asked. "How can you… Shit, Jason, what just happened?" He held out his hand, but she backed away.

"I'll tell you—I promise I will." He took a step towards her. "Just don't run—not from me."

She might be scared silly, but one thing she knew for sure: this was her Jason. Hers. So when he pulled her into a rough embrace, she let him, even if his hands were uncomfortably hot on her back.

"Come." He coaxed her towards the car.

"When will you tell me?" she asked, buckling her seatbelt.

"Tonight." He looked grim. "We must wait for the dark."

"The dark?" She tried to laugh. "What, your hands glow as well?"

He pulled his brows together. "Must we do this now?"

"I just saw you burn a guy!" Helle hissed. "So excuse me if I'm a bit upset, okay?"

He exhaled. "I have a gift."

"A gift? You blistered his skin!"

"He shouldn't have touched you!" Jason scowled. "Not like that." He turned fiery eyes her way. "I can't…I won't stand by and watch you hurt—ever again." Well, that oblique comment didn't exactly help.

"What, so you did that last time round?" she asked, loading her voice with sarcasm. Jason's face paled, eyes suddenly very dark.

"Yes," he whispered, and the single word was loaded with so much pain Helle allowed him to take her hand.

"How?" she whispered, feeling the warmth in his fingers diminish.

"I just… well, I can channel heat to my hands."

"What else can you do? Lift cars one-handed? Fly?"

"Don't be ridiculous," he snapped. He took a deep breath, took two, and reclaimed his hand to change gears. "I'll show you tonight."

Jason wasn't sure this was a good idea, but Helle had made it eminently clear that either he explained, or she would walk away. He had to close his eyes at the thought, grimly recognising there was a big chance she would do so anyway—walk away, that is.

They'd met up after six at the south-western entrance to Kensington Gardens, she arriving flushed and damp after her walk through the park. She'd looked delectable, all pink and rosy, but she'd been wary, an apprehensive set to her shoulders that had something twisting inside of him. To postpone things, Jason suggested they duck into one of the smaller coffee shops on Kensington High Street. With two large lattes and a slice of carrot cake to share, they sat down at one of the rickety tables. Jason took her hand, playing with her fingers.

"The first time I ever saw you, you were about eight years old. Your reputation had preceded you: everyone knew you were a wild and silent girl. In retrospect, I think you were a bereft child."

He stared off, smiling at the image of Helle the child, regarding him from under her lashes.

"That first time you were standing beside your father, your hands clasped in front of you and your hair braided into a long golden plait."

"With a red ribbon in it," Helle filled in, a small pucker between her brows. "You were the Wanderer's son and you were beautiful."

"Well," he said, somewhat embarrassed.

"A lanky suntanned boy with mahogany hair and eyes the colour of sunset." She shook her head, muttered something that sounded like 'unbelievable', and spent some time stirring her coffee.

"You remember," he said, squeezing her hand.

"Not really," she disagreed. "I just saw a fleeting picture, then it was gone. Why do you say I was bereft?"

"Because you were." He caressed her arm, noting how the golden down on her forearm rose at his touch. "You missed your mother." He studied the street outside. It was completely dark by now, the streetlights reflecting off the wet asphalt.

"My mother?" She sounded incredulous, amused even. It irked him, that she would one moment concede she remembered some details, then pretend she found the whole thing utterly ludicrous. So he chose not to say anything, by the simple expedient of stuffing his mouth with the last of the carrot cake.

"What happened?"

"Hmm?" He took a deep swallow of his coffee.

"Back then—with my mother."

"Do you really care? Or believe me?" It came out sharper than he intended, and she shrank away, watching him with certain caution.

"Is it so strange if I have problems with all this? It's not exactly the easiest of stuff to get your head round, is it?"

No, he agreed silently, studying his hands, now flat on the table. He flexed his fingers. And once he'd shown her what he could do…He swallowed noisily.

"You're nervous." She covered his hands with hers. Jason gave her a crooked smile. In his experience, his particular talent either had people fleeing in fear or dragging him off to a stake to burn him to death. Cold shivers travelled up and down his spine as he recalled the last time this had happened—1442 in Nürnberg.

"Your mother was one of the Amazons," he said, to steer them away from the subject.

"An Amazon? One of those women who rode around with their breasts uncovered?" She laughed.

"That's hearsay—stupid Greeks. No, the Amazons were fighting queens, brave and fierce in battle. But they were

97

practical, and where is the practicality in riding around with your chest exposed?"

Helle grinned and wiggled her brows. "Distraction?"

Jason shook his head, smiling, and went on. "I never met your mother, but from what I heard she was a pretty frightening lady with a mercurial temper. But your father adored her, and she him. It almost killed him when she left, riding off to God knows where."

"She left?" Helle's brow furrowed.

"Supposedly, one day your tantrums made her snap. She was so angry she threw you at the wall. Your nurse said that she saw you slithering down to the floor and was certain your mother had killed you.

"The next day, she was gone, back to her people. She couldn't trust herself to be around you. She never came back. I don't think your father ever got over her leaving, and it took a long time for him to want to see you. It was easier to blame you than to blame her." He leaned forward to touch her cheek. "You don't remember any of this?"

"Nope. No major loss, I gather. Not exactly the happiest of childhoods." She tilted her head. "But I do remember you. They called you the fire boy, didn't they?"

"They did." Here goes, he thought. He glanced at his phone and wondered how many minutes it would take before she ran.

"Strange nickname," Helle said, placing a finger on his hand. "Did you have pyromaniac tendencies? An urge to burn things to the ground?"

"No, not even close." He stood up. "Showtime, I guess." He felt a surge of heat flood his arm and race towards his hand. He so did not want to do this. "I'm going to trust you with this, but I'm not comfortable doing it."

She gave him a piercing look. "I wonder why." But at least she took his hand, walking in silence beside him as he led the way towards St Mary Abbots Church, a few blocks further down. He came to a halt, led her through the churchyard and round to the back of the church. Some clambering and they were in the church gardens, at this time of the night empty of anything but the odd cat. He pulled them further in, shielding them behind a tangle of shrubs. With a deep breath, he released her, and shoved her to the side.

"I need space," he explained, and extended his hands in front of him. He set his teeth.

Helle was not quite sure what she'd expected. Jason stood before her, arms raised, and thanks to the light spilling from the distant street lamp, she could see he was rigid, his jaws working rhythmically. She could feel the waves of apprehension that emanated from him, smell his fear. Shit: this had to be really, really bad. She strangled a yelp when electricity crackled to life between his palms. Jagged bursts of flickering light coalesced into a little ball of fire, burning merrily before Jason clapped his hands together, extinguishing it. He looked up at her and grimaced.

"Party trick," he muttered depreciatingly. Helle's legs tensed, ready for flight, and she kept a cautious distance from him.

"How do you do that?"

He tried to take her hand. Helle retreated, not really wanting him to touch her with those hands—at least not yet.

"I was born with it, it's just something I can do. When we lived our first lives, many people had… capabilities that have somehow got lost over the ages. My gift was valuable in a world without light switches or electrical stoves." He shrugged deprecatingly. "And of course, having a firefighter on your side was useful in all the endless small skirmishes we lived through." He extended his hand to her. "Please, don't be afraid of me. You know I wouldn't harm you."

Helle remained where she was.

"Please," he repeated.

Reluctantly, Helle moved closer. His shoulders relaxed, his mouth softened into a smile.

"Does it hurt?" she asked.

"No. But it can become a tad too warm at times. I've never made a snowball in my life—lives."

She touched his hand. "Do it again."

"Why?"

"I just want to see." She wasn't about to admit she was as fascinated as she was frightened.

"Fine." This time, he didn't extend his hands. He just snapped his fingers and light and heat crackled through the air.

"Wow." She couldn't stop herself from grinning. "Amazing!"

"Not always," he replied, sounding curt. Jason wiped his hands down his jeans. "Takes some time to learn to control it."

"I can imagine."

"No you can't." He frowned. "You have no idea what it's like to wake up in the night with your hands on fire—or how it feels when you burn your mother by mistake."

"I'm sorry," she muttered.

Jason shrugged. "Shall we go?"

He suggested they take a cab, but Helle wanted to walk, despite the light drizzle.

"It's a long walk back to Salem Street," he warned. Good. Long enough that all this stiffness between them could somehow melt away. They trudged in silence for a while, holding hands as they made their way up the elegant, tree-lined Kensington Palace Garden Street. Security guards lounged by most of the houses, a couple of joggers breezed by, and still they said nothing. Helle peeked at him. Her three-thousand-year-old fire boy. She had to shake her head, muffling a little laugh.

"What?"

"Nothing." She glanced at him again, and this time she couldn't quite contain the laughter.

"What's so funny?" But his mouth was twitching, eyes crinkling at the corners.

"You. Me. All of this." Helle took his hand. "The Helle and Jason freak show, that's us."

He just tightened his hold on her hand.

They talked a bit about Woolf and the odd events of the day.

"Curtis says they had real IDs," Jason said when Helle voiced her suspicion the whole thing was a set-up.

"Yeah, and we all know good, honest policemen make enough to walk around in matching top quality black suits." They took a right onto busy Bayswater Road. She kicked at a stone, sending it skidding across the pavement. "What was he up to? He knew I hadn't stolen anything."

"Intimidation," Jason said drily. "Samion's preferred cup of tea."

"Tell me about it."

"Hey," he said gently. "I'm here, Helle."

They were quiet the rest of the way, his arm tight around her shoulders. At her door he bent his head to hers and kissed her repeatedly, hands holding her still. His tongue flitted carefully against hers, and her gut pulsed with heat. The temperature rose exponentially when he pinned her back against the door, exploring her mouth thoroughly. After some time he gently loosened her hands from his hair and planted one last kiss on her forehead.

"Sweet dreams," he said with a half-smile, "see you tomorrow."

What? He wasn't coming in? Damn the man! Well, she wasn't about to beg, so with a little wave she pushed the door open. Inside, she sank down to sit on the stairs.

"You shouldn't have done that," Jason chided her when he finally caught up. She turned and frowned.

"Why not? I simply told him the truth."

Jason sighed, wondering if this impulsive being would ever learn caution.

"You humiliated Prince Samion in front of the whole court." He took her hand to make her stop. "That was unnecessary."

She was bright red with fury. "If my father thinks he can decide who I'm to marry," she began, but Jason covered her lips with his finger.

"He can. You know that. He's your father, and he can give your hand in marriage where it suits him best."

Her eyes widened. "Don't you care?" Her voice broke. Jason drew her into his arms.

"Of course I do." His voice was muffled by her hair. "But I can't

101

challenge his authority. We have to have him on our side. Antagonising a potential suitor will not help."

She leaned back to look at him. "I'm sorry, but Prince Samion was so smug, looking me up and down as if I already was his." Her eyes flashed. "I'll never be his," she snapped, but then her face fell. "He scares me. I don't like how he looks at me."

Jason stood silent, tightening his arms around her. He had also seen Samion's gaze, seen how those dark inscrutable eyes had followed the contours of her body, how they hardened into shards of obsidian at her rebuff. An involuntary shiver ran through his body. Helle lifted her face from his chest and looked him deeply in the eyes.

"I love you," she said seriously. "I want no one but you."

He smiled down at her. "And I love you. From that first moment I saw you, I have loved you."

"So your mind was made up already at the age of twelve?" she teased.

"No," he looked away and released her, only keeping hold of her hand. "No, my mind is still not made up." He smiled crookedly. "But my heart is."

Chapter 10

Jason called on the following Tuesday afternoon. "I need your help."

"Sure." She heard his smile through the phone line.

"Shouldn't you ask what I need you to do first?" he teased. "Imagine if what I want you to do is rob the Bank of England."

"I guess I'd tell you it would cost you."

He laughed. "I was wondering if you'd be willing to come in and help us out. My M&A guy is in hospital."

"What happened to him?"

"A lorry." Jason sounded grim. "Bloody big one, too."

"Oh." She leaned closer to the mirror and lifted the tweezers. "When do you need me?"

"Now? I'll send the car round."

Thirty minutes later, Helle thanked the driver and exited the car. Ironically, Jason's offices on Queen Street were less than three blocks away from Woolf & Partner over on Cannon Street, but in difference to Woolf's premises, Jason's business was housed in a five-storey brick building, the windows framed by white stucco. Inside, the building had been carefully modernised, but Helle ignored the lifts and opted for walking all the way to the top floor where a discreet black on white sign announced she was entering the premises of Morris & Son. Some moments later, she was ushered into Jason's private office. Not at all on the same scale as Woolf's, it was a nice room, dominated by the large modern desk and a gorgeous Turkish carpet in various shades of red and blue. Two comfortable leather armchairs stood by the window, a little table between them.

Jason was in his shirtsleeves, rolled up to display his forearms. He stood when she entered, offered her a seat and threw himself back into his chair.

"God, what a mess." He placed his arms on the desk. Very

nice forearms, Helle reflected, watching the play of muscles under his skin when he fiddled with his pen.

"What exactly do you need me to do?" Helle opened her laptop.

"Review all this." Jason shoved a huge pile of paper in her direction.

"Seriously?" Helle laughed. "You've never heard of the paperless office?"

"Oh, I have. Steve hasn't." Jason drummed his fingers against the desktop. "Poor sod."

"How is he?" Helle had never met this Steve person.

"According to the doctor, he looks as if someone pushed him through a grinder." Jason looked away. "But he will live, they say."

"A grinder?"

Jason set his jaw. "As I said: it was a big lorry."

"And the driver?"

"Gone." He scrubbed at his face. "So, will you do it?"

"What's the going rate?" Helle was already sorting the stack. Five different companies. None of the info sheets carried the Woolf & Partners logo. Mr Morris, it would seem, preferred to have nothing to do with Woolf's set-up.

"100 pounds an hour."

"No way." Helle sat back. "150."

They compromised on 125, Jason rolling his eyes and saying these freelance types were quite the pain in the arse. But, he added with a smile, seeing as he was indebted to her, he would be more than happy to offer her tea and biscuits before she got started. He pressed a button on his desk phone, and moments later a nice woman he introduced as Angela popped in with tea and chocolate digestives.

Steve's files might be on paper, but there was a structure to them, and by the time Jason dropped by her temporary office to ask if she wanted a lift back home, Helle had made some headway, organising things in various neat stacks.

"Should I continue using my own laptop?" she asked Jason as they made their way down to the garage.

"Not according to our IT policy." Jason opened the door for her and placed his hand on the small of her back, guiding her in the direction of his car. "I'll get you one tomorrow." He came to an abrupt stop. "Continue using?"

"Via the guest network. Your IT guy Will helped me connect so that I could access the internet…" her voice trailed off. "Shit." Woolf's techies had been all over her laptop on the Monday. "Do you think—"

"Yes." Jason was already running back the way they'd come.

"But that would mean Steve's accident…" No, Helle couldn't quite conclude the thought. Jason didn't reply. He was already on the phone to Will, taking the stairs three treads at the time.

"How much damage?" Jason paced his office, eyes leaping from Will, to Helle.

"A lot." Will shrugged. "Fortunately, we discovered it before we did the daily backup." He scratched at his mop of red hair. "Restoring the office network will be easy. Recovering the lost information will be harder. Damn!"

"I thought you said we have an uncorrupted backup file."

"We do. But the activated virus managed to send off a lot of information before we shut everything down." Will gave Helle a black look. What? Was it her fault the security protocol on the guest wifi had been that easy to circumvent?

"What sort of information?" Jason glowered at them both.

Will squinted at his screen. "Not sure. I'll have to cross reference all the data packages."

It was well past midnight and Helle was studying Will's latest printout. Everything on her laptop had been sent off into cyberspace, including all her contacts, her bank details – everything. Jason's laptop had been equally raided, and other than that, most of the information stolen seemed to be from Steve's files.

"Damn!" Jason's hair stood on end, his shirt untucked and a five o'clock shadow darkening his cheeks. "He knows the name of every single target." He scowled at his desk. "Five years of analysis down the drain."

"But he doesn't know which ones you're going for," Helle tried.

"Of course he knows which of the companies are most important to me." Jason glared at her. "Sam Woolf is not stupid, and now he has all my strategy documents as well." He sounded as if it was all her fault. Helle crossed her arms over her chest. Jason muttered something, picked up his phone, turned her back on her and dialled.

"Hey, Arthur, it's me." He wandered over to the window. "Yeah, it's after midnight here… Really? Well, tell her hello… sure, sure. Look, Arthur, I need a favour." He swivelled to look at Helle. "Do you mind?"

Without a word, she grabbed her bag and left. Bastard.

He called her some minutes later. She didn't pick up. He tried again. She let it go to voice mail. By the time the cab drew to a halt by her door, she had ten unanswered calls from him. Tough. Let him stew. Slowly, she made her way up the stairs. Right at the top, she collapsed, sitting on the top step, staring down the darkened stairwell. Woolf knew everything about her now—down to the names of her half-siblings and her size in shoes. And her bank accounts—but Will was handling that.

She jumped when her phone rang. Jason. This time she answered.

"Hi." He sounded hesitant.

"Hi." She pressed a hand to her eyes.

"Will's sorted out the bank stuff – yours and mine."

Well, that was good, she supposed, but it was not what she wanted to hear. She didn't say anything. She could hear his breathing.

"I didn't mean to insinuate this was your fault," he said stiffly.

"Fine." She hung up.

Predictably, ten seconds later, her phone rang again.

"Are you mad at me?"

"Whatever gave you that idea?" Helle leaned back against

the wall. God, she was tired. And scared. "Do you really think Woolf planned Steve's accident?"

"Yes. But we will never be able to prove it."

"But why?" Except that she already knew the answer. Woolf had calculated on Jason turning to the financial analyst closest to him.

"I've placed a bid for the Turkish company," Jason said. "Arthur thinks they're eager to sell. As for the others, if Woolf goes after them, I don't stand a chance in hell of outbidding him."

"Oh." At least the five companies she'd been working on that day were safe. She'd spent the afternoon on building the Excel formats rather than on entering the information.

"Do you want me to come over?" he asked after a lengthy minute of silence.

Yes, of course she did. She wanted him to hold her, hear his heart beat. "Would you stay?" she asked.

"Helle," he sighed. "You know I want to, but—" Helle hung up. And when he next called she didn't answer.

Jason was tempted to throw his phone at the wall. Instead, he cradled his head in his hands and dragged at his hair. He hadn't handled this well. He scowled at the printouts. It would keep until tomorrow—there was not much he could do. Jason grabbed his car keys.

In twenty minutes he was at her door. She opened it immediately, he held out his arms and she fell into them. Without a word, he carried her to the bed, spooning himself around her. She fitted just as she should into the curve of his body, her hair tickling his face. She shifted backwards, pressing her round bum against him.

"I'm scared," she said.

He tightened his hold on her. This entire matter with Steve had him on his toes. If Woolf—and he was quite convinced Woolf was involved—could do something like that to an innocent bystander, what would he do to him, to Helle? He kissed her head; he came with some protection—to kill a Wanderer was difficult—but Helle?

She turned in his arms. "Why?"

Jason wasn't quite sure how to answer. He didn't want to tell her the whole sordid story, at least not yet.

"He hates me." He brushed a finger down her nose. "In our previous life, you were meant to be his but you chose me instead." He smiled slightly. Nothing had been quite as simple, and Helle's choice had left the mighty Prince Samion humiliated.

"And now I'm choosing you again," Helle said. Jason leaned back to see her face, only dimly visible in the dark of the room.

"You are?" It made him sing inside—despite the situation with Woolf. Damn! Was it too much to ask that he be allowed a life with Helle without Woolf hovering like an enraged demon over them? Soft laughter whispered through his brain: "*What the fates have joined, must stay joined*," he heard his Wanderer mother say, and he shied away from the memory of the haggard look on her face, the day he had begged her to help him find Helle again in a future life. After he had betrayed Helle and driven her to her death.

"Hmm?" Helle yawned and snuggled closer. Just like that, she fell asleep. Jason didn't. He spent the entire night watching her, thinking it was a miracle to spend a whole night with her. Their first night together, he thought with a crooked smile, smoothing her hair off her face. One of many, he hoped, but deep in his belly he knew that unless he could vanquish Samion, their time together would be as short this time round as the last. He rolled over onto his back and stared up at the ceiling. He would need help. God alone knew where he would find it.

November dawn was seeping through the white curtains when Jason finally fell asleep, Helle's head pillowed on his chest. In his dreams, they were running hand in hand, and to their right the coastline plunged to meet the deep blue of the Black Sea. She turned to laugh at him, her thick braid bouncing between her shoulders. A braid the colour of sun-ripened barley, held together by a bright blue band.

He didn't know who he hated the most: the golden girl who had just laughed his suit out of her father's court, or the red-haired Wanderer, the youth to whom her eyes strayed continuously. He swept the remains of his pride around him and walked out of the hall, deaf to Kantor's pleading entreaties. Let the old fool sweat, let him consider the implications for this little dung-ridden corner of the world if she wasn't given to him in marriage.

He was entitled to her. Samion, Prince of Kolchis had a right to demand her hand in marriage, to father sons on her who would proudly claim their descent from Helios through their mother. And once old Kantor was dead—an event Samion would be more than delighted to anticipate—Tarokyie's fertile lands would be added to his, thereby making his control over this part of the Black Sea shoreline complete.

He studied the defensive walls that enclosed Kantor's little citadel with the practised eyes of an aggressor. Impossible to penetrate without loss of many lives, easy to defend through an extended siege. Yes, a perfect building block in his strategy to become the overlord of this fertile area, powerful enough to treat with the Greeks and grow even richer in trade. And then, of course, there was the matter of Kantor's wealth. Everyone knew the man was sitting on a mountain of gold, his treasury bulging at the seams—gold Samion intended to claim as his own.

He saw the girl come out of the hall, those blue eyes of hers narrowing in the sun. The curve of her hips, of her breasts, spoke of fertility. She'd give him a line of strong sons. Besides, he wanted her, desired to wind those golden tresses round his wrist to hold her still as he mounted her, wished to hear her gasp her submission when he took her.

Her hand grazed the arm of the Wanderer. It was common knowledge that those two were straying too close to the line of decorous behaviour. How her father could allow it he didn't know, but the girl needed to be taken in hand. Samion smiled to himself. That was a task he would gladly take upon himself.

Chapter 11

It had been a bad week. With the exception of the Wednesday morning when she'd woken to find Jason beside her in bed, albeit as fully dressed as she was, the following six days had been a sequence of disconcerting events and hard work, with Helle spending as long days as Jason did in his office, trying to salvage what could be salvaged.

"He is paying you, right?" Alison asked when she and Helle shared a pizza well after midnight on the Tuesday, a week after Steve's accident. For a woman who had just spent 16 hours working on a psychiatric ward, Alison looked remarkably bright, her dark hair brushed to a lustre, her eyes glittering.

"Through the nose," Helle said, making Alison grin. She offered Alison the last slice, shaking her head when Alison neatly folded it together and stuffed all of it into her mouth.

"Talent," Alison mumbled through all the food.

"Disgusting," Helle corrected. She cocked her head. "Spill it, Alison."

"Huh?"

"Come off it! You've been grinning like a loon since you got home. I'm guessing this is due to some dark and dangerous doctor."

"Definitely dark and dangerous." Alison winked. "But I can't tell you more than that."

"Alison!"

"I can't—I've promised him." Her face softened. "He says it's for the best."

"What, he's married?" Helle gave her friend a worried look. Alison had a tendency to go for men most likely to break her heart.

Alison mimed zipping her mouth shut.

"You're really irritating at times," Helle said.

"Sorry, honey, if I tell you, I'll have to kill you." Alison grinned.

"Fine." Helle gave Alison's arm a little shake. "But be careful, okay?"

"Me? It's him you should be worried about." Alison stood, revealing an indecently short skirt that hugged her curvy ass.

"Ah: he's old enough to have a heart attack," Helle teased.

"That would be unfortunate," Alison said. "I'd like to have sex with him first." She stretched, arching her back so that her full breasts strained against her shirt. "I'm hoping that will happen sooner rather than later—it's so long ago I might not remember how."

Helle snorted. "Yeah, all of six weeks."

"Four actually." Alison smirked and waltzed out of the kitchen.

On Friday afternoon, Jason let out a whoop and came jogging over to where Helle was sitting, buried in yet another mountain of paper documents left behind by Steve.

"The Turkish deal is done."

"It is?"

"Well, not formally, it isn't, but we have a Letter of Intent." He looked happier than he had done in a week. "I'll have to go to Istanbul to sign the final documents."

"Istanbul? I've never been to Istanbul."

"You want to come along?" He grinned at her.

"I'd love to." Helle shoved at a tottering pile of documents. "I deserve a holiday." At least Steve was recovering, she thought. "Besides, if all that stuff about previous lives is true, then Turkey is my home too, isn't it?"

A shadow crossed his face. "It is." His frown deepened. "What do you mean, if it's all true?"

"Sometimes it all sounds so unbelievable." Most of the time, actually. "So now and then I prefer to take things at face value—you, me, no previous life, no odd baggage that you know so much more about than I do." She shrugged. "I like being normal."

"You are normal. We both are."

"So let's do normal things," Helle said. "Let's go clubbing tomorrow."

"Why, Ms Madsen, are you inviting me on a date?"

"Seeing as I might grow old and wrinkled before you take the initiative, yes."

His face fell. "I'm not being attentive enough?"

"I'm kidding, okay?" Not entirely. They seemed to spend more time walking and talking than doing fun stuff. She gave him a teasing look. "Do you even know how to dance?"

"Do I know how to dance? Ha, it will be my pleasure to dance you off your feet."

"Easy to say, harder to do." Helle gave him a challenging look. Jason put his hands on her desk and leaned over to kiss her on her cheek.

"You'll be begging me to stop," he promised. As if.

He looked her over when he came to pick her up.

"Nice," he said, sliding a hand down to where the short black skirt just covered the lacy tops of her stockings. "Very nice." He took hold of her hands and stood back, studying her intently. "You still run?"

"What do you mean, still run?" Helle gave him an irritated look. These oblique hints at a previous existence were disquieting, and, as she'd told him, she was still in two minds about all this reincarnation stuff. "Was jogging in the vogue back then as well?"

"No." He laughed. "But you were the fastest runner in the village." He winked. "Made it very difficult to corner you at times."

She might have asked him out, but Jason had chosen the venue, which was how they ended up at one of the more popular clubs in Soho. Jason breezed them through the line, a hand to her lower back as he guided her towards the music. On the dancefloor, Jason ruled. She had never met a man who danced with such abandon—but not once did he allow her to get too far away from him, a possessive presence at her side, in front of her, behind her. In jeans that hugged his hips and thighs, black chunky boots and a white shirt that looked blue

112

under the flashing lights, he attracted far too many admiring glances from the girls who thronged the dancefloor. Helle shimmied closer to him, glowering at a bony brunette who was smiling invitingly at him—not that Jason even noticed. His thick dark hair, the ear-stud, the five o'clock shadow—he looked hot and smelled divine, as Helle discovered when he pulled her close and swung her round, making her laugh. She felt young—heck, she *was* young—and she danced until her silk top clung to her back, ignoring the protesting whine from her toes.

"Drink," she finally gasped, holding her hands up in surrender.

"Loo," he replied with a grin. "I'll meet you at the bar."

She managed to catch the attention of the barman and gulped down a glass of water before ordering wine for them both.

"Helle," a dark voice said, and she almost jumped out of her skin, retreating so fast she banged into the nearby barstool. Woolf was standing no more than a couple of yards away, a black shirt tucked into black jeans. He crooked a finger. She shook her head. "What, has he told you to stay away from me?"

"He didn't need to." Helle sidled further away from him. "I prefer keeping clear of men who threaten to hurt me."

"Hurt you?" He sneered. "You walk into my office wearing the Wanderer's handiwork round your neck, and you talk about me hurting you?" He loomed over her. "Damn it, Helle! He stole you once, and now…" His nostrils flared. "You were supposed to be mine," he said in a calmer voice. "Mine, Helle."

"You tried to coerce me, threaten me," Helle protested. But something in his voice sparked a flash of remorse, a feeling quickly submerged by the panic she experienced when he trapped her against the bar, one arm on either side of her.

"I did? As I recall I did nothing more than kiss you."

"You blackmailed me!" The bar was digging into her back. "And that time in the club—what were you planning to do then?"

"You didn't protest, did you?" Woolf made an amused sound. "As I recall, you followed me quite docilely."

"I couldn't protest. You know that."

His brows rose. "I do?" He leaned closer, and Helle squished her eyes shut, hearing him laugh. "Afraid?" he jeered. "Trust me, had I wanted to really hurt you…" He cleared his throat. "So what has he told you, your red-haired Wanderer?"

"Told me about what?" She dared a peek. He was still standing too close.

"You, him, me. What has he told you of that former life? Has he told you how young you were when you died? Or why you died?" He studied Helle's face. "No, I can see he hasn't. I wonder why."

Helle threw her wine in his face at the same time as Jason gripped Woolf by the shoulder and tore him away.

"Don't touch her," Jason snarled.

Woolf laughed. "I already have, Wanderer. But you know that, don't you? It was you who hacked my system and stole the files—and the pictures."

What? Helle stared at Jason. His back was stiff with tension, hands curled into fists. She'd not asked him about the files, assuming he'd been the one to destroy them, but this was the first time she'd heard about pictures. What pictures? And then she remembered that evening when Woolf undid her shirt, and she wanted to die.

"Not that I'm surprised," Woolf went on. "It's not exactly the first time you've stolen from me, is it?"

"Steal?" Jason growled. "Look who's talking. And what about what you did to Steve?"

"Steve?" Woolf shrugged. "I have no idea what you're talking about—and even if I did, I'd say it's collateral damage." He sneered. "You want to play with the big boys, you have to take some pain." He glanced at Helle. "Isn't that right, Helle? Pain and pleasure, hey?"

"Bastard!" Jason shoved him. "You'll never—"

Woolf laughed again. "But I already have, haven't I, Wanderer? I've taken her where you will never take her, done things to her you'll never do. I've seen her crawl with pain, and still offer herself to me."

Helle made a strangled sound. What was he talking about?

Woolf smiled. "Do you remember, Helle?" She shook her head, and he laughed. "No? I can assure you it will be my pleasure to prod your dormant memories alive." With that, Woolf was off, gliding towards the lounge area.

"Has he?" she asked.

"Hurt you?" Jason nodded. "Repeatedly." He touched her hand. "But that was then, not now."

She chewed her lip. "What pictures?"

"Just pictures." He flushed. "Most of them were just snaps of you in the office."

"Not all, right?"

"No."

"And you looked at them?"

"I did."

Helle pushed off from the bar and bumped her way through the crowd. She had to get away, find somewhere to hide herself.

"Helle, wait!" His fingers brushed her sleeve, but she just pushed on, needing to get away from him. He caught up with her by the DJ booth. Electro house boomed from the loudspeakers, the bass reverberating through the floor. He caught hold of her arm. She tried to push him away. The music changed to something slower and without a word he swept her into his arms, pressing her as close as he could as he moved in time with the music. She hid her face against his shirt. He kissed her head, murmuring her name over and over again.

The music ended, and Jason steered her across the dancefloor, reclaimed their coats and, taking her hand, led her up the stairs and out onto the street. Chilly and damp November air made her overheated face tingle.

"Is that why you haven't touched me?" she asked.

"Because I've seen pictures of you half dressed? Of course not." He slipped a hand in under her chin, lifting her face until she had to meet his eyes. "But I wanted to give you time. Wanted to give us both time."

Helle gave him a wobbly smile. "I don't need time. I need…"You, she thought. "Why do you need time?"

He looked discomfited, shifting on his feet. "I'm…well, I suppose I'm scared."

"Scared?

"Apprehensive, rather. I can't count the times I've imagined finding you again, loving you again. And now that I have, I worry that—"

"You'll be disappointed?"

"No. I'm afraid I'll disappoint." He pulled her close enough to drape an arm around her shoulders. "You're shivering."

"I want to go home." The thought of running into Woolf again had her stomach twisting into knots. She took his hand. "To your place."

She was on him in the cab, grabbing at him as if she intended to have sex there and then, on the back seat. He didn't mind: he was done with waiting, and so he kissed her back, pinning her against the seat as he ravaged her mouth, kissed his way down to her cleavage.

"This is how I feel about you," he growled, pressing his erection against her. "All I want to do is love you, have you in my bed for hours until you disintegrate under my touch."

"So why all this waiting?" Her breath was coming in shallow puffs.

"I already told you—and I wanted you to be sure." He slid his hand in under her top and found her breast, cupping it, squeezing it.

"Idiot." She grabbed hold of his hair and kissed him— hard. "I've been sure since you walked in the door at Woolf & Partners."

He pulled back. "You have?"

She nodded. "You were my Jason. I had no idea what that meant—and truth be told, I'm still not so sure what it means— but I knew you were mine. Only mine," she added, biting his lower lip a tad too hard.

They tumbled out of the cab. She hugged him from behind while he struggled with the locks, she stood on her toes to kiss his cheek while he entered the alarm code, and then they were in the hall.

"This…is…not…how…" he panted as he pushed her back against the wall.

"Shut up."

So he did, kissing her until she seemed to melt into his arms. His hands on her legs, up her skirt. Thin, thin knickers, and he would never know just what they looked like, his fingers tearing them apart. It made her gasp when he pushed two fingers into her, his thumb kneading her clitoris. Her hands on his waist, his arse, fumbling with his belt, his fly. His erection was painfully large, and he groaned when her hand closed round it.

"Damn it, Helle!" He was going to lose it if she kept that up.

"Take me," she replied. "Here, now."

He found a condom in his pocket, but she shook her head.

"I've got it covered," she said hoarsely. "And I'm clean."

"Me too." And he wanted her, skin against skin.

He tugged at her top and her bra, baring her breasts to his hands and his mouth. Blood was thudding hot and hard through his head, through his cock, and she was so warm, so wet. He lifted her up, she wrapped her legs around him, and there. Oh yes, there! He pumped into her. She moaned his name. They crashed into the wall, he thrust into her hard, so hard, and she was clenching around him, her mouth at his ear, her hands in his hair. Jason groaned her name, holding her hips in place as he came in wave after wave. She sagged in his arms and he leaned his forehead against hers, reluctant to let go.

Slowly, they slid down to the floor. She pillowed her head on his chest, he threaded his fingers through her hair, trying to calm his roaring pulse.

"I need to pee," she said, sounding hoarse.

"I need a drink," he replied, before heaving himself upright and helping her to stand. He smoothed her skirt and tidied her top, which made her grin.

"You don't like dishevelled?"

"I love dishevelled." He zipped up his jeans. "But some

sort of standard has to be maintained." He chose not to button his shirt, took her hand and led her to the bathroom. "I'll be in there." He nodded in the direction of the large room that took up most of the bottom floor.

"If I get lost I'll call you."

"It's not Buckingham Palace," he said with a laugh.

He was standing by the windows, staring at the darkness outside, when she came to join him. He watched her reflection as she approached, noting with a little smile how often she smoothed at the short skirt—being naked beneath was not something she was entirely comfortable with. Jason stuck his hands in his pockets. He wanted her again, and this time he'd make love to her, not just bang her.

She stopped for a moment, studying the room. He followed her gaze as it swept the white walls, the few pieces of modern furniture, before coming to a halt on the huge circular fireplace, hovering a couple of feet above the floor.

"I thought you weren't allowed to light real fires here in London," she said.

"We're not." He tapped the fireplace. "Gas."

"Oh."

He led the way to the gigantic Howard—a nostalgic reminder of his parents, albeit now upholstered in a modern, grey striped fabric—and patted the cushion beside him.

"Umm." She squirmed. "What did you do with my panties?" In response, he produced the strands of lacy material from his pocket and dangled them from his finger.

"These?" He lowered his voice, smiling at the wave of bright red flooded her face. "Beyond repair, I fear. Come, sit." When she still looked hesitant, he pulled her down into his lap. "You okay?" he asked, swiping a finger down her face.

She just nodded, her hand sliding across his chest, down his belly. Jason threw his head back, thinking he would never get enough of her touch. Helle, with him—an impossible hope come true. She slid a finger under his waistband, then there were two fingers, her whole hand, exploring him.

"More?" he asked huskily, and already his cock was hardening.

Helle met his eyes. "More."

He led her up two flights of stairs. He'd remodelled the entire upper floor into one large loft—his private space, all in hardwood and white. A large bed at one end, and at the opposite end, below a roof of glass and with a view of the garden, was his bathtub.

"In your bedroom?" Helle giggled. "Seriously?"

"I like baths." He turned on the tap. "Don't you?"

"I—"

He kissed her silent, kissed her as he relieved her of her clothes—all but the lacy hold-ups. "I like you in those," he said, holding her at arm's length. The black nylon contrasted with her fair skin, lending an edge of sin he found more than alluring.

"Well, I can't exactly bathe in them," she said.

"No?" One swift move and he had her in his arms, making her laugh in protest as he deposited her in the water. He shed his clothes and joined her, sliding down to sit behind her. She reclined against him, he slid his hands up her arms, her neck, down the slope of her flanks, over her belly to rest just over her sex. Jason stilled his hands, exerting only the slightest of rhythmic pressure. His fingers explored downwards, through the patch of blonde curls. Helle sighed, her hips undulating in time with his fingers.

Steam beaded her skin, water collecting in drops to slide down her breasts. He kissed her neck and she pushed back against him, her arse warm and soft against his throbbing erection.

"Jason," she moaned, twisting so that she could kiss him. "Jason," she repeated, when he released her mouth. "My Jason."

Drying her was one slow exploration. He divested her of the wet stockings, wrapped her in a towel and carried her over to the bed. If he closed his eyes, he could hear the poplars rustling overhead, smell the ripening wheat and the distant sea, feel the heat of the day when he first loved her. So many years ago, and yet an indelible memory.

Time for new memories, a new life with her, the woman who'd haunted his innumerable lives. Jason brushed her face

119

free of wet hair and kissed her. He cupped her breasts and kissed first one, then the other nipple. They hardened under his warm mouth, and when he suckled, she arched her back, fingers knotting in his hair.

He held her still as he slid down her front, kissing his way to her pubic mound. She smelled of evergreens, but when he buried his nose in her curls, he caught the salty scent of arousal, of woman. His woman. He played his tongue over her clitoris, and her thighs tensed. He did it again, and her hips rose. Jason blew softly and she twisted beneath him. Slowly, he built the need in her, and just as she was about to come, he moved up, to kiss her breasts, her mouth. She gripped him, begged for him to take her. He thrust inside, and she stilled. Again, and he felt her clenching tight around him. He pulled out. He intended to extend this for as long as possible.

"Lie still," he said when she made as if to sit up, hands reaching for him. He pressed her back against the pillow. She rubbed herself against his leg, hips thrusting demandingly. "Not yet." A long kiss, and she gasped out loud when he pulled at her nipple. She laughed when he dipped his tongue in her navel, stopped laughing when he buried his head between her legs.

He nipped her all the way up to her neck, he nibbled at her jaw, her earlobe.

"Kiss me," he said, and she rose off the bed, clutching at him as she did. He pushed himself inside. So many sensations; her warm, wet mouth, her moist, hot sex. His pulse, thundering through his head. His cock, sinking deeper and deeper into her. Not yet, not yet.

Once again, he pulled out, and she moaned in protest. Jason arranged her like a work of art on his bed. Eyes dark with arousal, legs sprawled wide, her pink folds glistening with her moisture.

He cupped his balls and gave her a slow smile. "Touch yourself."

"Now?" She lifted her head. He met her eyes, closing his fist round his hard cock. She watched, lips parted, as his hand moved up and down, from root to tip.

"Now you," he said, and her fingers slid over her sex, her hips rocking back and forth. She threw her head back, eyes closed as her pelvis gyrated, and he knew she was seconds from coming.

"No," he said, grabbing her hand. He sucked her fingers clean before guiding them to his cock. A sigh escaped him when she pumped him, her hand hard and demanding. He batted away her fingers, leaned over her, sliding his erection over her clit. She moaned. He took her, one swift movement sheathing his entire length in her welcoming warmth.

"Jason!" she gasped, nails digging into his back. "Ja…" he covered her mouth with his and flexed his hips—hard. Again. Again. He came and went. Below him she bucked and called his name. Now. Yes, damn it, now!

It took a long time for him to find the energy required to do more than lie beside her, staring into her eyes. So long, in fact, that somewhere midway through he fell asleep, smiling at the way she'd gripped his thumb. He remembered that, he thought fuzzily. His Helle had always held his thumb as she drifted off to sleep.

In the earliest of dawns, when the dark night began to shift to grey, he rolled himself on top of her again, his legs spreading hers apart. And he held himself on his elbows, moving very slowly until she clung to him, hoarsely calling his name.

"This is how I want it to be," he said afterwards, with her a heavy weight in his arms, "every morning for the rest of my existence, I want to start like this." He wound a golden lock round his finger. "I want to spend every night with you, I want to bury myself in you and feel the thudding of your heart beneath my hand, I want to wake with your warm breath on my skin and know that you are here, beside me, forever, and that I am finally home."

Helle lifted herself up to look at him. "Me too," she whispered. "Me too."

"Jason?" Helle squeezed down on the bench beside him. "Tell me about the Wanderers."

"What do you want to know?" he replied, frowning down at the piece of driftwood he was whittling.

"Everything," she said solemnly, making him laugh.

"I don't know everything. There are many secrets my mother has not as yet allowed me to share. So I can't turn you into a toad or freeze a horse midair or raise a person from his grave." He broke off when he saw her horrified face. "Helle," he said reproachfully, "I'm teasing." He went back to his whittling.

"Wanderers heal, Helle. We heal the body and some can even heal the ailments that afflict a ravaged soul. My mother can." He smiled with pride. "But then she's probably the best of all alive. And she's gifted, of course."

"Like you," Helle nodded. Jason shrugged and looked away.

"No, not like me. She is far more powerful than I am. She probably could transform you into a toad or freeze that horse in mid-leap. I have very much more to learn," he added quietly, thinking that he didn't want to. Not anymore. He was sixteen and wanted other things in life, first and foremost the girl by his side.

"So, one day you will be a Wanderer too," Helle said, her voice wobbling, "and maybe as powerful as your lady mother." She gave him a brilliant smile, while her eyes shone with tears. "And then you'll leave, because that's what Wanderers do. They go to where they're needed."

Jason put a finger to her cheek and gently caught a trailing tear. "I don't know, Helle," he said hoarsely, "I don't know."

Chapter 12

Alison sucked the last of the milkshake through her straw and sighed contentedly.

"My kind of breakfast," she said, combing her fingers through her hair.

"Mmm." Helle wasn't too keen on burgers and fries this early in the day, but it had been Alison's turn to choose, and predictably she'd gone with her favourite burger joint, saying the food more than made up for the lacklustre interior.

"So," Alison said, looking Helle up and down. "You look absolutely radiant."

She put a sarcastic emphasis on the 'radiant' part. Helle threw a self-conscious look at her reflection, all frizzy hair, bruised eyes and swollen lips, and conceded Alison was right. She smiled, hugging the memory of last night to herself.

"Can you please stop grinning like an idiot?" Alison teased, jabbing Helle with her index finger. "One might get the impression think this was a first for you." Of course it wasn't, but it had almost felt as if it was. Just the thought of Jason had Helle's insides twisting with longing, and she shifted restlessly in her chair, feeling a dull ache between her thighs.

Alison finished the last of her fries. "I danced with Sam last night." She stretched and grinned. "Well, maybe we did a bit more than dancing."

"What?" Helle sat up straight.

"Yup," said Alison brightly. "Boy can he move."

Helle took her hand. "Stay away from him, okay? He's dangerous."

"Dangerous?" Alison smiled condescendingly. "For you, maybe. For me—I don't think so. I can handle men like him."

"He'll hurt you."

"Is that what he did to you?" There was a gleam in Alison's

eyes, a wetness to her mouth. "Did he belt you? Whip you? Tie you up?"

"No." Helle frowned at her. "Of course not."

"So what did he do to you?"

"Sexually? Nothing." And thank heavens for that. "But he…" Helle searched for a word. "He intimidated me, dominated me."

Alison laughed. "Well of course he did. The man's a dom, and I happen to like doms."

"Dom?" Helle blinked, seeing a rather weird image of Woolf in leather and with a whip in his hand. "You do?" she added, staring at Alison.

"My taste in men is much more mature than yours."

Well, Helle thought, that was probably untrue—at least if she assumed Jason was telling the truth.

Alison stretched again, arching her back. She reminded Helle of a cat, the similarity emphasised by Alison's green eyes. "In my opinion, the great lovers are always doms—men who know what they want and what I need."

"What, you need to be whipped?"

"It's not all about restraints and whips." Alison gave her an annoyed look. "But yes, I like the…well…the conflicting sensations."

Helle's mouth fell open. Her best friend—her assertive, loud best friend—some sort of submissive?

"Don't look at me like that. It's not as if I'm some sort of freak, is it?"

"No, no, of course not." Helle swallowed. "But Woolf… Alison, he'll tear you apart if he feels like it."

"Don't be ridiculous. There are rules, okay? But you wouldn't understand—Sam's too intense for people like you."

"Too intense?" Helle felt a spurt of anger. "Yeah, you can say that again! He's a fucking bully, and what he tried to do to me—"

"Tried to do to you? He says that first you came on to him, then you went all ice maiden on him. You've only yourself to blame if you play the cock-tease with a man like Sam Woolf."

Alison's mouth softened. "Mr Woolf does not tolerate such behaviour."

Helle planted her hands on the table. "I never came on to him. Never."

"That's not what he says."

"Then he lies."

Alison snorted. "He said you'd say that, blame it on him rather than on losing your nerve."

"And who do you believe?" Helle asked, still trying to assimilate the fact that her best friend had been discussing her with Sam Woolf.

Alison lifted her shoulders. "Both, I think. You sent out signals he misinterpreted, he reacted accordingly, and you misunderstood." She grinned. "Not, I assure you, an issue where he and I are concerned. Want some pie for dessert?" she asked, thereby cutting off any further discussion.

Once they had pie and coffee in paper mugs in front of them, Alison returned to the subject of Jason.

"You still haven't told me when you met him."

"Yes we did; Frankfurt."

Alison wagged a finger at her. "Bullshit." She leaned forward. "So where?"

"None of your business." Helle sipped her coffee, avoiding Alison's eyes. Should she tell her? No way, her brain scoffed, Alison would never believe her. True. But Helle needed someone to talk to—had needed that for weeks—and Alison was the closest thing she had to a sister. And it wasn't as if she could tell Mum.

"Helle!" Alison kicked her under the table. "You can tell me, you know that."

Usually, yes, but with Alison mooning over Woolf, Helle wasn't that sure. Still, Alison was her best friend, had always been there for her. She pursed her lips. No, she decided, it was all too weird, and Alison was way too pragmatic—and fixated on Woolf.

"I'm not sure I should," she said.

Alison looked as if she'd been slapped. "What? You don't trust me? Me? The friend who's been there for you since you were four and managed to poison every single koi carp in your dad's precious fishpond?"

"By mistake," Helle protested. She'd fed them detergent instead of fish food.

"Still. I didn't say a word—even when he asked me." Alison mimed zipping her lips closed. She covered Helle's hand with her own. "You're insulting me, Helle. And making me nervous. What can possibly be so bad you can't share it with me?"

"You have no idea," Helle muttered. "If I tell you, you must promise you will never tell. Never." Wrong thing to say: Alison's eyes lit up, but she crossed her heart like they'd done when they were kids and swore she would never utter a word. Helle gnawed her lip. Alison had never betrayed her confidences before, but this was...No: she shouldn't. Alison squeezed her hand. "I'm here for you, okay? And I can handle it. You know I can, BFFs forever, right?"

"Forever," Helle echoed with a little smile. The desire to discuss all this weird stuff with someone won out: taking a deep breath, she began to talk.

For the first time ever, Alison was mute. Her mouth hung half-open, the pie forgotten. After what seemed an eternity, she cleared her throat.

"You can't be serious," she said flatly.

"I am." Helle traced a long, loopy J on the table. "Well, at least he is." She threw Alison a look from under her lashes.

"And you think Sam is weird?" Alison hissed. "Damn it, Helle, he's just an ordinary control freak. But this...The man belongs in an asylum somewhere."

"Who does?" Jason said, appearing at Helle's shoulder. "Hi, lioness," he murmured, kissing her cheek. Alison gawked. Rightly so, Helle thought, looking her man over. Jason was hot in his three-piece suits, but in hip-hugging jeans, Timberland boots and a sweater he was to die for. "Alison," Jason said in greeting. "Your choice of venue, I gather. Is the coffee any good?"

"Good enough for me," Alison replied. She studied him openly. "It doesn't show, does it?"

"Alison," Helle warned.

"What?" Alison gave her a belligerent look. "You don't want me looking him over?" She smiled frostily at Jason. "Good-looking men always attract my attention."

Jason averted his eyes, his cheeks flushing. Alison leaned towards him, undressing him with her eyes.

"Remarkable," she said. "He looks totally normal."

"Alison!" Helle flew out of her chair.

"Sheesh, keep your hair on." Alison held up her hands in an apologetic gesture. "Having listened to Helle yammering on about you, I was starting to wonder."

Jason lifted his eyebrows and threw Helle a look.

"She yammers? Is that good or bad?"

"It depends," Alison replied, "borderline obsessive if you ask me, but then maybe you don't mind, right?"

"No, I don't mind," he said, smiling at Helle.

"Interesting," Alison mused. "Helle seems totally knocked off her feet today, don't you think? You, on the other hand look fantastic. Different night lives?"

Alison was right: Jason did look fabulous. His whole body was less tense, more at ease. His eyes were calm as he looked at Helle, a little smile playing on his lips. He winked and sent her an air kiss before turning back to Alison, one long leg extended to rub his foot slowly along Helle's shin.

"So, from what I hear you're the actual God's gift to women," Alison said, lowering her voice. Jason's face smoothed into a bland mask: rather coolly he asked her what she meant.

"Well you know," Alison fidgeted, bumping her elbow into Helle's chair, "young body, old mind."

The mood plummeted from good to totally disastrous in less than ten seconds, and Helle silently cursed Alison to hell and back. She could have snapped icicles off Jason's voice when he asked Alison what she meant by that, and Alison said something sarcastic about misunderstandings before she abruptly stood up to get them refills.

"Care to tell me what that was about?" he said.

"I told her." Helle eyed him cautiously. "I had to tell someone, and I figured she was a better choice than Mum."

"And did she believe you?"

Helle shrugged. She wasn't too sure she believed everything he said, so how could she expect Alison to believe in it?

"I don't know. At least she didn't call the psychiatric ward and have me committed," she tried to joke, deciding not to share Alison's comment about asylums.

"It wasn't your secret to tell," he said angrily, getting up.

"Hey," she snapped. "I've only told one person, and in confidence. What's the big deal?"

"It makes people look at me as if I'm an abnormal freak." He dragged both hands through his hair. "I don't like that. I don't like being told I'm a—what was it—gift to womankind because I'm young in body but old in mind."

Helle felt a flare of anger. "I didn't ask you to dump all this on me, you know," she hissed, trying to keep her voice down. "And by the way, as a come-on tactic it has its drawbacks. It would scare the shit out of most people."

He jerked as if she'd slapped him. His hands closed over her arms, sending waves of uncomfortable heat through her.

"It wasn't a come-on tactic. It's the truth!" A moment later he was walking away from her, shoving Alison out of the way.

"I'm sorry Helle. I shouldn't have abused your confidence," Alison said, setting down a brimming mug in front of Helle.

"No you're not. You did it on purpose." Helle forced the tears back into their tracts.

Alison sighed. "I did—and maybe I was wrong to do so, but all that reincarnation shit, well—"

"You did it out of spite," Helle interrupted.

Alison raised her brows. "What? Just because I have problems believing his crap, I'm being spiteful?"

"It's not crap!" Helle glared at Alison. "That's the last time I tell you anything."

"Fine, see if I care." Alison tossed her hair. A heavy silence descended. Helle had no intention of breaking it—in fact, she was considering getting up and leaving, when Alison cleared her throat.

"I was out of line, okay? And whether delusional or not, he's carrying a torch the size of the Statue of Liberty for you."

"You think?" Helle muttered, looking sideways at her.

"Oh yes," Alison assured her. "He looks at you so intensely it actually hurts."

Helle pulled her coffee cup towards her and sipped, looking morosely through the window. She wasn't going to call him. If he wanted to be with her he knew where to find her, she thought, staring at the people walking by on the sidewalk. All of this was so complicated it made her head ache.

A hand on her neck made her start. "Save some for me." Jason sat down beside her, his arm heavy on her shoulders.

"There's plenty left." Helle handed him the cup. "I've kept it warm for you."

He grunted and took a sip. "I'm sorry," he said gruffly, looking at no one in particular.

"So am I." Alison narrowed her eyes. "But if you hurt Helle, I'll come after you with a scalpel." She collected scarf, handbag and coat and leapt to her feet. "Thanks for breakfast. I have to run." With a wave in their direction she took off. Moments later, she was outside, waving down a cab.

"Where's she off to?" Jason asked.

"Boyfriend, I guess." Helle gritted her teeth. "Woolf, I think."

"Woolf?" Jason sounded confused.

"You heard me. Apparently, my best friend likes it rough." Her stomach tightened at the thought.

"You have to warn her."

"I have. But Alison is quite convinced she can handle him."

"Idiot! No one handles Woolf." He frowned. "Did you tell her about Steve?"

"How can I? We've got no proof, no nothing."

"But she knows he came to your apartment, doesn't she? You told her, I hope."

"Of course I did. But she tells me I'm overreacting, that all he wants to do is make amends." Helle traced the veins along the inside of his wrist. "I'll just have to keep an eye on her."

"Hmph!" Jason captured her hand. "She's playing with fire."

"She's a big girl." At present a rather irritating girl, a constant case of snarkiness and PMS tantrums. Maybe that was

Woolf getting to her, bringing out the resentful jealousy that always simmered just below the surface in Alison—in general not directed at Helle, even if now and then there'd be a bitchy comment about some being born with silver spoons in their mouths, while others had to work for their living. As if. Helle sighed. She might have a trust fund, but her father had made it very clear he expected her to work and work hard. With an effort, Helle shook off all these thoughts and stood, gesturing at the bright day outside.

"Walk? We can go to my place."

"Or you come home with me and I cook you dinner." He took her hand. "Besides, I have to work—and I need your help."

"You have to polish your pick-up lines, Mr Morris," Helle chided.

"Why?" He smiled at her. "They're working."

Three hours later, Helle stood up to stretch her back. They were in Jason's study, a room lined with bookcases crammed with books, and with a gigantic antique desk presently littered with papers and laptops—new laptops. Jason was frowning down at the document in his hand, pen in his mouth.

"Time for a break." Helle wiggled into his lap, curling up against his chest. She needed his proximity after their recent argument over whether he should bring in the police or not in relation to the virus attack. Jason had refused, saying he had no intention of having a dozen police officers turning his office upside down—besides, they'd never find anything.

"A break?" He dug his chin into her head. "I don't have time for breaks." But he sat back, arms wrapped around her. On the opposite side of the room hung a huge world map, with hundreds of small red pins stuck across it.

"What's that?" Helle asked. "Your world dominion plan?"

"No." He kissed her hair. "That's my 'looking for Helle' map."

"Seriously?" she sat up.

"Every one of those pins indicates a place I visited looking for you, based on hours of research."

"Wow." She snuggled back down. "And here was I thinking you seemed almost normal today."

"I am normal."

Helle laughed into his chest. Sure he was normal; all guys she knew were reborn, fire-spouting magicians who made her want to hold them forever.

"Alison was right, you know," she mumbled, embarrassed. "You're God's gift to women, and I bet there are plenty of girls who'd love to get their share." Not that she'd let anyone get close. She'd tear their hair out first. Helle's very new acquaintance, Mr Greeny, shook his coils deep in her belly and nodded. At the very least tear their hair out.

"Poor them. I'm all yours." He pointed at the map. "It proves my point, I believe."

She bit her lip. "But why, Jason? Is it because you like me as I am now, or is it because you once loved that other me, a long-gone ghost?"

He was silent for a while. "I don't know," he finally answered. "I can't separate the one from the other." He tightened his hold on her. "I do know that when I'm with you, when I touch you, I feel whole. When your eyes meet mine it jolts me to the core of my being, and to be without you would be unbearable. Had I known you forever or just met you, I think I would have felt the same."

What could she say? Helle pressed her lips to his neck in a soft kiss.

One kiss led to another—and another. Warm, strong lips devoured hers, an insistent tongue penetrated her mouth, and Helle sank her hands into his hair. Jason lifted her onto the desk, hands sliding down to her thighs. He spread her legs, Helle moaned, rubbing her denim-clad crotch against his hands.

"You should only wear skirts," Jason said, leaning over her so that he could kiss her. "Skirts and no underwear." He pulled her forward, so that she was right at the edge of the table. "These are a nuisance," he continued, deft fingers unbuttoning her jeans. "As are these," he growled, slipping his hand into her panties.

She reached for his belt, he stepped back, shaking his head. "Lie back." Helle did as she was told, the papers rustling beneath her. Her jeans and panties came off, and every single nerve in her body stood on end when he knelt before her, his warm mouth on her sex. Oh, God! Those lips, those strong hands on her thighs holding her immobile. His stubble on the sensitive skin of her inner thigh, his tongue, stroking, probing. It was unbearable, it was wonderful—no, it was quite, quite unbearable.

Jason's mouth was suddenly on hers. He tasted of her. She heard the soft sound of his zipper, and then he plunged into her, one hard thrust that had her skidding backwards, her buttocks sliding over the soft worn wood of his desk. Jason gripped her hips and slammed into her again.

"Jesus," she gasped, trying to find something to hold on to.

"Not Jesus. Jason," he said tightly, ramming into her. Yes, yes, yes. Jason—her Jason—and the way he gyrated his hips, the way he thrust himself into her, making her his, made her blood pound through her veins, each and every cell screeching his name. More. She wanted—needed—him deeper, harder, faster, and Jason complied, eyes locked on hers. Up, up, up and suddenly everything burst apart, Helle free-falling as Jason called her name.

He collapsed forward, lying spent in her arms. It felt so good to hold him this close, hear his heart thunder in time with her own. After some moments, he propped himself up on his elbows, staring down at her. Long fingers traced the outline of her brows, her nose, her mouth.

"Good?" he murmured, a smile tugging at his mouth. She just nodded. At present, she couldn't quite find the energy required to speak.

She liked it that he could sweep her into his arms and carry her to the shower. It made her feel safe, somehow, to be cradled to his chest.

"You didn't even undress," she stated when he set her down in the white tiled bathroom. He just smiled in response, helping her out of her shirt and bra. His pants, his shirt, they came off and landed in an untidy heap on the floor. Helle just had to reach out and touch him, trace the outline of his muscular arms, of his taut abdomen. They stood close together under the warm water, holding each other. Helle's stomach rumbled, making him laugh.

"Hungry?" He stretched for the shower lotion.

"I could eat a horse," she replied, soaping her hands before washing him. He hummed under her touch, and then it was her turn to be soaped and rinsed, her turn to be wrapped in a big towel and kissed on the nose.

She was still in her towel an hour or so later, but now perched on a stool in his kitchen, watching his hands fly as he whipped together a meal consisting of fried cod with an olive and bacon topping which he served on a bed of couscous, fried asparagus on the side.

The modern appliances and stainless steel-topped counters contrasted with the old chopping block in a corner, its scarred wooden top covered in an assortment of candleholders. Like so many English kitchens, it was situated in the basement, with a large, multi-paned window giving onto what Helle considered to be a light-shaft, no more, even if some people used these enclosed concrete spaces as miniature terraces.

"No dessert?" Helle asked once she'd finished her fish. She didn't hold out much hope. Her recent inspection of Jason's fridge and pantry revealed a man with little interest in anything he deemed unhealthy, which, to Helle's chagrin, included chocolate and peanut butter. In response, Jason threw her a passion fruit. Whoopee. He grinned at her obvious disappointment.

"Next time, I'll make you a pavlova," he promised.

An hour or so later they were back in his study.

"Will you come with me tomorrow?" he asked. "I really need your help with this."

"Sure." Helle sorted papers into different piles.

"Maybe you could come and work for me," he suggested in a casual voice. Helle's hands stilled.

"No way," she said. "It's not right—not when all I want to do is jump your bones." She wagged a finger at him. "One shouldn't sleep one's way to the top, you know."

"You want to jump my bones?" He looked gratified.

"All the time." And there it was again, that little voice inside her head that screamed at her to not waste one single second of her time with him, because who knew, it might be cut short as brutally this time round as it had been last time. Helle drew in a long, shaky breath and just had to touch him. Something must have shown on her face, as Jason's eyes softened.

"Hey," he said, "it'll be fine, lioness."

"You must do as Samion asks and give her to him in marriage," Nefirie said as she moved her piece into position, after peering at the dice.

Kantor looked at her in surprise. "She says she loves Jason, and will wed no one but him."

Nefirie nodded. "But her marriage is not a question of love, is it? She must be wed as it benefits your people She is destined to be a royal consort, give her husband a line of male heirs." Kantor frowned at her words, but didn't reply, juggling the dice in his hand.

"I've promised her I won't force her," he said, throwing the dice and moving his pieces from one hollow to the other on the rectangular board.

Nefirie studied the board in silence. Her son was meant to be a Wanderer, like her. He had gifts to develop, lives to save. He should wed within his tribe, not this wild, golden-haired girl who would tie him to one place. Not this one love that would lead to so much pain, so much loss.

Nefirie shook her head. "You must, Kantor. She'll forget Jason. She'll be kept busy by all those future children." She studied the board and resigned herself to defeat. "It will be for the best," she whispered, thinking of her son. He would survive if she was wed elsewhere. And Helle would as well, she thought, ignoring the twinge of dark fear the mere name of Samion inspired.

Chapter 13

In Helle's opinion, the Monday morning started out perfectly. After a leisurely hour in bed, Jason dropped her off at her apartment on his way to work, having elicited a promise she'd join him as soon as she'd changed.

She breezed into Jason's offices just before ten, in a vintage Diane von Furstenberg dress that she knew for a fact clung to all the right places. Heels, lacy bra, lacy hold-ups and nothing more. Just thinking about it made her blush, a pool of damp heat collecting between her thighs.

She said hello to Angela, shook her head at the offered tea, and was ushered into Jason's office, Angela closing the door on her way out.

"That was quick," Jason glanced at her, looked again, and stood up. "Wow." His eyes ate her, lingering on her breasts and hips. "A dress?"

"A random choice," she tried, but from the way his mouth curved into a smile, he didn't believe her. His eyes narrowed and he folded his arms over his chest, leaning back against the desk.

"Come here," he said.

She did.

"Kiss me," he added. She did, feeling how his smile widened into a huge grin. He placed a hand on her hip, moving it slowly downwards. "What have we here? Really, Ms Madsen, no knickers?" His hand explored under her dress, finding her naked bottom. "How naughty," he murmured. "How very, very naughty."

"Naughty?" She felt breathless and hot, even more so when he cupped her sex.

"Very." A finger slid over her folds. "We shall have to decide what to do with you, Ms Madsen." To her frustration, he took his hand away, sticking his finger into his mouth. "Later, I fear," he added with a little frown, and Helle turned just as his office was invaded by four men, two of whom were in police uniform.

"You told them?" she asked, assuming they were there about the virus attack the previous week.

"No." He cut his eyes to Angela, hovering at the door. "Call Curtis," he told her, before focusing on the most senior-looking of the policemen, a man in a dark rumpled suit, who had over-large eyes the colour of weak tea. The man held up an ID, introduced himself as DC Bennett and sat down.

"Gentlemen, what can I do for you?" Jason asked.

"A warrant." Bennett slapped a paper down on Jason's desk.

"For what?" Jason asked, all of him radiating irritation.

"We have received information regarding money laundering activities," Bennett said with a shrug. He smirked. "Found your offshore account."

"My what?" Jason's voice dropped into a low growl.

One of the other policemen held up a manila file. "Account statements. You've stashed away quite the tidy little amount in that Belize bank. 157 million to be precise."

Jason laughed out loud. "Don't be ridiculous."

"We have it all here," the policeman said. "Transaction history, dates—there's even CCTV footage of you entering the bank some six months ago."

"Fascinating, seeing as I've never set foot in Belize." Jason speed-dialled a number, his phone on loudspeaker. "Will, get over here."

Will ambled into the room. His red hair was topped by a beret in yellow, red and green, and he wore ripped jeans hanging so low Helle had to avert her eyes every time he turned his back on her. Will was going commando. "What?" he asked, sounding grumpy.

"These gentlemen have a warrant," Jason said. "Give them access to whatever they need, but make sure they don't do anything—anything—to our data."

"Really, Mr Morris!" Bennett's nostrils flared. "How dare you—"

"We were subjected to a virus attack a fortnight ago," Jason interrupted him. "You will forgive me if I find it suspicious that some days later, I am accused of financial crimes."

"And did you report this incident?" the youngest of the policemen asked.

"What's the point?" Will yawned. "You blokes wouldn't be able to help anyway, would you? But I've documented everything, starting with just how we were infected." He jerked his thumb in Helle's direction. "Her laptop."

Thanks a lot. Helle glared at Will, who merely shrugged.

"And you are?" Bennett asked, looking Helle up and down.

Jason scowled, adopting a protective stance. "My girlfriend." He took Helle's hand and squeezed. Warmth radiated from his fingers up her arm.

"I was rather hoping for a name," Bennett retorted.

"Helle Madsen." She caught a spark of interest in the officer's eyes.

"Ms Madsen? Your name seems to have a nasty habit of cropping up in investigations such as these."

"And what's that supposed to mean?" Helle demanded.

"I'm referring to the purported data theft at Woolf & Partners." Bennett looked her up and down sneered. "You don't look like the typical hacker."

"Her?" Will gave Helle a disdainful smile. "*She* wouldn't have been able to do it. That virus was planted by a pro." He sounded quite admiring, earning him a warning look from Jason.

"She was set up—by that bastard Woolf," Jason said.

"Really?" Bennett drawled. "Why would Mr Woolf do that?"

"I have no idea. Jealousy? Boredom?" Jason's face hardened. They eyeballed each other in silence, the officer being the first to break eye contact. There followed a number of questions, aggressively phrased and just as aggressively answered, with Jason's face growing darker by the minute.

"You're going to have to come with us," Bennett finally said.

"By all means. But I'll wait until my solicitor joins us." Jason turned to Will. "Help Angela put together a comprehensive list of where I've been the last eight months."

"We'll be taking all your laptops," Bennett said.

"No. The laptops don't leave my premises."

"Too right." Will snorted. "We've just managed to repair the damage done, and damn if I'm going to risk some ham-fisted plodder undoing all that hard work."

"We have—"

"…a warrant," Curtis said from the doorway. "So by all means, go through the laptops. But as Mr Morris said, they stay here." He gave Helle a brief smile as he sauntered over to the policemen. The jacket of his pinstripe suit strained over his massive shoulders, a tie the colour of ripe aubergines contrasting rather nicely with his pale pink shirt.

"I—" blustered Bennett.

"You heard my client." Curtis crossed his arms. Sheesh, he must do some serious weight lifting, Helle reflected, watching his muscles shift with his movements. "Now, gentlemen; I believe you have an interview you wish to conduct?" He gestured in the direction of one of the meeting rooms.

"Not here," the DC snapped.

"Fine," Curtis loomed over the officer. "Lead the way then." With one last squeeze, Jason let go of Helle's hand. For some idiotic reason, it left her feeling bereft.

The hours dragged. Angela and Will were busy with their assignment, three policemen commandeered the main meeting room and all the laptops, and Helle tried to keep occupied by working her way through Steve's files, but without a laptop there was little she could do to bring structure to Steve's creative mess.

"I'm taking a walk," she told Angela around two, receiving a vague nod in reply. She stepped outside into a surprisingly balmy November day—so warm she unbuttoned her coat. She strolled up Queen's Street and took a left onto Cannon street, making for the imposing silhouette of St Paul's and the small gardens that surrounded it. A bench, some sun—just what she needed to recover some composure.

Helle leaned back on the bench and closed her eyes. 157 million… Imagine owning that much money! She yawned, wondering how things were going for Jason. The fact he'd been gone for so long did not bode well, but Will had looked quite pleased with himself when he put the final touches to the file he and Angela had put together, and Curtis had not looked overly worried.

A shadow fell over her, and an icy tingle moved up her spine. Moving so fast she snagged her coat on the armrest, Helle flew to her feet, backing away from Woolf's dark presence. Black suit, black shirt, no tie, gold cuff links and well-polished black boots—he looked dangerously attractive, the key word being the adverb rather than the adjective.

"Helle," he said, and her name rolled off his lips, his voice that dark rich velvet that had her knees wobbling.

"What are you doing here?" She slid behind the bench. Woolf raised his brows. Dark eyes trapped hers, sucked whatever air she had in her lungs out of her.

"I work here, remember?" He gestured towards Cannon Street. He took a step towards her and crooked his finger. No way. But there was no air in her lungs, and those eyes drilled holes into her brain, his low seductive voice whispering that it would be better for her to come than disobey. Helle shook her head to clear it of his voice, and in that moment of lost concentration he pounced, hands closing on her waist. She gasped. He yanked her towards him, hands sliding down her hips, and she suddenly remembered she was almost naked underneath.

"For him?" he growled, grinding his pelvis against her. His lips crushed hers, and she wanted to protest, but his voice was thudding through her head, and dark desire pulsated through her veins, flared into red-hot heat when he plundered her mouth. Woolf's grip tightened to a vice, fingers sinking into her flesh. The pain cleared her head.

"Let me go!" She bit him and pushed herself free.

Woolf cursed. "Bitch." He wiped at his mouth.

"Look who's talking!"

He looked amused. "No one's called me a bitch before." He made a grab for her. This time she managed to evade him. Helle cast a look around. Why were there no people? Woolf chuckled.

"No help there. In fact," he took several steps towards her, "no help anywhere." Yet again, he tried to catch her eyes, but this time Helle was prepared. The bead in her necklace hopped and burned, her elbow creases prickled with icy sweat and in her head she heard him calling her name, demanding that she come to him. It was so hard, so damn hard not to obey, not to succumb to his will. To disobey was to risk harsh punishment, he reminded her, his voice rippling like smooth silk through her head.

It was an effort to breathe, to keep on moving so as to ensure she remained out of reach. She scanned the little park, hoping to see Jason coming towards her.

"He won't be coming," Woolf said. "They'll stick him in a cell and throw away the key—tax evasion is a bigger crime than murder in this damned country."

"It's a set-up!"

He laughed. "Of course it is—but who's to prove it? Besides, it doesn't matter if it sticks—no smoke without fire, right?" He reached for her, she slapped his hand away.

"Don't touch me."

His voice rose to a roar in her head. Helle staggered back, her heel caught in a crack between the flags, and down she went, landing on her bum. Woolf's voice burrowed into her brain, it whispered and cajoled, it threatened and promised, and when he held out his hand, Helle stretched out to take it. Her other hand closed on a shard of glass, and when she fisted her hand round it, the resulting stab of pain cleared her head.

She scrambled to her feet, noting out of the corner of her eye that a woman was coming their way, her cane tapping out a steady rhythm.

"Saved by the bell, eh?" Woolf said with a crooked smile. Helle didn't reply. As long as she squeezed her hand around the glass, the resulting throbbing kept her head free of his voice. He frowned, glancing at her hand.

"Just leave me alone," Helle managed to say in a level voice. "You've got Alison now."

"Alison?" His eyes went pitch black. "What do I care about her? She's a distraction, no more. A way for me to work off the edge of my appetite while I wait for you to come to me."

"I never will."

"We'll see about that." He gazed at her intently, his voice slithered into her head, and Helle tightened her hold on the shard until she gasped in pain—but at least it kept his voice out. His fingers brushed her cheek, and she recoiled. "One day the Wanderer will be gone—for ever," he said, and she quaked at the threat in his tone. And then he was gone, making for the closest exit.

Tension drained out of Helle so fast she became lightheaded, the park spinning around her.

"Are you all right, dearie?"

"I'm…" She had to sit down, before she fainted.

"Here." The unknown woman beside her guided her to a bench.

"Thank you," Helle mumbled, receiving a light pat on her back, no more. When she looked up, the woman was already moving away, her cane beating a steady rhythm on the stone flags.

By the time she made it back to the office, Jason was pacing the foyer like an enraged tiger, his phone pressed to his ear. That magnificent hair of his stood in a shaggy mess around his face, eyes narrowed into slivers of bright amber as he loudly told whoever was at the other end that he had no comments— beyond saying that there was no substance whatsoever to the accusations.

"Damn!" he snarled. "Who the fuck leaked this to the press?"

"Woolf," Helle said from the doorway. "Who else?" She leaned against the door-frame. "Who else?" she repeated, sliding down to sit on the floor. She looked down at her hand, still clenched round the piece of glass. One finger at the time, she loosened her grip, staring down at the blood that welled in surprising quantities from a number of deep cuts.

Jason fell to his knees beside her. "What have you done?" He produced a handkerchief and wrapped it round her hand.

"I had to." She gave him a wobbly smile. "Pain helps concentrate the mind."

Jason's eyes darkened to the deep orange of a smouldering fire. Helle's nostrils flared as she drew in the spicy scent of his cologne, top-notes to his own personal scent, a heady mixture of man, sun-warmed wood and sea. Her man. Without much thought, she kissed him—hard.

"Hey," he murmured, leaning out of her embrace. "Are you—"

No talk. Not now, when she needed to reassure herself he was here, wipe away the vestiges of Woolf's unwelcome kiss. This time, he kissed her back, and from Angela's desk came a loud cough. Jason tucked his arms round Helle and rose, grunting under his burden.

"No calls," he said over his shoulder as he carried Helle into his office. He kicked the door closed, and lowered her slowly, holding on to her until she was standing firmly on the floor. She threw herself at him, and there was a most satisfactory bang when he crashed into the door.

Strong arms round her waist, and she was being carried over to the carpet. His mouth welded itself to hers as he guided her down onto her back. No foreplay, no undressing, just the sound of his trousers and underwear being shoved out of the way, and then he was in her, the sheer size of him causing her to groan out loud. He wasn't gentle, and she twisted below him as he pounded into her, a life-affirming force that pinned her to the floor, ignited her blood and had her exploding around him.

"Wow." She had sufficient energy to turn her head his way, finding him on his elbow.

"What was that for?" He spoke quietly, but there was an edge to his voice. Helle pulled her dress down, suddenly very aware of her partial nudity.

"He kissed me," she blurted, and Jason just looked at her. One second, two seconds, three seconds.

"And did you enjoy it?" he finally asked, winding one of her curls round his finger. She didn't reply. He yanked. "Answer me, Helle."

She decided to go for insulted. "How can you even ask me that?"

Jason just shook his head and placed a finger over her lips. "The truth."

Helle quaked at the icy look in his eyes. "Yes," she breathed. "At first. But then I bit him."

"Ah." He rolled towards her, bent his head and kissed her viciously, his teeth scraping over her lips. "I don't share my woman," he said when he released her mouth. "Not with anyone."

"I—"

"Hush." This time, his lips touched hers softly, his tongue darting out to lick and tease until she allowed it access. The kiss deepened, a hand slid down her back to press her that much closer to him. Helle moulded herself against him, turned on by his possessive touch, his equally possessive words. A sigh escaped her when he finally let her up for air, making him smile. His eyes softened, and he took hold of her injured hand. "Let's get you cleaned up," he said. "And then let's go home and pretend this shitty day never happened."

She ran. Like the wind through the night, fleeing from him, from the man with eyes like jet and hard, hard hands. The man her father had given her to, insisting his daughter deserved better than a Wanderer. Helle wiped at her face, at the snot running from her nose. The sound of voices far below had her redoubling her efforts up the heavily wooded slope. A full moon lit up the night, the restless waters of the sea glittering like silver to her left.

Her lungs hurt. Her cheek thudded with a blossoming bruise, and she tried to hold the torn linen closed over her sore breasts. His soon-to-be concubine, he'd said, laughing at her when he entered her tent, brusquely dismissing her two handmaidens. He, Samion, would have her that self-same night, and when she protested that her father had meant her to be treated honourably, he'd laughed, asking her if she thought him that big a fool.

"I know all about you and that accursed Wanderer whelp." He'd spat to the side. But from now on, she belonged to him, he'd added, and once she disappeared into the women's quarters in his palace, no one would ever see her again.

Helle choked back a sob. He'd hurt her, touched her where no

143

one had touched her before, and she'd been helpless under his weight, incapable of shifting him when he spread her legs with his. Her groping hand had found the engraved brooch that adorned her tunic, and without hesitation she'd sunk the sharpened pin into his neck, causing him to scream and throw himself to the side. Enough for her to scramble to her feet, to fight her way out of the tent and run.

She could hear him calling orders, and Helle's legs failed her for a while. His voice echoed through the dark, screaming to the heavens that he would make her pay. And then she was over the top of the hill, and far below she could see her father's house. Home. Helle broke into a run, calling for help, for Jason. From behind her came the sound of a horse, approaching fast.

She flew down the incline. He rode after her. One glance over her shoulder, and she lost her footing, tumbling like a ripe melon down the hillside. Helle landed on her back, all air knocked out of her. Samion drew his horse to a brutal halt. She couldn't stop the whimper from escaping her when he leapt off the horse, his sandaled feet loud on the gravel underfoot.

"I'll teach you to run," he snarled, reaching for her.

"Don't touch her!" Out of nowhere came Jason, in only his loincloth.

"And you will stop me?" Samion sneered. His horse whinnied, shifting nervously on its hooves.

"No." Jason gestured at the nearby shrubs. "They will."

Three large feline shapes slipped from the dark into the moonlight. Samion pulled his sword. His horse neighed, wheeled and bolted. Two of the lionesses set off in pursuit, the horse shrieking when they pulled it down. The third lioness remained where she was, regarding Samion out of eyes that shone silver in the moonlight. Samion backed away. The lioness pounced. He got his sword up, yelling for his men.

Belatedly, Helle heard them, many sandaled feet trotting down the hill towards them. She regained her feet, scampering over to where Jason was standing, hands tight on a primitive cudgel.

"Go," he said.

"Not without you." She pulled at his arm. "I will never leave you again, no matter what my father says."

The lioness roared, rose on her hind legs and struck with her claws. Samion cursed, staggering back as blood flowed down his face.

"Come." Helle took Jason's hand.

"Take her!" Samion yelled, pointing his men at Helle. "I want her…" He broke off, slashing wildly at the lioness. Helle spun on her toes and fled, dragging Jason with her. Behind her, the lions roared. Men screamed and cursed, voices rising in panic, cracking with fear. Helle just ran, speeding like a gazelle through the underbrush, Jason's hand in hers. Moments later, three silent shapes caught up, running effortlessly at her side. In the distance, she heard Samion screaming her name.

Chapter 14

Jason spent most of their run thinking, uttering no more than monosyllabic replies to Helle's occasional comment. The winter dusk was turning into night by the time they jogged up the last stretch, with Helle setting off in a burst of speed to beat him to the shower.

Jason slowed, dropped to the ground and did a series of push-ups. He frowned. Three days after that initially very uncomfortable interview with the police, he had been formally cleared of any charges, the account statement declared a fraud as were all the electronic transactions. The final nail in that particular coffin had been Nigel's deconstruction of the CCTV footage purportedly showing Jason in Belize and opening a bank account while incongruously lugging around a fortune in a suitcase. Bennet had gone the colour of a Victoria plum during Nigel's Skype presentation, squirming like a hooked worm when Nigel dropped words such as "credulous amateurs" and "IT incompetents". A friend indeed was Nigel but unfortunately the damage was already done. So far this week, Jason had received a number of curt if polite calls from potential partners, in essence telling him to sod off.

Not that he needed to work. One of the few benefits of multiple lives was the possibility to create hoards, and Jason's most recent parents had left him well off to begin with, but to Jason his father's company was more than a job, it was an heirloom, a carefully constructed little empire that concentrated on investing in alternative technologies. And now… damn!

Even more worrying was the visit he'd received earlier that day. The man, who'd waved an identity card at him and introduced himself as Mr Smith from Her Majesty's Revenue and Customs, had been all understated elegance, vigilant eyes darting this way and that as he followed Jason to his office. Once seated, the man had crossed his legs and regarded Jason in silence. Jason was not easily flustered by silence, but the way Smith looked at him, as if he were some sort of nasty grub, got to him.

"What?" he'd said, and from the way Smith's mouth curled into a satisfied smile, he knew he'd lost a point or two.

"Oh, nothing, Mr Morris. This is just a friendly visit from your own personal tax inspector."

"Personal tax inspector?" Jason had asked.

"We have this little adage," the man continued, brushing at his leg. "No smoke without fire." Pale eyes met Jason's. "Something you're familiar with, Mr Morris?"

"Yes."

"As of now, we will develop a very close relationship, you and I." Smith smiled. "I will be here at least on a monthly visit and expect to be kept abreast of all major financial transactions. All of them."

Jason had attempted to protest but the flinty look on Mr Smith's face had him swallowing his heated words. Something told him Mr Smith was a man it was best not to annoy. The so called tax inspector—Jason had serious doubts Mr Smith was anything as mundane as that, no matter his ID card—emanated a contained menace, reminding Jason of the very dead Francis Walsingham, Elizabeth I's faithful if somewhat unscrupulous spy-master. He even looked a bit like Walsingham, what with his neat little beard, and while Smith might not be wearing a starched ruff or a padded doublet, just like Walsingham he oozed determination and intelligence. And just like Walsingham, Jason suspected this Mr Smith had the powers that be at his back.

He finished the last set of push-ups and leapt agilely to his feet. All of this would keep—at least until tomorrow. He walked slowly up the dark stairs to Helle's apartment, pulling off his damp sweatshirt as he went. Helle was singing in the shower. He slipped in to join her, making her squeal in protest when he wrapped his arms round her warm and slippery body.

"You're icy!"

"Then do something about it."

By the time they left the shower, the bathroom was

shrouded in mist. Helle drew a heart in the condensation in the mirror, making him smile when she added an H and a J. She wiped the heart away and met his eyes in the mirror.

"Give it a week or two, and it will all be forgotten."

"Give it a week or two, and it might be too late." Arthur had called today, sounding hesitant as he explained that the owners of the Turkish company had asked a number of pointed questions. He wanted that company—and in particular their innovative approach to portable energy, pocket-sized gadgets that ran on patented little chemical tablets the size of a pound coin and produced sufficient energy to recharge a phone.

"My, you're moody today." Helle dug him in the ribs.

"I'm entitled, don't you think?" He adjusted the towel round his waist. "At one point, even Curtis looked at me as if I was guilty."

"But you're not." A statement that was much more of a question, Jason reflected.

"No," he replied. "Not in this particular case."

Before she could ask, he muttered something about getting dressed.

Alison was sprawled on the sofa, balancing a bowl of popcorn on her belly.

"Hi," he said.

She gave him a surly nod, no more. "Here again? Maybe you should start paying rent."

"Or maybe I should convince Helle to move in with me and leave you to pay it all by yourself," he retorted, knowing full well Alison paid only a nominal share of the costs.

"Whatever." She tossed her head. "I can always move in with Sam." She gave him a challenging look.

"If you have any sense of self-preservation, you'll ditch Sam Woolf and run for the hills."

"No need," she muttered. "He's in the US for the next few weeks."

"Well, thank heavens for that," Jason said, and the knot of anger and tension that had lain in his stomach these last few days softened somewhat.

He'd considered confronting Samion about the bogus charges, wanting nothing more than to shove the bastard into the Thames, there to drown, but he knew from past experience that one should never underestimate Samion—to do so was to risk ending up dead or worse. He traced the faint lines that decorated his left wrist, recalling an endless sequence of days at Samion's mercy. Heat pooled in his hands and when he closed his fists he heard the crackling of the static electricity, a bodily reaction to memories of pain and humiliation. He exhaled with a loud hiss, banishing the recollections to the furthest reaches of his brain.

"You okay?" Alison sounded more curious than concerned.

"Yes." He wiped his hands on the damp towel. A wisp of steam uncurled, but Alison didn't notice. "Look, I really mean it: Woolf's bad news."

"Surprise, surprise—he says the same about you." She gave him a cool look. "And you're apparently some sort of financial crook as well."

"I am not." Jason clenched his teeth. "Ask Helle about that."

"Yeah, as if she's objective." Alison snorted. "Every time she looks at you, miniature hearts appear in her eyes." Jason ducked his head to hide his pleased smile.

"Woolf set me up."

Alison rolled her eyes. "Of course he did. After all, Sam Woolf has nothing else to do with his time than hassle an insignificant competitor like you."

"Apparently not," he said lightly. "Unless he is hassling defenceless women."

"I'm not defenceless." Alison bristled. Compared to Samion, she most definitely was.

"Neither is Helle, and yet—"

She cut him off. "I'm not listening to that. She misunderstood, that's all. Sheesh, the way she goes on, poor Sam is some sort of devil."

"The man is an abusive bully!"

"For those of us with more sophisticated tastes, he's a demanding male, no more."

"Demanding? You have no idea." Jason wanted to shake her until her teeth rattled. "One day, he'll beat you to a pulp."

Alison laughed. "As if." She cocked her head. "You'll have to excuse me, but seriously, you expect me to believe you over him?" She snickered. "It's not Sam spouting all that shit about reincarnation, you know."

That was rich: Jason was tempted to tell her the truth about Samion, but doubted she would believe him.

"I am not, as you say, spouting any shit. As far as I know, I haven't talked to you about anything related to my past." Jason leaned back against the countertop and crossed his arms. "But as to Woolf, take my word for it; if you don't stay away, you'll burn."

"Yada, yada." Alison pulled a face. "Just butt out, okay? If I need an Agony Aunt, I'll sure as hell not turn to drop-dead Reincarnation Man."

"Fine." The more time he spent with Alison, the less he liked her, irritated by her open scepticism and sarcastic comments. With her long dark hair and slightly slanted eyes set in a heart-shaped face, she might look quite the angel, but so far Jason had not found anything angelic about her behaviour.

"What are you two arguing about?" Helle had wrapped her head in a towel.

"Woolf," Jason and Alison said in unison. Helle paled.

"I don't want to talk about him." She turned to Alison. "And I'll not have him here—ever. If you're into him and all his weird stuff, fine. But don't bring him here."

Jason frowned. The moment Woolf set foot back in England, he would insist on Helle moving in with him.

"Okay, okay!" Alison scowled. "I got the message, all right?" She sighed loudly. "Look Helle," she said in a calmer voice. "I know what he did upset you—"

"Upset me?" Helle's voice shook. "That's putting it mildly." She glanced at her hand, still bandaged, and flexed her fingers.

Alison hauled herself to her feet and gave Helle a hug. "I'm sorry, hon. But what's bad for you is working out great for me."

"He's dangerous," Helle said, sounding angry. Jason knew

for a fact she'd spent hours trying to convince Alison to stay away from Woolf—with zero success.

"Tell me about it: dark, dishy and dangerous—just how I want them." She glanced at Jason. "You, on the other hand, seem to prefer moody and delusional redheads—although I have to admit he's not too bad."

"Or delusional." Jason met Helle's eyes over Alison's head and raised his brows. Was she always this rude, he wondered, or did he bring out the devil in her? Or maybe it was Samion's influence. God knew that man could drown anyone's soul in black pitch.

"Not your call, buster," Alison retorted. "Generally the mentally insane don't recognise their delusions."

"Watch it." Jason pitched his voice low.

"I should know. I work with loonies, remember?"

"Alison!" Helle voice was like a whiplash. "What the fuck is the matter with you?"

"Right, that does it." Jason headed for Helle's bedroom. "We're leaving. Now."

"I can't believe she said that." Helle kept pace with him as he strode down the street, making for his car. He slid her a look.

"You shouldn't have told her."

Helle hunched together, making him regret his tone. "Too late," she muttered.

"Yup." But he took her hand, and after some initial resistance, she let him, fingers interlacing with his.

It was not a good evening. Jason resented the way she worried about Alison and how often she pulled out her phone to see if she'd received a text.

"Why don't you call her instead?" he finally suggested—not because he thought she should, but because he didn't want her this distracted when she was with him.

"She should be the one calling me." Helle gnawed her lip.

"But you're worried—and she knows you are." Manipulative. Yet another sin to chalk up on Alison's account.

Helle shrugged. "What if she's with him?"

"Fat chance. He's in the US—or so Alison tells me."

That had her brightening, even more so when Alison sent her a text, blaming PMS for her behaviour.

"Not," he pointed out, "an apology."

Helle laughed. "She's stubborn as hell. This is as good as it gets with her." She snuggled up to him. "Bed?"

"What's wrong with the sofa?" He nuzzled her hair, slid a finger along the column of her throat. Helle hummed and pressed herself closer.

"I was thinking sleep," she said.

"Were you?" His fingers found her breast. She arched and yawned at the same time, making him laugh. "Sleep it is, I see."

He liked having her in his bed, he thought, pulling the duvet up round her bare shoulders. They'd never shared a bed in their previous life, it had all been snatched moments of lovemaking outside, an odd nap here and there, now and then extending into an hour or two. The last time, they'd fallen into deep sleep, and by the time they woke up it was too late, whatever hopes and dreams they'd shared torn apart by Samion.

Jason rolled over onto his back, staring up at the ceiling. Not that it served any purpose to play the 'what if' game, but he couldn't help himself, wondering how their lives would have played out if the sun hadn't been quite so hot that day, the shade not quite as cool and inviting. Would they have lived happily ever after, he and his Helle, in a simple existence of hunting and farming, of babies that came along as regular as clockwork? Would they have died old and satisfied, content with being absorbed into eternity, rather than trapped in this exhausting sequence of lives?

He scrubbed at his face. At times, he felt so old. He laughed hollowly: eternal life had very little going for it after the first few hundreds of years. Except for her, sleeping beside him, his thumb held firmly in her hand. Jason held his breath, listening to her soft snuffling. Was it fate, he wondered, that had at last brought them together again? If so, was it fate that had decreed they be torn asunder in their first life?

"Fickle," he muttered. And cruel, he added bitterly, his chest constricting with remembered pain and loss. Not, he vowed, how things would play out this time. He turned on his side, careful not to dislodge her hold on his thumb. They were no longer as naïve as they'd been back then, both of them older and wiser. And while Woolf might retain some of his ancient powers, he was no longer the mighty Prince of Kolchis, well-nigh invincible when he came thundering towards them in his chariot.

She sighed in her sleep, twisting so that the duvet slipped down, revealing her breasts. When he touched them, her nipples hardened and she sighed again, shifting towards him. His Helle—but not quite his Helle. Truth be told, he didn't really know this woman, making the presumptuous assumption that she was a carbon copy of the girl he'd known so intimately all those years ago. And yet he was helpless before the tidal wave of emotions she woke in him, sweeping him so off his feet he felt as if he were drowning when she wasn't nearby.

There was no question in his mind: he loved her, would love her until the sun sizzled and died. But as to what she felt for him…he stroked her hair. Helle Madsen didn't love him—not yet. At most, she was *in* love with him: an ephemeral emotion at best, a heady rush of hormones that sometimes coalesced into lifelong love, just as often ended in a dead end.

"Love me," he whispered to her. After all these existences, did he not deserve her? But she had loved him once, sacrificing everything she had to keep him safe—and he had spurned her for it, driving her to despair and death.

"I love you," he said, brushing his lips over her brow. Helle smiled in her sleep, her mouth soft and wet. He kissed her tenderly. She mumbled his name, and when his hand slipped between her thighs, she widened her legs, still mostly asleep when he entered her. He loved her slowly. She wound her arms round his neck and held him tight. Afterwards, she lay rosy and warm on his chest, her hair tickling his nose. He didn't care. He lay awake and held her in his arms, and only when the first streaks of dawn lightened the sky did he finally fall asleep.

They were lying close to each other, staring up at the sky. Jason enfolded her hand in his, squeezing softly. She smiled and turned her head to look at him, the whites of her eyes shining in the moonlight.

"Tomorrow the year turns," she said, stretching up an arm to point at the sky. He pulled her closer, wrapping her cloak tightly around her. They were quiet, looking at the stars.

"It will all change this year," she whispered, letting her hand run down his chest.

"Yes," he agreed, trying to ignore her touch, but failing. "You'll be my wife—at last." The pure joy those words sent through him silenced him, and he propped himself up to look at her. Kantor had finally acquiesced to their union. A reluctant agreement, to be sure, wheedled out of him by his persistent daughter.

"Maybe we'll have a child," she smiled up at him. "A son with amber eyes."

He traced the contour of her face, caressing her cheeks. "Or a blue-eyed daughter."

"Or both," she said.

Or both. Or many, many more. "Will you love them better than me?" he teased, a slight twinge inside. She raised her fingers to his lips and ran them over the curve of his mouth, her eyes almost black in the weak light.

"No," she said quietly, "I don't think that is possible."

Chapter 15

There were worse ways of waking than to the smell of something cooking. Helle's stomach grumbled happily as she skipped down the three flights of stairs to the kitchen, only to come to a surprised halt at the sight of an unknown man, sitting on one of the chairs as he watched Jason cook.

Helle felt severely underdressed in only Jason's t-shirt and panties. From the way Jason's brows rose, he agreed, even if he didn't say anything, gesturing at his visitor with his spatula.

"Helle, meet Nigel Hawkins."

"Hi." She tugged the hem of the t-shirt lower.

"Yo." Nigel held out his hand. She shook it, and the two dozen bracelets on his arm jingled in response.

"Yo?" A man more different to Jason was difficult to envision. As thin as a rail, with hair that was shorn in front, long at the back, dyed in various shades of neon pink and orange, he looked like an over-age punker. His nose, his bottom lip, his brow and right ear were all pierced. The leather jacket he was wearing looked as if he'd slept in it, and the ancient KIZZ t-shirt was worn so thin in places she could see his skin. Very white skin.

"Isn't that how you Americans greet each other?" There was a twinkle in his brown eyes.

"Not all of us." She gestured at one of his necklaces, a broad leather thong decorated with a blue bead like hers. "I have one of those."

"Do you?" Nigel picked at his bead. "Very ancient form of protection."

"Against what?" Helle asked.

"Evil." He nodded. "Demons and such."

"Oh." Helle shared a look with Jason. Was he for real?

"Nigel is an expert in the occult," Jason explained. "And he's also one of England's brightest mathematicians." He set down a plate before her, laden with creamy scrambled eggs and smoked salmon. "He writes very, very complicated algorithms."

"Ah." She had the vaguest idea what this might mean.

Nigel grinned. "I am also the best hacker Jason knows— which is saying a lot, as he isn't too bad himself."

"A hacker?" Helle frowned. "That's illegal."

"Yup. But a useful skill at times." Jason carried over two more plates. "Like with Woolf and his files," he added in an undertone, "it came in handy there, don't you think?" A reprimand that had Helle ducking her head. Jason settled in the chair beside her, pressing his thigh against hers. She shifted away and concentrated on her plate, listening with half an ear while Jason and Nigel talked about everything from the upcoming padel tennis game to the latest results in the Premier League.

"…so what do I do?" Jason said, and the tone of his voice had Helle pricking her ears.

"No choice, is there?" Nigel sounded serious. "What exactly do they want?"

They? Helle shoved the plate to the side. "Who?"

"Ah! Welcome back to us," Jason said.

"I was hungry," she muttered. And angry with him for making her feel as if it was her fault Woolf had been able to blackmail her.

"I like women who like their food," Nigel offered, nudging a basket of flaky croissants her way. He waggled his brows. "The rounder the better, if you ask me."

"I'm not sure how to take that," Helle retorted.

"As a compliment." Nigel grinned, a contagious smile that broke his narrow face in two.

Jason draped an arm round Helle's shoulders. "Back off." His fingers caressed the bare skin of her upper arm. She sat stiff and silent. "Hey," he murmured. "You okay?"

She shrugged off his arm. "Who?"

"Who what?" He frowned at her.

"You said they want you to do something."

Jason twirled his spoon, eyes never leaving her. "I had a visit the other day. The tax authorities require full disclosure."

"And the hitch is?" She didn't understand why he looked so troubled.

"The hitch is that they have demanded access to all my transactions, all the time. I don't like it, when sensitive information leaves my office."

"So just say no."

"Not an option, I believe," Nigel put in. "You don't want them coming down like a ton of bricks on Jason—they might find the remnants of a neat little electronic highway leading all the way to Woolf's laptop."

"You know about that?"

Nigel sipped his coffee. "I do. I helped him." He studied her from under his lashes. Helle felt naked. Without a word, she left, half-running as she made for the bedroom and her clothes.

"Helle!" Jason caught up with her on the top floor.

"Did he see the photos?"

"No." He tried to pull her into an embrace, but she fought him off.

"It wasn't my fault," she said. "How was I to know he was doctoring those damn files?"

"You knew he was off—you told me you felt it the first time you met him. But you were so blinded by what he could do for your career, you chose to ignore all those alarm bells, didn't you?" His tone was the equivalent of being sucker-punched. Helle staggered backwards, groping blindly for the door to the bathroom.

"Asshole!" She slammed the door in his face, slid down to the floor and covered her ears to shut out Jason's voice, entreating her to open up. At long last, she heard Nigel's voice, and Jason moved away, his voice growing fainter as he descended the stairs. Helle opened the door as noiselessly as she could and made for her clothes.

She was pulling on her hoodie when Jason reappeared at the top of the stairs.

"Going somewhere?"

"Home." She pushed past him.

"Helle, wait." His fingers grazed her cheek. "I was out of line. Of course it wasn't your fault."

"Too right." She jerked her face away.

"Please don't go." His hand closed round her wrist, fingers tightening when she made as if to descend. He drew her towards him, reeling her in like a recalcitrant fish. "I keep on forgetting that you didn't know who he was."

"Oh, for God's sake! He's Sam Woolf, okay? An overpowering bastard who enjoys intimidating the people around him." What else was there to know, she wanted to add.

"He's also Samion, the all-powerful Prince of Kolchis."

"Whatever." She extricated herself from his arms and stood looking at him. "There's something else bothering you about that Smith guy, isn't there?"

Her abrupt change of subject made him blink. With a loud exhalation, he nodded.

"I don't trust him. And the fact that he's there indicates the authorities don't exactly trust me. I'm getting the impression he will push all my wrong buttons, wanting to provoke me." He spread his hands wide, turning them this way and that. "And I won't like it, and sometimes, when I don't like it—or feel threatened—I can't quite control what happens to my hands." He gave her an anguished look. "Can you imagine what they'd do to me if they found out?" He cupped his hands and closed his eyes, and just like that, electricity crackled, little flames dancing over his palms. Helle watched, mesmerised. With a rueful smile, Jason clapped his hands together. A faint smell of singed paper lingered in the air.

"So, will you stay?" he asked lightly, arms held open. She hesitated. Did she want him to touch her right now? But the look in his eyes, the vulnerable set to his mouth, had her walking into his arms, resting her head on his shoulder while his hands slid down to grip her butt and pull her impossibly close, the heat in his fingers fading back to normal when she stood on her toes and kissed him.

Helle was pleasantly surprised when Jason suggested they take off, leave London behind for the weekend.

"I have an ancient great-uncle in a care-home just outside Warwick," he explained, "so how about we take in the sights, stay the night and visit with him in the morning?"

"In Warwick?" Helle had already been to the castle, and had no desire to revisit what had come across as a theme park, complete with a huge number of kids running around pretending to be knights and princesses.

"We can go to Kenilworth." He grinned. "Would an American know anything about Kenilworth?"

"Huh." Helle wagged a finger at him. "My dad is a history nut, okay?" A pang of guilt rushed through her. She'd not spoken with Dad for over two weeks. "And as he's very much into the development of democracy, yup, I've heard of Kenilworth and what's his name, that thirteenth century dude Simon de something."

"Montfort." Jason rubbed at his neck, brows pulled together.

After a brief stop at her apartment and a stilted conversation with a surly Alison who muttered she was still feeling like crap, Helle threw a small bag into the minimal back seat of the Aston Martin and slid into the passenger seat.

"I could drive," she suggested an hour or so later. Jason had taken the M40 only as far as Oxford before opting for the more picturesque route offered by one of those smaller A roads and now they were driving towards a place called Moreton-in-Marsh which sounded as if it could be very swampy.

"What, you want me to turn over my baby to you?"

"I'm a good driver."

Jason glanced at her, found a lay-by and parked. "Fine." He tweaked her cheek. "One scratch, and you're on car washing detail for a year."

Helle eased into the driver's seat and spent some time acquainting herself with having the gear stick to her left.

"Feels weird," she said. She released the clutch and the car surged forward.

She hooted with joy and pressed the accelerator to the floor, grinning at the responding burst of speed.

"Careful!" Jason winced when she wove her way across

the lanes, cursed when she stood on the brakes to avoid overshooting their turn-off, and after an elegant overtaking, he yelled at her to pull to the side.

"You have a death wish?" he asked.

"I had it under control," she protested—although she had to admit it had been a bit too close for comfort, that damned truck—lorry—suddenly appearing round the bend.

"Speed maniac." He leaned forward to tug at her hair. "You always were."

Helle rolled her eyes. Not again. "Stop it," she said. "Just stop it, will you?" For the rest of the ride, Jason sat silent, staring stubbornly out of his window.

"I'm sorry," Helle said, once she'd parked the car and they'd got out. "It's just that at times, I find all of this quite impossible to believe." Most of the time, really. For all she knew, Jason might just be a fantastic storyteller. Maybe he was some kind of telepathic person who could plant images in your brain, starting with sending all those recurring dreams. *Nope*, her reptilian brain informed her proudly, *that was all me*. Helle's rational mind rolled its non-existent eyes, telling Mr Reptile to please crawl away and hide under a rock before it did any more damage.

"And yet it's true." He gave her a belligerent look, hands in his pockets, shoulders hunched against the wind. He looked away. "It's never going to work between us if every time I make a reference to my past you look as if you're about to have me committed. I can't live like that."

She tried to take his hand, but he merely shook his head, walking towards the entrance.

"Shit." Helle decided she had to make amends—damned difficult when he maintained a brooding distance as they crossed the long causeway. They were standing in what used to be the former lower bailey when she asked him if he'd ever been there before.

"Here?" Jason studied the remaining ruins. "Nope, it never ended up on our sightseeing list."

"That's not what I mean, and you know it." Helle tried to take his hand again. This time, he let her.

"I was here before this," he said, waving his hands at the soaring walls of the great hall, still impressive despite their ruined state. Helle tilted her head to the side, studying the few remaining windows, narrow and tall: they must have flooded the hall with light.

"How much before?"

Jason gave her a crooked smile. "You don't really care, do you? You're just asking to apologise."

"Maybe." She followed him along a length of perimeter wall. "Why do you think I don't remember anything?"

"Because you're lucky," he replied harshly. He turned to face her. "All those in-between lives, they're irrelevant—after all, you were lost to me. So I lived and died, lived again and died again, hoping that in the next life I would find you again."

Helle considered this for some time. "So, this is really a lucky chance, isn't it? I mean, here we are in the same place and at compatible ages, you twenty-nine to my twenty-four."

Jason made an amused sound, his eyes shading. "Lucky chance? Yes, I suppose so, but it's taken very many misses to get here."

Helle raised her hand to his face, traced his high cheekbones, the line of his brow. "Isn't it terrible to get old, over and over again?"

Jason squirmed. "I wouldn't really know."

"Why not?" She cupped his cheek, smiling at how he leaned into her touch, eyes half-closing.

"I always set myself an age limit. If I didn't find you before I was around fifty I would sort of start again."

Start again? Helle tried to catch his eyes, but he kept his gaze on one of the fortification towers.

"What, you killed yourself on a regular basis over the years?" Her voice was shrill with shock.

"Shh, people are staring." He pointed at the nearby group of tourists.

"So, did you?" she hissed. He shrugged, obviously very uncomfortable.

"Um, yes, I suppose I did. But it's also part of moving

on," he spoke quickly, "I have to be very concentrated in the dying to get to the being born again with my memory of you intact."

Helle stared at him, trying to grasp what he had seen and done throughout all those stunted lives. It made her heart break.

"So, time and time again, you committed suicide, for me?" She bowed under the guilt. For her: he'd lived and died, wanting only to find her.

He blushed furiously and looked away. "Yes, for you." End of discussion, his body language told her. Not bloody likely, but she decided to let it rest, for now. Instead, she listened while he told her of a distant life, when he was one of the men-at-arms who withstood the siege of Kenilworth in the aftermath of Simon de Montfort's death.

"I've never been back here since," he said as he steered her towards the car park.

"Why not?"

He shrugged. "No point, I guess."

She studied the meadows, the reddish stone of the ruins. "Did you die here?"

"No." He fingered his neck again. "A woman did..." He glanced at her. A woman? Deep inside her, Mr Greeny snarled in anger, but Helle kept her face impassive. "I cared for her, and she died. She was shot through the neck by a crossbow-bolt."

"What was her name?"

Jason shuffled his feet. "Juliet."

They drove to Warwick and found a pub. Jason ordered beer and steak-and-ale pie, leading the way to the secluded pub garden, surprisingly warm despite it being November. It was a tense meal. She kept on sneaking him looks. He ignored them, concentrating single-mindedly on his food. Could someone really love you that much, enough to die repeatedly? It made her choke, and she pushed the half-full plate away. He raised his eyes and met hers, but this time he didn't look away, this time he held her stare, his eyes a shimmering mixture of copper and gold.

"What?" he said, daring her. Helle pretended confusion, but he smiled, his eyes veiled, and wagged his finger at her. "You're thinking hard, so what is it you want to know?" Everything: she wanted to know how he could bear it to spend life after life looking for her, how he had lived and how he had died—but no, she didn't really.

"Isn't it difficult to make the transition into a new life?" she asked instead. Jason grimaced and rubbed his collarbone, closing his eyes slightly.

"I don't think it is," he replied after some time. "I don't really know. I'm not born with an awareness of my memories." He fell silent, looking away at nothing, his face expressionless as he collected his thoughts. In his current life, he had been an easy, happy child, he explained, giving her a fleeting impish smile. He'd excelled at school and sports.

"And is history your favourite subject?" she teased.

He shook his head. "No, mathematics. I even have an ancient degree from Cambridge – back from the 19th century," he said proudly.

"Whoopee." But she smiled at him, encouraging him to go on.

"Over time I've become quite good at selecting my parents," Jason went on. "It helps if they're well-to-do. Unfortunately, rich people aren't in any way kinder than others." He absently rubbed his collarbone again, a flicker of something unpleasant crossing his face.

"How select?"

He tilted his head to one side and studied her thoughtfully. "Generally, the soul dies, waits for a while and then goes on. And while I wait, I look through the prospective parents."

"Seriously?" She burst out in incredulous laughter, imagining a sterile pale blue room with a lot of see-through glittering souls, all of them busy paging through huge catalogues of potential moms and dads and ripping out the entries that interested them so that no one else would get at them first.

"Not quite" he said drily, his lips twitching as if he could read her mind. "I was very lucky this time round."

"So, what do they do?" she asked, curious. He hadn't really talked about his parents.

"Did," he said morosely, "they died in a car crash three years ago." He rubbed at a stain on the table. "I loved them a lot.

"Once the memories come back, it's awful. Whatever my childish dreams might be, they're suddenly wiped away, replaced by the horrifying comprehension that I have only one purpose in life: to find you. Rather frightening when you're about twelve years old." He laughed hollowly, drawing invisible eights with his finger. "You don't know how often I've wished that someone would permanently erase the image of you from my head, leaving me free to live an ordinary life. But from the moment you dance into my dreams, your hair spilling down your back, your eyes flashing as you smile, there's no choice—I have to search the world for you."

Helle's heart ached at the image of a small boy starting awake one morning after a vague dream, not knowing what it was he was seeing or why. Jason was still staring down at the table, the corners of his mouth drooping slightly, and Helle moved her chair close enough to brush her arm against his.

"It sounds like a curse."

His shoulders slumped. A sudden gust of wind ruffled his hair, and Helle clasped her hands against the desire to smooth it off his brow. Jason gave her a lopsided grin.

"A curse, definitely—but not one of your making."

His words cut deep. She increased the distance between them and his hand flew out, closing round her wrist. "It doesn't matter anymore: we're here now—together."

"I don't want to be a curse."

Jason placed a soft kiss on the inside of her wrist. "You're not the curse. You're the cure."

"Why?" she asked, her mouth dry. "Why must you find me again?"

"You died too young," he said without lifting his face, "there was so much left for us to do." Not the whole truth, she knew instinctively, but she nodded and stroked his hair, swamped by a grief she didn't understand. Maybe she should ask him about how she died and why, but she didn't want to, shrinking back from vaguely remembered pain. Besides, it didn't matter anymore, not now that he was sitting beside her.

Jason took her by the hand as they walked up the hill.

"You've done something with your hair," he said, looking at the intricate braiding so different from her normal heavy plait. She blushed, making him smile. They reached the little dell and the late evening sun blazed across the grass, creating miniature rainbows in the glittering waterfall. She seemed agitated, her hand trembling in his hold. He looked at her questioningly.

"What is it?"

She shook her head and hid her face against the rough linen of his tunic. He cupped her chin, lifting her face so that he could see her eyes. Her pupils were huge, and she raised herself on tiptoe to brush her lips against his. Brush them softly but suggestively. He gently pushed her away. "What is it you want, Helle?" he asked, his voice rough with emotions.

"You," she answered simply, undoing the ties that held her tunic in place and letting the garment float down to the grass. He backed away from her.

"We're not yet wed. Your father..."

She put her fingers on his lips, shushing him. "We will be, come the first summer moon, and I have waited long enough." He hesitated, unable to tear his eyes from her as she pulled the undergarment over her head, leaving her naked in front of him.

"Oh, Mother," he said and lifted his hand to carefully cup her rounded breast. She took a step closer.

"Don't you want me?" she asked quietly, her pulse thudding visibly in the hollow of her throat.

"You know I do," he replied, his voice a hoarse whisper. She smiled and took his hand, guiding them both to the ground.

Chapter 16

That conversation in the little pub was a turning point. During the rest of their afternoon in Warwick, Jason kept a cautious eye on Helle, worried by her silence, reassured by how she clung to his hand, refusing to let go even when they registered at the hotel.

No sooner were they in their room, but he pounced on her. He toed off his shoes as they moved towards the bed, leaving a trail of discarded clothes in their wake. He needed her, wanted her. Her bra flew to land on one of the chairs, her breasts filled his hands. Fumbling fingers on the buttons of his shirt, and he loved how her nails raked his shoulders in her haste to undress him. The lacy things she called panties were easily discarded, and when she fell to her knees before him, looking up at him with eyes as blue as bluebells, he shivered in anticipation.

Slowly, she pulled down his briefs. Damn it, woman! He grunted with impatience, but she just laughed, sliding her hands down his thighs. He kicked free of his underwear, she gripped his arse. Her hands, her mouth—God, he wanted her mouth, and his hands closed in her hair, holding her still as her lips and her tongue sent waves of heat through his balls. He hissed when she sucked, her tongue dancing over the sensitive tip of his cock.

Jason rocked on his feet, fighting the urge to push too deeply. Her hair tickled his skin, but most of all it was her hands, and that goddamn wonderful mouth, teasing—always teasing. She would pay for this, he vowed, he was going to do to her what she was doing to him.

Helle half-rose, kissed his belly, moved upwards to kiss his neck, his mouth. Strong fingers tugged at his chest hair, moved slowly over his arms.

"You're going the wrong way," he told her. "I want you down there, my lioness." He guided her back down, caressing her cheek as she settled back on her knees. His woman. She was so beautiful, kneeling naked before him, her hair shimmering in the lamplight. She licked her lips. A soft kiss to his glans, that teasing tongue caressing his cock, over and over again. He shuddered, rocking on his feet in an effort to stop himself from ramming into her mouth. Her lips closed over his cock, enveloping it in the moist heat of her mouth. He closed his eyes, savouring the sensation. Her hair tickled his belly, her hands urged him deeper and he was incapable of controlling himself, thrusting into all that wet warmth.

"I'm going to come," he gasped, hips flexing of their own volition. So good, so very good, and when she used her hands to cup his balls, one finger sliding backwards along the seam, he groaned out loud. He tightened his hold on her hair. Her exploring finger found his anus, a jolt of pure pleasure surging through him when she slid it inside.

"Damn!" he hissed. His cock in her mouth, her finger moving oh, so gently up his rectum—a wave of dark green jealousy washed through him. Had she done this with anyone else? And then he no longer cared, his buttocks clenching as he filled her mouth with his ejaculation.

"Good?" She smiled at him, before padding over to the bathroom. Good? Fucking, bloody great was what it was. The moment she emerged, face and hands damp, he swept an arm under her legs and carried her over to the bed. He kissed her, and she tasted faintly of him. He ravaged her mouth. She clung to him, giving as good as she got.

"Open your legs," he said thickly, sliding down her body. Her breasts, her belly, he kissed and teased, making her squirm when he bit a tad too hard. Her nipples stood like pebbles, and she was already deliciously wet, all of her quivering when he pushed a finger inside of her. First things first; he used his weight to pin her to the bed, lapping slowly at her tender flesh. He nibbled gently on her clit, and her hips rose off the bed. Again, and she gyrated. Back to licking slowly, and she groaned in frustration. Well, she could wait. He wanted her desperate for release before he finally gave it to her.

"Oh, God!" she moaned. "How much longer, Jason?"

He blew at her sex, laughing at the way she trembled in response. "Until I say so."

"But Jason—" she broke off, making wordless sounds when he suckled her clit. Her hips bucked, and he could feel her about to explode. He tightened his hold on her hips and lifted his face.

"Not yet."

"I'm going crazy here," she whispered.

He chuckled. "You will before I'm done with you." His cock was so hard it ached, but until she was close to unravelling, he would wait. Once again, he kissed her bud, and once again, her body responded, her fingers clenching on the counterpane.

"Please." She sounded hoarse—desperate even.

"You don't come until I tell you to," he said against her folds. "Promise."

"Anything," she gasped, making him smile. In her present state, she'd give him whatever he wanted. For now, what he wanted was to stoke her fire, drive her to the brink and then leave her to simmer. So he did, revelling in her sounds, in the way her body responded to his every touch and kiss. She was wet and ready, her face and chest as flushed as her genitals, her pubic curls damp with her arousal. He just had to taste her once again, causing her to arch her back and hips entirely off the bed.

"Turn over," he said.

Helle complied with alacrity. He lifted her up on her knees and entered her slowly, his fingers teasing her sex.

"Ah!" She pushed against him, legs trembling uncontrollably.

"Not yet, my lioness."

"I can't—"

He stilled. "I said, not yet." He waited until she stopped trembling before pulling out. This time, he thrust into her forcefully, and she groaned his name. Again, and she was shivering, hands clutching at the counterpane. He touched her, and she moaned.

"Shh," he murmured into her sweaty nape. "Who holds the key to your pleasure?"

"You do," she gasped, "but for the love of God, Jason, please…"

He laughed, increasing his pace. "Soon, lioness," he crooned, "wait for it, wait for it…" It was building inside of him, a tidal wave of sensations centred round his buried cock.

"Now!" he said through gritted teeth. With a hoarse cry she came, and he exploded inside of her.

"I swear, I don't think I can move as much as a finger," she said some time later.

"Mmm." He wanted to sleep before taking her again, but clearly Helle had other ideas, rolling over to face him.

"You must have had sex millions of times."

Now where did that come from? He threw her a cautious look from under his lashes.

"Maybe not quite that many." He ran a finger down her nose. "But none of them mattered." An image of Juliet rose before him, her dark hair a veil that hung all the way down to her waist.

"But I was your first, right?"

"My first love, definitely."

Helle sat up. "What, you had other girls?"

Jason laughed. "I was four years older than you. So while I was waiting for you to grow up…"

"Huh. That's the kind of behaviour that gets a girl branded a slut."

"While a man earns the accolade of being a stud," he shot back, grinning at her.

All this late afternoon activity had whetted their appetites, and it was with a happy sigh Helle attacked the steak on her plate. Jason studied the rustic interior of the restaurant, pleased with his choice.

"So when are we going to Turkey?" she asked, reaching across to nab a mushroom from his plate.

"In a few weeks." Arthur had phoned some hours earlier, to say things were progressing as they should. "I just need to get the financing lined up." He poured her some more wine. Not a major issue, in his case. "Wrong time of the year, though."

"Why?"

"Winter in Turkey is not so picturesque." He sipped

at his wine—an excellent Nebbiolo. "Spring, however, is an entirely different matter." Jason smiled to himself, lost in vivid memories. "Where we come from, the Black Sea ensures the winter is mostly rainy. With spring, the air lifts, and the sea sparkles bright blue under the sun. Red dust, green hills—to the distance the hills become mountains, covered in forests so old they say they've been there since the world was new."

"Wrong tense," Helle said in a light tone. "I bet you those forests no longer exist."

"Some of them do. But you're right, these days the slopes of the hills where we grew up are covered with *camellia sinensis*."

"Camellia what?"

"Tea." He leaned forward. "One day, I'll take you to Trabzon."

"Trabzon?"

"Home," he said, hearing the soft yearning in his own voice. "Well, the place closest to home. But we can't go yet. First we have to deal with that damned Woolf." The idea of encountering Samion on the Black Sea coast had every single hair along Jason's arms rising in alarm. On his home turf, Samion would be far too powerful.

"How do you mean, deal?"

Jason avoided her eyes by picking at his salad. "He'll do anything to stop us from being together."

"Anything?" Her voice shook.

"Anything at all." Which was why there was no choice. For them to be safe, Woolf would have to be dead—but he didn't tell her that.

To judge from its exterior, the residential home catered only to the well-to-do. Jason squirmed a bit when she pointed this out, muttering that what was the benefit of having money if one couldn't use it to make life easier for those one cared about? True enough—and from the way his uncle lit up at the sight of Jason, the affection was mutual. Helle liked Jason's great-uncle immediately, a wizened old man who called her 'dear heart' and complimented her on her excellent teeth.

"Dentist," he explained with a laugh. "Can't help myself, I'm afraid."

Jason brought his uncle up to date on the business—Helle was more than surprised to realise this old man had an eight percent share in Jason's company, as did an unknown cousin named Spencer who lived the good life down in New Zealand.

"Clive Morris was a bright young man," Uncle Everett explained with a grin. "Somewhat short of cash at times, so my younger brother and I helped him out." He laughed. "He was always wanting to buy back the shares, but we refused. Irked him no end, it did."

"I can imagine," Helle said. "Does it irk Jason?"

"Why should it? He'll get my shares soon enough."

Everett was something of a science geek, and he and Jason had a long discussion about the technical merits of various techniques for bone marrow replacement before he went on to ask Jason if he'd been down to Glastonbury lately. When Jason said he'd not found the time, old Everett looked very disappointed.

"The house deserves some TLC, Jason. You know Anne would have wanted you to take care of it."

"Mother's not here anymore," Jason retorted, "so she probably doesn't care."

"But I do," Everett said. "Tor Cottage is where I grew up."

"Sorry," Jason muttered. "It's just that since she died...I miss her more there."

"You have a house down in Glastonbury?" Helle asked as they were driving home.

"Yes." He glanced her way. "My mother grew up there, as did her mother and Everett. And their mother was, apparently, some sort of white witch." He chuckled. "Everett insists his mother has put sufficient protective wards on the house to keep the devil himself away."

"But you don't believe in stuff like that?" She hid a smile, thinking that the rational side of Jason was in severe conflict with the actual fact of who he said he was—an ancient reborn soul.

"Not really." He smiled to himself, eyes on the road. "But I've always been happy there."

The drive home was uneventful, the coming days were equally uneventful, even if Jason walked about with a constipated look on his face after each of Mr Smith's frequent visits. After careful prodding, she got Jason to admit that there were other reasons for his distrust of Mr Smith. Helle gawked when he explained just how much he had in his various accounts in Switzerland, a banking relationship that went back well over a century, plus the substantial assets he had placed in various locations around the world.

"Tax evasion?" she chided.

"Yes. I can't very well declare them, can I?"

At home, Alison's mood remained mostly foul, but on Friday Helle returned home to find Alison singing, her deep alto voice carrying all the way down the stairs from their apartment.

"Happy?" she asked, not even trying to keep the edge out of her voice. Alison had a lot to make up for, in Helle's opinion.

"I've got a date." Alison rolled up her stockings, adjusted the aqua-coloured dress and turned so that Helle could zip her up.

"Really?"

"Yup." Alison was borderline bouncing on her toes. She ducked into the bathroom.

"Is it Woolf?"

"Sam?" Alison's voice sounded vague. "He's in the US." Alison returned, lips now a bright red. "Look good?"

"Yeah." She looked awesome.

"Don't wait up." Alison grinned. "I'm planning on action tonight."

"…so I'm not sure if it is a good thing or not," Helle said to her mother, adjusting the earbud. "I mean, I'm really glad if she hooks up with someone else than Woolf, but sometimes she's just too—"

"Free with herself?" Miriam suggested.

"Makes me sound like the Moral Majority," Helle muttered, jumping a puddle. They'd left the apartment together, she and Alison, but where Helle had turned due east, Alison had remained at the street corner, waiting for her ride.

Miriam laughed. "Alison is a big girl. Her life is her life."

"Let's hope Woolf isn't the jealous type." Huh. Sam Woolf was beyond jealous, but given his comments when last they met, he wasn't all that into Alison. A good thing, all in all.

"Still working for Jason?" her mother asked, a tinge of disapproval in her voice. Helle rolled her eyes. Mum had very strong opinions about keeping professional and private lives apart—even more so since Dad had left her for his marketing assistant.

"Consultancy basis only, Mum." She rang off and increased her speed. She was running late, the consequence of preferring to walk rather than take the underground. The reflecting patches on her sneakers caught the headlights of a car, motionless by the kerb on the opposite side of the road. She adjusted the bag she'd popped her high heels into, wove her way through an elegant group of people just outside the Portman and crossed the road, darting in front of the idling car.

Further down Gloucester Place, she caught sight of Jason, pacing impatiently. He'd promised her an excellent meal at a restaurant on Dorset Street.

"Jason!" She waved, rising on her toes. Behind her, the car revved its engine. "Jason!" she hollered, but he didn't hear her, turning his back just as the car came abreast with her. A black car, tinted windows, but Helle had a glimpse of a gold watch, of a heavy golden ring, and just like that she knew.

"No!"

The car shot off like a bullet. So did Helle. The sidewalk blurred under her feet, her legs pumping at an impossible speed. The car engine roared. Helle shrieked, and flew towards Jason. The car pulled ahead. Helle caught up. Jason! He was going after Jason! The car swerved dangerously, two wheels on the pavement, forcing her to break her stride. People were yelling, and still Jason remained where he was, oblivious to the danger approaching. Turn around, Helle begged silently. Goddamn it, turn around!

Things slowed. Helle registered every crack on the sidewalk in front of her, every breath she took, felt her heartbeat reverberate through her. The car glistened in the dark, the wet asphalt below its wheels glittering with rain. An Audi, aimed like a cannonball towards her man. Her man. She was close enough to make out the heavy sweep of his hair, to see the little white wires disappearing into his ears. She had to reach him first, she just had to… People were leaping to the side, staring at her. She kept her eyes on Jason and redoubled her efforts.

She drew alongside the car. Her lungs were on fire, her legs stumbled, and still she ran—faster than she'd ever done in her life, faster than should have been possible. A long, low tackle and she sent Jason and herself sprawling among the garbage bags standing neatly stacked to the side.

"Ouff!" Jason went limp. There was a loud screech. Voices, so many voices, and someone was yelling, calling for the police. The engine roared and the wheels squealed as the car reversed, before high-tailing its way down the street.

"Jason?" She shook him, none too gently.

"Helle?" he sat up abruptly, gripping her by the arms. Searing heat scorched her.

"Ow!" she protested in a low voice. He let go immediately.

"Sorry, I…" He looked at her. "What happened?"

"Your little lady saved your life, mate." A large man helped Helle to her feet, giving her an admiring look. "I've never seen anyone run that fast before."

"Absolutely unbelievable!" someone else cried. There was a flash and Helle shielded her eyes. More flashes, and she shrank back against Jason.

"Cut it out," she said.

"I have it on video," someone called out. "That's the most amazing thing I've ever seen!"

"Shit!" Jason said in an undertone.

"Hey!" The large man stepped in front of them. "Back

off. Give 'em some privacy." He turned to Helle. "You all right, dearie?"

"I smell funny," she said, looking down at her best skirt, now smeared with stuff she didn't really want to look too closely at.

The man laughed. "That washes off." He looked at Jason. "And you? If you don't mind me saying so, you look concussed."

"Stunned, rather." Jason stretched to his full height, thereby resuming some of his natural authority. "We need a taxi."

"Consider it done." The large man was as good as his word, and a few minutes later they were in a taxi. Jason enfolded her in his arms, pressed his cheek to her head and they sat like that all the way to his house.

They undressed in his hall, leaving a heap of ruined clothes that Jason kicked aside.

"Come here," he said, and she clung to him, ear pressed to his heart. A steady reassuring beat, soothing her own panicked pulse. But he had to support her up the stairs, because her legs were as unmanageable as cooked spaghetti, and she just couldn't stop crying, silent tears running down her face.

"Shush," he said. "Don't cry, darling, it kills me when you do."

"You could have died," she sobbed.

"But I didn't—thanks to you." He managed to run a bath while still holding her to his chest, and then he helped her in, sliding in to sit behind her.

"It was Woolf," she said once she'd calmed down. But she doubted her testimony would hold up in court—what could she say? A vague shape behind a tinted window, but she was certain she'd seen his ring?

"Who else?"

"I thought he was in the US." She leaned forward to allow him to shampoo her hair.

"Samion rarely allows such things as geographical borders to restrict him."

Helle twisted to look at him. "What do we do?"

His chest expanded. "I don't know. But we will work it out." He raised her hand to his mouth, kissing it softly before placing it over his heart. "Somehow, we will."

And this time, Helle did believe him.

Nefirie started at the sound of footsteps, but relaxed once she saw who it was.

"Son," she said, inclining her head. She patted the stone beside her, inviting him to sit. He came over, his hands busy tying back his long, windblown hair from his face.

Nefirie reverted to her previous silence, her eyes unseeing on the water burbling across the pebbles at her feet.

"It doesn't please you." Jason said, turning to see her face.

"No," she agreed, "I would've preferred if you'd found another wife. Not her."

Her honesty made him flinch. "But I love her," he protested, "I've loved her since that first day when I was but a boy."

Nefirie nodded sadly.

"You don't always love what's best for you," she said, and turned to look at the sea. "She was meant for him," she added, ignoring the stony silence from her son. "He'll never forgive you for stealing her. Never."

Chapter 17

They woke to ringing phones. Jason fumbled for the lamp switch.

"What time is it?" Helle sounded half-asleep.

"Three a.m." He lobbed her phone at her. "Yours, I think."

"Mine?" Helle rubbed at her eyes. The phone began ringing again. "Mum?" Helle sat up straight. "Are you okay? Has something happened?" Miriam's response was so loud even Jason heard it.

"Me?" Miriam screeched. "What about you?"

"What do you mean?" Helle lowered her voice, as if hoping this would calm Miriam. Not a chance. The tinny voice filled the room.

"I saw the video!"

"What video?"

"What video? What are you, a moron? Seriously, Helle—"

Jason took the phone. "Hello Miriam."

"Jason? What are you doing there?"

"Helle is with me," he replied, shaking his head as Helle gestured she wanted the phone. "And yes, we are both fine."

"Well, thank heavens for that," Miriam said, her voice reverting to normal. "That video—"

"We haven't seen it," Jason said, making for his laptop.

"Like two million hits on YouTube," Miriam informed him drily. She took a deep breath. "I guess it's been doctored, right?"

"I have no idea." Jason moved the mouse a couple of times and the screen blinked into life.

"She…" Miriam made a sound that sounded suspiciously like a sob. "No one can run like that."

"Mum?" Helle took the phone back. "I'm okay, honestly." Silence. "Mum," Helle said softly, "don't cry." She moved over to the window, talking in a low, hushed tone.

Jason listened with half an ear, fingers flying over the keyboard. The video was all over the place: on Facebook, on Google+, on Twitter... BBC Online had it, Channel Four had it. Jason groaned. This was not good—not good at all.

Helle finished her call and joined him at the small desk. "Have you seen it?" Helle leaned against him, her bare skin cool to the touch.

"Not yet." He met her eyes and pressed the link.

At one level, he supposed it was magnificent. Helle, streaking along like a cheetah in full hunt mode, easily keeping up with the car. At another, it was simply terrifying.

"You always said I was fast," she said in a small voice.

"But not that fast." He clicked on the video again, staring at her as she flew along the street.

"Adrenaline?" She peered at the blurry image that was herself. "At least it's difficult to see it's me."

"There yes. Here..." He clicked on another link, revealing Helle's face bared under the flash of a mobile camera. "...it is not."

"So what do we do?"

"We hope no one recognises you." He tapped at the photo. "You're not entirely yourself here. But if they do, we blame it on adrenaline," he said with a false smile. They'd cart her off somewhere, lock her up as they subjected her to one test after the other. No, he couldn't let that happen. He scowled at the image on the screen.

"How did Mum find out?" Helle frowned, reading the caption. Nowhere did her name appear.

"I have no idea." Jason studied Helle's face as captured by the mobile camera. If he could somehow erase these images— or at least corrupt them... "I have to call Nigel." He kissed Helle's hair. "Call your Mum and ask her."

Nigel answered immediately. Not to wonder; the man kept strange hours, and since his recent trip to India they were stranger still. He listened in silence as Jason explained the situation, but Jason could hear his fingers tapping away as they spoke.

"The video is too blurry to pose any danger," Nigel said once Jason was done. "I've run it through a number of enhancement programs, but the dark and the rain make it damn difficult to see anything beyond a running figure. The photos, however…" He hummed, and Jason grimaced in exasperation. Whenever Nigel did deep thinking, he hummed the same ditty over and over again. "It's so easy, these days, to find someone's phone," Nigel added after a while. "Click, you're dead,"

"Dead?"

"Relax. The phone." Nigel went back to his humming. "I'll have all of these wiped—or permanently damaged—within the hour. So unless someone has printed out a copy she'll be safe." He breathed heavily down the line. "What is she on? Some sort of steroids?"

"Don't be an idiot. She's scared silly by all this and has no idea how it happened."

"A female hulk," Nigel said, laughing, "Has she gone green yet?"

"I sincerely hope not." Jason smiled despite himself. The female hulk herself came over, draped in a blanket, and curled up in his lap. He ran his hand up and down her back in soothing movements.

"Do you want me to wipe the video as well?"

"Too late," Jason said, frowning at the rapidly increasing number of views.

"Yeah." Nigel fell silent. "It's absolutely fucking marvellous," he said in an awed voice. "I've never seen anything like it."

Jason clicked the view icon again, eyes locked to the screen as Helle sprang into action. Nigel was right. Feline grace and surging power combined into something lethally beautiful. In his lap, Helle squirmed. Jason paused the video and switched to screensaver mode. She relaxed.

Nigel cleared his throat. "Just so you know, you owe me—big time. All this stuff is going to keep me up well after my bedtime."

"Which is when precisely?"

"Oh, I don't know. Eight in the morning?"

"You're a very odd creature."

"Says the man whose girlfriend apparently is Wonder Woman."

"Shut up."

Nigel laughed. His voice softened. "Take care of her. This must be messing with her head."

"And mine."

"Tell me about it." Nigel yawned and rang off. Jason dug his chin into Helle's head.

"Bed?" He was cold—and bone tired. With a grunt he stood, with her in his arms.

"Alison told her."

"What?" Jason urged her in under the duvet and crawled in after her, spooning himself around her. She pushed back, her arse round and warm in his groin.

"Mum said Alison called her and told her about the video."

"And how did Alison know…" He didn't finish the sentence. There was only one way she could have known.

"Exactly. She must have been there." She turned in his arms. "How could she?"

"What was she to do?" he said, even if he totally agreed: how could the stupid cow ignore their warnings and go out with Woolf?

"She could have told me he was here!" Helle sounded agitated.

"She could." He pulled her close enough that her nose was pressed against his clavicle. "We can ask her tomorrow. But now, I think we need to sleep."

"As if," she muttered, but she turned over again, allowing him to shield her with his body, keep her safe in the hollow provided by his limbs and his torso. "What am I?" she whispered, just as he was dropping off into sleep. "What sort of a freak can do that?"

He nuzzled her nape, planting a wet kiss just below her ear. "My freak." He extended his hand, snapped, and sent a spark of fire through the air. "Welcome to my world, lioness."

To his relief, she laughed. "Mum is going to go ballistic once we tell her everything."

"If," he corrected drily. "The fewer the better, Helle."

"Which shows you don't know my mum." He heard the proud smile in her voice. She yawned and snuggled even closer.

"Tomorrow. We talk about this whole mess tomorrow."

"Mmm."

Alison was a wreck. She sat huddled in a corner of the sofa, staring at Helle and Jason when they came through the door. In the background, the TV was on, showing yet another re-run of the video.

"You were there," Helle stated. Alison nodded, eyes on the cushion she was holding. "For fuck's sake, Alison, look at me!" Helle surged across the room and slapped the cushion out of Alison's hold. "You were sitting in that goddamn car, when Woolf tried to run Jason over."

"Yes," Alison croaked, pulling the blanket she was wearing closer.

"Did you try to stop him?" Helle grabbed her by the shoulders. "Did you?" She shook Alison, who didn't try to defend herself.

"No." Alison's eyes filled with tears. "What could I do?" She whimpered when Helle sank her fingers into her bare arms. "He would have hurt me if I disobeyed him."

"Let her go." Jason's strong hands slid down Helle's arms. "You're hurting her."

"And should I care?" With a disgusted sound, Helle released Alison. "Serve her right!"

"I didn't do anything," Alison protested. "I was just there, with him."

"I thought you said you could handle him," Helle snarled. "And why didn't you tell me he was here?"

Alison gave her a defiant look. "Why should I? He was here to see me."

"Really? To me, it seems he was here to murder Jason."

"That…" Alison swallowed. "It was a spur of the moment thing. He just saw—"

"Jesus!" Helle kicked at the coffee table, sending Alison's coffee mug flying. She turned to glare at her so-called best friend. "You're coming with us to the police."

"The police?" Jason and Alison spoke in unison.

"We can't go to the police," Jason began.

181

"No way am I going to the police," Alison interrupted. "To say what?"

"You were there! You saw it."

"We are not involving the police." Jason's voice was firm. "The moment we do, your name will be linked to that." He waved his hand at the TV, where yet again Helle was running at breakneck speed. She stared at herself—again. Impossible. Helle's thighs trembled, her mouth drying up. Jason was right, she didn't want her name associated with *that*, she just wanted to forget it had ever happened.

"Hey." Jason's breath was hot on her cheek, his voice low and comforting. "I'm right here." His lips brushed the top of her head, arms slipping round her waist to pull her close. "And I'm here because of you," he added in a whisper. On the screen, Helle had just tackled Jason to the side, the bumper of the car so close it almost glanced against her legs.

"I..." Alison said from behind them. "I thought he was going to kill you both." And then she began to cry. "I didn't understand, at first," she said through her sobs, "but then I saw Jason, and—" She broke off, took a deep gulp of air. "I screamed. He just laughed. And afterwards, he was so angry." She shifted on the sofa, and the blanket rode down, uncovering a huge bruise on her upper arm. "He... Well, let's just say I won't be going out with him again." Her eyes flickered to the door, hands clenching on her blanket. "Things got out of hand."

Helle's anger cooled a couple of degrees. "He hurt you."

Alison shrugged. "He did. But he'd argue it was consensual." She looked away. "After all, I never said no. It's sort of impossible to say no to him when he's all over your brain." Helle knew just how that felt. She sat down beside Alison and took her hand.

"You'll get over it."

Alison nodded. "Of course I will." But her voice sounded dull and tired.

"Why did you call Miriam?" Jason asked.

"I saw the video. Sam played it over and over again. I couldn't exactly call you, so I did the next best thing." She gripped Helle's hand hard. "I wanted to warn you."

"Good thing you did," Jason muttered, eyes on the TV where yet another expert was expounding on the need to find the runner, analyse her DNA. "Look," he said to Helle, "I have to see Nigel, make sure we've killed all the pictures." He brushed at her cheek. "You look tired. Stay here and get some rest."

"But what if Woolf…" Helle clung to him, not wanting to finish the sentence.

"It'll be fine," Jason said. She still wouldn't let him go, making him smile, those amber eyes of his lightening into gold. He leaned towards her, soft warm lips covering hers. "Let me go, lioness," he murmured against her mouth. No way. Not right now. She ran her tongue over his lips, Jason responded in kind, and suddenly she was squashed to him, one large hand at her waist, the other in her hair as he kissed the living daylights out of her, leaving her reeling and breathless when he finally let her go.

"Wow."

"That's what you get when you play with fire." His eyes heated, the copper tones flickering like miniature flames. A smile, his fingers grazing hers, and he was gone.

"Sheesh," Alison said. "You're really into him, aren't you?" She gave Helle a hesitant smile, and for the first time in weeks she sounded more like her normal self, as if she really cared.

"I am." Helle wasn't quite sure how to explain, but suddenly the words gushed out of her, impossible to stop. She told Alison of how she'd wake in the night and watch him, afflicted by a suffocating fear that he would suddenly fade away into nothingness. How at times it felt as if her heart would leap out of her chest at the sight of him, and how sometimes she would break out in a run in her haste to get to him, swamped by the conviction that he would have gone, melting back into the world of dreams.

"I love him so much, and it scares me. I'm scared that this will all be too much for me and I will crack open. Scared of failing him, of not living up to the dream he has created for himself over these long, never ending years of searching for me. Scared that…" She stopped, already regretting having shared all this with Alison given her recent behaviour. And then she saw Alison's bruised arm, her drawn face, and it was her friend, not the nasty bitch of late, who was sitting beside her.

"Hey," Alison took her hand. "You love him, don't you? The rest will work itself out."

"Let's hope so." Helle gnawed her lip, her gut tightening at the thought of Woolf.

She was still in a reflective mood when Jason returned, looking more than satisfied with himself. With half an ear she heard him explain to Alison that all photos of Helle had been wiped, and that even better, he'd found Woolf's name on a passenger list destined for the US.

"That's illegal," Helle put in, somewhat distractedly. She was sitting beside Jason, his arm a comforting weight round her shoulders.

"So?" Alison said, looking much happier now that she'd heard Woolf wasn't around.

"You could get caught," Helle admonished.

"Not likely." Jason grinned.

She was quiet all the way back to Jason's house, quiet throughout the evening, her throat clogged with words she wanted to say, but didn't quite know how to enunciate, wanting them to sound new and unused. She'd told previous boyfriends that she loved them, a quick kiss and a hurried 'I love you' as she hurried off to class or work or wherever. What she felt for Jason was much more complex, so much more permanent. This was not just love—this was a need, a pulsating ache when he wasn't close, a paralysing fear that one day he would leave. It was a want, a sense of incompletion in his absence, a glowing sense of wholeness in his presence.

"You all right?" he asked, sounding concerned as they made their way up to his loft. "You've been very quiet."

"That's because I don't know how to say what I want to say."

"Then show me," he said, his hands sliding oh so gently down her body.

He undressed her. She undressed him. They stood for a long time just looking at each other, not touching, not speaking. At long last he took her hand and led her to the bed, and all those feelings she couldn't put words to, she showed him instead. She kissed her way across his body, she used her hands and mouth, her eyes, to show him just how much she loved him.

She needed him in her, on her, over her. His weight pinning her down, reassuring her he was real, the way he pounded into her, filling her, stretching her, as he buried himself so deep she could feel his balls against her sex. She needed more—so much more—and he laughed, calling her wanton as he kissed her burning, swollen lips.

That night, she gave herself up to loving him—completely, irrevocably—and her heart thudded with fear. It was like going from a tremor to a full-blown earthquake, her foundations shaken, destroyed and rebuilt around him, only him. Jason noticed, and his need mirrored hers, his eyes locked with hers as he used his body to anchor her to him, enthral her forever.

In the safety of his arms, she finally found her voice. "I love you," she whispered, and it was no longer a platitude but a certainty. "I exist for you, only for you."

"I know," he whispered back, smoothing her sweaty hair off her face. "But it makes me very glad to hear you say it." And he held her to his heart, her hand firmly closed around his thumb as he rocked her to sleep.

Over the next few days, they became hollow-eyed through lack of sleep, because time was so much better spent exploring each other, time and time again. They barely kept their lives together, going through the motions of working, of eating. She had drowned herself in him, he in her, and neither of them was in a hurry to break the surface again.

"I won't be able to walk tomorrow," Helle groaned as she lay in his arms. He chuckled, a smug self-satisfied sound.

"Does that mean you're done for tonight?" he teased, kissing her head. Helle nodded, pressing herself against his chest, yawning hugely.

"Mmm, I think so—unless you have some interesting ideas to share."

"I could do sleep," he said, "I think I need sleep. I'm not a rabbit, you know."

She laughed softly. She most definitely knew he wasn't a rabbit.

"If you were," she said, "we'd be drowning in baby rabbits by now."

That made her laugh out loud; a whole house full of small baby rabbits. Boy, was she tired.

Jason stiffened, unwrapped himself from her and half sat up. "No baby rabbits. Not yet."

"Of course not," she said, turning her back on him. But she was overwhelmed by a yearning for his child. *No time to waste*, her reptilian brain said, *look what happened last time*, it added, trying to nudge her memory. Vaguely she remembered a red-haired baby, and the pain as someone tore it out of her arms. *Nope, not going there*, her mind replied very firmly, heaving itself hard against the opening crack.

Jason put one hand on her shoulder. "Helle?"

She didn't reply, still trying to grasp at the blurred memories of a small, warm child that floated through her head. Hormones, she scoffed. She'd better be careful before she said something pathetic like 'I want to have your babies.' But she did, oh God, she did…

"So do I," Jason said, apparently in one of his mind-reader modes, and turned her to face him, "but not yet." She just nodded, not trusting herself to speak, and let him pull her close, his fingers threading through her hair.

"All of you smells of me," he murmured drowsily later, "your hair, your skin. I can taste myself on you."

"Is that good or bad?"

"Good," he replied, rolling her over onto her back. "It makes you mine."

"How primitive," she said hoarsely, hearing him chuckle against the skin of her chest.

"Extremely," he agreed.

She hissed when he came inside, and he stopped.

"Are you very sore?"

Yes, she nodded, biting back at the burning sensation between her legs.

"And still you don't say no?" He moved slowly inside of her. She smiled and shook her head, placing her hands on the small of his back to keep him where he was.

"And you?" she asked him some minutes later, "aren't you sore?"

He nodded, pressing himself deeper inside with a slow, flexing movement of his hips.

"But still…" she whispered.

"But still, I just had to."

Yes, she agreed, they just had to. The candles guttered and flared, their shadows threw themselves against the wall and they said nothing more. They just were—here, now, together.

It was already hot. The dust swirled in a sudden gust of wind, and in the courtyard Jason paced, waiting for Helle.

Elessa sighed as she watched Helle wind her hair into an untidy plait before covering it with her veil, and wondered how much of the day would be spent hunting. She had seen it immediately, in the pink cheeks and suddenly shy looks Helle gave Jason, in the young man's glowing face and the way his hand lingered too long on the small of Helle's back.

Now she regarded her grandchild with a penetrating glance, noting with a reluctant smile how Helle ran her hand down her stomach, her face suffused by an introverted glow. She shook her head in exasperation. They should have waited.

"Should you really be going?" Elessa asked, putting a restraining arm on Helle's sleeve. "What if you have an accident, so close to the wedding?"

"We'll be back before night," Helle replied, hugging Elessa. "We're only going up the mountain."

"Be careful," Elessa said, putting her hand insinuatingly on Helle's flat belly. She smiled at the responding blush, and patted Helle before she moved away.

Evening deepened into twilight and they were not home. The skies darkened into night, and still they did not come. Elessa stood for hours, her eyes scanning the horizon for them both. Neither of them came back to Tarokyie. Not that night. Not for many, many, months.

Chapter 18

A week or so after the car incident, Helle had almost succeeded in convincing herself it had never happened. These last few days had been so intense, so full of Jason, all other aspects of her life relegated to a fuzzy background sound, no more. Well, with the exception of Mum, who had developed an irritating protective streak, calling so often it made Helle feel supervised.

"You are," Alison told her with a grin when Helle shared this with her. "Miriam is keeping a close eye on you, my girl." She made a gargling sound. "And she'll slit the throat of anyone who hurts you." This said with a meaningful look in the direction of Jason, who ignored her.

"Alison," Helle said with a glare. Talk about throwing stones in glasshouses.

"Just sayin'." Alison's face softened. "At least you have a mother to look out for you."

Ouch. Alison's own mother had died when Alison was ten. "You're welcome to a share of her," Helle said.

"I know." Alison grinned. "I think I already have one." She buttoned her coat, pulled her new woollen hat down over her ears and hunted about for her gloves.

"Yeah. She thinks the sun shines out of your ass." Helle smiled back, followed Alison to the door and locked it behind her.

They were in Helle's apartment, where Jason commandeered the kitchen while Helle sorted through her clothes. This living in two places had its drawbacks, and Helle was considering taking Jason up on the offer to move in with him. Alison had looked less than pleased at the idea, but while Helle had forgiven her—almost—for the Woolf thing, she no longer felt obliged to take Alison's opinion into account. Something in their friendship had broken over the last few weeks, and Alison's constant ribbing of Jason wasn't improving things.

Helle tossed a number of rolled up socks into her duffel bag and sank down on her bed. The one thing that had her holding back from permanently moving in with Jason was something else entirely: he was driving her nuts with all his references to a past she didn't remember and definitely didn't want to be defined by. It was as if their new-found intimacy had breached some sort of floodgate on memories he'd previously kept very much to himself, and now he was constantly sharing some little insight or other into what their past life had been like.

Every time he did, Helle could feel him assessing her reactions, and every time she told him she didn't remember, he would look at the same time disappointed and relieved. Helle was mainly irritated.

She wandered out to the kitchen, drawn by the smell of the bouillabaisse presently simmering on the stove. Jason sliced up bread, added the final touches to his homemade aioli, and motioned for her to sit down. The soup was delicious. And in the light of the candles, Jason looked delicious, black shirt rolled up to display his muscled forearms, strong legs encased in tight jeans. He grinned when he caught her staring, did a little twirl before sitting down opposite her.

The white Alsace wine was excellent—a low-key celebration of the fact that the Turkish lawyers had approved the proposed Share Purchase Agreement, this after the fourteenth draft or so.

"Do you think the present owner will stay on once you've made him a millionaire?" Helle asked.

"Probably." Jason refilled her bowl before serving himself. "These innovator types tend to be very protective of their babies." His face lit up. "It's such a neat thing! It's almost like magic—in goes the little tablet, out comes electricity."

"Sounds like a gas meter to me," Helle said, laughing at his excitement. "And I can see it isn't only the innovator who cares about this particular baby."

"Obviously," he replied drily. "Given the amount of money I'm paying for it." Off he went again, explaining just how ingenious the device was, offering offline recharging possibilities. Helle propped her chin in her hand and just listened, smiling at his enthusiasm, at the way he raked his long, strong fingers through his hair, making it messier by the minute. Midway through a sentence, he came to an abrupt halt.

"Listen to me," he said, rolling his eyes. "Obsessed."

"I am," she replied. "Obsessed, I mean."

He reached across the table to touch her cheek. Helle half closed her eyes, rubbing her cheek against his hand. Jason chuckled.

"Just as always, hey?" He tugged gently at a strand of her hair. "My lioness, preening like a lovesick kitten under my touch."

Helle sat back, frowning slightly, but Jason's face had acquired that dreamy look it always wore when he was about to share yet another unwanted insight into their previous life.

"I especially remember one occasion," he said, "you must have been around thirteen, old enough for your grandmother to insist you cover yourself with a veil, and—"

"Stop." Irritated, Helle stood, stacking the dishes. The spoons clattered when she threw them into the uppermost empty bowl. "I don't want to know, okay?"

Jason sat back. "Well, excuse me. I'm simply sharing a memory with you."

"A memory you have—I don't. So how am I supposed to react? How do I even know they are true?"

"True?" Jason's eyes darkened. "Are you calling me a liar?"

"I don't know!" Helle threw her arms up in the air. "But I'm so tired of living under this…this…cloud of previous existences—existences I don't remember at all. Sometimes, all this stuff about previous lives just seems a load of mumbo-jumbo." She dumped the dishes in the sink.

"Mumbo jumbo?" Jason got to his feet. "How dare you disparage my memories like that? Do you think I want to remember? Have you any idea what it's like, to wake up life after life to the realisation that I've lived before—several times, by the way—and know that my single purpose is to find the woman I lost three thousand years ago? Three thousand years!" He laughed mirthlessly.

"Well, I didn't ask you to come looking, did I? And just

for your information, I'm not that girl you once knew. I'm me, Helle Madsen, and every time you start dragging up your so-called memories, you're not exactly making me feel as if you love me, it's more as if you're in love with a damned ghost." She might just as well have kicked him in the face. For a moment he just stood there. Her heart clenched at the way he looked at her, his love, his torment, shining out from his eyes, but then he whirled, and like a tornado he tore through the flat, collecting his keys, his phone and jacket.

"What are you doing?"

"I'm leaving," he said through gritted teeth. "After all, you don't want a freak in your life—you've made that damned clear."

"I never called you a freak!"

"No? I guess it's a matter of interpretation. And believe me, I've had ample experience of people who look at me like you just did, as if you think I'm crazy."

"I don't think you're crazy. You're just—"

"What?"

Helle hitched her shoulders. Too intense, she wanted to say. Somewhat delusional, perhaps. Jason shoved her out of the way and wrenched the door open.

"Jason!" She almost stamped her foot. "Don't leave like this."

The door shivered in its frame and he was gone.

The night air was cold enough for his exhalations to rise in gusts of mist before him, but he didn't really notice, striding away at speed. He heard her shove the window open, heard her call his name, but he ignored it—why shouldn't he, when she'd just accused him of being borderline insane? Jason shoved his hands into his pocket and slowed his pace. To some extent, she had a point—however reluctant he was to admit it. Maybe he did love her more for who she once was than for who she was today.

He came to a halt and turned his face up to the sky and closed his eyes. There she was, his Helle, the girl-child he had loved all those years ago, and his stomach tightened with familiar pain, his mouth wobbling as the long-ago Helle danced before his eyes. But superimposed on this ancient image was a vivid, vibrant woman, and she was also dancing, her shirt half-unbuttoned to reveal the lacy bra beneath, her short skirt showcasing her legs, her bottom. This Helle challenged him, she was no child, no hazy memory—she was his future. The faded image of ancient Helle seemed to nod her approval, blowing him one last kiss before she released him to love and embrace the new her.

"Insane," he muttered with a crooked smile. "Damn it, Morris, she's right, you're seeing ghosts." Not ghosts; a spurt of anger rushed through him. He was remembering, goddamn it, and he couldn't help it that he did and she didn't, could he? And to expect him to bottle it up, wasn't that demanding too much? Was it so strange that he needed to share his precious memories with the woman who'd inspired them, fettered him to her forever?

He sighed. He was burdening her with his recollections— he knew that—but he felt entitled, after all these lonely years. Also, he was working up to telling her; bit by careful bit he'd been attempting to lay the groundwork to tell her what really happened. She needed to know, because of Woolf. It made him inhale unsteadily. Would she still love him, once she knew all the sordid details? Or would the past reach out across the divide of time and smite him, leaving him eviscerated when she walked away?

To his surprise, he'd retraced his steps, standing almost directly under Helle's window. The soft glow of candlelight had been replaced by the harsher light of electrical fittings, and he supposed he should go up and make things right. But at the same time maybe it was good if they had some time apart. These last few days they'd been more or less joined at the hip and perhaps she needed time to figure out what she felt. He already knew, he thought, eyes on her window. Besides, she had to take him as he was: he could not, would not, suppress his memories in her presence, pretend they didn't exist. He squeezed his eyes shut. None of them, not even the ones that could potentially tear them apart for good.

His phone rang. Will. With a relieved shiver, Jason set his dark musings aside and escaped into the far simpler world of business and IT.

She had expected him to come back. She had at least expected him to call, but as the evening progressed, she came to the conclusion that this was him punishing her. She sent him a text. *OK?* An hour later, he replied with a *Yes*. Nothing more. Helle threw the phone aside. If he was hoping she would call, well then he could damned well keep on waiting—she wasn't the one who'd stormed out, was she?

So she made herself some hot chocolate with marshmallows, did some channel browsing before ending up watching *Love Actually*—very apt, a mere three weeks before Christmas. Her mind wandered. On the screen, Colin Firth was swimming about in some dank pond, salvaging sodden papers. On the sofa, Helle was having unwelcome flashbacks. Most of them were hazy and unformed, all but those of the young man leaning against a wall, his arms folded over his chest. His dark mahogany hair was tied back off his face, and his golden gaze followed her, a soft smile on his face. She smiled at this very young Jason, so unformed as a man, still a boy, but tall and well-built, his body a collection of taut muscles—as it was now.

She saw small, squat houses, each windowless except for a series of square holes just below the roof, a verdant hillside that rose steeply from a glittering sea. She could feel how her breath came in shallow gasps after having run all the way to the top, laughing at Jason when he sulked because she'd beaten him again.

"Tarokyie," she said out loud. Her first home, a little place that breathed heat and peace. "Shit," she muttered. Imaginations, she told herself, the random product of a brain titillated by the concept of former lives, further stimulated by Jason's references to a shared past. Deep down, she knew they weren't. The old woman who regarded her with so much love, wrinkled hands wiping at her cheeks—she was real. She was Nana, and the man with hair as riotous as Helle's own, he was her father. "Kantor," she said, sounding out his name before deciding she needed something stronger than hot chocolate.

She was still awake when Alison came home.

"Where's Jason?" Alison asked the moment she came in, taking in the bottle of whisky, the empty Ben & Jerry ice-cream carton.

"He left." Helle gave the whisky a considering look. Should she have a third? "We had a fight, and he just upped and left. I guess one could almost say we broke up." No, she wasn't going to cry. Helle pinched herself hard, blinking back the tears.

"So what happened?" Alison handed her a tissue. Those damn tears were running silently down Helle's face.

"I told him I was sick and tired of all these references to a previous life," Helle said, and there was a twinge of shame as she recalled just how devastated he'd looked. "Seriously, Alison, I just—" She bit off.

"...don't know if you believe it," Alison filled in.

Helle nodded, eyes on the tissue she was tearing apart. "Sometimes I do. Sometimes it feels as if we're dragging this whole load of baggage around, and even worse, I have no idea what it is." She gave Alison a beseeching look. "He'll come back, won't he?"

"You've just told him you don't believe in him." Alison handed her another tissue. "Not so strange, given what he's telling you, but for him..." She shrugged. "He believes it." Helle nodded. He most certainly did, and sometimes she did as well—like when Kantor and her Nana sprang into life inside her head. But she wasn't about to tell Alison that.

"Call him," Alison said.

"Or I wait until he calls me. He's the one who took off."

"We have to be getting back," Helle jiggled her thighs. He made a discontented sound and scrunched his eyes tightly.

"I don't want to. I want to stay like this a little while longer."

Helle smiled and ran her hands over his face, using her braid to tickle him softly over his long straight nose, over the twitching corners of his mouth and across the paler skin of his throat. "I'm glad that you're clean-shaven," she told him, tracing his square jaw with her fingers, "it would have been a pity to hide something like this under a wild beard."

"Something like what?" he teased, his lips curving softly.

"Like this," she ran a finger along his full lower lip.

He sat up and cradled her head, holding her still against his mouth.

"I love you," he whispered through their kiss.

"And I you," she smiled back. For a moment she considered telling him, sharing the secret she knew would make him overjoyed. No, she smiled to herself, she'd wait until she was entirely sure. Maybe she could tell him on their wedding night.

They didn't hear the men until it was too late. Close to a dozen or so, they charged into the clearing. When Jason leapt to his feet they were already surrounded, and a well-placed slingshot brought Jason to his knees.

"Run, Helle," he yelled, "run while you can, my heart." But she couldn't leave him alone to face them all, not when blood ran down his face and dripped onto his linen tunic. Not when Samion himself appeared, guiding his chariot across the uneven ground.

Samion threw the reins to one of his men. "So," sneered, "look what I've cornered. The lioness and her chosen mate." He spat out the words, the emotions flashing through his eyes making her quail in terror. "She was right, my informant, well worth her price." He leapt off his chariot and came striding towards her, and darkness shrouded his shape. She held her chin high, trying to stare him down. Jason was still dazed, his head wound bleeding. He tried to stand, but all Samion did was point his finger at him and it was as if Jason had been bolted in place.

"Take him away," Samion snapped, "and make sure he can't use his hands."

"Don't you dare hurt him," she growled, still unconquered.

"He comes with his own protection," Samion said. "If not, his blood would already be seeping into the ground. Even I know the cost of harming a Wanderer."

Helle watched them dragging Jason away. He stumbled and turned, trying to find her with his eyes. For one moment their eyes met and held, unspoken words flying between them.

"And you," Samion walked closely around Helle, while she tried not to flinch. "You're of course also protected by your blood." He leaned closer, his breath on her cheek. "To an extent." He laughed gratingly and grabbed hold of her braid, forcing her towards him.

"They'll come looking for me," she said, staring at the four parallel marks that disfigured his face. Claw marks—the marks of her lioness.

"Eventually, but will it be in time?" His hand forced her chin up, his lips suddenly very close to hers. She tried desperately to turn her face away, but his eyes froze her to the spot, incapable of twitching as much as an eyelid. Samion laughed and sauntered over to the nearby shrubs where he cut a long switch. It whistled through the air when he swung it back and forth. Helle tried to wrest herself free from the man holding her.

"Never, you said, little Helle." Samion smirked, returning to his circling of her. "Never would you lie in my arms." She stiffened her spine, determined not to let the fear his words caused show on her face. He chuckled drily. "And this time, you can't turn and run. In fact, you'll never run from me again."

His hand closed around her wrist, an iron manacle she was unable to break free from. At first she struggled, but when he turned the full force of his eyes on her, her legs wobbled. It was useless to fight him. Meekly, she followed him towards the large rock in the middle of the clearing.

"Disobedient women must be punished," he said, forcing her down over the rock. His fingers brushed her cheek. "Don't you agree?"

Those eyes hovered far too close for her to do anything but nod. At his command, she pressed her cheek against the rough surface.

"Lift her up and hold her," he barked, and other hands pulled Helle higher onto the rock, fettering her hands and her calves. It wasn't until he undid her sandals that she understood. It wasn't until she heard the soft swoosh of the switch parting the air that she fully grasped what he was going to do to her. It wasn't until the stiff length of wood hit the blades of her feet that she knew. Time and time again the switch came down, cutting bloody stripes into her feet, tearing into the vulnerable muscles and tendons. He was right; she'd never run from him again. She would barely walk.

Chapter 19

He didn't call. Helle kept on checking her phone, hoping she'd missed a call, or a text, but Jason seemed quite happy to maintain some sort of silence. It got to her, but with an effort, she stayed silent too. At least for the entire Tuesday.

On Wednesday, she gave in. A quick text, no more.

U ok?

His reply was instantaneous. *Fine.*

Not exactly a reply to invite further texts, but she tried. *Meet up later?*

Once again, he responded within seconds. *Why? You like hanging out with delusional peeps like me?*

Well, sod him too.

So instead of walking about with her eyes glued to her phone screen, she went for a long run, throwing a careful look over her shoulder before she blazed off in a finishing spurt. Phew! Fast, yes. Abnormally so, no.

After she showered, she visited the dry cleaner, scrubbed the cooker clean of the remains of last night's bolognese and read the three back-issues of *The Economist* she'd pilfered from Jason's office. She sat for a while at the laptop, debating with herself whether she should drop by his office on the pretence of finishing off her work. But what if he ignored her as much there as he'd been doing since Monday evening? Her nerve failed her and she went back to checking her phone.

Finally, she couldn't stand it.

What, you're going to kill me with silence? she wrote.

If you want to talk, you know where to find me, he wrote back.

Not me who walked out, she replied. He didn't respond.

Thursday, she woke with a burning need to call him—well, to make love to him, if she was going to be honest—but she managed to fight the urge by going out for yet another long run, this time doing close to twelve k before she returned home, agreeably tired physically, but totally wired emotionally. No, she promised herself, she wouldn't call him. Or text him. It was Jason who'd walked out, leaving their argument hanging in mid-air. He should take the first step, right?

"He should," Mum agreed when Helle carefully raised the subject during their call. She couldn't exactly tell her what it was they'd argued about, and from her mother's sceptical silence, she didn't buy Helle's thin cover story. "But men are men. Sometimes, their pride gets in the way of doing the right thing."

"So we're not entitled to our pride?"

"Hey, us women are the emotional brains in any relationship."

Helle chose not to say something about Dad and Mum. As she recalled things, it was mostly Dad smoothing out their disagreements by coming home with flowers, or simply taking Mum in his arms. His arms. Helle gave herself a little self-hug. All of her missed Jason, however ridiculous that might sound.

"Have you booked your ticket yet?" Mum asked and Helle didn't know what to say. She wanted to be here, in London— and hopefully with Jason—over Christmas.

"Yeah," she lied, deciding she would send her mother an e-mail instead. She'd go ballistic.

The afternoon dragged on. As Alison was off at some conference or other in Birmingham, Helle decided to treat herself to a huge bowl of popcorn and a marathon session with *Lord of the Rings*. For the first time ever, it didn't work, and while Gandalf was telling the Balrog he couldn't pass, while Aragorn was leading the defence of Helm's Deep, her thoughts kept straying back to Jason.

And then, during her favourite scene, the one where Theoden urged his men to ride to death, a collective suicide almost, given the opposition, she sat up so abruptly she spilled popcorn all over the sofa. It was four a.m. She groped for her phone. No new texts, no sign of life from him since that last text, well over thirty-six hours earlier. Suicide. What if...? Helle looked without seeing as the Riders of Rohan mowed down the orcs, were mowed down in turn by the Oliphaunts.

No, she tried to tell herself, he wouldn't—not over something as silly as this.

She gave up on sleep at six. She tried to call him several times, but he didn't pick up. She sent him a text, a short *ok?* but there was no reply.

"Inconsiderate asshole," she muttered, trying to stop herself from picturing multiple suicidal scenarios. Rationally, why would he do it, she asked herself. After all, here they were together—sort of—for the first time in three millennia, according to him. But she remembered his quiet voice, the anguish in his face when he told her that once he gave up on ever finding her, he moved on.

She was in his office at nine. She hadn't bothered dressing up, wearing her faded green hoodie over a clean tee and her favourite jeans. From the way Angela studied her, this attire was not in line with company expectations.

"Is Jason here?'"

"No." Angela frowned. "I thought he'd be with you. He hasn't taken any calls this morning." In fact, he hadn't spoken to anyone at the office since the previous afternoon, when he'd left abruptly, saying he had matters to take care of.

"Matters?" Helle asked.

"His solicitor—you know wills and deeds and stuff," Will said in passing. He grinned at Helle. "You look hot in jeans."

"Wills?" Helle felt sick.

Will just shrugged. "Yeah, paperwork in general."

"Oh." She left without a word. She needed a cab.

The doorbell rang. Jason was tempted not to answer. His head was ringing, his mouth dry and sticky with the residue of last night's binge. The doorbell rang again. With a groan, he levered himself upright in the Howard. Juliet was snoring beside him, bare legs tangled with his. Had they...? Jason blinked and scrubbed at his face. No, he decided. She'd wanted to, he hadn't, and so he'd kept plying her with wine until she fell asleep—like a nanosecond before he followed suit.

The doorbell again. "Turn the fucking thing off," Juliet moaned.

Someone pounded at the door. "Jason?"

Damn! He shot to his feet. That was Helle. He tucked his shirt into his jeans as he went, cinching the belt. He needed a restorative drink. The sunlight that filtered through the coloured glass of the window over the door hurt his eyes.

She pounded again.

"I'm coming," he told her, struggling with the locks before swinging the door open. The sight of her sobered him up fast. She'd been crying, and she'd clearly wiped at her face with something none too clean, leaving a faint smudge of mud just below her right eye. She was also wet, her hair plastered to her head.

"What are you doing here?" he asked, sounding gruffer than he intended. He winced at how hurt she looked and tried to make amends by holding his hand out to her. She ignored it, but at his gesture stepped inside. Water puddled on the floor below her, dripping off her hair, her red jacket.

"You walked in the rain?"

"No, I took a spontaneous shower with my clothes on." She stepped out of her shoes, leaving damp footprints on the floor. "There were no cabs so I had to walk from the closest tube station."

"Ah." He ducked into the downstairs bathroom, found a towel and handed it to her.

"Jason?" Juliet called from the living room. "Who's that, honey?"

Helle froze, towel in hand. Blue eyes widened and turned his way. Jason closed his eyes at the look in them.

"It's not what you think."

"How would you know?" she bit back, throwing the towel at him. "Is that why you haven't answered my calls, Angela's calls? Is that why you haven't replied to my texts? Because you've been busy elsewhere?" She was already trying to stomp her feet back into her sodden trainers.

"Of course not!" He'd forgotten to recharge his phone,

it was lying in some pocket or other. He frowned. "Why has Angela called?"

"How the fuck would I know? But I do know why I called, you bastard. But I guess you don't care about that, do you?'"

"Jason?" Juliet sashayed down the long hallway in their direction. In only her shirt, her dark hair hanging in a lustrous mess down her back, she looked as if she'd just got out of bed—his bed. Well, to some extent he supposed she had—but not like that, not in any way that should have Helle looking at him as if all she wanted to do was wrench the door open and flee.

"This is Juliet. Juliet, meet Helle." He'd hoped to have introduced them under different circumstances—had even hoped they could like each other, but from the way Juliet looked at Helle, and Helle looked at Juliet, it was obvious neither of them had any intention of voluntarily spending any time with each other.

"I'm his aunt," Juliet purred, stroking Jason's back. He shrugged her hand off, irritated by her possessive behaviour. Helle was studying Juliet, all the way from her bare, lean legs to the cream silk shirt, her gaze lingering on the tumbling hair, on her tanned face and the bright red fingernails. It made his heart lurch when Helle folded her hands together, hiding her own less than perfect nails.

"You're very young to be an aunt," Helle said.

Juliet shook out her long, dark hair. Beautiful hair, Jason reflected. He liked long hair. Helle used to have hair as long, a mass of curls he'd loved to sink his fingers into.

"I'm his aunt by marriage, not blood." Juliet laughed, a low, sensual sound. "Fortunately, as otherwise we'd have been dabbling in incest, wouldn't we, Jason?" He shot her an angry look, she raised two perfect brows, an amused smile on her mouth.

"You've never mentioned an aunt." Helle backed away. "Of course, now that I've met her, I understand why."

"It's not what it seems," he repeated.

"No?" Helle was already at the door, groping for the

handle. "Put yourself in my shoes, buster. What would you think if you found Mr Stud in my living room?"

Jason winced. "Don't go. Please." He made a grab for her but she evaded him, and just like that she was outside, running through the rain.

"Helle!" He splashed barefoot through the puddles on the pavement and managed to catch up with her at the corner with Argyll Road. "You're overreacting—listen to me!" He took a deep breath. "I don't have many friends," he explained. "Juliet is one of them."

"Yeah, you're bed buddies as well."

"Used to be." There was no point in lying. "But not anymore. Not now that you're—" He broke off. "And why should you care? You made your opinion of me pretty clear."

"I came, didn't I?" She was crying now, those wonderful green-flecked eyes of her narrowed with hurt. "I was worried that you'd—"

"Do what?" He pushed her back against one of the parked cars, caging her within his arms. "Kill myself?" Helle nodded, wiping at her eyes. "You're an idiot, Helle Madsen. You think I've spent three thousand years leaping through lives to find you, only to give up when you throw a tizzy?" He shook his head. "I am far too persistent." He rested his forehead against hers, slipped his hands round her waist and drew her so close that their hips met. "So why are you here?"

"I…" Helle hesitated. "I have memories too."

Jason tightened his hold on her. She believed him.

The rain turned into a downpour and they ran back to his house, hand in hand. Jason helped her out of her jacket, steadying her as she wriggled out of her sodden jeans.

"Here." He handed her the towel, but took it back to pat at her hair, her face.

There was a sharp cough from behind them. A fully-dressed Juliet was standing some feet away, studying Helle as if she very much wanted to poke her eyes out.

"I'll be leaving, then," she said, but her voice and her body begged Jason to tell her to stay.

"Good idea," Helle muttered.

Jason placed a finger over her lips. "Hush." He directed himself to Juliet. "Drive carefully. Give me a call when you get home."

Juliet gave him a hug. He patted her back, all too aware of Helle's gaze on them.

"Dinner soon?" Juliet asked.

"Sure." Jason disengaged himself, pulled Helle close. "I can cook for the three of us."

Juliet didn't comment. With a nod, no more, in Helle's direction, she left.

"So, your aunt." Helle's voice demanded an explanation. She shrugged out of her hoodie and wound the towel round her waist.

"In this life, she is. She was married to my father's brother, but he died several years ago."

"Oh. And is she happy being your aunt?"

Jason grimaced. "Not really. We've run into each other in several lives, and yes, she wants more, much more than I can give her. But I've always told her that's not on the table—she knows you always come first."

"Didn't seem that way just now," Helle said, following him into the living room. Two wine bottles on the table, one on the floor, and the Howard was a rumpled collection of cushions, the indentations of two bodies clearly visible. Helle studied them without saying anything. Her nostrils widened, and he took a careful sniff. The room smelled faintly of sour wine, of scented candles and Juliet's perfume.

"We drank too much last night." He'd invited Juliet over to talk about Helle but had ended up fending off Juliet's very determined seduction attempts. Best not share that with Helle.

"No, really?" She kicked at one of the smaller cushions littering the floor, looking vulnerable in only her t-shirt and towel. "Was that all you did?"

"What the hell is that supposed to mean?" he bristled.

"Have a guess." She looked at him from under her lashes. "It's not as if she would have said no, is it? I bet she was begging for it last night."

"Fat good it did her. I'm not interested—not anymore."

She sat down on the Howard, grinding her arse into the upholstery as if staking a claim on it.

"She's the Juliet who died at Kenilworth?"

He nodded.

"She's gorgeous." Helle sounded grudging, eyes on her tightly-folded hands.

"She is, but that's beside the point." He sat down beside her. "You're the one I've been coming back for, life after life."

"Why?"

"Why?" He didn't understand.

"Why have you spent your life—excuse me, your lives—looking for me?"

"I told you—I had to. We deserved more than we got that first time round."

Helle grimaced. "But I'm not her, Jason. God knows what pictures you've painted of me over the ages, but what if I'm not like her, your beloved long-dead girl?"

"But you are," he said, trying to take hold of her.

Helle stood up and began to pace. "Of course I'm not! I'm a modern woman who has no desire whatsoever to be defined by what I might have been three thousand years ago." She took a deep breath, backing away when he got to his feet. "You don't know me, Jason. You just think you do. In fact, I bet you know that Juliet much better than you know me."

"Stop!" He grabbed hold of her shoulders. "Stop it, now." Her words filled him with panic. She was going to leave him, walk away from him, too frightened by the impossibilities that linked them. "Of course I know you're not the girl I once knew—you are older than she ever was, you have the benefit of an education, you're a product of the people who raised you and the times you live in. But you're as vibrant, as brave and obstinate as she was. You make me care as much as she did, and you—you, not the faded images of long gone Helle—make my heart sing every time I see you."

"Hmph!" Helle leaned away from him.

"What, you don't believe me?" He lowered his voice to a husky drawl, gratified to see the responding flush crawl up her neck and cheeks. One hand slid down her back, cupping her arse with enough force that she rocked into him, the other slid up to sink into her hair, holding her perfectly still as he kissed her. Softly.

Her arms came up around his neck. He caught hold of her wrists and disengaged himself. "Well, do you?" he asked, walking her backwards towards the sofa.

She licked her lips. "I—"

He didn't let her finish. Pinning her hands to her side, he kissed her again, and this time he demanded entry. Her mouth softened—all of her did. As he ended the kiss, he bit her lower lip, hard enough that she made a protesting little sound.

He yanked the towel off her. She reached for him, but he evaded her hands. "Take your clothes off," he said, moving so that he was standing behind her.

"What about you?" She looked at him over her shoulder before pulling off her t-shirt.

"All in good time, my lioness." He ran a finger up and down her nape and she shivered, hands trembling as she struggled with the clasp of her bra, the lacy garment landing on the floor. His hands cupped her breasts, fingers playing with her nipples. She rested back against him, her head on his shoulder.

"I love you," he said, kissing her shoulder, her ear, her neck. "Do you believe that?"

"I do. Agh!" She jerked when he tightened his hold on her nipples. "Jason, I—" She ground her arse against his crotch, and he smiled against her skin.

"Bend over." He wanted her now. "Take hold of the armrest on the sofa."

"What? I'm not sure—"

"But I am. Do as I say." He guided her hands to the soft pile of the upholstered armrest. "Place your elbows on it and stay that way," he said, a hand on her back as she lowered herself further, her arse now being her highest point. "You're beautiful," he murmured, stroking her buttocks. "So very beautiful—and mine." He ran his hands down her thighs, up to the golden curls that adorned her pubis. A finger through her folds, and she was wet and warm, her legs dipping when he touched her clit.

Jason fell to his knees behind her. She uttered a loud gasp when he buried his face in her sex. She shifted on her feet, a number of urgent little sounds spilling from her when he kissed her, licked her. He could feel the tightening of her internal muscles, could sense her clenching rhythmically. One last kiss, and he rose. Helle moaned, made as if to touch herself, but he caught her hand.

"No. I thought we'd agreed your pleasure is mine to give you."

"Then get on with it!"

He chuckled, drew a teasing finger up and down her cleft, up to her anus and back down again.

"Jason!" Once again, here came her hand.

He slapped it away. "I told you to keep your elbows on the armrest." He leaned over her, his mouth at her ear, a finger on her clit. "Do I have to tie you up to keep you still?"

"Would you want to?" she asked breathlessly, grinding her hips in time with his finger's movement.

"Maybe." The thought was arousing, but not as arousing as the vision of Helle in his arms, clutching at him, raking her nails down his back. He withdrew his finger and she protested, telling him he was a damned tease. That made him laugh.

He pressed his jeans-clad erection against her arse. His hands followed the contours of her hips, slid round to grip her upper thighs and pull her back against him. She threw her head back and moaned.

"Does it turn you on to stand like this, stark naked in my lounge?" he asked.

"Yes." Her voice shook.

"Turns me on too. My woman, driving me crazy with her smell, the warmth of her skin." He undid the buttons in his fly and knelt on the sofa, just in front of her. She reached for him, but he shook his head.

"Ah-ah. Your mouth only."

He could have kept this up a long time. The sensation of her lips, her tongue, on his cock, had him floating in a sea of red colours. One part of him wanted to come in her mouth. The other wanted to come inside of her, feel her unravel under him as he gave himself over to that excruciatingly short moment of time when his mind was wiped free of any thoughts, every single cell in him striving towards physical release.

His hips jerked. So close, so very close. He released his cock from her mouth. It bobbed when he got to his feet, heavy and hot with his seed. Did anyone use the word seed anymore, he mused distractedly as he positioned himself behind her. Helle lifted herself up on her toes, thereby displaying her moist sex.

"Hold on," he said, before burying his entire length in her. Hard.

"Yes!" Helle lifted herself higher. He pulled out, pushed in. Fast and hard, his hands holding her hips. She was calling his name, all of her tightening around him. More. He needed more. Jason picked up pace, flexing his hips so that every thrust had his balls slapping into her damp skin. Her legs folded, he pulled her up to stand. He wasn't done yet, damn it! And here, at last, it came. He felt his face contort, mouth widening into a soundless shout as he spurted into her.

It was anyone's guess how they made it from the living room to Jason's precious tub. Helle had no recollection of making it up the stairs, her head still swimming in a euphoria of sensations that precluded as much as twitching her nose intentionally. But here they were, immersed in hot water and the scents of lavender.

"Why did you just walk out?" she asked, breaking their comfortable silence.

"It guts me when you deny our past."

"But how can you expect me to buy into it?" She half-turned so that she could see his eyes. "I don't remember, Jason."

"But you said—"

She placed a finger on his mouth. "I have fragments, half-formed images of another place, another time. But it's like sitting with ten pieces of a 5,000-piece jigsaw."

"I suppose you're right. Maybe I'm expecting too much from you, but it's just that I've been so lonely, for so long, and finding you—well, I hoped that it would be like it was."

"What? Me a crazy girl who ran about with lions, and you the boy with fire eyes and hands that could set the night alight?" She sat up abruptly, sloshing water over the side of the tub. "I remember that," she said. "How you spun globes of fire between your hands and flung them upwards, lighting up the skies for me."

Jason laughed. "So do I. You were quite the little pest about it, begging me to do it over and over again."

"But you didn't mind, did you?" Helle sank deeper into the water, snatching at recollections of balmy nights, of standing barefoot in only a linen garment while Jason stood before her—a boy whose teeth shone white in the dark as his fingers spilled little sparks. She took his hand and turned it over, pressing a kiss to his palm. "Would you do it again? For me."

"I will." He pressed his cheek to the top of her head. "The first time in this life my hands crackled with electricity, I thought I would die. I almost pissed myself when sparks jumped between my hands."

"I can imagine." No, not really. But given how her recent burst of speed had unnerved her—still scared her silly—she supposed discovering you could start fires with your bare hands would be terrifying.

"Yeah. My adolescence wasn't exactly a happy time. I spent too much time daydreaming as I sorted through all the strange memories that flooded my brain. I thought I was going crazy. I wanted to find a girl with a thick blonde braid who teased me as we ran around with lions."

"Didn't you tell someone? Your mother?"

"About the dreams yes. But I definitely didn't want to share my magic." He extended his hands, clenched them, opened them, and above each palm a flame flickered. He laughed hollowly and submerged his hands in the water, which hissed and bubbled. "I've never told anyone about the fire."

"Not even Juliet?"

"Nope. Not even her." He used his toes to open the hot water tap, steam wafting off the surface. "That's why it was so important to me that you believe me. I'm so sick and tired of always being alone with my memories and hopes."

"You're not." She climbed into his lap, clasping his face between her hands. "Not anymore." In response, he kissed her nose.

They were as wrinkled as prunes when Jason's phone began to ring. Repeatedly.

"What now?" he muttered, sloshing water all over the floor as he got out and hurried over to where the phone was charging.

"Hello?" He frowned as he listened. "Damn!" The frown deepened into a scowl. "Yes, yes, I will, Angela. Right now." He rang off.

"What?" Helle handed him a towel.

"I have to call Arthur." He booted up his laptop, the phone pressed between his ear and neck. "Arthur? Jason here." He listened, his mouth tightening. "But we already have a contract! Yes, I know, but…Fine… Yes, of course… I'll call Selim Bey right now." The phone flew in an arc, landing on the bed. "Damned Woolf!" Jason stalked over to retrieve his phone. "He's going after the Turkish deal—after he's screwed me over on two of my other targeted companies."

"But that's not his thing."

"What? Screwing people over? Seems to me he does that all the time." Jason was scrolling down his contacts.

"The Turkish set-up. He generally goes after companies that have come further in the commercialisation phase."

"I'd hazard he's making an exception," Jason said.

"To get at you."

Jason just nodded, the phone already pressed to his ear. "Selim Bey?" He switched to Turkish.

There was no point in listening when she couldn't understand anything, so Helle went in search of clothes, touched to find he'd laundered all the stuff she'd left behind. She was tugging his comb through her damp curls when he came to find her, still stark naked. She studied him through the mirror. He really was a most amazingly handsome man, his face a collection of sharp planes and defined lines. The soft lower lip and the golden colour of his eyes only served to underline his stark good looks, as did the shaggy mess of his dark red hair.

"So, you ready to go to Istanbul?" he asked, grinning. "We're concluding the deal on Wednesday and I was thinking we could stay for some days so that I can show you the sights."

"Combining business with pleasure, huh?"

"Always." He took the comb from her. "Life is too short not to."

"Mother," she whispered in the dark, drawing her knees up to her chin. "Please Mother, keep him safe for me. Bless him with your strength, cradle him to your chest and keep him alive."

She hugged herself, trying to blank out the pain that shot up from her feet and the waves of nausea that accompanied it. She heard the door creak open and shifted away, burying her face against her knees. Here he came again, and she knew the coming hours would be terrible.

"Mother," she added hoarsely, "help me bear it."

The door swung shut. She kept her face hidden, hoping that this time he would leave. The heavy folds of his garments rustled as he came towards her, his sandals almost soundless on the packed earth floor. The scent of precious sandalwood tickled her nose, and she tightened her hold on her knees. His hand on her hair, and her head was craned back. The weak light of the lantern illuminated her tormentor's eyes, no more. He studied her, and she cringed under the weight of his stare. Casually, he stuck a hand down the front of her torn linen tunic, finding her breast. He squeezed. She gasped.

"I am going to punish you," he said, "and we both know you deserve it, don't we?"

She wanted to shake her head. But she knew it was better to nod—for her and for him, the man whom she loved and who was presently hanging in chains somewhere in the nearby dungeons. She was forced down on her back. She begged him with her eyes, but he just smiled, his long oiled curls falling forward as he lowered himself on top of her. Dearest Mother, she thought, help me. But there was no divine intervention. There was only him and his black, black eyes.

Chapter 20

"You really should have a Brazilian," the girl presently waxing Helle's legs said.

"You kidding? This hurts enough as it is."

"You know what they say: no pain, no gain."

In which case Helle was more than happy to do without the gain.

She was exiting the salon when a large car with tinted windows pulled up beside her. One of those new BMW SUVs, she noted, thinking her father probably already had one to ensure pouty Janine and his sons were transported safely through their lives. That reminded her: Callum wanted an Arsenal shirt for Christmas and she'd promised Janine she'd fix it. And then she wasn't thinking all that much of Janine—in fact, her mind was wiped clean when someone grabbed hold of her and threw her into the back seat. The door slammed, the locks clicked.

"Hello, Helle." Woolf was sitting beside her. Helle's heart pounded, her nostrils widened, inhaling his distinctive scent. She made a mewling sound and pressed herself against the door. Woolf stretched, took hold of her seatbelt and fastened it. "Drive," he ordered before raising the partition. He smiled at Helle—an ice-cold stretching of lips that revealed his teeth. "Alone at last, hey?" He held her eyes, she tried to close them. His voice echoed in her head, there was an increasing thudding behind her ears, and her back broke out in a sweat. The car hit a bump, jolting them both. He cursed, she squished her eyes shut.

His fingers grazed her cheek. "Afraid of me?"

"Yes," she croaked, without opening her eyes.

He laughed. "Wise girl. But just so you know, so far I haven't even tried to frighten you." He moved closer. "Imagine just how terrified you will be when I do." His leg pressed against hers. "Open your eyes."

She refused.

"I said, open them." He gripped her leg, the pressure of his fingers making her suck in her breath. "Open them, Helle."

She obeyed. His face was far too close, his beautiful mouth curling in a satisfied smile. He ran a finger over her lower lip. "It doesn't have to be like this. I am protective of those who belong to me."

"I don't belong to anyone," Helle managed to say. "Let me out—now!"

"Now?" He leaned over her and swung the door open. She screamed and clung to her seatbelt. The car was speeding along. He barked out an order to the driver: the speed dropped sufficiently for him to pull the door closed.

"This is abduction," Helle said.

"Abduction?" Woolf raised his brows. "I'm not about to carry you off by force. This is just a little afternoon drive." He fingered her hair. Helle jerked her head away.

"How did you know where I was?"

He gave her an enigmatic smile, no more, a finger travelling down her neck.

"How?" she demanded, futilely trying to evade his gentle touch.

"Well aren't you the curious one." Woolf tapped her forehead. "I'm in here, Helle."

No. She shook her head firmly. She didn't want him there.

He chuckled. "There's little you can do to stop me." He moved even closer. "You hear me, don't you? My voice, it seeps through your brain, and you can't ignore it." His fingers gripped her chin, lifting her face so that their eyes met. "Like now," his voice boomed in her head. "I am inside you, speaking to you, and yet my lips aren't moving, are they?" He released her face and straightened up. "Best get used to hearing me there," he said with a smirk. "There's nothing you can do about it—well, as long as that accursed Wanderer is not around." Or if she was in pain—but she didn't tell him that, sinking her nails into her palm.

Woolf studied her in silence. "It's time you make your choice."

"Choice?" She tried to lean out of reach, but that just had him moving closer, his big body squashing her against the seat.

"Me or him, little Helle."

"That's a no-brainer," she replied. "I will never choose you over him."

"No? That would be very, very foolish."

"What can I say? I have a problem with overbearing assholes who try to intimidate me into obeying them."

He blinked. Then he began to laugh, sitting back sufficiently for Helle to be able to straighten up.

"A woman with spirit, hey?" he said once he'd calmed down. "That will make it all the more fun to tame you." He leaned closer, the ice in her voice giving her a major brain-freeze. "You have two options: either you come with me voluntarily or I'll carry you off anyway."

"So why don't you?" she demanded, hating it that her voice squeaked.

That lovely mouth curled into a smile. "Because it's much more fun this way. If you choose to come willingly I shall have the pleasure of watching the Wanderer have his heart crushed—by you. If you don't, I'll force you to watch as I crush it—literally." He held out his hand, and in his palm lay a beating heart. He grinned, closed his fingers round it and squeezed until blood seeped between his fingers.

"You're sick," she whispered, incapable of drawing her gaze away from his bloodied hand. He laughed, shook his hand a couple of times and gone was the blood, the massacred heart. A fucking trick. She fell back against the seat, trying to calm her racing pulse.

"You have no idea, little Helle," he said. "No idea at all. So, what will it be?"

"I will never come to you. Never. I would rather die first."

"Brave words, little Helle. But unless you do, your precious Wanderer will die a slow and painful death. I'll dismember him first and you will hear his every scream, hear him beg and plead for death before I finally..." He closed his fist again and squeezed. Once again, blood seeped through his fingers.

"Bastard!" She made as if to slap him. His hand shot out, closing round hers like a vice. The fragile bones in her wrist protested loudly. She gasped. He lifted her hand to his mouth and kissed each of her knuckles in turn.

"I can be tender too, you know."

Helle snatched her hand away. "Stop the car. Now." For an instant longer, his eyes burned into hers. Then he tapped at the partition, and the car slowed.

Woolf opened the door for her. "As of now, no more kid gloves, Helle. Your choice, of course. You've got twenty-four hours to make up your mind." The door slammed shut, the car took off, and Helle belatedly realised he'd left her several miles from home. To be precise, just behind London Zoo.

It was dark when she came home—it must have been quite the extended session at the beauty parlour, Jason thought with a smile, tasting his curry before replacing the lid and going to meet her. She was standing by the door, balancing on one leg while gingerly pulling off her high-heeled boot, dropping it to the floor to join its mate. She was dirty, she limped as she walked, and when Jason swept her into his arms, she winced, muttering she was stiff with cold.

"Where have you been?" He licked his thumb and rubbed at a smudge on her forehead. "And why haven't you returned my calls?"

In reply, she held up her dead phone. "I need a shower." She ducked under his arm.

"Helle." He stopped her. "What's the matter?"

"Woolf," she said, and a torrent of words spilled from her, an incoherent story that had Jason stiffening with fear—and anger. He'd snatched her! The bastard had snatched her, and what was to stop him from doing so again? He pressed her to his chest and she hugged him back, clinging to him. "He says he'll kill you." She looked up at him. "But he wouldn't, right?"

"He'll try." And Samion would ensure it was a slow death that made it difficult to progress onwards. Helle's throat worked, eyes wide with fear. "This time, things will be different," he added.

214

"This time?" It came out breathless, Helle's eyes never leaving his.

"He's threatened you with my safety before," was all he would say. She opened her mouth, but he placed a finger on her lips. "Not now. First, we get you warm and clean."

A hot shower and clean clothes had her regaining some of her buoyancy, and as she insisted she was starving, they ate first, sitting in a kitchen lit only by a sea of candles. She devoured the lamb curry, tearing chunks of naan bread to dip in the sauce.

"You did this?" she said, her mouth half-full.

"I always do my own cooking." He served her some more spinach, laughing at her face. "In my home, if you want dessert, you eat your vegetables first." She brightened at the word 'dessert', lighting up when he set down a panna cotta in front of her.

They'd not spoken a word about Woolf during the meal. Not until they were curled up in the sofa, watching the gas flames, did she raise the subject.

"Why all this hate?" Helle lifted her tea mug and regarded him over its rim.

"Why? Three thousand years of rivalry, I guess." He studied the fire, thinking that it was strange how much more comforting it was to sit before a real fire, hearing logs crackle with heat

"Something started it. What?"

Jason dropped his eyes to his hand, presently running up and down her arm. "You," he muttered. "It all started because of you."

"Me?" Helle sounded amused.

"Two possessive men, one desirable woman. Happens all the time."

"Desirable?"

"Oh yes." In his mind, he saw her as she'd been then. Graceful and curvy, the folds of her garments clinging to her hips. "And you chose me."

"But that in itself doesn't explain things. So what happened? Okay, so I chose you over him, but why this anger? He's had eons of time to get over it"

"He can't."

"But why?" she insisted.

He pursed his lips, considering what—and how much—to tell her. "He wants revenge."

"For what?" She tried to sound relaxed, but her hands were tight around her mug.

"I'd best start at the beginning."

"An innovative approach," she teased.

He tweaked her hair. "Want me to tell you?" She promised to be silent.

"His father was the king of the former kingdom of Kolchis, surrounding your father's little land, and it was a permanent thorn in Samion's and his father's sides to have this breakaway country controlling the best port in the area. Your father grew rich on trade, while they sat by and fumed. It had been that way for centuries, and your father lived in a very uneasy peace with his much larger neighbour."

"Kantor," she said. "My father's name was Kantor."

"Yes." He smiled, recalling that huge bear of a man. King of a kingdom so small he could ride from one end to the other in half a day.

"I remember," Helle said hesitantly. "A huddle of whitewashed houses, and in the summer we would sleep on the roofs, the stars close enough to reach up and grab them." She smiled. "And there were poplars lining the wheat fields, but just by my house was a cluster of pine trees."

Jason nodded, taking her hand.

"And the sea," Helle said dreamily. "So blue it shifted into the deepest of purples and black in the distance." She looked at him. "You were always fishing!"

"Not always. My mother wouldn't have allowed it."

"I wouldn't know." She sounded sad. "But I do remember the courtyard, the bench with the huge rosebush beside it." She frowned. "I get the feeling I spent a lot of time on that bench—unhappy hours."

Jason didn't reply, haunted by the sudden image of Helle sitting in the shade of the rose, her feet bandaged, the hollows of her eyes bruised after nights without sleep. And when she saw him, she lit up, as if an inner sun rose behind her face. She extended her hand, mouthing his name, and he…Jason choked. God help him, he'd ignored her, walking past her without as much as a look. But out of the corner of his eye, he'd seen her slump, arms coming up to cradle herself, and he'd been glad that she was hurting.

"It was a beautiful little place, wasn't it?" Helle said. "And mostly, I think I was happy there."

Mostly. Except for the last months of her life. Jason cleared his throat and went on with his story.

"It wasn't only beautiful. Kantor's kingdom was strategically placed. Its excellent defensive position allowed him full control over trade in the eastern part of the Black Sea. Your father had no son, and Samion, encouraged by his father, came up with a brilliant plan. He'd marry you, and any issue would be rightful heir to both countries. Kantor was, to be fair, not happy about it, but such a marriage would buy his people peace. You were a royal princess and your usefulness was precisely that: as a pawn in a dynastic marriage."

"Didn't he want me to be happy?"

"Happiness didn't come into it. You were an asset to be used in negotiations. Arranged marriages have been the norm in all ruling families, duty taking precedence over personal likes or dislikes. For both sons and daughters, I might add.

"During the negotiations Samion never thought about you as a person. You were a name to him, heiress to an illustrious house, a woman to bed and breed from. So he was totally unprepared when he saw you the first time. I was there." He couldn't stop himself from smiling at the recollection. "You were twelve, and your long hair hung unbound to your waist. Your grandmother had washed it in chamomile water to bring out the gold in it, and you were so beautiful.

"It was the day I finally understood that the heart I'd given you four years before was indeed forever yours," he added, squeezing her hand. "Anyway, Samion saw you and he was smitten. His eyes smouldered as he watched you move, and whenever you passed by him his hands twitched, as if he wanted to reach out and grab you, there and then.

"I hated him," he hissed, "and luckily for me, so did you. Well, perhaps hate is too strong. You were polite to the extent it was necessary, but otherwise you just ignored him, your eyes darting to me as often as possible. Every time you looked at me, every time you smiled at me, I felt like crowing, my heart ready to burst. And Samion noticed."

Oh yes, he had most certainly noticed, dark eyes flitting from Helle to Jason. Even now, so many years later, Jason couldn't quite suppress the tremor that rushed through him, remembering eyes black with hatred and disdain. Where Jason had still been a boy, Samion was already a man—an impressive man, muscled arms banded with gold rings, oiled hair hanging in black curls well down his back.

"That first time, you laughed when he said you were destined to be his, and if anything, that made him even more determined to have you. Your father warded off Samion's suit for some years, referring to your youth. Not really a valid excuse in an age when girls as young as eleven were wedded and sent off to fulfil their marital duties. Samion took it well, to begin with, but in your fifteenth year he returned in full regalia. This time he came to request your hand in earnest." He picked up Helle's hand, caressing the finger that he hoped would one day be adorned by his ring.

"I could see no way out. Everyone knew he was coming to make you his wife, and you begged me to run away with you before it was too late. I couldn't. My hands were tied, out of convention and also because of class. I was a Wanderer and my kind didn't marry royalty. In retrospect, I should've done as you said, stealing away under the cover of the night.

"The day he was supposed to come, you came to me in the morning and begged me to love you. I couldn't even do that. I just…I held you as you wept."

It was among the hardest things he'd ever had to do, to witness Helle's departure. The donkey she was to ride was decorated with flowers, and as for Helle herself, she was a graceful figure swathed in layers of linen and silk. Already veiled, the only thing he could see were her eyes—as blue as the sea, they locked with his, a wordless farewell that tore the heart out of his body. When she was lifted up onto the donkey, the veil parted and her braid became visible, threaded with the blue ribbon. His blue ribbon.

"I had never before seen you so silent. Even your father was affected, even more so when you refused to bid him farewell, your hands curled into fists so tight your knuckles were white. Elessa, your grandmother, refused to speak to Kantor, standing beside me instead. She held my hand." He rubbed at his fingers.

"Already then, Samion was perfidious. Your father gave you to him as a wife, but that same night, he tried to take you by force, humiliate you before you were formally wed. You fled." He shifted on his rump. "You never told me if he…well, if he…"

"Raped me," Helle said baldly. She looked away. "I remember it hurt, that's all. And I remember running for my life." She had paled, enough that the freckles he rarely noticed on the bridge of her nose were visible.

"I heard you screaming my name." He studied her. Had she just said he'd raped her? As he recalled, Helle had been covered with bruises and welts. "I came." He gave her a fleeting smile. "I ran towards the sound of your voice, and your lions came too." Jason laughed hoarsely. "Samion ended up marked for life and when he reappeared at Kantor's gate the next day, demanding admission, Kantor turned him away, saying he'd given him his daughter as a wife, not as a concubine. When Samion called your name, you climbed up the ladder to stand beside your father, chin raised, back stiff. He commanded you to come out. You told him—"

"…that I had promised myself to someone else." Helle smiled.

"Yes." He smiled back. "I realised when I was helping you climb the wall around your father's enclosure that I couldn't let him take you again. So I slashed my thumb and yours, and we made a blood vow."

"How infantile," she laughed. "And then what?"

"Samion was livid, even more so when you leaned over and told him that you'd rather mate with a donkey than have him anywhere close to your bed again." Jason tweaked a strand of her hair. "Too outspoken, you were, and Kantor tried to smooth things over, but you were having none of it, adding that as far as you were concerned, Samion of Kolchis was no man, he was a vile beast, a drooling animal."

She'd been frightened out of her wits by what had happened the previous night, but too stubborn and proud to show as much as a glimmer of weakness. An adolescent girl, challenging a full-grown man, humiliating him before his men with her taunts—until Kantor ordered Jason to drag her out of sight. But not before she'd upended the bucket of bodily waste on the oiled head of Samion, covering him in urine and faeces.

"And Samion?"

Jason shrugged. "You paid the price for your defiance in the end. A very heavy price." He was relieved when she didn't ask.

"Because I chose you?"

Jason twisted his lips into a crooked smile. Yes, she had chosen him—and he had betrayed her, crushed her like a worm underfoot.

"Partly. You humiliated him, and he never forgave you for the scars your lion left behind."

"And is that why he's looking for revenge?"

"Not only that." He drew in a deep breath. "I killed him."

"What?" Helle sat up straight, tea sloshing down her front.

"For you. I killed him for you." And for himself. For months of torture and whispered evil, for extinguishing his hope, for filling him with corroding bitterness.

"What did he do to me?" Helle asked.

What hadn't Samion done to her? He decided to go with the abbreviated version. "He stabbed you to death. So in revenge, I took his life." A euphemism. He'd done more than that. He'd destroyed Samion's bloodline, he'd sent every affliction known to man to ravage his house. Jason wiped his hands. He'd done wrong—a Wanderer turning his healing skills into a weapon of vengeance.

Jason cleared his throat. "And you stepped all over his pride. With every life he's lived, he's had an even greater hunger to avenge himself. He can no more stop himself coming after us than I can stop myself from looking for you."

"Great," she said. "Our own personal Nemesis."

He took a breath. He had to do this. "Do you want me to tell you the whole story?" He didn't want to tell her—ever. So when she shook her head, he relaxed, falling back against the cushions.

"I don't think I want to know too much about our first life," she said. "I have problems enough coping with one life. I guess I'm worried that once I start peeking into those hidden corners of my mind, I might find myself having to handle more memories than I want."

"Tell me about it," he muttered darkly.

"It must be pretty terrible at times, mustn't it? All those memories crowding your poor head."

"Yes, sometimes it gets too much. Thank heavens I don't remember everything."

Helle set the mug down. "And I don't remember more than fragments." She settled herself beside him, her head on his shoulder.

"No, it seems you don't—yet." He stroked her face. "Whether you like it or not, many of the memories from your first life will come back. I'm afraid that's because of me. I've breached a door that you've kept very firmly closed. I'm so sorry for that, lioness." But dear Lord, don't let her remember it all, he prayed silently, for her sake, but also for his.

"Let them come when they do. I'm not really in a hurry to know how it all ended back then, because obviously something went very wrong. So tell me about the good bits when you feel like it, but leave out the bad bits, okay?"

"All right," he promised, yet again inundated with relief.

"Do you think all people are travelling souls?" she asked later, rousing him from his doze. She'd been quiet for so long, he'd assumed she'd fallen asleep, a welcome and comforting weight on his chest.

"No. Most people living today are first timers, and I think in general you only get that one chance at getting it right. To push your soul onwards requires determination, or desperation." Tons of both, actually.

"So why you and me?" She yawned, snuggling closer. Jason toyed with her hair, thinking.

"You out of desperation, me out of determination," he finally said. "I had to make it up to you. I had to keep you safe from Samion, may he be cursed." He spat out the name in disgust.

"Well, you've already saved me from him this time round."

He decided not to tell her that so far, Samion hadn't even started trying.

He sat in his hole and raged, wrenching futilely against his chains when he heard her voice echo faintly across the courtyard. He ached at the wobble of panic in her voice. It was all his fault. If only he had not insisted that they go alone, if only he had been more on his guard. He threw himself forward, his fists clenching as he tried to break loose.

He lost track of time, he hung suspended in the dark, dank hole. Her voice was gone. He no longer heard her, and he feared she was dead. He roared her name until he was hoarse, whispered her name until he fell asleep.

Jason hung in permanent darkness, never properly awake, never properly asleep. Sometimes he was whipped, and the manacles chafed and burnt, a constant source of pain. He chanted her name to himself, he murmured it over and over again. Sometimes he hoped she was alive. Often he wished she had died and escaped her cage.

And then the visits began. Every night, the heavy door opened, and Jason blinked in the torchlight, his hands clenching uselessly in their fetters. He didn't want to hear. He didn't want that soft voice whispering in his ear, conjuring up visions he didn't want to see. He wanted to die, be whipped to shreds, rather than hear the velvet voice he couldn't close out telling him things that drove nails into his heart.

Still, every evening Samion came. Every evening he sat by Jason's side and his dark voice told him in detail about how he spent his nights. With her. A snap of his fingers, and no matter that Jason squeezed his eyes shut, he still saw her—his Helle, writhing with passion in Samion's arms. Every evening as Samion left, he would smile at the heartbroken Jason and bid him a good night.

Sometimes, she came to him in his dreams and he was so glad when she told him how much she loved him. He would wake to darkness and to the knowledge that she shared another's bed. It drove him insane. He no longer wanted to live, his heart a beating wound inside his chest.

Once during all those months he saw her sitting in the courtyard, her face raised to the sun. For a moment he felt the pull of her. If only she would open her eyes and meet his. Then he saw. The swollen belly and the heavy breasts, her hand caressing the bulge with a soft smile fluttering at the corners of her mouth. He had never felt so alone in his whole life.

Chapter 21

Next morning, there was a message on Helle's phone. *Time is ticking. Tick tock.* It made Helle's stomach shrink, to the point that she couldn't eat, no matter how good Jason's Sunday frittata smelled.

"What's the matter?" Jason's hair was still damp from his recent shower, all of him glowing after their morning workout. Mr Morris took his body seriously, and had a state of the art gym installed just off the utility room in the basement.

In reply, Helle held out her phone.

"Shit." Jason threw down his fork. "So now it starts."

Starts? Helle's stomach shrank even further. To her, it seemed plenty had happened already.

"Could we call the police?" she asked.

"And tell them what, precisely?"

"He threatened me! He forced me into his damn car yesterday."

"And when the police appear at his door, you can bet on Sam Woolf having an unbreakable alibi." He sighed. "Trust me, he doesn't play fair."

"So then what?"

In reply, Jason flexed his hands, studying each individual finger in turn. "I'll think of something." His dark voice sounded determined—and calm.

One text per hour followed. *Nineteen. Twenty. Twenty-one. Twenty-two. Twenty-three.* And then the last one: *Twenty-four. Bang, bang he's dead.*

"Right," Jason said, looking at the last text. "We're getting you a new phone." He shrugged on a worn leather jacket, making him look a poster boy for bad and beautiful, and taking her by the hand, led them outside. Helle scanned the street, the cars, the windows of the neighbouring houses. "He's subtler than that," Jason said drily. "Our Sam prefers the dark."

They walked along the street, hand in hand, in the general direction of Sloane Square. The sunny December day had brought out a lot of people, the pavement crammed with strollers—Jason called them pushchairs—and with mothers dragging toddlers along. Despite Jason's comforting grip, Helle couldn't relax, head swivelling this way and that as she attempted to catalogue potential dangers. Futile, she realised, but she couldn't stop herself, all of her tensing whenever she saw a man looking in their direction.

An hour or so later, she had a new phone, programmed with the contacts she needed. She sent off a text to her parents advising them of their new number, wrote one to Alison, but hesitated just as she was about to send it.

"No." Jason's hand closed over her own. "If Alison knows, it is only a matter of time before Samion does."

"She wouldn't tell him—not now." But even as she said it, Helle realised she didn't quite believe it. There had been a couple of instances the last week when Alison had been on the phone, only to immediately cut off her conversation when Helle came through the door.

"Maybe not voluntarily." He draped an arm round her shoulders. "And no, he wouldn't resort to force. He'd just hypnotise her." Well, that was a relief, Helle supposed, deleting the drafted text. She pocketed her new phone and pulled out the old one. A new text. Jason took it from her. "I'll hang onto this in case someone else tries to contact you."

"Yeah, like the job agency."

Jason snorted. "You're not working anywhere else, Helle. I need you close—and I need your brains and business sense."

"That last part saved you from coming across as totally Neanderthal."

"Well, I'm not that old." He tightened his hold on her. "But if you want, I can grab you by the hair, drag you back to my cave, and have my wicked way with you."

"Yes, please."

Monday in the office started with a flurry of work. Steve Darrow phoned to say he'd be back in a week, making Angela break out into the biggest smile Helle had seen since she first met her.

"She's sweet on him," Will confided. "Well, she was, with him all floppy hair and bespoke suits. Not so sure how he'll live up to the image of the anaemic upper class type when he's in a cast from hip to ankle."

"Upper class?"

"Old money." Will tapped his nose. "As I hear it, not so much old money, which is why Steve has been forced to become a wage slave."

Helle laughed out loud. "Wage slave?" She gestured at their surroundings. Modern and contemporary, Jason's premises bathed in light, its dark hardwood floors decorated with an array of beautiful Kelim carpets.

"It's relative," Will said. "If you're used to swanning about with a butler at your heels…" He winked and slouched off, still in those low-hung jeans, but thankfully today he was wearing underwear.

There was a pretty tense moment just before noon when Juliet showed up.

"Jason," she cooed, entering his office without as much as a knock on the door. She came to an abrupt halt at the sight of Helle, sitting side by side with Jason with multiple spreadsheets open on their screens.

"Hi," Jason said, standing up to greet her. Much too affectionately in Helle's opinion, noting just how slowly Juliet's hand slid down Jason's back as he stepped out of Juliet's embrace. In something short and clingy, dark stockings and Louboutins— of course Louboutins—she looked intimidatingly beautiful, all of her oozing wealth, from her discreet diamond earrings to the antique sapphire ring on her finger.

"I hope you haven't forgotten we're doing lunch today," Juliet said with a purr, fingers moving up and down Jason's forearm. Damn that woman, could she stop touching him all the time? Fortunately for Jason, he frowned and leaned out of reach when Juliet made as if to brush his hair out of his face.

"Sounds like fun," Helle said. "Where are we going?"

Juliet gave her the Death Star look. "It is our little tradition," she explained, "just Jason and me."

"Really?" Helle slipped her arm in under Jason's. He bit his lip, his eyes sparkling. He found this amusing, did he? Stung, she released his arm. "Be my guest."

Juliet smiled triumphantly and did her catwalk thing, waiting for him at the door. Jason hesitated.

"What do you want to eat, Helle?" he asked, holding out his hand to her. Ha! Helle swayed her hips as she moved towards him. Juliet looked as if she'd bitten into a giant lemon.

"Italian would be nice," Helle said. "But you go ahead, I have work to do." She stood on her toes and kissed Jason—a full tongue-and-everything kiss—before returning to the desk. One-nil to Helle Madsen, she crowed silently.

It was a short lunch, Helle noted an hour or so later.

"Did you have fun?" she asked when Jason stopped by her desk to give her a kiss.

"Not really. I missed you."

Smart man.

"I brought you dessert," he said, setting down a little paper bag on her desk. "Something very sweet and chocolaty." He kissed her again before disappearing into his office.

Nigel came by halfway through the afternoon, an apparition in black and purple with so many necklaces of varying lengths around his neck it was a miracle he could move under the weight of all that metal. Worn cowboy boots matched the leather vest he was wearing over his Desigual t-shirt, a silver ring adorned each finger—and thumbs—and he was chewing on an unlit cigarette.

"You smoke?" Helle asked, sniffing discreetly. He didn't smell like a smoker.

"Do I look like an idiot?" he replied. Helle tilted her head to the side and considered him. Intelligent dark eyes looked right back at her, his narrow face struggling to contain the smile that was lifting the corners of his surprisingly plump mouth.

"So why the cig?"

"Makes me look like James Dean."

"He's dead."

"As I said, it makes me look like him—not be him." Nigel gave her a little wave and made for Jason's office, dangling his worn backpack by the handle.

When Jason asked her to join them, he was looking grim. Without a word, he sat her down and gestured for Nigel to speak.

"This is a security feed from Saturday noon—in Frankfurt airport." Nigel pressed the 'play' icon. Blurry people rushed back and forth, most of them a collection of dark clothes and dark bags. Now and then, someone would look straight at the hidden camera, but mostly it showed a sequence of shapes rather than features. Until Woolf came strolling down the passage, head held high, in full view.

"That's…Impossible. He was here!"

"So you say," Nigel said.

"He was!" Helle glared at him. "I tell you, he was here, in London."

"Helle," Jason cut her off. "We believe you—well, I do at least," he qualified. "But this just shows how skilful he is."

"Yup." Nigel's fingers flew over the keyboard. "If one didn't know exactly where to look, it would be difficult to spot this has been doctored."

"So how can you prove it?"

"I didn't say I could prove it. I said I could spot it—but it's flimsy at best." Nigel shot her a look. "And for the record, I believe you too." He frowned at Jason. "It would really help to know why Woolf is coming after you."

"I already told you: business rivalry." Jason spun his chair and stared at the window.

"So why threaten Helle?" Nigel asked. "That sounds personal to me."

"I used to work for him," Helle pointed out.

"Ah. An industrial spy."

Helle bristled. "I was nothing of the sort! I'd never—"

Nigel grinned. "God, you're touchy, aren't you?" He

closed his laptop. "Jason is my best friend. If he says you're good, as far as I'm concerned, you are. But should you screw him over, I'll come find you, Helle Madsen."

"Oooo, look, I'm shivering in my shoes."

"You should." Nigel stood up. "I may not look much, but I can assure you I can be quite the avenging angel when I have to be." Somehow, Helle believed him. Those long, spindly fingers were probably capable of handling a number of things, including a gun.

"Nigel," Jason groaned, "give it a rest."

"Hey," Helle said, "I can say the same. You hurt my Jason and I'll whip your ass."

"Jesus," Jason muttered, "my own little Ninja team." But his mouth twitched, eyes softening as he looked from Nigel to Helle.

Jason had planned on leaving earlier, but an unannounced visit from that damned Smith had him detained until well after seven o'clock. Helle was still working at her desk, a pool of light in the otherwise dark office, and when he'd showed Smith out, he came over to sit on her desk.

"What did he want this time?"

"Same, same. He presented me with a long list of transactions he wanted explained, and then he dug into a lot of questions about Woolf & Partners. He seems to think we're in cahoots, somehow." He scrubbed at his face. He needed a shave, a hot shower and some wild sex—not necessarily in that order.

"So what did you tell him?"

"To go and fuck himself." Jason rolled his shoulders. It had been an unpleasant meeting, even more so when Smith had alluded to the possibility of reopening the investigation into money-laundering. Not that Jason had anything to worry about in that respect, but a tenacious financial investigator could turn up his real stashes, no matter how carefully he'd covered his tracks.

"Very proactive." Helle closed down her laptop.

"Well, I didn't phrase it quite like that." He fiddled with

his ear-stud. "But I did suggest he spend some time researching just how Woolf made his money, and what he might have tucked away in Jersey." He leaned over the desk to turn off her lamp. "Coming? I'm starving."

"He doesn't like me, does he?" Helle said as they made their way down the stairs to the garage.

"Who?"

"Nigel."

Jason shrugged. "Why wouldn't he?"

"Oh, I don't know. It may be the way he threatened me today."

Jason turned, causing her to bump into him. "He's a tad protective. We've been friends for a long time, and other than my mother, he's the only one who's seen me in the grip of my nightmares."

"Nightmares?"

"When my memories came back." He didn't want to talk about this. Fortunately, any further conversation was interrupted by Helle's phone.

"Mum?" she said. "Hello, Mum?" She came to a halt, while Jason continued his descent.

Just by the door, he checked the little screen mounted beside it. Since Samion's threats, Jason had increased security, with webcams installed not only in the office but also here, in the garage. He peered at the screen. Other than his Aston Martin, the garage was empty. He shoved the door open and flicked the light switch. Wide pillars marched down the centre of the underground space, lit by flickering light fixtures that reluctantly came alive. He frowned. What use were webcams if the lighting was this deficient? He made a note to speak to Will about it when out of the corner of his eye he saw something move. He set down his briefcase and tensed. Nothing. He almost laughed at himself: spooked by shadows, no less.

Jason relaxed. From behind, came the sound of Helle's voice, still on the phone with her mother. Jason smiled when Helle groaned out a loud 'Mum!' This was followed by a laugh and a much softer 'Yeah, he's great," that made his smile wider. It didn't take a genius to work out who she was talking about.

He was halfway to the car when glass crunched underfoot. Instinctively, he halted, dropping into a crouch. There were shadows behind his car, a madly flickering fixture above it giving little useful light. Jason licked his lips, his hands pulsing with heat. He rose and took a step forward just as two men dropped down from the ceiling. In black leather, with ski-masks and gloves, they looked like Special Ops. One of them kicked at his head, a glancing blow that had Jason reeling back, thereby avoiding the other man's swipe. A blade grazed his forearm. Jason ducked, got a good grip on the closest assailant and increased the heat in his hands. A muffled yell, and the other man kicked out, Jason's entire body exploding with pain when a heavy boot connected with his ribs. His hold slipped, and a series of kicks drove him backwards, away from the man who was rolling on the floor, clutching at his burning arm.

He had one of the pillars at his back, and when the man kicked again, Jason threw himself to the side, ignoring the protesting twinge up his side. The foot slammed into the concrete, enough to throw his attacker off balance. Jason leapt forward, hands ablaze.

The man retreated. Jason was breathing hard, blood trickling from a split eyebrow and from his arm. The man on the floor had pulled a gun, and it struck Jason that Woolf had no need to kill him himself—he could have others do it for him, thereby avoiding the curse that came with the spilling of Wanderer's blood. He threw himself to the floor. The bullet whined through the air, burying itself in the pillar.

"Jason?" Helle stood outlined in the light of the stairwell behind.

"Get down!" he yelled, and she threw herself flat. Jason was back on his feet. Fire dripped from his hands, and with a low growl he attacked the man still standing. The resulting scream echoed through the empty space. Leather hissed and spat, the man sank to his knees, still screaming. His arms, his legs were on fire, and the man's companion uttered a whimper, eyes flickering from Jason's hands to the bloody, blistered mess that was the other man.

"How…" He didn't get to say more. Jason was on him, burning hands wresting the gun from him. From somewhere to his right, he heard the sound of a shotgun being cocked. Woolf appeared from behind the car.

"Back off, Wanderer," he said.

"You!" Jason raised the gun.

"Yes, me." Woolf chuckled. "I told her, didn't I? Either she comes back to me, or you're dead meat."

"Not about to happen."

"Oh, it will, Wanderer, unless she returns to me."

Jason wasn't aware of having pulled the trigger, not until Woolf staggered back. The shotgun hung awry, Woolf's right arm disabled.

"Helle, call the police!" Jason called, ignoring the way his fingers dripped fire on the man at his feet. He lifted his hand, fingers curling round a globe of spitting flames. He sent it flying, an arc of sparks that had Woolf stumbling backwards. Another, and a slick of oil on the floor caught fire, causing Woolf to retreat further. "Got you," Jason sneered, advancing with his hands held high.

"I don't think so." Woolf brushed a hand over his wounded arm and raised the shotgun. Jason flung out his arms, sending a wave of heat his way. The shotgun whitened with heat and with a curse, Woolf dropped it. Jason snarled and took a step towards him. *End it!* his brain hollered. *End it now!* Jason raised the gun. Woolf twirled on his toes and a thick fog enveloped him. Not fog, some sort of gas. Jason fell to his knees, coughing. He had to get away, before he lost consciousness. The car. He dragged himself toward it, holding his breath. He had to hide. He had to….

Helle's eyes were the first thing he saw when he came to. She was kneeling beside him, pressing a tissue to his eyebrow. Jason attempted to sit up, groaned at the pain in his side, and lay back down.

"Woolf?" he managed to say.

232

"Gone. Once the smoke cleared, they were all gone." Her hands were shaking so hard she couldn't get a new tissue out of the little pack. "They almost killed you." She gave him an anguished look. "I couldn't live with myself if he did."

"And I couldn't live with myself if you went back to him because of me." This time he succeeded in sitting up, ignoring his protesting ribs as he pulled her close. "Promise me you won't. Whatever happens, promise me you'll never return to him."

"How can I promise that?" Her voice was uncharacteristically high. "Do you expect me just to watch as he tears you apart?"

"No." He cradled her face. "I expect you to help me destroy him."

She just looked at him. And then she began to laugh, a high-pitched sound that sounded more like wailing at a wake than laughter. "I—" She wiped at her eyes. "I don't know how to do this."

"Me neither." He handed her one of the tissues. "But as long as we're together, we'll work it out."

They sat at the kitchen table for hours, silently sipping tea, both of them lost in their own thoughts.

"Let's go to bed," Jason finally said in a tired voice "it's almost one in the morning." He looked awful, his face a collection of bruises and cuts, his torso taped by the nurse in the emergency room. Bed sounded like a good idea. Helle swayed to her feet, took his hand, and followed him up the stairs, one tread at the time.

Jason fell asleep the instant his head touched the pillow. But Helle didn't dare to sleep. She was afraid of closing her eyes and waking up to a world where someone she loved had died, her mouth wobbling at the thought of a life without Mum, or Dad or even worse, Jason. She shifted restlessly and turned to find Jason looking at her, his eyes mere glimmers in the weak light.

"I can't sleep," she admitted, raising a hand to his face. "I think I need you to hold me."

"That makes two of us." He shifted so close she could feel

the length of him from knee to chest. They lay like that, nose to nose, for some time.

"If you only knew how often I wake up wanting you," he whispered to her.

"Me too," she replied just as inaudibly. "There are nights when all I want to do is wake you up and make love to you again and again and again."

"Why don't you?" he smiled, kissing her softly. Helle shrugged and tried to look away.

"It's just that I'm not sure if it's supposed to be like that, you know? That I want you so very, very much."

"Supposed to be?" he echoed, easing her onto her back. "You think there's a norm?"

She opened her legs to him, a sigh escaping her when he entered her. "I don't know. But should I want you this much? Always? Do you want me as much?" She felt exposed asking this and turned her face away. One large hand cupped her cheek and forced her to meet his eyes.

"Always, my lioness. I want you and need you all the time." They didn't say much more, making love slowly and steadily until they fell asleep, safe in each other's arms.

Helle woke up well before him, and eased up to sit and watch him sleep, her heart swelling with emotions. She ran her fingers through his hair, and his mouth twitched into the slightest of smiles. She curled up as close as she could without touching him, inhaling his scent, that familiar mixture of warm man, of sundried brine and brisk winds. He was sleeping on his back, sheet and duvet tangled round his middle, and she just had to pull the bedding off, see him naked and alive. She traced the shape of him with a hovering finger, not wanting to wake him with her touch, and her eyes filled with tears.

"What is it?" he asked, making her drop the sheet. He sat up and put his arms around her. "Helle? Why are you crying?"

"It's just that…" Helle broke off and hid her face against him, rubbing her cheek against his warm, live skin.

"What?" Jason insisted.

"I'm scared," she admitted in a whisper, "scared that I'll wake up and find that these last weeks have just been one long dream."

"I'm very real," he assured her softly, tugging his hands through the tangles of her curly hair. "And you're definitely not asleep." He put his hand on her bare skin, chuckling when she muttered an 'Ow' under the heat of his fingers. "See? I'm real, and you're awake." He lowered his head, brushing his lips over hers. "And this time, my lioness, I aim to spend an entire lifetime with you. And I am thinking at least six children."

"What?" She sat up straight, and he smiled, clearly pleased with how effective his distracting manoeuvre had been. "Six? You're nuts." He pulled her down to lie beside him.

"And if I want six?"

She rolled her eyes.

"Hmm?" He nuzzled her neck. "If I insist on six?" Helle shivered under his touch, his mouth. She licked her lips.

"Well then, six it is," she replied, ignoring the way her rational brain was howling with laughter at this very submissive statement.

"Good." He kissed her again. "Your pleasure, your children—for me to give you, only me." And for some odd reason, that turned her on.

Samion threw himself down on the one chair and regarded her speculatively. Her feet were wrapped in rags, the recent whipping reducing her to shuffling. She looked unkempt, her hair wild around her face. She had a rip down her linen tunic and the undergarment was turning to a dirty grey after too long use. He wrinkled his nose at the musky smell emanating from her corner—she needed a thorough scrubbing. He poured himself a goblet of wine, turning the earthenware vessel round in his hands. He glanced at his forearms, the gashes from her nails still stinging. She wasn't giving up without a fight, he thought, with reluctant admiration.

"It doesn't need to be this way." He could entrance her into submission if he wanted to, but for some reason that was not enough.

She spat in his direction, pressing herself against the wall. He sighed, the slight flicker of compassion hardening into determination. He stood up and stretched, downing the last of the wine.

"I won't kill him," he informed her conversationally as he unbelted his tunic, "but there's nothing to stop me from maiming him."

Helle covered her ears with her hands. He looked at her contemptuously. She was so weak when it came to the Wanderer, handing him the sword with which to destroy them both.

"What will you do, I wonder," he said, lying back on the bed, "to keep him safe and whole?"

He flashed a cruel smile at her. She forced herself up onto her damaged feet.

"Anything," she whispered, bowing to the inevitable.

He was obsessed with her. Sometimes he tried to be gentle, using soft hands and soft words. He made her forget at times. Some nights she burned inside his arms, her mouth urgent on his—a spark of passion that died as quickly as it came, the blank look returning to her eyes.

He hated it when she escaped from him to run with her memory man, her mouth softening into the slightest of smiles. She should smile that way at him, not at the fading recollection of the red haired, golden-eyed bastard presently languishing in the dark.

One night she moaned his name.

"Jason," she said, and the love in her voice cut him to the quick. He slapped her hard, feeling a vague satisfaction at her cringing fear.

"Never utter his name in my bed," he hissed, and she promised, shying away from his raised hand. "Whore," Samion went on, suddenly so much angrier than ever before, "you lie in my bed and open your legs to keep him safe. Do you think he will ever want you back?" He laughed at her expression, knotting his fingers in her hair. "Whore," he repeated. "My whore."

When he left her that night, she was covered in bruises and welts, her thighs and buttocks sticky with his seed. Tamed, he reflected, when she scrambled to her knees at his barked command. A sliver of bright blue showed under her swollen lids. Not tamed enough, he concluded, and something black and hot stirred at the thought of making her submit completely. If it took him weeks or months, he would succeed, wiping that last glimmer of defiance from her face.

Everyone breaks eventually. Over the coming weeks he reduced her to *his plaything, and the fire in her eyes was quenched, replaced by the wary look of a cornered doe. Samion liked it when he saw the flicker of dread in her eyes, heard the slight choking sound when she understood what he was going to do to her. It whetted his physical appetite to hurt her, to know she would docilely accept whatever he did to her.*

She gasped in pain, her eyes filling with tears, and he smiled, releasing his hold.

"Did it hurt?"

No, she shook her head, giving him a wobbly, insincere smile, no it hadn't hurt. He did it again, seeing her grit her teeth not to whimper, not to cry out. Inevitably, sooner or later she did, and he had the added pleasure of punishing her for that. And yet, at times he watched her sleep, his hand brushing gently over her cheek.

He was elated when he understood she was with child—his child, not the Wanderer's. Once the child was born he'd release the red-haired bastard from his hole. He smiled in expectation. He would show him the child and laugh at the Wanderer's naked pain.

He watched her belly swell. His hooded eyes studied her as she moved, saw the smile playing on her lips when she placed a hand on her womb.

"You love the child," he stated. Helle nodded and ran her hands over her bare distended skin. Samion put his hand over hers. "Then you must love me a little too."

She nodded, averting her eyes. But he saw the flash of unveiled dislike and was torn between wanting her and hating her.

Chapter 22

It was a good thing, in Helle's opinion, that they were going to Istanbul. The further from Sam Woolf, the better.

"Mmm," Jason said when she shared this with him, a preoccupied wrinkle on his brow. He was revising the last draft of the share purchase agreement, pen in hand, and he looked very much the business tycoon in his black suit, his blue shirt open at the neck.

"I have to pack." Helle grabbed her laptop and shoved it into her backpack. All day, she'd been making an effort to forget the events of the previous evening, but now, with dusk quickly turning into winter night, she wanted to leave the office while there were still people around.

It hadn't been a surprise to discover the security cameras had been wiped. Poor Will had been subjected to such a bollocking by Jason, Helle had seen no option but to intercede, which only earned her scowls from both men. Now, apparently, the cameras in the garage were impossible to hack, the overhead lighting had been upgraded, and the ancient ventilation drum through which the men had entered had been sealed—a bit like locking the stable door after the horse had bolted in Helle's opinion, but as Jason got some satisfaction out of doing all this, she hadn't said as much.

"You coming?" she asked.

"Can't. Not yet. Take Tim with you."

Tim Burns was the latest addition to Helle's life, a man with cauliflower ears and the grace of a panther—albeit a rather overweight panther.

"And you?"

"Pick me up when you're done." He gave her a distracted wave before punching a sequence of numbers on his phone. "Arthur? Hi, it's me. Look, about the earn-out, I was thinking…"

Helle left him to it.

The apartment was dark, and Helle breathed a sigh of relief. She didn't really want to talk to Alison, still uncertain as to how much to share with her. And she couldn't quite quash the suspicion that anything she told Alison would one way or another end up with Woolf.

For all her worldliness, for all her kick-ass attitude, Alison was as defenceless as a newborn fawn when faced with Woolf, even if lately she'd been making noises along the line that she'd really told him off for the 'Jason thing' as she called Samion's attempt to run Jason down. Huh. From the way Alison avoided meeting Helle's eyes while saying all this, Helle had concluded she was lying, big time. Just as she'd lied the other day when she'd said she was having no further contact with Woolf, at least to judge from her vivid blush—and all those hastily interrupted phone calls.

Helle had just finished folding the last of her clothes when Alison stormed into the apartment, coming to an abrupt stop at the sight of Tim, standing with his arms crossed in the living rom.

"Who are you?" she asked.

"He's with me," Helle answered, hurrying over to the bathroom.

"Hi, 'He's with me'," Alison said, following Helle. "Where are you going?"

"I'll be out of town for a few days," Helle replied, rushing back to her bedroom, still with Alison at her back.

"Out of town? Like where?" Alison studied the sunglasses perched on top of Helle's bag.

"Surprise." Helle stowed one last sweater in the bag.

"You don't want to tell me, do you?" Alison said in a flat voice.

Helle shrugged.

"Damn it, Helle! What will it take to regain your confidence?"

"That you stop seeing him, for a start," Helle replied, not at all surprised when Alison averted her face. "Because you still are, aren't you?"

"Maybe." Alison gave Helle a defiant look. "He's kind of addictive. And anyway, everyone can make a mistake. He just lost control when he saw Jason—not exactly surprising, given that Jason had stolen all that info from him."

"There was no data theft—not from Jason's side." Helle gritted her teeth. "Woolf's the one—"

"That's not what he says!"

"And you believe him over me?"

"Not normally, no. But since Mr Reincarnation walked into your life, things aren't as clear-cut." Alison lowered her voice. "How the fuck do you expect me to believe anything he says? He's delusional—you told him so yourself."

"At least he isn't hurting people for fun." Helle zipped up her bag. "Woolf, on the other hand…" She looked at her friend. "You're playing with fire."

"Yeah?" Alison snickered. "That's rich, coming from the girl who's dating a guy who thinks he can start a blaze with his hands."

"Who, Jason? Are you for real?" Helle managed to laugh. "What, and this is information you've received from that oh, so reliable source, Sam Woolf? The same source who told you I was begging for him to come on to me? The same guy who twisted your arm until it bruised because you objected to him trying to kill my guy?"

Alison flushed. She opened her mouth to say something but Helle held up her hand. "I don't want to hear. And once we're back, I'll be moving out." She shouldered her backpack and picked up her bag. "I'll pay my share of the rent for three more months, that's it."

Alison took hold of her. "You know I can't pay for this place on my own."

"Ask Woolf. Maybe he'll be glad to chip in." But she sighed at the look on Alison's face. "We can talk when I get back, okay?"

It took exactly five minutes before Helle's phone rang.

"Hi Mum." She settled back against the leather upholstery of the SUV.

"What's going on with you and Alison?" Mum asked. No preamble there.

"Ask her."

"Seeing as she was crying her eyes out, it was kind of difficult to do that." Her mother sounded reproving. "How can you treat your best friend like that? If Jason has a problem with Alison, then he needs to get over it."

"Jason?" Helle made a face at the phone. "It's Alison who has a problem with him."

"But—"

"Look, Mum, you have no idea what's going on with her, okay? But let's just say that no way am I going to live with someone who's likely to have Sam Woolf staying the night."

Mum fell silent. "Alison and that jerk? Again?"

"Yup."

"But you have to stop it! She could get hurt."

"According to Alison, Woolf is her preferred type of poison. She likes it rough."

"She does?" Mum fell silent again—sort of a record. "Well, I guess it takes all kinds." She laughed. "Anyway, I didn't call you just to yell at you for throwing your best friend out onto the street—"

"I did no such thing! But she—"

"Yes, I got all that. As I was saying, I wanted to talk about something else. Christmas."

"Yeah?" Helle swallowed. Mum was going to be so disappointed. She took a deep breath, but before she could say anything, her mother beat her to it.

"I know you're looking forward to coming home, but Phil and I have been trying to find a weekend for ourselves and the only weekend we could find was Christmas, and I promise I will make it up to you once we're back in London." It came out so rushed Helle had to spend some time deciphering it.

"You're abandoning me?" she asked. With her mother, one had to milk what one could.

"Oh, darling, of course not! But I—"

"It's okay, Mum." Helle smiled. "But I expect a major dinner when you get here, okay? I'm thinking champagne and caviar as a starter."

"Really, Helle, how clichéd. Everyone knows it's vodka and caviar."

241

"Whatever." She sent her mother a loud kiss and hung up. The stewardess gestured with her elegant manicured hands, directing most of her warmth towards Jason. Blood-red nails indicated their seats, and Helle slid in to sit by the window.

"Champagne? Turkish lemonade?" The stewardess was back, the tray held in front of Jason. When he thanked her in Turkish, the beautiful face cracked into a delighted smile, a volley of incomprehensible sounds spilling from her lips.

"Chick magnet," Helle muttered. In response, Jason grabbed her hand and lifted it to his lips. The stewardess stuttered to a halt. Jason raised a brow, saying something that sounded like bitumen. They were talking about coal tar? The stewardess smiled and nodded.

"Bitumen?"

"*Birtanem*," he pronounced slowly. "My only one."

"Oh."

After that excellent start to their Turkish adventure, Helle dozed for most of the flight, the rustling sound of Jason's papers restful rather than disturbing. When the seatbelt sight came back on, she pressed her nose to the window, with Jason leaning over her shoulder.

To fly into Istanbul on a sunny day really was something. The huge city spread in all directions, straddling the narrow waterway that separated Europe from Asia. From above, the buildings were a uniform drab reddish colour, dotted with spires and domes and bisected by water. Miles upon miles of similar houses, cradling the jewel that was the Sea of Marmara, a blue sapphire in a heap of gravel, its irregular diamond shape tapering up into the narrow gash of the Bosporus to the north, while to the south the straits of the Dardanelles connected it with the Mediterranean proper.

Helle was entranced, in love with the city from an altitude of ten thousand feet. Beside her, Jason was silent, but she could sense how thrilled he was as he stared down at the deep blue of the sea beneath us.

"Welcome to Turkey," the stewardess said politely once they'd landed. She smiled at Jason. "Welcome home, sir."

"Home?" Helle laughed softly. "Somehow I don't think you have a valid Turkish passport."

The combination of an ancient city with modern means of transportation resulted in utter traffic chaos, and it took them well over an hour to reach the hotel.

"Seriously, the pasha suite?" Helle was enchanted by the elegant décor, and especially by the four poster bed, draped in various shades of pink.

"Comes with its own hammam," Jason said, standing by the window. "And an impressive view. Behold the Hagia Sofia." He undid his tie. "Selim Bey has rescheduled the meeting for tomorrow—his mother is ill. So let's go and do some sightseeing."

The old town of Istanbul was a sequence of narrow streets, clapboard houses painted in every shade of pastel colour imaginable climbing the hilly ground. A steady wind from the sea brought with it a faint smell of brine which mingled with the scents of warm bread, waterpipes and strong coffee—there seemed to be a café or a teahouse in every other house.

"It's quite ugly," Helle said, looking at the façade of Hagia Sofia. "Too squat, too faded, too…" A huge cupola adorned the reddish building which seemed to bow under its weight.

"Big?" Jason suggested. "And how can you say it is ugly?"

"It doesn't soar. Other churches, well they lift themselves towards the heavens. This one looks as if it is cowering under divine rage."

But when she entered, she took it all back, gawking at the rounded ceiling, at the mosaics – well, basically at everything. In difference to its exterior, the interior of the ancient church was an explosion of colours and patterns, of gilded icons and Arabic writing.

"Have you ever been here before?" she asked, admiring the vaulting of the nave.

"Here?" Jason shuffled his feet. "Do you really want to know?"

"I do."

He did a slow turn. "Yes. Once in the first years of the thirteenth century—really bad timing—and once in the early twentieth century. Equally bad timing."

"Why?"

243

"In the thirteenth century, the Crusades. You know, brave Christian knights who were supposed to free Jerusalem but got distracted into sacking Constantinople instead." His face set. "Organised murder, that's what it was." He shook himself. "Ready for the Grand Bazaar?"

"Do they sell magic carpets?"

"They don't exist," Jason said, smiling down at her.

"How do you know? Aladdin had one."

"Fairy tale stuff," he snorted, making her grin.

"You know what?" she told him. "So are fire boys. And girls that run like the wind." He chuckled and ruffled her hair.

Okay, so they didn't find any magic carpets, but otherwise the bazaar was a treasure trove, displaying everything from spices to the most amazing lamps Helle had ever seen. She wanted all of them, she thought, caressing the rounded glass lanterns. So immersed was she in a display of blue lamps that she didn't notice Jason leaving, only discovering his absence when she turned to tell him something.

"Jason?" She took a hesitant step away from the shop, scanning the thronged passageway in both directions. Nowhere did she see a man of his distinctive height. She dithered. Should she stay and wait for him? Make her way back to the hotel? And where was he? Could he…? No. Helle took a deep breath. No one knew they were here. Although come to think of it, a man as determined as Sam Woolf could easily find out, couldn't he? The hitherto so perfect day was marred by the bitter taste of fear.

"Helle?" Jason's voice made her jump. "Finished with your lamps?"

"Where were you?" She heard how accusing she sounded.

"Over there, by the chessboards." He touched her cheek. "Did anything happen?"

"No." She felt silly. "I just didn't know where you were."

He saved the best bit for last, holding her hand as they walked down to the water, just beyond the Topkapi Palace. The evening breeze was chilly and out on the Sea of Marmara, ships were queuing up to enter the Bosporus, an endless line of vessels. Jason closed his eyes. Instead of the ugly metal ships before him, he saw the smaller vessels of his time, wooden ships that used wind or oars to propel themselves along. Ships mostly filled with those accursed Greeks, he thought, in a colonial endeavour as ferocious as any other.

"What are you thinking?" Helle touched his hand, recalling him to the present, to the suspension bridge over the Golden Horn, the distant bridge over the Bosporus. Ferries darted back and forth, on the eastern side the buildings were already sinking into the shadows of approaching night. They strolled along the waterfront, the setting sun gilding the choppy waters.

Jason came to a halt, gazing towards the east. "I've never been back to where we came from," he said. "Not once."

"Do you want to go?"

"I do." He drew her close. "But not this time. We will wait for spring." And for that accursed Samion to be well and truly out of their lives. To return to Trabzon before that—no, it would be far too dangerous.

"Something to look forward to," she said lightly, gazing out across the Sea of Marmara. Jason closed his hand around the little box in his pocket, acquired in the bazaar. Yes, something to look forward to. A honeymoon perhaps? He laughed at himself: he was a hopeless romantic, he told himself, but it was the fact of being here, with her, that had made him act so spontaneously, leaving her engrossed in lamps while he sneaked off to the neighbouring goldsmith's shop. "And anyway, Istanbul isn't too bad," she added.

"Too bad?" He nibbled her ear. "This is one of the most magnificent cities of the world. Ancient and the worse for wear, it still entices. And despite all this," he said, waving his hand at the metropolis surrounding them, "it's still as beautiful as ever." Jason's eyes lingered on the Galata Tower, and under his feet he could feel the tremors caused by cars and trains. Like a pulse, he reflected, the city's ancient heart beating to the same rhythm as always.

"Was there a city here already back then? You know, when we were kids together."

He smiled at her euphemism. She still had problems

accepting the notion of multiple lives, and he supposed that was to be expected.

"No. The Greeks had a trading post here, and the barbarian people would at one time or another come down in huge caravans to trade and barter." He looked down at her. "We were the barbarians."

"Of course," she murmured.

"My mother and I walked all along the coast, from beyond Trabzon to here," he went on, "and wherever we came we were received with respect—respect for her, not for me. She was the most renowned Wanderer alive." And not above pointing that out to the people she met on her travels, he recalled with a fond smile. Nefirie was not exactly a shrinking violet, and her startling looks, her dark red hair contrasting with the pallor of her skin, attracted plenty of attention.

"Well, not to the Greeks of course," he added acidly. "They had no patience with a barbarian female healer, no understanding of her art. They called it magic and black arts, and accused her of conjuring evil spirits." More than once, they'd had to leave under the cover of the night, him a small boy who didn't understand why he was yet again dragged away from new friends. He stared off across the water, seeing not the bustling city before him, but a rickety boat, a woman sitting silent in its prow as it cast off, her son huddled in her lap. "So, we avoided this side of the strait."

He could sense that she was bursting with questions about Nefirie, but he didn't feel like talking about his mother— not here, where suddenly she felt closer than she'd done in three millennia. Was she still walking this earth, another soul condemned to wander through time? He hoped not.

The bed, according to Helle, was too small. According to Jason, it was perfect, making it impossible for her avoid tangling her legs with his. They were warm after their shower, replete after a late dinner, and Helle was blinking drowsily, hand closed around his thumb.

He stroked her hair.

"I want to make love to you. Here, so close to the place

we once came from." Rising on his elbow, he leaned over her to kiss her shoulder. "Call it closure, call it a new beginning, but I need this."

"I'm too tired," she objected.

"You don't have to do anything." He slowly pulled the sheet off her body, a slow caress of fabric against skin. "All you have to do is let me love you."

He punched his pillow into shape and sank down beside her. Eyes burned into eyes, and all he did was look at her, while whispering in detail just what he intended to do to her. As he spoke, her hitherto drowsy eyes widened, the pupils dilating when he described where he intended to kiss her. He could almost taste her arousal, her nostrils widening as she began to shift in bed.

"Are you just going to talk?" she murmured

"No." But he wasn't going to touch her yet. He sprawled and fondled himself without breaking eye contact. Her hands moved of their own volition towards his erection, but he shook his head. "You may only look, lioness."

"Well, how about I do the same?"

He grabbed her wrist, kissed it, and placed it on her pillow. "You're not allowed."

"No fair," she grumbled.

"To those who wait, great things will come," he said with a smile, stroking his cock. Her eyes darted from his face to his sex and she licked her lips, pressing her thighs together. "On your back," he said, and she complied with alacrity. "Spread your legs for me." He lowered his voice to a dark growl, fully aware of how affected she was by it. Helle's thighs widened, the soft folds of her sex already glistening with moisture.

Jason got to his knees and sat back, studying her. Despite being this far into winter, her skin retained a golden hue, further highlighted by the fair down on her arms, as fair as the hair on her pubic mound. He leaned forward, breathing gently into her moist curls. In response, goose bumps appeared along the outside of her thighs. Oh, he was going to enjoy this, he thought, blowing gently on her nipples, her neck, the curve of her hip, her navel.

"Jason," she said, hands reaching for his shoulders.

"No." He pinned her hands to the mattress. "You may not touch, you may not speak. I want you only to feel."

"I am," she groaned when he licked along her collarbone. "I am."

"Shhh." He placed a finger on her mouth.

"Jason, I—"

"Jason, I—" She stared up at him, eyes glazed with desire.

"I know, lioness, I know." He returned to his gentle torture. He alternated between exhaling and inhaling, his nose hovering a millimetre above her skin. She arched towards him, her legs splayed even wider in a silent request that he take her. Not yet. From teasing her with his warm breath, he went on to use his tongue, his teeth. She made a series of guttural sounds when he suckled on her nipples. Her hips bucked beneath him, her arms tense with fighting the need to touch him. He liked her this compliant, liked it even more that she allowed him to lead—he needed to, and she seemed to understand that.

He was back to kneeling between her legs, one finger rubbing gently up and down her cleft. She'd already climaxed once, was well on her way to a second orgasm, would probably have a third before he took her. Hard, he thought, he was going to bury himself so deeply inside of her she'd be incapable of moving, of doing anything but taking what he gave her.

The second orgasm rippled through her. She opened her eyes and lifted her hips in an open invitation. It made him smile, recalling their first time together, both of them so much younger, so inexperienced. He'd been at most twenty, she sixteen, and while they knew very little about making love, they already knew quite a lot about being in love, so his first exploration of her had been tender, if hurried. After all, young men rarely have the patience required to excel as lovers—it is an acquired art, to learn to pleasure the female body.

He positioned himself on top of her, and she held her breath in expectation, eyes locked onto his. Most of his weight on his elbows, his hands holding her still as he powered into her, a hoarse gasp escaping him. So warm, so soft, so…so his.

248

Yes, she was his, had been meant to be his since the dawn of time. His.

She hooked her legs round his, giving him better leverage. He filled her, each flexing of his pelvis bringing him that little bit deeper. She ground against him and in response he gyrated his hips so that she shook beneath him, helpless in the throes of yet another orgasm. He covered her mouth with hers as he came, her name echoing in his head.

"To new beginnings," Helle whispered. "May they always be as spectacular as this one."

Jason slid her a look. Now he was the one on the verge of sleep, while she was regarding him with shining eyes, her skin rosy, her mouth soft and inviting. It was an effort to find her hand, clasp it and raise it to his mouth.

"*Birtanem*," he said, and was rewarded by a smile so wide it made his heart crack—just a little.

Jason no longer tried to avoid Samion's soft voice, his amused laughter. There was no point. Faithless, he raged in silence, she had been faithless. While he sat in the dark, she slept in another's arms. While he called her name, she loved another.

Helle rarely spoke. She sat on the window seat and willed him to appear by magic in front of her. Strong and golden, his fires keeping her safe. He never did. Her body was heavy, and the child turned and heaved, restless in its shrinking space. Soon it would all be over, she thought, her mind shrinking back in fear.

When she slept she dreamed of him. When he slept, he dreamed of her. In their dreams their hands would meet, their fingers braiding together. When they woke they were alone. He in his hole, she in her golden cage.

Chapter 23

Helle woke to a bed empty of Jason but filled with the most deliciously erotic memories. There was a slight twinge of regret at not finding him beside her—she'd hoped to return the favour and then some—but on the other hand there were certain parts of her that could do with a break.

When she emerged from the shower, he was at the little table, immersed in his laptop. His Chelsea boots smelled of new polish, his grey suit looking somewhere between strict and casual when combined with a colourful hankie in the breast pocket and a pink shirt worn with the top two buttons unbuttoned.

She hugged him from behind before smoothing his thick hair back off his brow.

"Good morning."

He tilted his head back to look at her. "Is it, Ms Madsen?"

"Morning or good?" she teased, before kissing him. "I'd say it is an excellent morning—except for the fact that I'm hungry."

"That," he said, standing up, "is easily sorted. Allow me to introduce you to the joys of a Turkish breakfast."

"As opposed to those of a Turkish bed?"

"The one does not exclude the other."

After breakfast, they hurried down to the waterfront and took a ferry over to the Asian side. From the water, Istanbul was even more impressive than from the air, its shores lined with buildings that varied from positively ancient to so new the glass in the windows was tinted. Helle was hanging over the railings, trying to take a photo, when out of the corner of her eye she saw a man watching her. She had an overall impression of black—all the way from the shoes to the sunglasses—but when she turned to properly look at him he was gone.

Helle stood on her toes, trying to find him. A man with a

bald, tattooed head should stick out like a sore thumb, but it was as if he'd gone up in smoke.

"What are you looking for?"

"Nothing." She frowned. Maybe she'd just imagined him.

As they were getting off the ferry, she saw him again, standing two levels above them. He was definitely looking at them, a phone pressed to his ear.

"Jason, look!" She tugged at his sleeve. "That guy, he was watching me before."

"What guy?" Jason shaded his eyes. The man was gone.

"I'm telling you, I saw him!" Helle half ran to keep up with Jason, who was walking rapidly towards the taxi stand.

"I'm not disputing you did." He hurried them along. "But just because a man looks at you, that doesn't mean he has sinister thoughts. Especially not when you're looking like you're doing right now."

"You think?" She smoothed her skirt into place.

"Smoking hot," he assured her, making her laugh at his phony American accent.

A small delegation welcomed them to the premises of PillEL. A man somewhere between forty and fifty stepped forward, extended his hand, and introduced himself as Selim Demir.

"I thought his name was Bey," Helle whispered.

"Honorary title. Bey is like Don in Spanish."

"Ah." She smiled at the distinguished gentleman who as a matter of course stepped aside to allow her to enter first.

Jason and Selim exchanged words in Turkish, but after a while Jason held up his hands in defeat. "Sorry," he said, "my Turkish is simply not good enough."

"You speak excellent Turkish." Selim Bey beamed at him. "You know our country?"

"I had family in Smyrna."

"Smyrna?" Selim Bey raised a brow. "Greek family?"

"At the time, I think they were Ottoman citizens," Jason replied with an edge.

"Ah, yes, and then came Atatürk." Selim Bey smiled thinly. "And afterwards, there was no Smyrna. There was Izmir."

"Yes." The muscles along Jason's forearms bunched.

Selim Bey exploded into more unfamiliar language. Jason tilted his head to his side.

"Is that Greek?" He shook his head ruefully. "Afraid I don't speak it."

"But you speak Turkish—how strange."

"Strange? My ancestors spoke Turkish."

Which, Helle assumed, was something of a stretch. Whatever language the people along the Black Sea had spoken in antiquity, she seriously doubted it was anything like modern Turkish. And then she realised he was talking about the relatives he'd had in Smyrna, a bitterness lacing his voice when he tersely described how the family had had to flee.

"The mother died," he said. "Bayoneted in the back by a Turkish recruit." His eyes met Helle's for an instant, the amber colour drowning in fiery copper. Shit. Somehow she got the impression he had been very much there.

"Such things happen," Selim Bey said. "But it is history now."

The conversation turned to technical aspects, both men relaxing visibly. Helle went back to taking notes.

"Done and dusted!" Jason high-fived Helle once they'd left Selim at the notary's office. The short December day was quickly darkening into night, but to the west the silhouette of the ancient citadel stood stark against a sky shifting in green and pale yellow.

"Congratulations. You now own an electrical pill company." She grinned. "Sounds very weird."

"But is borderline magic." He looked happy, eyes bright as he launched himself into a little speech about how his new company would revolutionise the world. Once back on the ferry, he ordered tea served in thimble-sized glasses and gazed towards the south.

"I'm guessing Smyrna was in that direction," Helle said, snuggling up to him. With the sun gone, the temperature was falling fast, making her choice of jacket feel inadequate.

"It was."

"So, in one life you're a Turk, in the next a Greek. Must be confusing, keeping your prejudices in order."

Jason laughed. "One of the drawbacks of multiple lives, I guess. It's difficult to root for one side only when you've lived with both."

Helle didn't reply. Over Jason's shoulder, she'd caught sight of a distinctive tattooed head. Twice might be a coincidence, but three times? She stepped closer to Jason.

"He's here again."

"Who?"

"The man I told you about."

Predictably, when Jason turned, the man was gone.

The incident with the man made Helle jittery. Jason, however, stilled, eyes narrowing as he inspected the approaching docks. His whole body was coiled as if in expectation of an attack, and when she slipped her hand into his, he squeezed in response, making Helle retract her hand as if she'd been stung. He was burning hot.

"Sorry," he apologised. Helle carefully touched his wrist. Sizzling.

"It's the fire," he explained, "sometimes I overheat." Helle nodded. Of course. Happened all the time. He gave her an anguished look, muttering something about not being able to help his damned condition.

"How will I ever be able to tell if you're overheating or running a fever?" she asked him, to lighten the mood. He looked very irritated.

"My hands and arms overheat. Not my head." Good to know.

"So where exactly did you see him?" Jason said, interrupting her tangential excursion into the consequences of living with your own personal water boiler.

"There." She pointed in the direction of the prow. As if she'd conjured him up, the man popped into sight, saw them staring and legged it, with Jason in pursuit.

The ferry had not moored yet, but Mr Tattoo Head wasn't about to let something as immaterial as a missing gangway stop him. Like a stag in flight he jumped, slipped on the concrete of the dock, went down, but was up an instant later. Jason cursed, made as if to follow, but was detained by two burly sailors.

"You know him?" Helle watched the man disappear into the murky darkness of the ancient bridge arches.

"No. But it doesn't take a genius to work out who he is working for." He frowned. "We have to leave."

"Leave? Like right now?"

"Yes." He offered no further explanation, hurrying her down the gangway.

"Why?" Tired of being dragged along like some extra piece of luggage, Helle dug her heels in. Besides, it was easy for him to jog, he wasn't wearing platform heels.

"If Woolf finds out we're here and comes after us…" He shook his head. "I was a fool to come here."

"You're being ridiculous," she said. "Woolf has other things to do besides persecuting us, running his business for one. He is far too busy conquering the world of mergers and acquisitions to be able to rush off after us." She didn't really believe this herself, remembering the recent events in Jason's garage, but that had been opportunistic behaviour, while traipsing off to Turkey in pursuit was way high on the Richter scale of seriously disturbed behaviour.

Jason gave her an exasperated look. "We're in Turkey!"

"And?"

"This is his home ground." He took a deep breath. "Samion comes from blood so ancient it is welded to this land. This is where his powers are at their strongest, this is where he comes closest to reverting to the wizard prince he once was. And believe me, he would jump at the chance of wiping me off the face of the Earth here, where the three of us first saw the light of the day."

Helle studied the cobbles at her feet. More mumbo jumbo, more incomprehensible shit that made her toy with the thought she might be sleeping with a lunatic. An uncomfortably warm hand closed on hers.

"We have to go, Helle."

She followed him mutely, more than aware of how deserted

the narrow streets were, not at all as they'd been the previous day. A sudden movement in a doorway made her halt. Beside her, Jason hissed in warning, pulling her back the way they'd come. Another shadow appeared, holding something that glinted in the weak light of the street lamp. A gun. Holy shit, Mr Tattoo Head was pointing a gun at them.

Someone laughed, and ice trickled through Helle's veins. Sam Woolf was already here.

"So, Wanderer, it is time." Woolf bowed slightly. "For you to die, that is."

"Not today," Jason said, shoving Helle behind him.

"Oh yes, today." Woolf smirked. "The deadline expired on Sunday, so you're already on borrowed time." He glanced at Helle. "You should have done as I told you to. Now it's too late."

Helle's mouth was dry, her hands shaking uncontrollably. Three men, two of them with guns. And from the look on Woolf's face, he had every intention of ensuring Jason died. Here. Now. At his command, one of the men raised his gun.

"No!" Helle stumbled towards them, was arrested by Jason's arm. "Don't shoot!"

Woolf laughed, snapped his fingers. The gun went off. The bullet slammed into a nearby tree. Helle blinked. At such close range, even she would have hit the target.

"Stay where you are," Jason said in an undertone. "Whatever you do, don't move!"

"But…"

"Do as I say, Helle!" He didn't look at her, standing with his arms extended. Energy crackled through the air, and when the next bullet hit the same tree, Helle understood. Well, no, she didn't, not really, but she guessed that whatever Jason was doing was acting as some sort of heat shield.

Woolf whirled on his toes. He spun like a dervish, and with every spin it seemed to Helle he grew in size and darkness, eyes glittering opals in a face as pale as the distant moon. The night air resonated with his voice. Helle's vision blurred, the ground beneath her feet tilting this way and that. She had problems remaining upright, seemed to have forgotten how to breathe, and in front of them, Woolf grew into a horrifying apparition, dark smoke swirling around a face that narrowed and sharpened, mouth wide open in a snarl.

Helle tried to back away and bumped into Jason. Woolf flung out his arm: something small and dark came flying through the air towards Jason. It exploded when it crashed into the barrier of heat Jason had created, the air filling with the scent of gunpowder.

"Stand still! And stand behind me." The tendons in Jason's neck, in his hands, were rigid. He moaned and shivered when Woolf's next two projectiles exploded against the invisible shield, and when Mr Tattoo Head chose to open fire, for a moment Jason lost his concentration, the bullet whistling by far too close for comfort.

"We have to back away," Jason said. Back away where? Helle ducked when two guns went off simultaneously. Woolf bombarded Jason with his miniature bombs, and with every hit, Jason reeled, arms shaking with the effort of maintaining their protection. Helle couldn't think, the ground vibrated, and Woolf's voice was in her head, roaring at her to step aside and leave the Wanderer to his fate. No. She tried to shake her head, and the voice inside of her sank razors into her brain, causing her to bend forward. Agh! She had to obey. Helle took an unsteady step away from Jason, heard him say her name. No choice. She had to… Another step.

"No!" Jason leapt towards her, grabbing at her. Her skin flared with the heat of his hand, but she didn't care. Pain. Pain would block him out. She shook her brain clear of Woolf's voice and straightened up, in time to see one of those dark explosives come flying towards them. It exploded an arm's length from Jason's face.

Jason exclaimed and staggered back, arms flung out. Black smoke enveloped him, and when Woolf threw his head back and laughed, Helle screamed. Woolf came loping towards them. Jason was clutching at his chest, wheezing like a punctured accordion. Helle's hands closed on the strap of her heavy shoulder bag. Sheer instinct had her swinging wildly, hitting Woolf full in the face. The force of the blow propelled him backwards. Helle swung again, and there was a sound of something breaking, blood spurting from Woolf's face as he fell to his knees, his goons rushing to his aid.

"Jason?" She tried to prop him up. "Are you hurt?"

"Can't breathe," he groaned, "my lungs…" She clapped him on the back and he coughed, spewing up what looked like soot.

Mr Tattoo Head caught hold of Helle.

"Jason!" she shrieked. A hand covered her mouth. She bit down. Hard. The man swore, but didn't let go. She kicked and flailed. He pinched her nose closed, and she couldn't breathe, couldn't think. Her pulse thudded in her ears, her feet struggled for purchase on the slippery cobbles. Something was on fire. Someone was screaming. Jason? Was that Jason? The hand over her mouth disappeared. Helle gulped air, bracing herself on her knees. Mr Tattoo Head was rolling on the ground, burning like a torch.

She was hauled upright. For a moment, she feared it was Woolf holding her, but she recognised the touch, the long, strong fingers so hot they blistered her skin. She didn't care.

Woolf had regained his feet, if anything looking even more terrifying now that his face was bloodied. He took hold of his nose, there was a sharp crack, and he shook his head a couple of times. When he next looked in Helle's direction, his face was undamaged.

"Shit!" she squeaked.

Jason stepped in front of Helle. Two men facing off—it could have been a movie starring Clint Eastwood, except that in this particular duel the odds were stacked, two more men appearing behind Woolf. A snap of his fingers, and two became four.

"What, no backup?" Woolf sneered. "So how long do you think you'll be able to hold us off, Wanderer?"

"Don't underestimate me, Samion."

"Prince Samion to you, cur!"

"You lost the right to be called prince ages ago," Jason snarled. He edged backwards, and Samion came after, growing in stature with each step he took. How did he do that? Jason came to a halt, and Helle felt his stance relax. Why? Nothing seemed to have changed.

Woolf was standing like four yards away, flanked by his men. Jason raised his arms, spread them wide, and fire crackled between his hands, leapt downward to sizzle on the cobbles. One of the men jumped, but at Woolf's growled command he froze, the gun in his hand shaking madly.

"I don't have time for your fire shows." Woolf sank his eyes into Jason and began to speak, a language so ancient it caused the stones under Helle's feet to crack apart. The street tilted, the houses sagged, and out of every crevice, every hole, came an army of snakes.

"They're not real," Jason said. "Nothing of what he's doing is real." His arms were shaking, hands glowing like embers. He held them palm downwards, little tendrils of steam rising from the ground below his feet.

Helle was not convinced. When something slithered over her foot she choked back on a scream. "I can feel them." They were everywhere, undulating towards her.

"It's all in your head, Helle." Jason did not take his eyes off Samion, arms still held in a protective stance. "My gift, however, is real." He brought his arms down swiftly. The heavy iron drain-cover at Woolf's feet exploded upwards. The nearby lids followed suit, vaporised water enveloping Woolf and his men in huge clouds of hissing steam. The men screamed, Woolf yelled.

"That was you?" Helle gasped.

"Run!" Jason yelled. Helle kicked off her heels and flew up the nearest street, dragging Jason along.

Samion stood in the doorway, ablaze with pride; a daughter, to be followed by many sons. He smiled at her, the mother of his child, and strode over towards the bed. She kept her eyes on the swaddled infant and clutched her tightly. The women in waiting fell away as he drew closer, faces averted. Samion noticed the tense atmosphere and narrowed his eyes in suspicion. Helle cradled the baby defensively.

"Give her to me," he snapped. She held onto the child, hiding its face against her breast.

"I said, give her to me." He loomed over her. "Or do you want me to rip her off you?"

She kissed the fuzzy little head and held out the baby. He took her gently and crooned to her as he lifted her to his face. The baby opened her eyes and gazed at him through amber coloured irises. His eyes. Samion staggered back and looked venomously at the whore lying in his bed.

"This is not my child," he hissed. She smiled weakly, managing to look defiant despite her ravaged state.

"I know. I've always known."

In that moment his ambivalence towards her solidified into hate. She had duped him, allowing him to hope that she might one day love him, and all the time she had known that the child under her heart was the Wanderer's. What a fool she must have thought him when he came with his precious pomegranates, so proud of her swelling body, so gentle in his caresses. He had tried to love her—she had laughed at him behind his back.

The serving women huddled by the door. They were waiting for him to erupt, to give in to his infamous temper and crush the tender little skull underfoot. Samion looked down at the child and made his decision.

"You," he pointed to one of the women, "take this child to the nurseries. Find her a wet-nurse."

"No!" shrieked Helle. "No, she's mine. Give me my baby, please Samion, give her to me." She clutched at his leg, one arm outstretched towards the child. "I'll do anything," she pleaded. "Please Samion, anything, just don't take my baby from me."

Samion sneered and passed the infant over to the waiting hands. He bent down and wound his hands into Helle's hair, tearing her off him. She gasped.

"I don't need you anymore. She'll do fine instead," he snarled. "She'll be dancing at my knees in no time, obedient to my will, not like you. She will love me because she'll have no choice."

"She's a baby," she stuttered.

"But not for ever," he smirked. "Get the guards," he said to the women, "tell them to throw this one out. Tell them to cart her back to Kantor, if he'll have her. Oh, and throw the other one into the cart as well."

Helle fought all the way, screaming for her baby. She bit and tore, kicked and punched. Samion stood watching, his hands clasped behind his back. He had won, he thought triumphantly, ignoring the painful cracking of his soul. He had finally broken through to her heart. She was begging now, begging and crying for her child, but it was too late, at least for her.

Jason tried. They jeered at him, laughing at his tottering attempts to walk. Eight months in the dark, eight months in a hole. His legs shook. They laughed and heaved him up on the cart, throwing him carelessly into a corner. And then they brought her. A spitting, fighting beast, screaming for her child. He watched with blinking eyes as she alternated between begging and hitting out wildly around her. He shrank away from her as they threw her wailing into the cart. Someone slapped her into stunned silence. He didn't care. He averted his eyes from her.

Helle collapsed, lying delirious through the two days' journey. She never noticed Jason sitting huddled in a corner, never saw him jump as if he'd been stung every time she called his name. She didn't see him clasping his hands, controlling the urge to comfort her and hold her. He would never touch her again, he promised himself. He would never lay hands on the harlot lying beside him, despite her repeated calls for him, only for him.

Chapter 24

He refused to stay in the hotel. At his barked commands, Helle packed together their stuff, carrying both their bags when they left. Jason flexed his hands, at present so swollen and sore they were almost useless. Should Woolf come after them now... A matter of time only, he conceded, and it made his blood run cold. This time, he'd taken Woolf by surprise. Next time, Woolf would not underestimate him.

They took a taxi to the airport, but once there, Jason didn't go inside the terminal.

"What?" Helle asked.

Jason nodded in the direction of a group of policemen. "They give me a bad vibe." She studied them in silence, gnawing at her lip.

"You're right," she said. "I don't think they're the real thing. So now, what?"

"We rent a car."

The paperwork took far too long. Jason kept a careful watch on whoever approached, and only once they were safe in the Golf did he relax. He shoved his seat back and looked at Helle. "We're going west."

"West." She made a helpless gesture. "Which way?"

He would have preferred to drive himself, but his hands made that impossible. He picked at a huge blister on his palm and glanced at her, grimacing as he saw the mark his hand had left on her arm.

"Does it hurt?"

"A bit." She kept her eyes on the traffic, hands tight on the wheel. "But it helped." She sounded distant.

"Are you all right?"

"All right?" A sound very like a sob escaped her. "How the fuck can you ask me that?" She glared at him, and the car swerved dangerously before she got it back under control. "I

261

just saw… Heck! I don't even know what I saw, but whatever the case, it was damned scary." She didn't say anything more for the coming half-hour, her profile cold and forbidding as they drove steadily northwest.

Jason dozed, resting his head against the window. The heat in his hands abated, and he knew from previous experience his blisters would be gone by the morning.

"So, Greece or Bulgaria?" she asked. He looked out the window at the darkness that surrounded them, pulled out his phone and studied Google Maps.

"Greece," he said. "Make for Alexandroupoli." 25 miles or so from the Turkish border, it should only take them a couple of hours to get there.

"Make for it? I have no idea where it is or where I am!" She burst out crying, long, heaving sobs that shook her entire body.

"Hey," he said. "We're okay, Helle."

"We are?" she wiped at her eyes. "You might be, but I'm not."

"Pull over."

She shook her head. "We're going to Greece, remember?"

"Pull over. Now."

This time, she complied, clambering over the central console to sit in his lap. "He really does want to kill you," she hiccupped, hiding her face against his shirt. "He won't give up, will he?"

"Probably not. But I'm not an easy man to kill." He stuck his nose into her hair, inhaling her scent, at present overlaid with a tinge of sweat and the odour of fear.

"Is this how it's going to be? Will we spend our entire life looking over our shoulders?"

Jason drew in a ragged breath and closed his eyes. "I hope not." It would be unless they managed to destroy Samion but he didn't think she wanted to hear that. "Look, let's find somewhere to sleep first. Then we'll talk."

It was after midnight before they found the hotel Jason had googled, just by the port in Alexandroupoli. It was off-season, so the options were restricted, but Jason was pleasantly surprised by the standard of the room, the modern décor and comfortable beds a welcome end to an exhausting day. It had been a long drive on narrow Thracian roads bordered by wilderness, and Helle's eyes were huge in her pale face, her normally so soft mouth set in a grim slash.

"I have to lie down." She threw herself on the bed, shoes and all. He fiddled with his water bottle, undressed, and joined her, all the time aware of her assessing eyes.

"Let me help you," he said, easing the shoes off her feet. She wriggled out of her skirt, pulled her top over her head, and slid in under the covers. She turned this way and that and finally sat up. "I can't sleep. I'm dead on my feet, but I'm not sure I dare close my eyes. What if he finds us here?"

"Not likely." He'd turned off both their phones, using only the burner phone Nigel had provided him with before they left London.

"When it comes to Woolf, anything is likely," she muttered. She ran a careful hand over her blistered skin, courtesy of Jason. "My grandmother would have put butter on it."

"Which is of no use at all." He took her hand. "I didn't mean to, but when I saw you move towards him, I didn't stop to think. I…" His voice faltered. "To see you walk away from me, to him, it was too much of a déjà vu, and I…"

"I left you for him last time round?" She sounded horrified.

"Not as such. You were forced, but all the same, I couldn't take the chance you'd get too close to him." He rolled over on his back, staring up at the cream-coloured ceiling. "The day he took you away was two days before we were to wed. We'd been up in the woods, at one of the hot springs, and you were…" he smiled sadly. "…delectable."

Half-naked, her hair cascading undone down her back, she'd been rosy after their recent nap, her lips red and swollen from all his kisses. A young woman full of life, the sunlight gilding her hair, her curves visible through the linen of her under-tunic. And next time he saw her, she'd become a wraith, thin and grey, her defiant spirit crushed by months under Samion's tender care. Not that he'd cared or noticed—he'd been too busy hating her for abandoning him to hang in chains in Samion's dungeons. But he didn't tell her that.

"So what happened?"

"You already know: he stabbed you." But first he had crushed her vibrant spirit, then he had made Jason hate her. The final beating and the stabbing was only the conclusion to a carefully orchestrated destruction of a young woman which ended when Helle went after Samion with a knife—only to die at his hand.

Helle shifted closer. "Here," she said, touching herself just above her right breast. "And here." She indicated her back.

"Yes. And here, and here, and here…" So much blood, staining her garments, staining the ground, her hair. "But he paid." Jason studied his hands. "Tenfold." Even now, so many years after the fact, he felt a twinge of shame—not because he'd killed him, but because he'd enjoyed it.

Helle was looking at him with an expression he couldn't quite decipher, eyes unreadable under her lowered lashes.

"You have to understand," he said, "that when you died, I was left a hollow man. There was nothing inside of me, no feelings, no needs, nothing. My mother tried everything, but even the power of a Wanderer has its limits. I was a husk, a husk that ate and slept, but no longer lived. I didn't care what happened to me and I volunteered for every dangerous raid, hoping for the relief of death. I tried to fulfil my promise to you, but I was too late. I could find no trace to follow."

"What promise was that?"

"Does it matter?" He shrugged. "I'm not quite sure I remember myself," he lied, because if he told her about his promise, he'd have to tell her all the rest, and he had no idea how she would react.

"No matter what dangers I faced, I came out unscarred, as if the gods had ordained that I would find no release from pain. I was pathetic, spending my nights pressing my only keepsake of you, a ribbon, to my cheek, trying to catch a scent that was no longer there. Only one thing drove me on: to find Samion and eradicate him and his from this earth, as he had destroyed you." He looked away, disturbed by expression on her face. Was it pity or disgust? It was a fine line separating one from the other, and besides, he didn't want her pity, he didn't deserve her disgust—not for grieving for her.

"I hardened into a parody of the man I was destined to be. Everything light and sweet in me was wiped away, replaced by this corroding anger, this ever-swelling hatred."

She squeezed his hand—a gentle reassuring pressure. He returned it in kind, would have preferred to not tell her the rest, but there was no going back now.

"I destroyed him. His children I afflicted with disease, his crops I set on fire." He smiled coldly. "And finally, one day I had the pleasure of taking from him what he had taken from you. I took his life, slowly and painfully."

There was a muffled gasp from Helle, her fingers tightening into a vice round his. He threw her a quick glance before going on.

"He didn't deserve to live, not after what he'd done to us. The revenge was sweet, but short-lived. As he lay bleeding, his breath coming in short gasps, he turned his malevolent stare on me and told me this was but the first of many games to come. *'I will kill you uncountable times in the lives to come, and as to her, I will find her and tame her, bring her to heel like a disobedient bitch. She will be mine, Wanderer, and she will pay for all eternity for what you just did to me.'* My anger was such that I set his bed alight and left, leaving him to scream his life away."

He wanted her to say something. Instead, she sat mute, mouth hanging open. Her hand lay unresponsive in his, and she had problems meeting his eyes. Shit. The silence lengthened as he tried to gauge her reaction, but there was none, just this blank face regarding him as if she had no idea who he might be. Before he lost his nerve completely, he plunged on.

"I didn't understand what he meant by his last words, so I turned to my mother. Poor Nefirie, how it must have hurt her to see her son become one of the living dead, to know that I had broken all rules of her tribe as I tortured Samion to death." He threw her a challenging look. "I had to, Helle."

She nodded. "Go on," she said hoarsely.

"Anyway, I told Nefirie what Samion had said, and she just deflated, like a pricked balloon. I'd never seen her like that before, and it scared me more than anything ever had. After what seemed like an eternity, she turned to me, her eyes full of tears and told me that Samion, as all of his clan, Aeëtes' house—your house as well, by the way—knew how to push the soul onward through time. It was a mindboggling concept."

"We're kin? Woolf and me?" She sounded disgusted.

"You were kin—very, very distant kin."

"Thank heavens for that. So then what?"

He was relieved by her animation, by the way she leaned forward.

"I didn't understand at first—how could I? Nefirie didn't want to explain, knowing full well what I would do once she'd told me." He fondled her hand. "Suicide was as frowned upon then as it is now." He picked at the coverlet, seeing before him Nefirie's ravaged face, her hands raised in supplication that he not leave her. But there'd been no choice—not for him.

"Nefirie taught me to die, Helle. To die to go after you." He covered his face with his arm, drained by all this talk.

"Did it hurt? To die?"

Jason shook his head. "Not that first time. After all, there was a hand to hold on to and I kept my eyes on the evening star. That's all you need, I think, to die peacefully: the hand of someone who loves you and a patch of the infinite sky on which to rest your eyes."

"Has there been a hand in your other lives?" she asked, her voice breaking.

"Occasionally, but mostly I've died as I've lived—alone." Atonement, he supposed, for the vengeance he'd wreaked on Samion.

"How sad."

"It is as it is." He tapped at her nose. "Don't cry, lioness, it's all ancient history."

"Not all of it." She found a tissue and blew her nose. "So what's the secret? To die and travel onwards on purpose?"

Jason ran a finger down her cheek. "To die while conscious. No lingering morphine-induced sleep. To die, knowing you're dying, living the pain of dying, and to rise above it, thinking only of you."

For some reason, that had her throwing herself at him. Jason hugged her back, pressing her head down to rest on his chest, just above his heart.

"Have you run into him in other lives?"

"Repeatedly."

"And has it always ended badly?"

"Not always," he replied, "but often."

"And who usually wins?"

"He does," Jason groaned the words, his body clenching with remembered pain. "You see, he remembers who he is all the time. From the moment he's expelled from the womb, he knows who he is and why he's here. I don't. It always takes me years to remember. So it's been too easy for him sometimes."

"Oh." She tugged at his chest hair—a tad too hard. "And what about me? Have he and I met up?"

"I'm not sure. Maybe. Ow!" He caught hold of her hand. "I know of only once."

"And that, from the tone of your voice, didn't end in wedding bells and happily ever after."

Jason shuddered at the thought. His Helle, happy with Samion? "No. It ended with a premature death in a Paris canal."

"Nice." She pressed herself closer. "So it's him or us?"

"Yes, but this time I must end it. It must stop." He caressed her cheek. "Sleep?"

Helle shook her head. "Tell me about her—your mother."

As a distracting manoeuvre it was transparent, but Jason was happy to oblige.

"I guess she'd qualify as a good witch," he began, "an old soul—and a damn restless soul. Most of my early childhood was spent travelling through the countries of those times, from one ailing patient to the other."

"So no friends?"

"Not really." He wound a tendril of her hair round his finger. "Not until I met you and you made it your vocation in life to cling to me like a vine."

"Huh. I bet you liked it."

"Of course I did."

"She was beautiful, wasn't she?" Helle said, sitting up beside him. "I have this image of someone very tall with hair the colour of…cinnabar." She smiled. "And her eyes were just like yours, except that they were always a golden yellow, while in yours the copper flecks sometimes take over."

"What, you've been studying my eyes?" he teased.

"Always." She traced his brows. "Such beautiful eyes."

"Hmm. I'm thinking you're only saying that because you know I've got a Snickers bar in my bag."

"You do?"

"I come prepared for everything," he quipped, but it fell somewhat flat. "I'll get it for you."

They shared the Snickers as Jason continued with his tale.

"Wanderers were sacrosanct, their healing skills and insight valued by all. Nefirie was exceptionally gifted and she had a standing invitation to most of the local courts, so during my first few years we moved from courtyard to courtyard, part of a small band of Wanderers that would stay for a few months before the itch to go on became unbearable. That was why we were called Wanderers: always unwilling to settle, ever on the road… I don't really know why she decided to stay at Kantor's court, particularly as she wasn't too happy about how close we were." He threw her a cautious glance. "But maybe she recognised the workings of fate and knew better than to intervene."

A soft wrinkle appeared between Helle's brows. "I think she loved him, that's why she stayed. And he loved her."

Jason gave her a baffled look. "How would you know?"

She blushed. "Well, I see them, and the way he's looking at her, it's sort of obvious he worships the ground she walks on." She frowned. "They're quite old, though. So maybe it happened after… Sheesh, it feels strange talking about this!"

"After we died, you mean."

"Yeah. Sort of comforting each other, you know?"

He hoped so. He'd always feared Nefirie had spent the rest of her life as alone as he'd been ever since. To think of her sharing a bench with Kantor, maybe with a jug or two of that awful sour wine Kantor was so fond of, lightened his heart.

"Did she like me?" Helle asked, arms behind her back as she undid her bra.

"Why do you ask?" Nefirie had never warmed to Helle, regarding her with as much affection as she would a toad.

"I don't know. It's just an impression I have, that she didn't like me much."

"I think she was prescient enough to understand that you and I would have it tough, and she wished us both an easier life. You were easy to like," he said, toying with her hair, "wild and wayward, as your father used to say. With pride, I might add."

"And were we ever married?" she asked.

"No, we weren't. Your father had agreed to it, but it was not to be. You died."

"I was pretty young to die, wasn't I?"

He stroked her head. "You could say that. You were not yet eighteen." He yawned. "Enough talking. I need to sleep."

She snuggled up to him, her breasts soft and warm against his side. "Sweet dreams, honey," she murmured.

"And you," he replied. But he spent most of the night hoping she wouldn't dream at all, praying that the memories she'd kept repressed for so long remained safely buried in the darker corners of her mind.

Nefirie saw the cart trundling up the hill before anyone else. She ran to meet it, her heart leaping with joy. Nothing had prepared her for the pain that coursed through her when she saw her son. Dearest Mother, her son, reduced to a wreck. Shame at what she'd done coursed through her. She'd done it for him, but look at him now, and Helle...no, she hadn't intended anything like this.

Jason was sitting in the furthest corner, his face an impenetrable mask. But she could see the anguish beneath, she could see it in the way his knuckles were tight with tension and in the new lines that flared from his eyes. She wept inside at the sight of him. So pale, so gaunt, his cheekbones razors in his face.

When he saw her, his eyes softened and she saw a tremor run through his body. When she placed her hand on his arm he stiffened as if in fear. Nefirie stroked his warm skin. He was alive—now it was up to her to heal him.

Elessa hurried towards the cart, her heart filled with hope. Hope that died when she saw Jason stagger unsteadily to his feet and walk away, leaning heavily on his mother. Nefirie was the colour of day-old curd, her usual composure ripped off her. When Elessa tried to meet her eyes, Nefirie looked away, and something small and toothy twisted in Elessa's belly.

"Helle?" she asked Jason, as she crossed his path. He just pointed silently in the direction of the cart.

Elessa cried at the sight of the girl. She called for a litter and helped lift her from the soiled straw. She raged when she saw the mangled, ruined feet, raged even more when Nefirie shook her head at Elessa's plea to come and look, help her heal their Helle. But mostly she wept at the dead and empty look in Jason's face as his gaze followed the litter to the door.

Chapter 25

It was a crushing dream, a dream that had her protesting that no, she didn't want to... please, don't show me this. All she wanted was to die, her heart shattered as she rode along the heaving sea, the plunging mountains to her left. He had spurned and shunned her, looking at her with contemptuous hate. She was numb, wrapped in a cloud of despair so deep she could barely breathe.

Helle woke up, silent tears streaming down her face as the vague and painful dream hardened into memory. And so, unwillingly, Helle recalled how she came to die in that long ago first life, sitting for a very long time with her knees drawn up to her chin as she stared unseeing at the wall.

She was tongue-tied all morning, side-stepping his every attempt to touch her. Jason kept on throwing her concerned looks, dark brows pulled down over eyes that were predominantly golden in the bright light of the December morning. The hotel restaurant was almost empty when they entered, but there was a promising smell of food, and the room bathed in sunlight, the large windows to the south offering a magnificent view of the Thracian Sea looking towards the distant island of Samothraki.

Helle poured herself some tea and added a largish dollop of honey. She kept her eyes on the cup as she stirred, all too aware of the weight of his gaze.

"What's the matter?" he asked, neatly decapitating his egg. She considered what to say—or if to say it—but she was drowning in vague recriminations. She needed to know.

"Last night I had a dream," she said, looking at Jason over her mug. He stilled, lashes coming down to shield his eyes. "And when I woke, I remembered." Jason paled slightly under her scrutiny, but otherwise remained immobile, waiting.

"You never listened to my side of the story, did you?" she said, feeling the bile rise. Jason flinched and in the look he gave her, she saw panic. Helle set down the cup, studying its plain decoration with an interest it didn't merit.

"Not once did you try and talk to me, convinced as you were that I'd been faithless. You took his word over mine. His, Jason!" She struggled to keep calm. It wasn't really important, she tried to tell herself, not now, not anymore. But it was tearing holes in her heart and filling her mouth with the acrid taste of humiliation. "All those times when I stumbled in your direction, just to see you turn away…" Helle's voice tailed off as she saw, replayed in her head, his eyes passing quickly over her, the curtest of nods as he deftly sidestepped her and went to join other women instead.

"I'd sit across the hall from you and see you fondle other girls, hear you laugh with them. You'd once said you loved me, but now you avoided me, and the pain you caused me was worse than anything Samion had done to me." Her breath caught. "I survived eight months in hell believing you loved me. And now that you no longer did, I wished he'd killed me, allowing me to die with my faith in you intact."

"Helle, I…" Jason tried to take her hand but she snatched it away.

Jason groaned and hid his face in his hands. "Helle, let me explain."

She stood up. "You had no idea what I went through!" she yelled, throwing her cup so that it shattered at his feet. "And you never bothered to ask."

Jason rose to put his arm around her, but Helle shoved him away.

"You killed me," she spat, "almost as surely as if you'd driven the dagger in yourself."

Once again, he tried to embrace her. She swung at him, her fist connecting with his mouth. She winced when his lip burst open, ashamed of herself for hurting him, but wanting to hit him again and again. So instead she wheeled, threw the door open and ran. Who cared that she was only in jeans and a t-shirt, who cared that her feet were bare—she had to get away. He came rushing after her, calling her name, but she just ran, barging through the stand of cypresses that formed some sort of hedge. Her skin tore, but she didn't stop. He had betrayed her. She'd thought he loved her but he had crushed her.

She ran until everything was quiet inside her, until she no longer could hear him call her name. Helle had no idea where she was, and the wind coming from the sea was bitterly cold. People were staring at her, nudging at each other as they pointed at her bare feet, her swollen face. She ignored them. Her heart felt as if it was bleeding with pain and all she could see was the way his eyes had widened when she punched him. What a fucking mess… Helle sank down on the sea wall.

She was halfway back to the hotel when she saw him, standing very alone on one of the stone piers that protected the harbour. The wind ruffled his hair, his eyes on the white-capped sea. A lonely man facing the world, shoulders bowed. It made Helle's heart lurch, her anger dissipating. He'd paid a steep price for the mistakes he'd made in that distant life, when he was not much more than a boy himself.

"Jason?" she slipped her arms around his waist. He closed his eyes. His thick lashes glistened with tears, his Adam's apple bobbing up and down. As underdressed as she was, he was chilled to the bone, and she wondered how long he'd been standing like this, buffeted by the wind.

He cleared his throat. "We'll come down with the mother of all colds if we don't get back." Without waiting for her answer, he moved off, keeping his distance as they walked back to the apartment. He limped slightly.

"Did you hurt yourself?"

He shrugged, indifferent.

He stepped aside to allow her to precede him up the stairs, handed her the room key and leaned against the wall, watching her fumble with the lock. Once inside, he slid down to sit on the floor, staring vacantly into space. Helle opted to do the same, their hands almost touching. Not quite, though.

"For eight months Samion kept me locked up in a hole,"

he said abruptly. "Eight months in darkness, fettered like a beast. Eight months with only myself as company, eight months where I slowly lost my mind. Every night, he came to visit, in the beginning to taunt me, whip me, but as time passed, to twist a far more cunning knife, shredding me to pieces without shedding one single drop of my precious Wanderer blood." He made a gagging sound.

"Sometimes I pretended to be asleep but he just kicked me awake, ignoring my gasps of pain, and then smiled pleasantly as he enquired how I was, settling himself on a stool beside me. And then he would begin to talk. He told me details of his life with you, of how pleasing it was to bed you, now that you were biddable. He would smile and tell me he couldn't stay too long, because you were waiting for him—eager for his kisses, for his touch."

Vague images of hard hands, menacing words crowded Helle's head. A never-ending violation, months in which her whole life shrank to one room and one bed. His bed.

Jason drew a long, ragged breath. "He described your breasts, the freckles dusting your back, the way your toes would curl and your breath would catch. Things a lover knows. He'd chuckle when he commented on how ticklish you were. He revelled in sharing the discoveries he had made—the birthmark on your left thigh, how you bit your nails when no one saw. He painted a picture of you as his willing, welcoming mate."

"I never was." She hooked her little finger into his. Jason nodded, no more.

"I know that now. But back then…For months, he recounted details of an intimate relationship. For six of those months, he described how your body changed as his seed grew in you. You loved that child, he'd say in that soft, unctuous voice of his. You had forgotten me.

"I saw you once in all those months. Once as you sat in the sun, a smile on your face as you held your hands on your swelling womb. It nearly killed me. I hated him, but God help me, I hated you too. I thought you'd rather die than have him near you and now apparently you were happily sharing his bed, night after night." He fell silent, resting his head against the wall.

"He won. He broke my heart by making me believe you had left me willingly, and then I broke yours, in revenge. All the way back to Kantor's court you lay delirious beside me in the cart, calling my name, and I refused to touch you, even to look at you. Had I been strong enough, I think I would have preferred to walk rather than to sit beside you."

Helle withdrew her finger, affected by the bitterness in his voice. He smiled sadly.

"I enjoyed it," he admitted huskily. "I'd see your eyes glue themselves to me, I saw how they widened when I flirted with other girls and I was glad. It was only fair that you should hurt like I did. But sometimes…" He choked. "…sometimes I'd watch you from a distance and wonder why he'd thrown you out, and I ached inside with the loss of you."

"You could have asked," she said, feeling a flare of anger.

Jason turned to look at her. "Yes. I should've asked, but I was so angry with you, and then there was the baby and I hated you, God how I hated you, for that." He leaned his head against hers, fumbling for her hand. "I'm so sorry, love. So very, very sorry." His eyes closed, her hand held hard in his. "When Elessa came to find me that morning, I swear I regretted it all, every single word, every cutting gesture. But it was too late. You were already on your way. Elessa said you'd ridden off to kill him, but…"

"That wasn't true. I was hoping to provoke him into killing me. It just hurt too much to keep on living, I couldn't take the pain anymore."

"Oh, God." He pulled her close in a one-armed hug, squishing her to his chest. Most uncomfortable, but Helle had no intention of moving. He pulled a twig or two out of her hair and then pushed her away, carefully inspecting her.

"You don't look too hot," he said, tracing a nasty cut on her right forearm.

"Look who's talking." Helle rubbed her thumb over a streak of dirt on his cheek.

"Shower?"

She nodded and got to her feet. "Yeah, a shower would be good—and a nap."

"He didn't win," she told him some time later. She was clean, she was warm, and he was lying beside her. He looked at her blearily, already half-asleep. "Don't you see? We're here, together. So he didn't win, did he?"

Jason's swollen mouth curved into a slight smile and he turned onto his side, drawing her close. "No, you're right. He didn't win, my lioness."

Helle stared up at the ceiling. "Did you ever find her? Our baby?"

Jason opened one eye. "No. I looked everywhere for her, but she was gone. The child was stolen from Samion's palace a few weeks after her birth. They said she'd been taken by the Wanderers, my people coming to claim back their own."

"Maybe she ended up with your mother," she whispered, hearing how much that sounded like a wish.

"Yes, maybe." He sounded unconvinced, but in her mind's eye Helle saw how a tall woman turned to smile at the little curly-haired redhead tagging at her feet.

"She had my curls," she said out loud. "My curls and your eyes." The child in her head turned, staring back through time at Helle, her golden eyes wide and calm.

She had finally found the strength to get out of bed. She tottered over to the window and studied the busy courtyard, looking for him.

"Where's Jason?"

Elessa looked uncomfortable and concentrated on folding the linen towels in front of her.

"I think he's out hunting," she replied.

"Nana? Why hasn't he been here? Has father forbidden him to see me?" Yes, that was it, she thought with leaping hope. Kantor had barred access to her room, and as soon as Jason heard she was better, he would come. Elessa sighed and put away the linen.

"No, child, he hasn't. We have both made it clear he was welcome to sit by your side."

"But then…" Helle turned away "why isn't he here?" Her shoulders slumped and she wrapped her arms around herself.

"Give him time. He has his own nightmares to lay to rest." Elessa patted Helle's shoulder and moved towards the door. "If you're

up to it, I can ask one of the guards to carry you to the courtyard. It might be good to get some colour in those cheeks."

It was nice to be out in the sun again. Helle sat back on the bench, resting her shoulders against the sun-warmed wall. She closed her eyes, inhaling all the familiar scents; lavender, sage and rosemary, the salty tang of the drying seaweed and the rotting sweetness of the grapes dotting the ground under the vines. It was good to be home. Now she just needed to regain her strength, so that she could go and find her daughter.

There was a commotion at the gate. The hunters were coming back. She tried to stand, but the pain in her feet made it impossible. So she sat, and her stomach came alive with butterflies when she saw him riding straight and proud among the others. A little gaunter, a little paler, but still her Jason.

He rode through the gate and she raised her hand in greeting. He saw her, a flash of something she couldn't identify in his eyes. Saw her and turned away, ignoring her. She didn't know what to do, stuck as she was on the bench. This close, she could see how ravaged he looked, deep grooves etched in his face. Her heart went out to him. What had Samion done to him? If it hadn't been for his tribe, he would've been dead. And if it hadn't been for her acquiescence, he would've been maimed... No, she mustn't think about it. She must forget it, all of it.

Jason was crossing the courtyard, his trajectory forcing him to pass by her bench. She smiled as he came closer, wanting nothing more than to rise and dance towards him. His eyes bore down on her, his mouth hard and grim. He nodded shortly and walked by, ignoring her pleading eyes and wavering smile. She didn't understand.

Once he was safely away from her, Jason moved over to the doorway, studying her as she sat on the bench. He could see that she was weeping, her arms wound tight around her midriff, as always when she was in distress. It shredded his heart, but he shut out the pain. She didn't deserve his love. But he couldn't tear away his eyes, noting how thin she was, how wan. After a while she stood, and it knifed him in the gut to see how carefully she walked. She could scarcely balance, every step an effort.

Kantor came to stand beside him, frowning at the sight of his daughter stumbling gracelessly towards the women's quarters.

"Her feet will never heal," he said gruffly. "May he be cursed forever."

Jason straightened his face, not wanting Kantor to see how difficult it was not to run to her, take her into his arms.

"Really? A side effect of childbirth?" he asked neutrally.

"Of course not," Kantor replied, scowling. "He had the soles of her feet whipped. Elessa says it's a miracle she manages to stand at all."

Jason swallowed, recalling her screams. But it had happened before she turned false. Before she welcomed Samion to her bed, eating his sweetmeats as her belly swelled. He turned away, looking for something to distract him.

Days became weeks, and from a distance he watched her slowly regain her strength. She would never be what she once had been, could no longer walk as she had once done, her former graceful stride reduced to a painful hobble that left her gasping for breath. It made his stomach turn, and he cried inside at her stumbling progress, cursing the man who had stolen her grace forever. Then he'd remember the child and curse her instead.

She tried to place herself so that he wouldn't be able to avoid her, and yet he always did, sidestepping her with the curtest of nods, as if she was nothing but a mere acquaintance. Her gaze followed him around the hall, she saw him flirt with other women, play with their tresses, and she didn't understand.

At night, she wept herself to sleep, her heart breaking as she thought of him, of him and their daughter. In her dreams, all was well again: they laughed and ran together as they had done since childhood. To wake up to her changed life was torture. She would never run again, her mangled feet would never heal. And he no longer loved her, and she didn't know how to bear it.

At night, he muffled his sobs in his pillow. In his dreams, all was well again, he would hold her in his arms and she would blush beneath his eyes. To wake up was hell. She had given herself to another and he didn't know how to bear it.

Finally, one night she cornered him. "I have to talk to you," she said hoarsely. "Please," she added placing her hand on his sleeve. Her turquoise-flecked eyes glittered in the torchlight. Jason shrugged and avoided eye contact, following her into a corner of the hall, where he leaned back against the wall, crossing his arms across his chest. He couldn't quite suppress the tremor that ran through him at the sight of her, so bleached of life.

"Well?" he said, shaking off the twinge of pity.

"You're leaving," she said.

He nodded. He couldn't stand it here at Kantor's court. Not anymore. He'd go west beyond the port of Trabzon, putting as many miles as possible between him and her.

"And you haven't told me why. Don't I deserve an explanation? What have I done to be treated this way?" For an instant, her eyes flashed. "Please explain to me, because I don't understand. We were to be wed and now I'm air to you. You seem to blame me, not that accursed Samion, and I…" Her voice broke, her teeth sinking into her wobbling lip. He was overwhelmed by a desire to pull her close and comfort her. But he didn't. He just looked at her, maintaining a mask of utter boredom.

"Jason, he took our child." She reached for him, her hand coming to a trembling halt midway to his arm. "He has our child in his keeping!"

Jason remained still, his eyes half closed as he squashed the flare of hope her words had kindled. She lied, she was faithless, he reminded himself. A whore—Samion's whore.

"Our child?" he lifted an eyebrow. "You must mean your child. Yours and Samion's," he snarled as his composure fell away. "After all, you seem to have found his bed most enjoyable."

Helle gasped. "Enjoyable? How can you say that? Don't you know me better than that?"

Jason looked at her disdainfully. Let her suffer like he had. "I thought I did. But then I didn't take you for a whore either, did I?" He sneered at her, ignoring the absolute shock on her face. Her hand dealt him a crushing blow across the nose.

"A whore? Is that what he told you? And you believe him—without even talking to me?"

Jason ran his hand over his tender face. "The facts speak for themselves, I think. And I don't share my woman with other men." With that he turned and left. Behind him, he heard her groan his name, a sound so filled with pain his eyes stung. Jason increased his pace.

The next morning, Jason woke to hands on his arms, shaking him roughly.

"She's gone," Elessa said.

Jason looked up at Elessa, bleary-eyed. "Who?" he asked, even though he knew immediately.

"Helle's gone." Tears were running down Elessa's cheeks. "So help me, I think she rides to her death."

Jason sat up. "Why would she do that?" he said, ignoring the pitching feeling inside his gut.

"Why?" Elessa scowled. "You ask why? Haven't you seen her following you around like a whipped cur?" Jason squirmed under her gaze. "Of course you have, and you've made sure she's seen you court other girls, laugh with them, fondle them, haven't you?"

Jason stood up, looking for his tunic. "And why shouldn't I? Isn't that what she did with Samion?"

Elessa stared at him and he quailed at the expression in her eyes. "Are you out of your mind? Have you talked to her? Heard her version?"

"I don't need to. I was there, remember? Samion made sure I knew every detail."

"Samion?" Elessa croaked. "And you believed him?"

Jason shrugged his tunic over his head. "She took him to bed, he got her with child. What else is there to know?"

Elessa laughed, a strange cackling sound, devoid of any amusement. "She was raped, Jason. Night after night, he raped her. He forced her to his bed and subjected her to everything he wanted."

Jason covered his ears. "No! Samion told me—" He sank back down onto his bed, his legs trembling too much for him to stand. What had he done? Oh, dearest Mother, what had he done?

"Samion lied!" she hissed. "He made a deal with her—her body for yours."

No. He tried to shut out Elessa's voice. No, it wasn't true, Helle had betrayed him!

"As long as she obeyed, you were left undamaged," Elessa continued. "So she did what she had to do, because to her it was so simple—she had to keep you safe and whole."

Jason cringed, shame burning through his body. Deep down, he had known, but he had chosen to listen to that poisonous voice instead of trusting his heart.

Elessa straightened up. "You may still be able to save her, but you have to hurry. She'll be riding towards Lizard's ford, making for his palace beyond." She threw something at his feet. "A parting gift, I believe." Her voice broke. "Bring her back, Jason." She ran from the room.

Jason picked up the thing she had thrown and felt his heart break cleanly in two.

It was her braid. And his ribbon.

Chapter 26

They arrived in Athens late in the evening two days later. It had been an uneventful journey—relaxed, even, once Jason got hold of Nigel who informed them Woolf was back in England.

He said something more as well, causing Jason to scowl at the phone.

"Did you hear me?" Nigel must have been yelling, given that even Helle could hear him.

"Yes, I did…yes, yes, you made your point." If anything, Jason's scowl deepened, brows pulled into a formidable line of anger. "Fine…I said fine, didn't I?…Oh, for God's sake, don't be such a twat, Nigel!…Yes! I heard you!…Damn!" He disconnected, staring stonily straight ahead.

"What?" Helle asked.

"He's just being difficult. Suddenly, the stupid man has developed a conscience."

"Ah." She steered the car carefully down the narrow road. "I'm guessing this is about Woolf."

"Yes." Jason scowled again. "He's concerned about invading Woolf's privacy."

"He has a point."

"A point? And what do you think Mr Sam Woolf is doing?" Jason held up his phone. "How do you think he found out we were in Turkey?"

"Called Angela and pretended he was a prospective client?" He just looked at her.

"Yeah," Helle muttered, "you're probably right."

"I've never been to Athens," Helle said once they reached the hotel. "Very picturesque."

"Sarcasm doesn't suit you." Jason signed the register and thanked the clerk.

"I'm just saying. We could have booked into something in

282

the city, not out here by the airport." She pouted, which only made him raise his brows.

The room was functional. No nice four-poster, no elegantly folded towels, no complimentary bathrobes.

"Maybe we shouldn't go home," Helle said, sitting cross-legged on her bed. "We could do a Jason Bourne or something and just drop off the grid."

He gave her a humourless smile. "That only works in the movies. Besides, I'm not going to let him dictate my life." He pummelled the pillow into shape.

"He already is," she snapped, regretting her tone immediately. These last few days she'd been walking about with her teeth gritted, always on edge, always with a wad of tears in her throat. Probably PMS, she reflected, but deep down she knew better. It all had to do with that dream.

She didn't fully understand what it was she'd remembered. Her brain was unwilling to release more than fragments; months in a small room, hands that held her down, night after night without Jason by her side. At times, the far more recent memories of Woolf, his body looming over her, superimposed themselves on those older, vaguer recollections, and she'd wake up feeling borderline schizophrenic, torn between her real self and that ancient Helle. And there was something else… a niggling feeling of loss, of something warm being wrenched from her arms. Her baby, a snuffling little life stolen from her the moment it was born.

With an irritated exclamation, Helle sat up. Yet another sleepless night, courtesy of her overactive brain. It was close to five in the morning, and the room was draped in darkness. Jason slept sprawled on his back, both arms thrown over his head, the hands softly curled. She sat beside him, arms wrapped around her knees, watching him sleep as she could not.

In the space of eight weeks, this man had gone from being a stranger to being a fundamental part of her existence. She craved him, every single one of her cells demanding his touch, his warmth, his smell. Like an addiction, leaving her less herself than she was before.

She was swamped with fear and resentment. Her life was being shredded to pieces, shrinking to revolve around Jason and their own personal pain in the butt, Sam Woolf. Helle sighed. She didn't want to be the heroine of a far-flung, time-spanning adventure best fit for a Hollywood fantasy, or have her fate tied down without any choice in the matter. She wanted to be normal Helle, with no strange baggage in the form of previous lives and vindictive jilted suitors.

She had no idea how long he'd been watching her, analysing every flickering emotion that crossed her face, but suddenly she was aware of his eyes on her.

"Hi," she said. "Sleep well?" He nodded but went back to studying her with undiminished intensity.

"What are you thinking?" he asked, running a hand up and down her bare leg.

She considered his question for a long time. His eyes never left her face.

"He took it all, didn't he?" she asked instead. "He took you, he took my baby and ultimately he took my life."

"Yes."

"And that's what he wants to do now as well, isn't it?"

Jason nodded and took her hand.

"I don't want this. I don't want to remember things from a long-gone existence, I don't want to live my life always looking over my shoulder, wondering if today is the day when he'll actually make good on his promise and kill someone I love." She expelled her breath, regarding him carefully. "I want a normal life. You know, dates, living together, fighting, breaking up, trying again… Not this overblown, intense existence." She squeezed his fingers, but his hand lay unresponsive in hers. "I want my life back. I want to be normal again. But it's too late, isn't it?"

He didn't reply for a long time. Finally, he cleared his throat. "I'll leave if you want me to," he said, his voice expressionless. "If that's what you want, I'll walk out of your life today." He pulled his hand free and turned his face towards the wall. "I'll take care of Woolf first, of course."

"Idiot." Helle trailed her fingers over his broad shoulders

and down his spine. "I don't want that. There's no purpose to me without you, not anymore." She nudged him, hard, waiting until he'd turned so that she could see his face. "You live in my heart, you dance in my blood. I want to fall asleep in your arms and wake beneath your eyes for all the remaining days of my life."

The scary thing was that she actually meant it. Her rational brain made disgusted gagging noises, muttering something about unhealthy dependencies, but she didn't care. Jason raised the back of his hand to her cheek and smiled, a slow, wide smile that lit his face from within.

Thankfully, Helle's phone rang before it all got impossibly mushy and emotional.

"Hi Mum," she said, trying to sound upbeat. "How are you? And why are you calling me at this hour? It must be like midnight over there."

"Where are you?" Mum asked, cutting her off. "I've been trying to call you for days."

"I forgot to charge my phone."

"Right. And I have little angel wings hidden under my shirt. You never forget to charge your phone!"

"I do when I've forgotten an adaptor plug." Helle congratulated herself on her quick save. It wasn't exactly an option to tell her mother they'd switched off their phones a couple of days to lead the big bad wolf astray.

"You're abroad?"

"I'm on a business trip." Helle felt no need to explain further.

"You are?" Mum sounded sceptical. "Why do I get the impression you're not telling me the whole story here?"

"Because you suffer from work-related damage, in your case excessive curiosity due to far too many years as an accountant."

"CFO, darling."

"Whatever."

"I'm still not convinced," her mother said, reverting to her no-nonsense voice. "Something is going on with you." Too right. Helle swallowed the urgent need to tell her everything.

"Yup, I'm helping Jason with an acquisition." A minor component in the last few days, but still.

"Jason, huh?" Mum sounded mildly disapproving. "So he is still your boss as well as your boyfriend?"

"Mostly my boyfriend." Helle slid over to the edge of the bed, turning her back on Jason.

"How serious is this?"

"Very." Helle lowered her voice. "The real deal."

"Huh." Mum's attempt to sound stern was ruined by the laughter in her voice. "Don't do anything rash."

"I never do." She smiled when Jason slipped his arms round her waist, his warmth surrounding her.

"No, you're too much like your father that way."

"Mum!"

Miriam laughed. "Listen, I have to run. Tell Jason hi, okay?"

"So I'm the real deal, am I?" Warm lips on her ear, on her neck. Helle tilted her head to the side to give him better access.

"Yup."

"How real?" His hands moved upwards to cup her breasts.

"Very." She turned to face him and he pounced, kissing her until dark spots rose before her eyes, leaving her dizzy and laughing.

They fell backwards onto the bed, she on top, and she was still laughing. She stopped laughing when he took hold of her hips and lifted her so that she straddled him, groin against groin. He was already hard, his hips arching demandingly. "I want you," he said, eyes glowing with an inner fire. "Now."

She rose to allow him entry, gasped when he gripped her and surged into her, impaling her on his erection.

"Ah!" It was almost too much, this sensation of being filled to the brim. He lifted his hips, and all of him was buried in her, his hands holding her still.

"I like this," he said. "You, tight and warm around me." He moved ever so slightly, nudging at her core. She wanted to move, ride him, but he wouldn't let her, setting a slow pace that had her groaning out loud. He sat up, wrapping his arms round her. "I like this too," he said, flipping them over, and he sent stroke after stroke reverberating through her. He lifted her right leg to rest against his shoulder, making it impossible for her to reciprocate his thrusts, and when he leaned forward she was locked in place by her limb and his weight, the look in his eyes burning little holes through her heart.

He remained inside of her, moving slowly as he fondled her, warm fingers circling her clit, the point at which they were joined.

"Taste yourself," he said, sticking his wet finger in her mouth. She sucked, hard, and he responded by flexing his hips, just as hard. It made her gasp. His fingers were back, teasing, touching. Her insides contracted in response. Close, so damn close!

"Not until I say so."

"But I need to—"

"I know. But not yet." He eased her leg down, pinning her to the bed with his weight. A series of soft kisses on her eyes, her mouth, and she took a firm grip of his head and shoved her tongue in his mouth, lifting her hips demandingly. Enough, already!

He took over the kiss. Lips sliding over hers, a tongue that thrust hard, and moments later she was clinging to him with everything she had as he drove into her, fast and furious.

"Not yet, not yet, not yet," he repeated like a mantra, eyes locked on hers. It was devastatingly erotic, to fight the urge to climax, to hold it back until he told her to let go. He slipped a hand in under her, lifted her that much closer. Damp flesh slapped into damp flesh, tremors flew up and down her legs, and still she didn't come, her body howling in frustration.

"Now!" he commanded, and with a hoarse shout she exploded, digging her fingers into his shoulders as he came, groaning her name.

Jason flopped over to lie beside her.

"Wow." Helle barely recognised her own voice, all dark and gravelly.

"Indeed." He took hold of her hand and raised it to his mouth, kissing it gently. "Marry me."

What? Helle blinked. "Now?" Shit, Mum would have an apoplectic fit.

"No." He smiled at her. "I want us to have a real wedding."

He rose on his elbow. "But I'd like you to wear my ring." He toyed with her hair. "Say yes, Helle."

"Okay," she squeaked, and in a fluid movement he lifted himself off the bed, returning some moments later with a little box.

"Seriously?" She held it gingerly. "Am I that predictable?"

"Maybe it's me being spontaneous." He poked at the box. "Open it."

A ring nestled inside, a wide band of white gold studded with miniature diamonds that glittered in the light. And right in the centre was a blood-red stone, frozen fire trapped in rock.

"So that whenever you see it, you think of me," he said, slipping the ring onto her finger.

"I think that's how things generally work," she replied, turning her hand this way and that. "It's in bad taste to think of someone else than your fiancé when looking at his ring."

"I should bloody well hope so," he said.

Chapter 27

They'd argued about Woolf on the flight home, with Helle insisting they had to go to the police, while Jason just as adamantly refused, repeating over and over that there was nothing the police could do.

"Once we involve them, we're hamstrung. The law has a nasty habit of insisting we play by the rules."

"So then what?" Helle wasn't sure she wanted to hear the answer—besides, she already knew the answer.

"We handle this ourselves." He gave her a dark look. "Maybe we can get him deported or something."

"Fat chance. He's a British citizen."

"So we take a page out of his own book." Jason pursed his mouth. "An impromptu audit from the taxman could help."

"The taxman? Woolf & Partners is squeaky clean—he's made sure of that."

"Probably." Jason shifted on his seat. "But Woolf & Partners is only the tip of Woolf's business empire—and the rest of it is safely hidden out of sight."

"What, like some sort of mobster?"

"Something like that." Jason shook his head at the offered coffee refill, giving the stewardess a distracted smile. "He owns clubs, restaurants, hotels—and supplies the additional extras his more discerning guests may require."

"Extras?"

"Girls, boys, drugs—you name it. He's good though, ensuring the legit side of the business is kept squeaky clean."

"Well then," Helle sighed. "Back to zero, huh?"

"Not necessarily." Jason's eyes acquired an icy sheen. "It's just a matter of presenting the authorities with a number of coincidences." He looked quite smug when he leaned back in his seat. "And I know exactly how to push it."

Helle thought about that for a moment. "Smith."

Jason gave her an exasperated look. "Smith? Absolutely not, I don't trust him. He's got Woolf among his contacts."

"And you know that how?"

Jason shrugged. "I just do. That's what happens when you leave your phone lying about."

"Of course," she muttered. "So who?"

"Curtis." Jason stretched, the cable knit he was wearing riding up to offer a glimpse of his tight abs. "He has contacts all over Scotland Yard."

It was a better plan than the alternative, Helle thought some time later, bracing herself before the landing. If Jason's idea worked, they'd get Woolf off their backs without actually having to do anything to him, which sounded great. She might hate his guts, might be willing to use force to defend herself, but to kill him…well, that was a bit too much.

"What's to stop him from putting out a contract on us?" she asked, once they were off the plane. "Just because he's in jail—or deported, whatever—doesn't mean he's destitute and powerless, does it?"

"Samion?" Jason snorted. "As a last resort, maybe. But he wants to be in at the kill, see us suffer and beg."

"How nice." Her throat itched—on the inside. "So this whole tax thing, it's more of a delaying manoeuvre than a final solution, isn't it? Even if it sticks, he wouldn't be locked up for ever."

"No." He tightened his hold on her hand. "But it buys us time."

She didn't want to buy them time, some snatched years of happiness. She wanted an entire life—with him.

After a short stop at the office which turned into a long stop as Jason brought Steve up to speed on the acquisition, did his e-mails and generally reverted to being the director of Morris & Son, they went home, stopping along the way for groceries.

"She might be at work," Jason said when Helle dialled Alison's number again. Yet another thing they'd argued about:

Jason did not want her to use her own phone to call Alison, but Helle had ignored him, saying Woolf probably already had her number—he probably had some contact at BT he could intimidate into giving him whatever info he needed.

"True. But she hasn't texted me back." Helle made an irritated sound and stuffed the phone back into her pocket. It was drizzling outside, the overcast skies killing what little there was left of daylight. Less than ten days to Christmas, and so far, he hadn't raised the subject. Alison was scheduled to go back to the States in a week, Mum was headed to wherever it was Phil was whisking her off to, and it struck Helle that maybe Jason had plans too. After all, he did have an aunt, didn't he? Helle pulled a face. Just the thought of perfect Juliet brought her simmering insecurities to a boil.

"You're looking as if you accidentally bit into something very nasty," Jason teased.

"I was thinking about Christmas."

"That explains it." He smiled. "Don't you like Christmas?" he asked over his shoulder, lugging their carrier bags to the kitchen.

"It's just…" She broke off.

"I was thinking we could go down to Tor Cottage." His voice came from the pantry. "You, me and an open fire." His head popped back out. "Does that sound okay?"

"Sure." She grinned. "Open fire, hey? Do you have a bearskin too?"

"Sorry." He made an apologetic gesture. "But I have a very nice carpet."

He sent her off for a shower while he busied himself at the range. A large chicken, chillies and bunches of coriander looked promising, and by the time Helle came back down again, it smelled just as promising. The table had been set, there was an open bottle of wine on the counter, and Jason was in the living room, fiddling with one of his loudspeakers. She browsed through his Spotify lists, smiling when she found one titled *Dawn with Helle*.

"Too mushy," he protested when she selected the first track.

"Mushy is good." Even more so when he swept her into his

arms and danced her across the floor. "Very good," she added later, licking her lips. This man of hers was a wonderful kisser, and if it hadn't been for the way her stomach was grumbling with hunger, she wouldn't have minded remaining in his arms a good while longer.

She picked up her phone in passing and sent off yet another text to Alison. Still no reply.

"Shit, can she sulk or can she sulk?"

Jason shrugged. "Maybe she doesn't want to talk to you."

"Duh." She frowned down at the display. "She could at least reply to my texts."

Jason set down a plate loaded with food in front of her. "Eat. And if you want, we can go over there afterwards. You can always pretend you just came over because you needed clean underwear."

"Which I do, actually."

"You most definitely don't. I want you without, remember?"

His tone made her fidget, a sudden pool of warmth deep inside of her. Helle stuffed her mouth with chicken to stop herself from grinning goofily at him. Or jumping his bones. Later, she promised herself.

Jason would have preferred to stay at home. The drizzle had turned into heavy rain, and even with Tim driving the car he felt exposed outside the house, eyes darting this way and that as he tried to identify any potential threats. Somewhat illegally—and with the help of Will while they were in the office earlier—he had managed to ping Samion's phone and now and then he surreptitiously slid out his phone, studying the little blinking spot that told him Woolf was still at his office, information further verified by the feed from one of the security cameras in Woolf & Partners's offices.

He gritted his teeth as he considered his options regarding Samion: the best thing would be to kill him, but he knew from bitter experience that Samion was adept at defending himself, and gifted with uncanny prescience. The idea of exposing him, however, had merits, one of the principal ones being that it would bring Sam Woolf into the public eye. It would require a lot of complicated work, one enticing lure after the other leading the authorities towards Mr Woolf. Jason studied his hands, clenching them a couple of times. It would be best to kill him.

"She isn't at home," Jason said, peering out of the side window as Tim parked the SUV. "Unless she's asleep, of course." The windows facing the street were dark.

"At nine in the evening? I don't think so." Helle slid across the seat and followed him outside. "She's probably at work—those double shifts are lucrative, and maybe she feels she needs the money now." Something flitted over her face, mouth thinning into a line. "Well, now that we're here, I might as well pick up some of my stuff."

The moment they stepped into the stairwell, Jason's hackles rose. A faint line of light was visible under Mrs Simmons' door, her TV blaring loudly, but the lamp over the stairs didn't work, and the higher they got, the more oppressive the vibrations. He drew Helle to a halt, nostrils flaring as he tried to isolate the cause of his unease. Samion wasn't here—he knew that for a fact, yet the air still held a remnant of his ridiculously expensive eau de Cologne.

Helle was hanging onto his hand, squeezing so hard his fingers were beginning to go numb. She edged closer to the door, set a hand to it and pushed. It opened with a squeak. From somewhere in the dark interior came a responding whimper.

"Alison?" Helle remained in the doorway. Jason groped for the light switch, stepping back with a low exclamation when the overhead lamp came on.

"Oh, my God!" Helle was already rushing in the direction of Alison, sitting on the floor behind the overturned sofa. The table had been reduced to matchwood, the cushions had been torn apart, spilling white downy feathers over a room that looked as if it had been struck by a hurricane.

"Don't touch me!" Alison shrieked, and blood bubbled from her mouth. Helle came to an uncertain stop.

"Alison? Oh, honey!" She fell to her knees in front of her friend, but when she reached for her, Alison shied away.

"Don't touch me!" she said. "Don't! Don't, don't!" Huge

sobs tore through her, tears running down her bloated and bruised face.

"You need help." Jason approached slowly, making soothing sounds, but Alison kept on screaming, wordless sounds of fear that had Jason coming to a halt.

"This is your fault, you bastard!" Her voice rose in yet another shrill shriek. "Why couldn't you stay away from her? Why did you take what he wanted?"

Jason stilled, seeking Helle's eyes across the room.

"His fault?" Helle said. "This is Sam Woolf's fault, goddamn it!"

"You don't understand!" Alison's breath came in short gasps, one arm cradling the other. "He did this to me to punish you for your disobedience." Her mouth fell open in a wail. "He doesn't want me, he wants you. You!" She slumped against the wall.

"We have to get her to hospital," Jason said in a low voice. Helle gave him a brittle look, hands shaking wildly as she fumbled for her phone. "She will live, Helle." He put a hand on her shoulder, but she shrugged it off, eyes fixed on Alison.

"Look what he's done to her," she groaned. A patchwork of dark bruises covered what was visible of Alison's body, one eye was swollen shut, the cheekbone below looking flattened. Her nose was broken, there was an encrustation of snotty blood around her mouth, and bruises ringed her neck. Jason bit his lip. This is what he'd done to Helle all those years ago, the bastard, and while Jason doubted Helle remembered, Samion knew full well Jason did.

Helle finished her call to the emergency services. "They're coming," she said, crouching down beside Alison. "You have to press charges."

"No!" Alison coughed, her lips staining a bright red. She grabbed at Helle. "You mustn't say anything." Her one good eye locked on Jason. "If you do, I'll tell them he did it! It's his fault, Sam told me this is because of him, that he had to hurt me because you wouldn't listen. Damn Wanderer, stealing what isn't his!" She tried to spit at Jason.

He rocked back on his heels, disturbed by the venom in her

voice, a flare of anger rushing through him at her accusation. He'd warned her, hadn't he? As had Helle, and the stupid woman had just laughed at them, assuring them she was fully capable of handling Woolf. Fool! But she didn't deserve this, and Jason's hands closed into uncomfortably warm fists, warm enough that Helle frowned at him, gesturing at the miniature sparks that leaked from between his fingers. He took a deep breath, relaxed his hands.

"Don't be ridiculous," Helle said, but she wouldn't look at Jason, keeping her eyes on Alison. "Woolf needs to be stopped, before he does this to someone else."

"I don't care! Leave me alone, I won't say anything, no, I won't!" She grabbed at Helle. "He'll kill me if I do." Alison dragged herself up to sit. "Promise me you won't say anything."

Helle pursed her lips. "Fine," she finally said. A quick glance in his direction, sufficient for him to see the disgust on her face, before her focus reverted to Alison. Jason slowly got to his feet. She was closing him out.

When the ambulance arrived, Helle insisted on riding with Alison.

"I'll meet you at St Mary's," Jason said.

"You don't have to," Helle replied, still without looking at him. "This may take some time."

"Hey," he said, a hand on her elbow to steady her as she climbed in behind Alison. "Of course I'll be there." Helle just nodded. The door closed and the ambulance drove off.

Jason remained in the middle of the street. She was blaming him for this, just as much as Alison was. His chest constricted, every breath a painful effort.

"Sir?" Tim stood beside him. "Aren't we going with them?"

Jason cleared his throat. "Yes, we are." He slammed the car-door as he got in and pulled out the phone. On the screen, the blip that was Sam Woolf remained where it was, a mocking blinking light that made Jason suppress the urge to hurl the phone out the window.

He was half-asleep in the waiting room when Helle finally came out. It was close to five in the morning, and Helle looked rumpled and grey, her hair a messy tangle.

"How is she?"

"Fractured arm, broken ribs, ruptured cheekbone, concussion, two front teeth gone, stitches to her inner lip—and that's just the parts I understand." She threw herself down on a chair opposite his and hid her face in her hands.

"Jesus." Jason wanted to touch her—needed it, to somehow bridge the distance between them. But when he moved over to sit beside her, she stiffened, leaning ever so slightly away from him.

"I need a cup of coffee," she said, "preferably one with a disgusting amount of sugar in it."

"I'll get it for you."

"Thanks." She rested her head against the wall and closed her eyes.

When he got back with the mug, she wasn't there.

"Her friend needed her," the nurse said. She patted Jason on the arm. "Maybe you should go home."

No. He wasn't leaving without her. Ever.

Chapter 28

It was close to noon before Helle left Alison fast asleep in her bed. They'd had to cut off most of her hair on one side to stitch up one of the gashes, and she looked so frail without it, her pale face adorned with bruises and bandages resting against the nondescript white of the hospital linen.

She had hoped Jason would be gone. She'd even texted him, telling him it was okay if he left. Instead, he was still waiting, looking as tired and dishevelled as she felt. Helle stood for a moment in the doorway to the waiting room, trying to make sense of the conflicting feelings rushing through her. Damn it, but he was a complication! Unfair, she chided herself: it was Woolf who was the complication, not the man presently regarding her with a hesitant expression in his eyes, his cheeks shadowed by a day's worth of beard.

"How is she?"

"Sleeping." Helle yawned. "They've pumped her full of stuff, so she'll probably sleep the rest of the day." She scrubbed at her face. "I'm so tired." Her whole body ached, a consequence of all those hours huddled on the chair by Alison's bed.

"Let's go home." He stood. "We'll have to walk, or take a taxi. I sent Tim home." He held out her coat.

"I was thinking of going to a hotel." Her insides twisted at the look on his face. "Look, it's just..." She twirled the drawstring of her sweats round her finger. "I need time for myself. These last few days, it's all been too much." In less than a week, she'd confronted Woolf in Istanbul, remembered things she definitely didn't want to remember, engaged herself to her long-lost fated lover, and seen her best friend beaten to a pulp. No wonder she felt as if she was coming apart at the seams.

Without a word, he took hold of her arm, marching her

towards the exit. "Don't shut me out," he said once they were outside.

"I'm falling to pieces! My entire life has become impossible and I just...I need space." She backed away from him, hating how she hurt him by doing so.

"This is him winning." Jason said bitterly.

"No, this is me trying to survive," she replied. "If he did that to Alison, what would he do to you? How can I risk anything happening to you?"

"And what does that mean? That you'll walk out of my life because you fear for me?"

"I—"

He grabbed hold of her, shaking her hard. "Goddamn it, Helle! Don't you see that nothing he can do will hurt me even half as much as that? If you leave me…"

"I'm not leaving you! I just—"

"…need time to think," he filled in. "The most classic break-up statement in the world." He shoved his hands in his pockets and walked off. "Take whatever time you need," he said, without turning around. "Let's just hope I'm still around when you've finished thinking."

"Jason! What the fuck does that mean?" She grabbed hold of him.

"It means precisely what I said," he replied, shaking off her hand. "Do you honestly think Samion will stop coming after me just because you're not around?"

"He wants—" She couldn't finish.

"You," he said. "And me he wants dead."

"Don't say that."

"Why shouldn't I? It's the truth, isn't it?" He dragged his hand through his hair. "So, are you coming with me or not?" There was a silent entreaty in his eyes. Helle clasped her hands together, noting distractedly how the small diamonds in her ring glittered in the light, the red stone blazing.

"I just need time."

Without a word, he spun on his toes and left. She knew he wanted her to run after him, but she just couldn't find the energy to do so, her feet rooted to the spot. He was receding, that glorious hair of his deepening into a rich mahogany when a beam of sunlight touched it. What was she doing? There went her future, walking away from her with a set to his shoulders that had her screaming inside.

"Jason!" she yelled. "Wait, Jason—wait!"

He didn't stop, but he slowed his pace. She ran flat out to catch up with him and when she came abreast, he held out his hand. But he didn't look at her, striding along at a pace he must have known was uncomfortable for her.

"Say something."

"What do you want me to say?" He kept his gaze straight ahead. "Do you want me to admit just how vulnerable I am when it comes to you? Fall to my knees and beg you never to leave me, because if you do it's the equivalent of having my heart yanked out of me?" He tightened his hold on her hand, sending uncomfortable flares of heat up her arm. "You slash me wide open with all that stuff about needing to think, and then you want *me* to say something? Shouldn't you be the one saying something?"

"I tried to explain," she said. "All this stuff with Alison, with Woolf—it's too much. I can't even think straight, I'm so mentally exhausted."

"Of course you're tired—and scared, and angry, and whatever else you're feeling. But that's no excuse to run off. We're supposed to handle things together, you and I. At least that's what I assume this means." His fingers closed on her ring. "Two days ago, you accept my proposal for marriage, and then today you just want to take off on your own to *think*? Damn it, Helle, you're killing me!"

"I'm sorry," she mumbled. "I didn't mean—"

"You're taking me for granted," he cut in. "Somehow you're assuming that just because I've lived through endless existences looking for you, I will always be there."

"You said you loved me," she protested.

"Just because I'll always love you doesn't mean I'll always be there. I have pride too, you know."

"This isn't about pride!" She dragged him to a stop. "Look at me, Jason." He kept his face averted. "Damn it, look at me!" She yanked on his arm. Reluctantly, he turned to face her. She took a deep breath. "I love you, okay? Love you so much the thought of a life without you paralyses me."

"Welcome to the club," he muttered.

"But all this shit—it freaks me out, and I don't know how to cope."

"So we cope together." he said roughly. "Together."

"Together," she echoed. She chewed her lip, not quite knowing how to phrase the question she had uppermost in her mind, but knowing she had to ask it. "If we were to break up, you wouldn't do anything stupid, would you?"

"Break up?" He dropped her hand.

"Oh, for God's sake, Jason, don't be like that!" She shoved at him. "It's just that at times that freaks me out too, okay? The notion that you've been…umm…offing yourself in life after life." For her, for another opportunity to find her. She felt suffocated by this, the resulting responsibility for his life and happiness a burden that at times was way too heavy.

Jason exhaled, inhaled deeply, and did it all over again. "No, I wouldn't do something stupid, as you so quaintly phrase it. I would just give up, try to find some contentment before I die, for good. No more lives looking for you, no more endless heartbreak. This is it, and either it works or it doesn't." He gave her a bleak look. "I can't do this anymore."

Oh. She felt disappointed—at some level. At another, her heart was breaking for him. He didn't say anything, his eyes lost in the distance. Finally, he shook himself.

"Coming?" But he didn't take her hand—or say a word—as they walked home in the weak warmth of the December sun.

He studied her out of the corner of his eye. She looked tired, her mouth drooping at the corners, her shoulders slumped. Now and then, she'd kick at something on the ground, but mostly she trudged along beside him, as silent as he was.

"You're angry," she said when they turned up his street. Well-tended if bare shrubs hung over wrought iron fencing, house after house set some ten feet back from the street. Expensive vehicles lined the street, the majority of them black.

Most of the houses were white—as was his—but here and there someone had gone for a daring mild yellow or a startling red door. He opened his gate and allowed her to precede him before replying.

"Disappointed, rather." Not true. It filled him with anger—and fear—that she would prefer spending time on her own to mull things over than share them with him.

"With me?"

He didn't reply at first, digging for his keys. The locks clicked open smoothly, and he stepped inside, deactivating the alarm.

"With your reaction." He held out his hand for her coat. "You're playing into his hands."

"Well, I didn't, did I? I'm here, right?" She stomped off, locking herself in the toilet. He sighed and wandered off to the kitchen.

Some moments later, he was busy at the chopping board, shirt sleeves rolled up. He heard her come in, felt her presence behind him, but he was still too upset, so he pretended complete immersion in the task of slicing the tomatoes, his hand tightening on the handle of the knife. He was so mad at her—irrationally so, he realised—wanting to take her by the shoulders and shake her until she cried, punishing her for the fear that raged inside of him, that hollow ache she'd caused by saying she needed distance from him. From him! The knife slipped in his clenched hold, slicing through the tip of his finger. Blood welled, and Helle exclaimed, rushing for the paper towels.

"Here." She handed him the paper.

He nodded, no more.

"Want me to take over?" she asked, moving close enough for him to feel her warmth. He didn't reply, going back to his chopping. "Obviously not," she muttered. She remained where she was for a while longer, making the odd attempt at conversation. He wasn't interested, the meaner part of him enjoying her discomfort. Instead, he piled the tomatoes to the side, added handfuls of finely-chopped basil, garlic and onions, not once looking at her. Finally, she gave up.

"Fine, have it your way. I'll just go and be alone somewhere else, shall I?" She wrenched the door to the refrigerator open, rifled through the upper compartments until she found the dark chocolate. Jason frowned as she tore the wrapping, breaking off almost half.

"I was saving that for later."

"Tough. That's what you get when you treat me like air." She made a face. "The way you're acting, I'm thinking there's no point in me staying, is there?" She popped a piece of chocolate in her mouth and made for the door. "Oh, that's right," she said sarcastically, halfway there, "I forgot; we're supposed to do things together, confront things together." She threw the chocolate she was holding at him. "Not seeing much of that at present, you jerk."

He whirled, throwing the knife into the sink. "It was his fault! It was Samion who did that to Alison, but you were going to punish me, Helle. Me. Not him."

"I wasn't punishing anyone! I told you, I needed time to think." Her mouth wobbled. "Look what he did to her, Jason. What if he does that to Mum or my dad? Or his wife, Janine?" She looked away. "What if he punishes the people I love, one by one? What then?" She swallowed audibly. "You said you were vulnerable, but so am I, so are they. Even worse, they are bystanders, dragged into all this mess by me—by us."

"By him," he corrected harshly.

"Whatever." She studied her hands. "How can I risk them? It's different for you, you only have me, and I'm stuck in this mess."

That hurt. "I have Juliet," he said.

"Oh, yeah, your gorgeous aunt." She scowled at him. "Not the same as a mother or a father, is it?"

"Maybe not. But if anything were to happen to her—because of me—I would be devastated."

"You would?" There was a cool edge to her voice. He just looked at her. "Sorry," she mumbled. He shrugged. This wasn't about Juliet—or her family.

"So what do you want to do? Leave me? Go to him?"

She looked so horrified he almost smiled. "Go to him? Never!" She approached him hesitantly. "I'm not leaving you, Jason." She rested her head against his shoulder, but he made no move to embrace her, standing as still as a rock.

"Easy to say. What if he hurts someone else you love, what then?"

She flinched, rearing back to see his face. "I…" She licked her lips. "I don't know."

Jason nodded, slowly. "So that's how it is, is it? I'm to live with a fucking Damoclean sword over my head for the rest of my life?" He scrubbed at his face, feeling utterly exhausted. "Maybe you should go."

"I don't want to go!" She sounded on the verge of tears. "Damn it, Jason, what do you want from me? One moment you're telling me to stay, the next you're more or less pushing me away."

"I want your commitment!" he yelled. "I want that ring on your finger to mean something."

"It does—you know it does. But when you ask me what I'll feel if he hurts someone I love—"

"I know what you'll feel. You'll feel guilt and anger—a lot of that directed at me." He crossed his arms over his chest in an attempt to keep his heart from ripping apart.

"No. Never at you. At him, Jason." She sank down to sit on one of the chairs, her back rounded, her face hidden by her hair. "No matter what, I wouldn't leave you," she said quietly. "In fact, I don't think I could. There's simply no choice—not anymore." Helle raised her chin and met his eyes.

Jason relaxed his posture. "No choice, hey?"

She shrugged. "Nope."

"A bit like me then," he said, smiling lopsidedly. "Tethered by fate to my one and only love." A soft blush spread up her face at his words.

"Sounds so romantic, when you phrase it like that."

"This isn't about romance. This is about the sordid reality of love in all its gritty, painful glory."

"Sounds wonderful," she snorted.

He pulled her into his arms. "You and me, Helle."

"You and me." She stood on her toes and kissed his cheek.

"Forever." He didn't give her a chance to respond. His hands came up to frame her face, holding her still as he kissed her breathless. He lifted her to sit on the counter and leaned his forehead against hers, relishing her proximity, the way she smelled and felt under his hands. She pulled his head down and kissed him. Not in any way a gentle kiss: no, this was rough and desperate, teeth knocking against teeth, lips bruising each other.

He pulled at her sweats and underwear, yanking them down her legs. He pulled her towards him so that she teetered on the edge, rubbing his jeans-clad groin against her naked sex.

"Haven't you forgotten something?" she panted, kissing his face, his ears, his throat, her hands busy unbuttoning his shirt.

"I think I'd notice if they still were on." He popped the buttons of his fly open. And then he was inside her, her legs hooked round his hips, and it was too fast, too urgent, but it didn't really matter. The important thing was that she was here, her breath hot in his ear as she murmured his name, her hands clinging to his arms. He came within seconds, his hips jerking spasmodically. She wrapped her arms around him and held him close, and Jason buried his face in the crook of her neck. He could have stayed like this forever, his jeans and boxers shoved halfway down his legs.

With a little grunt he pulled out. "Shower?"

"Bath. A long one, I think."

An hour or so later, they were back in the kitchen, Helle watching as he assembled his bruschettas. He heaped the fried bread with tomatoes and basil, drizzled some more olive oil on top and handed her the bottle of Chianti.

"I'm going to tell Mum," Helle said between bites.

"Tell her what?"

"Everything." She gave him a belligerent look. "I have to, okay? If I don't tell her and something happens to her, it'll kill me."

Jason studied his food. "Fine."

"You don't like it."

"Of course I don't. Somehow, I don't think she's going to be too thrilled with her future son-in-law, do you?"

Helle tapped her knife against his plate. "That's my decision, not hers." She nudged at his unfinished bruschetta. "You don't want it?" At his little head shake, she switched plates.

He sat back, nursing his wineglass. He yawned. Close to 36 hours awake were beginning to take their toll. Terrible hours, most of them, but at least Alison was doing as well as could be expected, this gleaned from Helle's hushed phone conversation with the hospital. A detailed image of Alison, sitting huddled in the corner of the destroyed living room, flashed through his mind. It could have been Helle, it could have been his woman, lying battered and bloodied. The stem of his wine glass snapped, spilling wine all over the table.

"Shit!" He leapt to his feet.

"You okay?" She was already dabbing at the mess.

"Yes." He carried the broken glass over to the sink. "Leave it, lioness. Let's just go to bed before I fall asleep on my feet."

"Sounds like a great idea."

He fell asleep with her head on his shoulder, his thumb held firmly in her hand. His last conscious thought was of her, of a young woman dancing with joy as the Black Sea beyond her caught fire in the light of the setting sun.

He found her thrown in a ditch, her garments stained by something dark and warm.

"You came," she said, and her broken mouth widened into a smile. A thin tendril of blood slid down the side of her mouth. He kissed her and smiled back, trying to convey with his eyes all the feelings rushing through him.

"Yes, I came. I've been such a cruel fool," his voice broke. "I—"

"Shhh, there's no time for all that." She lifted her hand to his face. "It's all forgiven."

She bit back on a cry when he lifted her, fingers sinking into his arm. He cradled her to his chest, and under his hand he could feel her heart, hammering against her ribcage. Her breath came in short gasps, a whistling sound accompanying each exhalation.

"I'm so sorry that I'll never lie with you again." She raised her hand to his cheek, her eyes filming. "I'll never feel your heart beat in time with mine again, never give you the sons we were destined to have."

"Helle." He kissed her cold fingers. "My Helle." A sob tore at his throat.

"Don't cry." She smiled—a dazzling smile, for all that her teeth were rimmed with blood, as were her lips. "I love you. I have since the day I first laid eyes on you." She inhaled, a loud wheezing sound, and pressed her hand to her side. "It hurts."

"Once I get you home, Nefirie can heal you, she'll—" Do what? He had seen wounds such as hers before, knew a punctured lung was impossible to repair.

She closed her eyes. "The damage goes too deep." She turned her face to the side. "It's not fair. I'm not ready to die."

He cradled her even closer, willing her to stay with him.

She coughed, blood staining her lips. "Find our daughter. Promise me you'll find her."

He nodded, rendered speechless by his tears. Her eyes closed, her breaths shallow efforts that grew successively weaker.

"Jason? Are you there?" Her voice was almost inaudible. He pressed his lips to her forehead.

"Yes, my love, I'm here."

"I'm frightened," she said. "It hurts, and I'm so cold." He hushed her, wrapping his cloak tighter around her. "Give me your hand" she said, widening her fingers to braid them with his and guiding them to her chest. "This is yours," she said, so softly he could barely hear her, "forever."

He lifted their joined hands to his chest. "And this is yours," he said hoarsely. She smiled once, and then her head fell back, mouth agape. She was gone.

He carried her back in his arms. Up the last incline, people came running, falling silent when they saw his burden. He tried to say something, enunciate her name at least, but there were no words, nothing but the heavy despair that made each breath an effort, each step an act of faith.

They were waiting in the courtyard. Elessa and Kantor, Nefirie standing to the side. He couldn't meet their eyes. Somehow, he slid off the horse. His knees folded and he sank down, still with his Helle in his arms. Jason pressed his lips to her temple, arms cramping round her. He just couldn't let her go, and Kantor had to wrest her from him, persuading him in a soft voice to let her go, to deliver Helle into her father's arms.

His life had ended and he moved through the motions of the everyday in a trance, his heart and mind in a dark, haunted place. He chopped off his hair, as she had done, and shunned them all, because each and every one of them reminded him of her, of his beautiful vibrant Helle who now lay dead. Dead because of him. The guilt drove stakes through him, pain twisting through his guts when he remembered his cruel words, his final rejection of her. If only he had listened to her! If!

His life shrank to a sequence of endless days to which there was no purpose—not now, not when she was gone.

He was sitting by the waterfall when Kantor came to find him. Jason struggled to rise at his approach, but Kantor gestured for him to remain sitting, lowering himself carefully to the ground beside him.

"She wouldn't have wanted this for you," Kantor said. "She wouldn't want you to live as if you're dead."

Jason shook his head, unable to reply.

"Jason," Kantor's voice was full of pity. "Son, look at me." Jason reluctantly turned to face him. "She loved you, Jason, she loves you still. Remember that." Kantor opened his arms and pulled Jason close, stroking his short, ragged hair. Jason turned his face into Kantor's shoulder and wept, his fist clenching and unclenching round the tattered blue ribbon that was all he had left of her.

Chapter 29

They were on their way to the hospital when Nigel appeared at the door. Helle gave him an irritated look, muttering something about being in a hurry.

"This won't take long," Nigel said brusquely, "but we need to talk."

"We as in the three of us, or just you and Jason?" But she gave a resigned sigh when he insisted it affected both of them, slouching after him to the kitchen. She sat down, straightening her skirt. It was work mode today, with Jason in a dark blue power suit, his hair still wet from his recent shower. Helle adjusted her holdups, hiding a little smile. It had been a very nice shower, preceded by a long session in his little gym that went on to become something else entirely before he was done with her.

She was feeling happier today. Alison was recovering. After two days of competent care the swellings were going down, the normal Alison re-emerging bit by bit, even if her eyes retained that constant shadow of fear, her whole body starting whenever a shadow fell over her bed. To Helle's frustration, she remained adamant about not pushing charges and when Jason agreed with her, Helle decided to drop it, however much it set her teeth on edge that Sam Woolf would get away with it.

"Are you listening?" Nigel barked, recalling Helle to the present.

"Umm…" She lifted her shoulders. "I was thinking about Alison."

"Oh, right." He looked ashamed. "Better, I hear."

"Much," Jason replied. "But not everything heals." He regarded Nigel steadily. "I thought you wanted out of all this."

"Wanted out?" Nigel's voice rose, the bracelets on his arm jangled loudly as he waved his arms about. "I want to know what the fuck all this is about!" He threw a folder on the table, pictures spilling from it. "And don't tell me it's about business. This is far more personal."

Damn right it was. Helle slid one of the pictures towards her. It showed her, walking half-naked down the corridor between Jason's top floor bathroom and the bedroom.

"I came as soon as I realised someone had compromised your security network." Nigel looked grim, fiddling with the most recent addition to his necklaces, this one a leather thong decorated with a huge lapis lazuli eye. "He's even hacked the alarm system."

"What?" Jason half rose.

"Relax." Nigel waved him back down. "I've fixed it. I've fixed all of it—but I want to know why your so-called business competitor wants to spy on you. Or why he's hacked her phone." He jerked his thumb at Helle.

"He has?" Helle asked.

"He has." Nigel sucked in his lower lip, teeth worrying at the stud. "I can't go on doing this, Jason. Not without knowing why. I am breaking every law there is about privacy violations—as is he—and sooner or later, something will backfire."

Jason stacked the pictures into a neat little pile. "When did he do this?"

"Two nights ago according to the logs." Nigel shrugged. "He activated one of my alarms this morning. He could have walked right in here, and something is telling me it would be a bad, bad thing if he did." From his backpack, he produced another file, this one substantially bigger. "Mr Sam Woolf is not who you think he is."

"Oh," Jason said, "I am sure he is exactly what I think he is."

"He's fucking dangerous is what he is." Nigel shoved the folder at him. "People who disagree with him have a nasty tendency to disappear, for good. Look at this!"

Documents, photos, printouts of e-mails—they all spilled out on the table. Young girls stared up from photos, most of them smiling. The same young girls in other photos, lifeless. Boys, emaciated men, women in cheap clothing—all of them looking as if any hope they'd ever had had been beaten out of them.

"Where did you find this?" Jason asked.

"Does it matter? There's a dark and deep side to the internet—and that's where the truly ugly fishes come out to play and trade." Nigel's hands shook, a long digit touching one of the photos. "Behold Woolf's main commodity—and when they're no longer any use, they end up dead." He scrunched one of the photos together. "Slave labour, girls, drugs, boys—he deals in everything!"

Jason frowned down at one of the e-mails. "We already knew that. The question is how to stop him."

"You can't," Nigel said flatly. "The man must have a number of people in his pockets. This is too big for him to handle otherwise."

"We have to." Jason sounded grim.

"Look, I'm all for crucifying men like him—preferably publicly and with a nail or two through his balls—but you have to back off. A one-man crusade will fail." Nigel fiddled with his long thin braid, legs bouncing nervously.

"We have to try."

"We do?" Nigel's dark eyes bored into Jason, into Helle. "This isn't about his criminal activities, is it?" Helle ducked her head. Nigel was Jason's friend, it was up to him how much to tell him.

"Damn it, Nigel! Isn't this enough of a reason?" Jason swept his hand over the table and the papers on it.

"Absolutely, but it isn't your reason, is it?"

"No." Jason chewed his lip. "If we don't get him, he'll get us," he admitted.

"Why? What is going on between the three of you?"

"What is this, some sort of Inquisition?"

Nigel sat back. "If you want my help—and just so you know, you need my help because Will can't hold a candle to me—you have to tell me why." Mulish silence met his remark. Nigel frowned. "Initially, I thought this was about Helle playing dirty with business intel—"

"Thanks a lot," Helle interrupted.

"...then I suspected it might have something to do with Helle herself." He did a quick up and down, eyes lingering over

Helle's breasts. "Not that I don't understand the attraction, but she isn't that special, is she?"

"You have no idea," Jason said, his hand covering Helle's.

"Whatever." Nigel's face collapsed. "What are you involved in?" He glanced at Helle. "What has she dragged you into?"

"This has nothing to do with Helle."

Nigel's brows rose into arcs of utter disbelief, the piercings wobbling disconcertingly.

"It's about Woolf and me, an old feud that goes years back," Jason said. "Helle is yet another ingredient in that particular stew."

"You forget that you and I go years back too," Nigel retorted. "And not once have you mentioned a Sam Woolf."

Jason shrugged. "I couldn't. And for some years, I hoped it would all go away."

"But it hasn't," Nigel stated.

"No. Woolf is a persistent bastard."

"And you're a lying one." Nigel made as if to stand.

Helle grabbed hold of him. "Sit down," she said, before turning to Jason. "You're going to have to tell him."

"I can't. He's going to think I'm crazy."

"You still have to." Helle stroked Jason's cheek. "He's your best friend. He deserves the truth." She gave Nigel a wobbly smile. "Hear him out, okay?" She stood, looking down at Jason. "I'll go and see Alison. We can meet up in the office."

"Stay," he begged, taking hold of her wrist.

"No, honey." She disengaged herself from his warm fingers. "It's better if you talk alone."

Nigel studied Jason before glancing at Helle. "Is it that bad?"

"Worse. But somehow, I think you'll like it." She poked at his necklaces, at the multiple charms that decorated his chest. "It's totally in line with New Age thinking." With a little wave, she left them to it.

When Helle arrived at the office, Jason was already there, stuck in a meeting with Steve and Mr Smith. Tim took a seat in the reception area, and Helle wandered off to find a cup of tea.

"Biscuit?" Angela held out a tin.

"Thanks."

"So, is she feeling better?"

Everyone at the office knew about Alison. No one knew who had put her in hospital.

"I guess." Truth be told, Alison had been in a foul mood, flying into a tantrum when she'd seen her reflection in the mirror. After she'd told Helle to fuck off for the third time, loudly claiming this was all Helle's and Jason's fault anyway, Helle had left.

In the car, she'd called Alison's father. He'd sounded a bit grumpy at first, but after complaining about his jetlag for a couple of minutes, he'd told her he hoped to be able to fly back home to the States in a couple of days with Alison. A good thing, as Alison had made it quite clear that she had no intention of staying in Britain—understandable, given the circumstances.

She'd also talked to her mother. Seriously, at times she wondered if Mum was telepathic, calling her just as Helle was considering whether she dared call her this early in the morning. It was a strained conversation, Helle growing more nervous by the minute as Mum's silence spoke volumes. Finally, her mother had cleared her throat, and Helle could hear the tears in her voice when she asked if they had any idea who'd done this to Alison.

"She says she doesn't," Helle sidestepped.

"But…"

"But nothing, Mum. Alison insists it was a random attack."

"And you believe that, do you?"

"No. But I can't exactly force her to say something, can I?"

"I suppose not." More silence. A very long silence. "You think it was Woolf?"

"I don't know."

Fortunately, Mum had left it at that, but Helle had few illusions when it came to her mother. The moment her mother saw her, she'd subject Helle—and Jason—to a barrage of questions.

A couple of hours fiddling with her latest Excel sheets

served to wipe her brain clean of any thoughts about Woolf or Alison. Now and then, she checked if Jason was available, but the meeting seemed interminable and Angela had no idea how long it would last.

"That Smith," she sniffed, "he just barged in here this morning."

"Ah." Helle decided not to worry about that. Not now.

Jason came out looking drawn. There was the merest of nods between him and Smith as they parted, then Jason retreated to his office, with Helle at his heels.

He didn't want to talk about his conversation with Nigel, beyond saying things had gone well, considering. Instead, he paced his office, a list of creative expletives dropping from his mouth whenever he referred to Smith.

"As if I don't any have other things to do but answer his damned questions!" He banged his hand down on the desk. "He insists on a detailed list of my expenses in Turkey and even went on to insinuate that I—"

"Lunch?" Helle suggested, cutting him off midstream. Jason blew out his cheeks, the angry look in his eyes abating.

"Lunch." He took her hand. "Vietnamese okay?"

They never made it out the door. Steve came hobbling in, saying Jason needed to review a Letter of Intent before he sent it off. Helle threw Steve an annoyed look. She got the impression he was trying to muscle in at every opportunity, and the day before she'd overheard him saying something disparaging about her files. Huh. Talk about the pot and all that—the man was supposed to be an M&A specialist and did it all on paper?

"I'll bring us something back." Helle stood on her toes to kiss Jason firmly on the mouth. There: see Steve better that. Jason's eyes were alight with amusement.

"I'm not into men," he murmured in her ear.

"No, but just in case he is." She kissed him again and under her lips Jason's mouth widened into a grin.

She hurried down the steps to the sandwich shop, presently packed with people. Tim was waiting outside, visible through the glass shop-front. Helle wriggled her way towards the counter, weighing her options. Italian ham and mozzarella on sourdough baguette, or bacon and scrambled eggs in a traditional bap? At last it was her turn. She had to lean over the counter to make herself heard—which was when she felt someone moving to stand behind her, his weight pressing her flat against the marble-topped counter.

Helle didn't need to turn around. The scent of sandalwood, mixed with the drifting notes of cinnamon and myrrh sufficed for her to know who it was who was pressing his pelvis against her bum.

"Let me go!" She tried to push away from the counter. His hands came down on her wrists.

"Why should I?" Woolf's voice rumbled in her ear. He shoved one leg between hers to spread them. She tried to protest. His voice slipped in through her ear and coiled itself like silk rope round her brain, robbing her of speech, of will, of anything but the urgent need to do as he pleased, as otherwise he would hurt her.

"I could unzip myself and take you here, and you wouldn't deny me, would you?" he said, licking her ear. "Maybe I should," he added, releasing her right hand to lift her coat and skirt.

Oh God, Helle couldn't breathe. The press of people around them hid what he was doing, but she felt his fingers on her skin, how they slid in under the edge of her panties. She wanted to throw up, to scream at him to stop, but that voice, those hands, that scent—she was incapable of fighting him, when his hypnotic bass rumbled through her mind. She felt his erection pressing against her buttocks. Helle made a weak attempt to buck him off.

"I've got a car outside," he said. "And when I tell you to, you will follow me outside and get in." No! She tried to shake her head free of his voice, but he tightened his grip on her hands—and froze.

"What's this?" His fingers closed round her ring. She tried to wrest her hand free. "I said, what's this?" His voice was like a whiplash, anger radiating from him. "Damn that Wanderer bastard! Who the fuck does he think he is?" He yanked at the ring, she curled her finger in protest. He did it again, and a flare of pain rushed up her arm, freeing her from the paralysis imposed by his voice.

"Help me!" she yelled, and the people closest turned to look at them. Woolf hissed a curse in her ear before releasing her. When she turned around, he was gone, a swirl of cashmere overcoat disappearing through the door.

"Miss?" Tim shouldered his way through the crowd. "Are you all right?" he asked, once his bulk was between her and the rest of the shop.

"I'm not sure." She pressed a hand to her mouth. "I think I'm going to be sick."

In a matter of seconds, she was outside, Tim holding her as she vomited in the gutter.

He must have called Jason. Long legs pumping, Jason came flying towards them in his shirt sleeves. He skidded to a stop beside her. No words, just his open arms, and she fell into them, hiding herself from the world against the warmth of his chest.

Chapter 30

"I don't want a new phone. What's the point? He'll find my number soon enough anyway." Helle sent her phone spinning across the table and cradled her face in her arms. Jason caught it before it fell over the edge, frowning down at the latest text. It was unsigned, from an undisclosed provider, but there was still no doubt who'd sent it—and the dozens of other texts she'd received over the last twenty-four hours.

I will punish you, this last one read. Not quite as gruesome as the one preceding it. *Everyone you love, I will smite to the ground*. Or the first one, the one that read *False bitches must be put on a leash and whipped*. Jason deleted this last one as well and lobbed the phone over to Nigel.

"Can't you block him?"

"How?" Nigel did some swiping over the touch screen. "He keeps on changing his number." He sank down in a crouch beside Helle. "I'm sorry Yo-Yo, but there's nothing I can do."

"Yo-Yo?" Jason eyed his best friend and his fiancée. When had they reached the nickname stage?

"Because us Americans always say *Yo* to each other." Helle raised her head enough to meet Nigel's eyes. "Except we don't." Something resembling a smile tugged at her mouth.

She'd been reluctant to tell him what had happened in the sandwich shop, and once she did, it had taken a superhuman effort to remain calm and soothing, when what he wanted to do was to rant—at Samion for being an abusive son of a bitch who used his considerable powers to immobilise her, at her for not having done something. Not that he had any idea what she could have done, but the thought of her being touched so intimately by Samion, in public, sickened him.

It apparently sickened her as well, and he'd had to use force to wrest the flannel from her last night, her skin abraded and red. When he applied lotion, she'd cried, arms round her midriff in a forlorn little self-hug. Only when he'd pulled her to sit in his lap had she quieted, eventually falling asleep in his arms. Jason hadn't slept. He had planned revenge, various alternatives of how to end Samion's days playing through his mind.

He'd been reluctant to leave her alone when he'd set off for work in the morning, so having had Nigel offer to babysit had been a godsend, even though he felt a twinge of jealousy when Helle smiled at Nigel, not at him. And as to that ridiculous nickname…

"Here." Nigel put the phone down. "Maybe you should let Jason screen the texts."

"Yeah." She hid her face again. "I have to call the hospital and check on Alison."

"I already did." Jason stroked her hair. "She's well enough to curse me to hell and back."

"Great news." Helle sat up, turning tired eyes his way. "Why won't she put the blame where it belongs?"

"Because that would be admitting that she is partly to blame. She should have listened to us." Jason went over to the fridge. "Hungry?"

"Yes," said Nigel

"No." Helle studied her ring—his ring—running a finger over it.

"You have to eat."

She looked at him, eyes brimming. "I want Mum. Silly, right?"

"Now, now." Nigel shook his head, making every single object he wore jingle. "Get your act together, Helle Lion-tamer." He grinned. "I rather like the sound of that—much better than Yo-Yo. You could wear a lion pelt and nothing else." His pierced eyebrows waggled.

"You wish." But she smiled, sitting a bit straighter. Jason shot his friend a grateful look. Nigel winked.

As he was leaving, Nigel pulled Jason to the side. "I left some photos on a USB stick that you should see."

"Of Helle?"

"No." Nigel looked uncomfortable. "Just look at them when you have a moment, okay?"

"Sure." He followed Nigel out in the hall. "The alarm is up and running again?"

"Yes." Nigel looked grim. "And this time, he won't get past the firewall."

"Unless he switches off the power." Just saying it made him feel insecure.

"Won't work." Nigel grinned. "PoE switches, man. If necessary, they're powered by the internet—and I've made sure that's on an isolated power supply." He sighed, the grin wiped away. "He's dangerous, Jason. And what you're proposing to do is the equivalent of grabbing a cobra by the tail and hope it doesn't twist round to bite you."

"You haven't held any cobras have you?" Jason replied in a light tone. "Because if you had, you'd know that once you have them by the tail, they're done for."

"Not this particular cobra." Nigel adjusted the little screen that controlled the security cameras. "This is one big motherfucker of a snake—don't forget that."

"Not about to." Jason nodded in the direction of the kitchen. "This time, he loses, we win."

Nigel rolled his eyes. "Totally irresistible; a story of love and revenge spanning three millennia." He poked Jason in the stomach. "I'm still in two minds about all this. Maybe you're just pulling my leg."

"Of course I am. All that crap about reincarnated souls, only an idiot would believe it, right?"

"Right." Nigel punched him on the arm. "And people like me, gifted with enough intelligence to embrace concepts that appear inconceivable to the normal man."

Helle helped him with the dishes once Nigel had left. Her phone buzzed and she jumped.

"I'll take it," Jason said. A new text. Jason deleted it unread. He gave her a hug. "How about we go down to the cottage tomorrow?"

She brightened. "Yes!" Her face fell. "Won't he find us there?"

"Maybe. But I can assure you he won't be able to touch us—not there."

"Really?" She heaved herself up onto the counter. "How come?"

"Protective measures," he said lightly.

She looked at him before bursting out laughing. "What, your great-grandmother's wards?"

"Hey, you shouldn't disparage stuff you don't know anything about," he replied, trying to sound stern. "My great-grandmother came from a long line of witches, so when she set up her wards, she knew what she was doing."

"Somehow Woolf doesn't strike me as a person who's afraid of spells and bunches of dried herbs."

"It doesn't matter if he's afraid of them or not. What matters is that he can't enter." Jason also relied on much more modern technology to keep his cottage safe, but he knew from experience that some wards were unbreakable.

"Can we go tonight?" She wound her arms round his neck.

"Now?" He glanced at the clock. It was well after eight. He'd have to call Mrs Hampton and ask her to swing by Tor Cottage with some essentials.

"I just want to get away, put some distance between us."

"Pack your stuff, lioness." He kissed her brow. "We leave in five."

He had hoped to arrive at Tor Cottage in daylight, wanting her to exclaim when she saw it nestling against a huge bank of bare lilac shrubs, with Glastonbury Tor rising behind it. Instead, it was in the middle of the night and a persistent rain made the dark impenetrable, the headlights weak beacons of light that swayed as he drove down the last stretch, a narrow lane, no more.

There was a cattle grid at the end of the lane. The car bumped across and when Jason switched off the ignition, they were engulfed in darkness.

"Very nice," she said, a trace of laughter in her voice.

"Oh ye of little faith. Come on, you."

The moment they stepped inside, his shoulders relaxed,

all of him imbued with the sense of peace that always stole over him whenever he came here. Helle looked around and he could see she was affected as well, her face softening for the first time since the previous day.

"Hall," he said. He gestured to the right. "Parlour." To the left. "Kitchen." He led the way there, stopping at the threshold. This was the oldest part of the cottage, the ceiling so low he could touch it without extending his arm. Whitewashed plaster walls, dark beams, and in pride of place a cream coloured Aga. The bricks on the floor were old and worn, arranged in a herringbone pattern, and Jason smiled to himself, recalling his father's creative cursing the summer he'd spent repairing the further corner.

"Oh!" Helle's fingers danced over the wooden tops, followed the contour of the porcelain sink, traced the antique delft tiles that decorated the wall.

"It's warm," she said when she reached the Aga.

"Courtesy of Mrs Hampton," he told her, "as is the well-stocked fridge."

Helle nodded distractedly. She did a slow walk round, and everything she passed, she touched, hands lingering on the worn wood of the table, on the shawl that hung on one of the chairs.

"My mother's," Jason explained. "She loved to sit here, but complained there was a draught." He smoothed his fingers over the soft wool. "She made it herself."

Helle sat down. "Home," she said, running her hands up and down the armrests of her chair. She smiled up at him. "This is home, Jason."

An image flashed through his head. Helle, a newborn child in her arms, a toddler playing at her feet. The kitchen was full of sunlight, the door to the garden was propped open, and the heady scents of lilacs drifted through the room.

"Yes," he replied. "You're right. This is home—our home."

She woke refreshed in an unfamiliar bedroom, Jason fast asleep beside her. The room was bathed in light, the large windows facing the east uncovered. The room was sparsely furnished with a large bed, a chair by the window, a little table and two stools. A magnificent circular rug lay in front of the windows, a study in greens and blues.

"Like your eyes," Jason said from beside her. "I bought it because it reminded me of them." He pulled her close, nibbling at her earlobe. "Did the light wake you?"

"I don't know. But if it did, I don't mind."

"My mother refused to cover the windows. It drove my father crazy, until she bought him one of those eye masks." He chuckled. "I'd sneak in, and she'd be sleeping with her face to the light, he'd be on his side, that black mask making him look like Zorro." He ran a light finger down her spine. "Feeling better?"

"Much." She curled into him. "So much better, that I'm thinking of making pancakes for breakfast."

"Sounds promising." He stretched, the sheet falling away to reveal him in all his naked glory. He was beautiful, her man, lean and hard, with muscles that rippled under his skin when he moved. She kissed his chest. He made a deep humming sound when she kissed him again, looking very disappointed when she slid away and hunted about for something to wear.

"Come back," he said.

"Too hungry." She attempted a smile and shoved her hair out of her face. "Later." He gave her a long, hard look and she ducked her head, anything to avoid those penetrating eyes. How was she to explain how sullied she felt by the incident with Woolf? He'd touched her—there—and she hadn't done anything to stop him.

Helle hurried down the stairs. Jason caught up with her before she reached the kitchen, still naked, still warm from bed.

"No," he said firmly, wrapping her in his arms. "This is not how we handle this, lioness."

"Then how?" She couldn't quite breathe, so hard did he squish her to his chest.

"Trust me," he said in her hair, slowly manoeuvring her towards the stairs. "Come back to bed, and I will show you how."

No one had ever touched her with such gentleness. No one had whispered such words in her ear. No one had kissed

321

away her every single tear, had placed his lips over hers so softly she could imagine it was but the touch of a breeze. The room shimmered with golden light, the sun's rays softened by a light fog that glistened just outside the windows. On the bed, Helle's body arched beneath his hands, her eyes lost in the ceiling above.

He enveloped her in his presence and warmth, his stomach pressing into hers, his eyes a hand's breadth from hers when he entered her. Stillness. His fingertips sliding over her face, tangling in her hair. All of him inside of her, a heavy possessive warmth that had her widening her legs, her pubic bone grinding against his as she strove upwards, needing him closer, deeper, everywhere.

He kissed her, his thick hair tickled her face when he nuzzled her neck, nibbled her ear, all the while holding perfectly still. Perspiration dewed his upper lip, and she rose off the bed sufficiently to lick it off, taste him, rub her nose against his face and smell him. He whispered her name. She traced the outline of his beautiful mouth with her finger.

God knows how long they lay like that. His hands braided with hers, his chest expanded on an inhalation, and then, at last, he began to move. All of him, pounding into her. All of him. All of him, all of him. Helle's body twisted, her nerves screamed and sang at the same time. Now. Yes, now!

She must have slept, her face pressed to his shoulder. Helle woke and she was sticky with him. All of her smelled of him, and on her right wrist a bracelet of miniature blisters showed just how hard he'd held her, the heat inside of him on the verge of spilling over when he came. Helle smiled, touching them lightly. She didn't mind. They were testament to the fact that it wasn't only him driving her crazy, it was just as much her testing his self-control.

Helle propped herself up on her elbow. In sleep, Jason's mouth was partially open, the normally so sharp lines of cheekbones and nose softened in repose. Dark lashes shadowed his cheeks, a lock of hair tumbled over his brow. She pressed her lips to the hollow at the base of his throat. It made him open his eyes, still dark and drowsy with sleep.

"Helle?" He brushed the back of his hand down her cheek.

"Lie still." She sat up. "This is for you. Only for you."

Sometimes the not touching is as inflaming as the touching. To run your finger almost, but not quite, across skin that puckers in desire, to blow a stream of warm air across a stiffening nipple, to allow your hand to hover millimetres from skin that is begging, no dying, to be touched. Jason's face flushed, his eyes darkened further. His breathing grew shallow, the muscles along his arms and legs tensed, but otherwise he remained as still as a statue, quivering under the shadow of her hands.

Helle set a hand on his abs and he exhaled in a sibilant rush. The hair on his chest glinted in reds in the sun, but darkened as it headed south, a narrow dark line connecting his navel with his groin. She kissed him there, a series of kisses all the way from his sternum to his pubic bone.

"Sweetheart," he whispered, his hands resting on her head. "Let me—"

"No." She raised her head sufficiently to look at him. "It is my turn to give."

His erection twitched. Helle closed her hands around it and sucked lightly on the glans.

"Jesus!"

"So you like this?" She did it again. He half laughed, half yelped.

"What an idiotic question," he answered unsteadily, "you know I do." She rubbed her face in his groin, inhaling the warm, salty smell of him. His balls moved and shifted, his sac tightening when she kissed her way up the length of him, moving her hand slowly up and down.

This time, she wasn't quite as gentle when she took him in her mouth.

"Agh!" His hips rose of their own accord, his thighs like stone under her hands. He gripped her shoulders. "No more, come here instead."

Helle didn't reply—she couldn't. She merely shook her head before biting down, ever so carefully, on his penis.

"Oh, God, Helle!" he moaned, fingers knotting in her

hair. "Damn it, woman, I—" He bucked into her mouth. She released him with one last, lingering kiss.

"Lie still," she told him, "I don't want to bite too hard by mistake."

"No," he laughed breathlessly, "that wouldn't be good. Not there."

His erection was throbbing with heat, hard and demanding as it jerked in her hands, and when she closed her mouth round it, he groaned, a hoarse wordless sound. And then he came, filling her mouth with the tangy taste of semen.

Helle stretched out beside him, her head on his chest. His heartbeat thumped loudly below her ear, his ribcage heaving with his breaths. Jason rubbed her behind her ear, and she stretched into his touch.

"Thank you, my *birtanem*," he said, his voice a soft caress. She dug her nose into his armpit and blew, making him squirm.

"You're welcome, hunk."

"Hunk?" He sounded very pleased.

"Well, I have to call you something complimentary now and then. Ouch!" She mock-glared at him. He rolled her over, tickling her mercilessly until she admitted that yes, he was a hunk, for real. Only then did he allow her to get up, telling her he was really looking forward to those pancakes.

"Chauvinist," she muttered.

Jason grinned and shoved her pillow under his head. "Absolutely. That's what you get when you shack up with an ancient soul." He made a dismissive gesture with his hand. "Run along, woman. Do what you have to do to keep your man happy."

"Yes sir." She stuck her tongue out, making him laugh.

324

Chapter 31

It was a wonderful Christmas break, nine days immersed only in each other, with the outside world held at bay. A short conversation with her mother, a longer one with Dad and his family and couple of exchanged texts with Alison—that was the extent of Helle's social interaction, the rest of her time spent absorbed in Jason.

Other than his long conversation with Juliet on Christmas Day—dear auntie was obviously disappointed by her nephew's no show, at least to judge from Jason's darkening expression—Jason had been as focused on her as she'd been on him.

That first day, they'd explored Glastonbury Tor, with Helle insisting they start by walking far enough away from it for her to properly appreciate the strangely shaped hill adorned with a narrow stone tower.

"Like a middle finger raised to the sky," she'd said, and Jason had rolled his eyes, explaining it was a chapel, named after the archangel Michael, and of course this meant Helle had to climb all the way to the top to inspect it. They'd returned to the chapel several times, but they also took long rambling walks around Glastonbury itself, they explored Wells, spending endless hours admiring the west façade of the medieval Cathedral and the statues that thronged it. But mostly they wandered about in partial nudity, each of them addicted to the way their bodies came together, like the missing pieces in a complex jigsaw puzzle.

He'd been right about the carpet before the open fire—it was soft. They spent entire evenings draped round each other while the fire crackled and spat, content to lie close together, while in the background one of Jason's endless Spotify lists filled the room with muted music.

"One moment it's Handel, the next it's The Human League," Helle teased him, once again surprised by his mixes.

"Both begin with an H," he replied with a grin, before going back to feeding her ridiculously expensive imported strawberries dipped in chocolate

Most of all, Helle spent time acquainting herself with Tor Cottage. Jason was right; it was as if a benign spirit was in residence, settling itself like a warm blanket round Helle's shoulders. The sensation was strongest in the kitchen, faded the further away from the old hearth she got, but was never entirely gone.

Directly above the kitchen was Jason's old room. A narrow bed, a desk close to the window, a bookcase crammed with books, some of them far older than Jason, two well-loved teddy bears on the bed—the room gave the impression of a lonely child.

"Were you lonely?" she asked, sinking down on the bed. Jason picked up one of the teddy bears.

"At school, no. Here, yes. I preferred it that way. It was mostly just me and Mum when we were here." He gave her a quick smile and sat down beside her. "She would have liked you. Poor Anne, she worried herself silly when my nights were invaded by strange dreams."

"And she believed you?"

"Eventually." He fiddled with the teddy's torn ear. "It helped that her mother had the Sight—she was used to not everything being explicable." He handed her the teddy. "This used to be hers."

The high point came when Jason led her out into the darkness of New Year's Eve, holding her by the hand as they made their way down to the bottom of the long garden.

"I promised you this," he said, brushing some leaves off an old stone bench for her. He stood before her, hands spread, and there was a soft glow round his fingers, the air between his hands crackling with energy. The glow intensified. He moved his left arm in an arc, and a wake of sparks lit up the night. He brought his hands together, and cradled in his palms, a flame burnt bright red.

Helle was entranced, a lump in her throat as she watched

him paint the darkness for her, his hands moving with the precision of a juggler's as he threw balls of glittering fire to light up the heavens. A final shower of fiery sparks and he clapped his hands together. It all went dark. She could hear him shift on his feet, but could only make out the general shape of him, her eyes still dazzled by his recent display.

"Say something," he said. She didn't. She just lifted his hands and kissed his hot palms.

Inevitably, the day came when they had to leave.

"I'm not sure I want to," Helle grumbled.

"It's your mum, not mine," Jason said.

"Yeah." But she perked up at the thought of seeing Mum again and said as much. Jason grunted, no more, driving the car carefully over the cattle grid. On either side of the grid ran a metal mesh deer fence, with the option of running a hefty electrical current through it should Jason judge it necessary.

"To reinforce the wards," he'd said with a shrug as he showed Helle how it all worked. The diesel-driven generator was connected to a complex tangle of wires and from what Helle gathered, the current was enough to stun a full-grown man. "My mother's idea," he said lightly. "She didn't like the sound of that Samion character I had such nightmares about."

They bumped up the lane, Tor Cottage already invisible behind its screen of trees and shrubs.

"Are you still planning on telling her?" Jason asked.

"I have to. Maybe she'll also want to put up an electrical fence round her backyard." It came out with more of a bite than she'd intended.

"Maybe." He shot her a look. "Will she be able to handle it?"

"Mum?" Helle really had no idea.

They stopped by the Kensington house first. There was a message from Nigel to call him, and Jason spent an hour or so on the phone while Helle caught up with e-mail and FB. Tons of holiday greetings, a short mail from Alison's father asking Helle to pack up Alison's stuff, a very long mail from Dad that Helle started to read—before slamming down the lid of the laptop.

It took Jason less than a second to realise something was wrong. He'd been intending to share news of Nigel's progress— electronic documents of all kinds had been pilfered from Woolf's various businesses and transferred over to a server hosted in Finland—but found Helle sitting on the bed, staring at her laptop as if it was a poisonous snake.

When she saw him, she flipped the laptop open and turned it to face him.

Jason read in silence. "Son of a bitch," he said once he had reached the end of the long missive from Ben, Helle's father.

Helle's eyes blazed. "If he touches as much as a hair on any of my baby brothers, I'll kill him." She held out her hand. "Give me my phone, I have to call Dad." Jason dug into the pocket of his jeans, by rote checking to see there were no new texts. There was: a picture of a grinning little boy, sporting an oversized Arsenal jersey and a head of curls as blond and riotous as Helle's. *So young, so vulnerable*, the text said.

"Callum?" Jason asked, holding up the text.

Helle paled. "Yes." Her hands shook when she scrolled through her contacts.

Jason covered her hands. "What exactly will you tell him?"

"That Woolf is a creep and took it really badly when I broke off with him." She looked at him. "He wouldn't hurt a child, would he?"

"I hope not." Jason heard himself how unconvincing that sounded.

"He does and I'll saw his balls off with a bread knife." This time, there was no fear in Helle's voice. This time, it was all rage. Jason ruffled her hair; his lioness was baring her teeth. Samion best beware, or he might wake a beast that had been desiring revenge for centuries.

He reclined against the headboard, listening as she spoke to her father. As he understood it, Woolf had appeared at the family home on Boxing Day, surprising Helle's father, his four brothers-in-law and their respective families. After apologising for the intrusion, Woolf had presented Helle's three brothers with gifts—from Helle, he'd said—insisted on taking some pictures of the boys for Helle and then left rather hastily.

"Damn him! This is him showing just how easily he can grab someone dear to me," Helle said once she'd hung up, having clarified to her father that if he ever saw Sam Woolf again, he should call the cops—or Janine's gun-toting brothers—after a description that painted Woolf as dangerously deranged. Dangerous, definitely; deranged, unfortunately not, Jason thought. She eyed Jason. "At least we know why he hasn't been texting me as much: he's been livening things up in the U.S."

"Apparently." Jason pressed his lips together. Not anymore, he wasn't. According to Nigel, Woolf was very much back in residence in his Chelsea home. "So, your Mum?" he said. Best get this done, he reflected, not that he had any desire of seeing Miriam's eyes narrow at the more improbable aspects of their story.

He parked the Aston Martin a block or so away from Grosvenor Square. "Phil lives here?" He whistled softly.

"Inherited it from a spinster aunt, together with a truckload of money," Helle explained. "It really killed his credibility as a vociferous proponent of the socialist model," she went on, amusement colouring her voice.

"Phil's a socialist?" Jason grinned, gesturing at their surroundings.

"Not anymore. But yeah, he used to be—or maybe that was just his way of getting Mum all riled up so that she'd notice him."

"Makes absolute sense," Jason said.

"It's like boys shooting spit-balls at the girls they like, or yanking their pony tails."

"Ah." He took her hand.

Miriam opened the door immediately. A warm, long hug for Helle, a somewhat more restrained greeting for Jason.

"Phil's out," she said, "picking up some wine." Jason handed her the bottles he was carrying, seeing her mouth twitch appreciatively. "Spanish. Helle's been sharing my tastes?"

"No, I like it myself." He hung up his jacket, helped Helle with hers, and saw Miriam's eyes grow round when Helle pulled off her gloves, displaying her ring.

"The real thing, huh?" was all she said, before hugging Helle again. She gave Jason an appraising look, all the way from his blue shirt to his black boots. "At least he scrubs up well."

"Mum!"

Jason laughed, meeting Miriam's eyes calmly. Helle's mother was in two minds over him, he could sense that. Well, he wasn't going anywhere, not without Helle, and the sooner Miriam came to terms with that, the better. Very much on purpose he draped his arm round Helle's shoulders, pulling her close enough to kiss the top of her head. Miriam smiled thinly.

After some minutes of small talk over wine and olives, Miriam sat back. "You said you had something to tell me, and I'm assuming it had nothing to do with that ring."

"Umm..." Helle fidgeted beside him. "I...we...well..."

"Helle?" Miriam's gaze bored into her. It made Jason suppress a surprised guffaw: the cobra look! He'd only ever seen his mother do it, but Miriam's version was just as bad. "Shit, Helle, you're not pregnant, are you?"

There was an astounded silence from Helle. They shared a look.

"No," Jason said, "no baby—not yet." This said with a belligerent edge, indicating it was none of Miriam's business.

"So then what?" Miriam asked.

Helle sighed. "Look Mum, it's a long story, and I don't know if you'll believe it anyway. It's all pretty incredible."

"Try me," Miriam said caustically. "I'm much more open-minded than you give me credit for."

"No you're not," Helle mumbled. "You're into facts and figures, remember? This is...well, at the very least it's weird."

"You're the one who wanted to tell me." She sipped at her wine. "I'm all ears."

Not once did she interrupt. Her grip on the wine glass tightened, her generous mouth flattened into a thin line, but other than that there was no outward reaction.

Finally, she cleared her throat. "So, in summary you're telling me Jason and you have been around for like ages, and now you've met up—at last." She shook her head, slowly.

"Wow." She settled back in her sofa. "And even worse, that bastard Sam Woolf is also some sort of reborn soul, out to get you."

"Nice and succinct," Jason said, attempting to alleviate the mood. Miriam fixed him with a glacial stare.

"Sounds like bullshit to me."

"But it isn't, Mum. Remember those dreams I used to have? The ones about lions and a boy—"

"…called Jason. Yes of course I do. But from there to buy this complicated storyline…" Miriam scowled. "And as to that nonsense regarding Woolf, come off it. The man harassed you, Helle. He also runs a major illegal business—or so you say. That makes him a major creep, not some sort of reborn avenging angel."

Jason shared a quick look with Helle. She'd been the one who'd insisted they focus on Woolf's illegal activities rather than give Miriam a blow-by-blow account of their recent adventures, saying she didn't want to scare her mother unnecessarily. Seeing as he'd have preferred it if they hadn't told Miriam anything, he'd allowed Helle to do as she pleased.

"He's dangerous, Mum. Look what he did to Alison. What if he does that to you? Or to Dad or one of my bro…his sons?"

Miriam's brows went up. "It's okay to call Ben's sons your brothers, darling. And yes, what happened to Alison was bad, although she seems to have herself to blame—"

"Mum!"

"Sheesh! Keep your hair on!" Miriam snapped. "Nothing excuses what that bastard did to her— nothing! But she knew he was bad news, didn't she? And just because Woolf has some sort of sick fixation on you, that doesn't in itself corroborate your crazy story." She sat back, levelling yet another penetrating look at Jason. "In actual fact, there's no proof, is there?"

"No," Jason said smoothly. "You'll have to take it on trust."

"A long professional life has taught me not to take anything on trust." She frowned at him. "Especially when unknown men pop up out of nowhere and sweep my otherwise so pragmatic daughter off her feet."

"Isn't that proof enough?" Helle interrupted.

"No." Miriam looked from one to the other. "It's just too incredible, and those 'memories' you refer to, they could be anything."

"Seriously? I would never invent something like this."

"Jason might." Miriam shrugged. "No offense, Jason, but—"

"Very much offense, actually." He stood up. "I told you this was a bad idea, Helle. Maybe I should leave."

"Yeah, maybe you should," Miriam muttered.

"No!" Helle took hold of his arm. "We have proof, Mum— of a sort. Jason has a gift, a—"

"Helle," Jason warned. "No."

"Why not? That will convince her."

"It will make her look at me as if I'm some sort of circus freak!" he hissed. "And, if you haven't noticed, she already does."

"No, I don't," Miriam said. "I haven't got to the freak stage yet."

"Jason's hands can spout fire," Helle blurted.

He disengaged his arm from her hold. "I'm leaving." He made for the door, she grabbed hold of his belt.

"I know you don't like sharing this, but I have to convince her. You know why!"

"Not like this. Not at the expense of me—me, Helle!" He shrugged off her hands.

"Jason, don't!" Helle moved to stand in front of the door. "I don't know what else to do. If he does to her what he did to Alison, and it's because she didn't believe us—"

"You could have told her what you told your father! A jilted ex-lover going ballistic is a hell of a lot easier to believe in, but instead you needed to tell her the truth—our truth. And now what? You want me to perform like some damned trained seal?"

"Hey!" Miriam's voice was sharp. "Stop it, both of you. I get it, that you feel Helle has betrayed your confidence, but the thing is, she and I don't have secrets from each other."

"Of course you do!" Jason snapped. "Parents and children don't share everything—and they bloody well shouldn't." He gave Helle a tired look. "I'm going home." She shook her head in mute entreaty, took a step away from the door towards him, and seconds later was sent flying into his arms.

Phil's unexpected entry had the benefit of allowing Helle to cling to Jason like a limpet, refusing to be dislodged even once he'd regained his balance.

"I'm sorry," she whispered in his ear, "I'm so, so sorry. I didn't mean to reduce you to a freak show, and I know I was wrong, but I just..." His stiff shoulders softened somewhat. "I need her to believe me," she admitted, still talking only to him. "Please, Jason."

"No." He set her down. "Don't ask me to do this."

"Do what?" Phil broke in. He extended his hand to Jason. "We haven't met. Phil Abbott."

The men shook hands. Helle tried to catch Jason's eyes, but he studiously avoided hers, a clear sign of how much she'd hurt him.

"What's going on?" Phil looked from Jason to Mum.

"Never mind." Miriam rolled her eyes. "Lovers' tiff." She placed a hand on Jason's sleeve. "Please stay."

Helle slipped her hand into Jason's to let him know that if he was leaving, so was she.

"I've made homemade pistachio ice-cream for dessert," Mum went on. Jason's mouth quirked into a little smile. "And there are two chickens in the oven, stuffed with—"

"...rosemary and lemon," Jason filled in.

Over dinner, the mood relaxed. No talk about reincarnated souls, just the normal chit-chat about the economy and the political situation in Europe. Phil went out of his way to put Jason at ease, keen eyes bright under bushy eyebrows as he moved the subject over to football. Helle spent most of the meal trying to make physical contact with Jason, with very little response. When he shifted to the side to avoid the pressure of her leg, Helle felt her face flood with heat. She stood up, so abruptly she jarred the table, and began collecting the dishes.

"Need help, love?" Phil grinned at her.

"No." Helle stooped to kiss him on his brow. She liked Phil, all the way from his crew cut hair to the designer shoes he kept polished to a shine. His shirt was a size or two too small—they always were, buttons straining over a torso that had more hair than muscle—and a bright fuchsia pink. She kissed him again, and Jason glowered. Tough.

"He's still mad at you, isn't he?" her mother asked when she entered the kitchen.

"Tell me about it," Helle said, bending over to load the dishwasher. She straightened up. "I know he's sensitive about it, but you're my mother—I trust you with anything."

"Can he really do what you said?" Mum rooted about in the fridge.

"Yeah, he can." Helle sat down on the table. "It's pretty awesome." She nibbled at one of her nails. "All the other stuff is true as well—especially the stuff about Woolf being a vindictive bastard." She gave her mother a considering look: time to tell it all. "He tried to kill us in Turkey."

"What?" Mum dropped the tray she was holding. Two of the plates shattered on the floor. "What the f... ? When? How? And why didn't you tell me this before?" Her fingers shook when she picked up the pieces of broken china.

"I didn't want to freak you out." Helle crouched beside her. "And that time when I ran so fast, it was because Woolf was trying to run Jason over."

"No." Mum swallowed. "No, Helle."

"He attacked Jason in his garage as well." She cut her finger on a shard.

"Jason! Always Jason—what if he hurts you?"

Helle shrugged, sucking at her bleeding finger. "If he hurts Jason, he hurts me."

"You can't stay with him." Mum pulled Helle to her feet. "Listen to me, Helle. You can't be with a man whose business dealings put you at risk."

"Business dealings?" Helle shoved at her mother. "This has nothing to do with business, it has to do with me."

"You? How can it? You've just met them both."

"I already told you."

"And I don't believe a word of it!" Miriam yelled.

"Don't or won't?" Jason asked, coming in with an overloaded tray and Phil at his heels.

"Both! I won't believe something as ridiculous as the story you told me before."

"What story?" Phil handed Helle a napkin.

"Never mind!" Mum snapped. "It's all hogwash."

"It's not!" Helle glared at her. "And you know it isn't. You remember my dreams, don't you? Damn it, you even sent me to a psychiatrist!"

"She did?" Jason and Phil asked in unison. "What dreams?" Phil added.

"Just stuff," Helle said. She wasn't about to tell Phil.

Mum snorted. "You might just as well tell him—I don't keep secrets from Phil."

"Figures," Helle muttered. "Look, the important thing here is that we have to stop Woolf—before he stops us."

Phil's face was a study in bewilderment. "Stop?" He sat down at the kitchen table, gesturing for them to do the same.

It took Mum a minute to give Phil an extremely abbreviated version of events, ending with a caustic comment that only someone who was borderline insane would believe any of it—this with a long look at Jason.

"Utterly unbelievable." Phil's gaze flitted from Jason to Helle.

"See?" Mum said.

Jason regarded them in silence. He glanced at Helle, extended his hand and snapped his fingers. For an instant, a little flame hovered in the air. Miriam hyperventilated. Phil rushed over to her. Helle took the opportunity to snuggle into Jason's lap. His arms came down to hold her close.

"At least she believes us now," he said.

"He really wants to kill you?" Mum asked over tea and coffee, gesturing at Jason.

"Either one of us will do," Jason replied. "He wants to destroy us, and he only needs to kill one of us to achieve that."

Mum looked aghast at his bald comment. Not quite as aghast as Helle felt, visualising Jason bleeding out in front of her while Woolf dragged her away to a future of black eyes and hard hands.

"So go to the police," Miriam said.

Jason explained that wasn't going to help—not against a man of Woolf's resources. Phil nodded in agreement, making Mum scowl.

"Then what?" she asked.

"We fix this ourselves." Helle leaned forward, outlining their plan. Miriam listened grimly.

"And you can prove his connection to this illegal business?"

"We can," Jason said.

"It won't help," Phil said bluntly. "If this Woolf bloke is truly out to get you, having him locked up will not solve the problem."

"No." Jason met Helle's eyes. "The only permanent solution is to kill him."

Helle's fingers tightened on her cup. He was right, Phil was right, but no matter that Woolf was a major bastard, the thought of murdering him… and then she remembered the picture of Callum, the look on Alison's face when they found her in the apartment. No choice. God help them, there was no damn choice.

"So why are we doing all this if it ultimately won't help?" She managed to sound matter-of-fact, ignoring the way her heart had seemingly lodged itself halfway up her windpipe.

"Distraction. Woolf enjoys being rich and powerful. He'll do what he can to salvage his empire—and it doesn't hurt if it absorbs all his energy for a while." Jason ran the back of his hand down her cheek. "I need the time. Samion is a difficult man to kill."

"Oh, so he has magic powers too?" Mum snorted, but there was a pinched look to her face that stood in stark contrast to her derisive tone.

"Yes," Helle replied on Jason's behalf, "he most certainly does." His voice, those eyes that burned holes in your skin, the way he had healed his broken nose…

"Go back home." Mum reached over and gripped Helle's hand. "Leave them to fight it out on their own."

Helle snatched her hand away. "No way! I'm not leaving Jason. Where he goes, I go, okay?"

"Even if it costs you your life?" her mother asked.

Helle raised her chin. "Yes."

Mum exploded.

Chapter 32

"Her way of apologising?" Helle suggested, when Jason held up two tickets to a West End show. They had arrived in an envelope addressed to him, not her.

"She isn't very good at it," he said, peering at the note that accompanied the tickets. "And her handwriting is atrocious."

Yesterday was not how it should have been, was all the note said, signed with a loopy 'M'. Helle shook her head with a little smile. Even that ambiguous sentence had cost Mum. Well, serve her right; she'd been downright offensive, demanding that Helle should leave Jason—do anything, in fact, to keep herself safe from that maniac named Sam Woolf. "No man is worth your life," she'd yelled. "Not even a circus freak like him." Which was when Helle went ballistic, telling Mum she would never speak to her again unless she apologised. Immediately. All in all, a bad evening, salvaged by Phil and Jason who somehow managed to calm both Miriam and Helle down.

"She worries," Jason said, retrieving the crumpled note from Helle's fist. "All mothers do."

"Maybe. But she doesn't get it, does she? Nothing can keep me safe from Woolf except submitting to him and letting him do as he pleases with me." The hair along her nape prickled at the thought.

"I'll not let him touch you." His hands slid over her hips, yanked her closer, until she was glued to him.

"Likewise." She fiddled with his ear-stud. Desire bloomed in her gut when he nibbled her lip in response.

"I have a meeting," he murmured against her skin. "But I can be dissuaded from attending."

"It's with Curtis," she said with a laugh. "He bills you what, 300 pounds an hour?"

"More—much more. But you're worth it."

She smacked his arm, rock hard and unyielding. "Insatiable sex fiend."

"Guilty as charged, Ms Madsen." He kissed her. His phone rang. He kept on kissing her. It kept on ringing. With an irritated sound he released her.

"You can make it up to me later," she said, pinching his butt as she wiggled out of his grip.

Helle was flushed with laughter when they left the show. "Great show, don't you think?" she said. Jason gave her an amused look.

"Not exactly intellectually challenging."

"Musicals rarely are. That's their appeal, honey."

He just shook his head and guided her through the crowds of Piccadilly to Lexington Street where he ushered her into a small tapas restaurant.

The restaurant was full, people sharing tables with virtual strangers—and enjoying it, to judge from the noise level. Bread, wine and olive oil appeared at impressive speed, and Helle was happily dunking her third slice of bread into the oil when a large party appeared at the door, several men in dark suits who called for wine.

She recognised the voice immediately and pressed herself into the shadow of their little corner. Opposite her, Jason was immobile, eyes on her.

"Oh, look! My favourite people in the world." The velvety voice was far too close. Woolf laughed and sat down at the head of the table, waving his companions off with a promise to join them in a minute. A blue shirt provided the only dash of colour, his three-piece suit and long scarf as black as his hair and eyes. "I do hope I'm not disturbing anything," he said, his voice as soft and luxuriant as always. Jason stood up, his hand extended to her, but Woolf's hand came down like an iron fetter on Helle's forearm.

"Come, come," he said, "stay a moment, stay and keep me company." Jason remained standing. "If you don't I'll break her arm," Woolf added sweetly. Helle uttered a strangled moan, wondering if he would be capable of pulverizing the bones should he want to. Probably, she decided, twisting in pain as he increased the pressure. Jason sat down slowly. Woolf's smile widened as he pulled his thumb back and forth over Helle's arm in the mockery of a caress. It made her skin pucker in distress.

"Take your hand off her," Jason hissed, his fists clenched tightly. Woolf laughed, and let his hand linger on her arm for a moment more before he complied.

"Well, isn't this fun?" he went on, a twisted mimicry of a smile on his face. "The three of us together." A glass of wine appeared before him, and he sipped at it, studying Helle intently. His eyes narrowed into slits. "You haven't learnt your lesson yet, have you? You belong to me, not him." His lip lifted in the slightest of sneers. "Disobedience comes at a price, little Helle."

"Shut up!" Jason hissed. "Get up and leave—now!"

"And you would make me, how?"

In response, Jason leaned forward and grabbed hold of Woolf's arm. His fingers glowed, but Woolf didn't as much as flinch. Smoke curled, Woolf's nostrils dilated, and the unpleasant scent of burning flesh filled the air.

"Jason!" Helle jerked her head in the direction of a nearby party, who were complaining about the odd smell. With a curse, Jason released his hold. Woolf immediately covered his singed sleeve with his other hand. He was in pain, a sheen of sweat on his upper lip.

"You'll pay for that." Woolf brushed lightly over the damaged sleeve, and before Helle's astounded eyes the frayed fabric knitted together. He faced Helle. "As will you. And this time, I'll not be duped by you." His face darkened. "For months you let me believe the child growing in your womb was mine, not his."

Helle gasped, overwhelmed by the memory of having her baby torn from her arms. "She wasn't even yours, and you took her. And I always knew the baby was Jason's. That knowledge helped me survive your repeated rapes." She stood. "Let's go, Jason."

Woolf rose, blocking her passage. "Rapes? It wasn't always

rape, was it? So many nights you lay in my arms moaning with pleasure. So many nights you asked for more, your hands insistent on me. But maybe it's easier to pretend you never enjoyed what we did, to forget those very special nights." He threw a sidelong glance at Jason before looking back at her. "But we both know the truth, don't we? A woman's body doesn't lie, and from the way you trembled in my arms…" he left the rest unsaid.

"Asshole!" Helle threw her wine in his face. Woolf made a grab for her, but she retreated, backing straight into Jason. Woolf snarled at them, baring his teeth.

"How does it feel to know I've fucked her far more often than you have?" he asked Jason. "There you were, rotting in your hole, and every night I had her. Have you ever fucked a pregnant woman, Wanderer? Have you felt her swell, watched her body ripen and grow soft? They become so sweet, warm and moist and oh, so wanton." He grinned, eyes glittering with malice. "And just so you know, she came every single time I had her."

Helle's face was on fire. "That's not true."

"No?" Woolf purred. "And for that lie, you will pay as well—once the Wanderer lies dead." He laughed. "Enjoy your evening. Next time we meet, Wanderer, it won't be in a venue crowded with people. No, the next time, it will be me and you—and you won't be leaving alive."

They barely spoke on the way home. Jason shrugged off his coat, stalked over to the ancient Chinese cabinet in which he kept his liquor and poured himself a generous measure of whisky.

"Is it true?" he asked, without looking at her. "Did you enjoy his lovemaking?"

"I don't know," Helle snapped, "I have no idea. I'm not the one who remembers." She pulled up the sleeve of her sheer top, staring down at the bruises left by Woolf's fingers. A vague memory of those same fingers travelling up her spine in a gentle caress, drifting over her breasts, had her blushing furiously.

He downed his whisky, poured himself another. He

scowled at her bruises, but didn't comment—or make any move to inspect them further.

"Does it matter?" she demanded. "It wasn't as if I was with him voluntarily, was it?"

Jason just looked at her, twirling the glass. Once again, her face heated. His eyebrows rose, his generous mouth thinning into a harsh gash.

"And if it were true, does it change the way you see me?"

"I don't know." He kicked off his shoes and sat down on the sofa.

That got to her. "What, you're going to judge me based on something he says?" She laughed hollowly. "It's just like it was last time round, isn't it? You're judging me without the whole story."

He turned to face her, his eyes blank. "Then tell me the story."

Helle wanted to hit him. "How can I? I don't remember!" She turned on her toes and escaped the room, coming to a halt in the hall. Maybe she should leave, take a cab to the apartment, but truth be told she was afraid to do so, didn't ever want to spend a night there again after what had happened to Alison. So she did the next best thing and locked herself in the upstairs bathroom.

She hoped he'd come and knock, wheedle her into opening. But the silence from the other side of the door was absolute, and Helle sank down to sit on the floor, resting her head against the tiles. She closed her eyes, and her brain flooded with unbidden images of the long ago.

Images of a man who leaned over her and explicitly described just what he would do to Jason unless she did as she was told. Dark eyes that regarded her with the intensity of a prowling cat, gauging her every reaction, her every emotion. Vague memories of nights in his bed, her body existing only to serve his needs. All of this to keep her man safe, knowing that unless she complied with Samion's wishes, Jason would be punished.

Helle staggered to her feet, overwhelmed with a need to shower, to cleanse herself. These new memories were like an oily residue, leaving her soiled inside and out. The water was hot—borderline too hot, but she stood in the steam, trying to soap away the pictures of her with him, all those years ago.

Anything he told her to do, she'd do. She'd undo her hair, undress, stand this way or that, sit, kneel, lie on her back—all the while smiling, even when it hurt. He liked to do that—to hurt her, watching as she bit back on her cries, knowing that if she cried out, Jason would be made to cry out as well. But at times he was gentle, his body, his mouth, eliciting reactions she did not want to feel—not with him.

She dried herself slowly, wiping away the condensation in the mirror to stare at herself. The person staring back was younger than her—so much younger, the hair a cloud of fuzzy gold that fell well down to her waist. Helle was suffused with pity for this younger, vulnerable self. She'd been a child, an innocent girl Samion tore to pieces—because of the man who was nursing his damned whisky and his bruised ego downstairs. Helle threw the towel on the floor and went to bed.

She was still awake when Jason tiptoed into the room some time later. On purpose, she'd left her clothes in a messy pile on the floor, and she could hear him pick them up and place them on a chair. The bed dipped when he sat down beside her, placing a hand on her hip.

"Helle?" he said softly. She pretended to sleep. The bed dipped again when he rose, padding over to his side. The sheets rustled as he slid in to lie beside her. "I know you're not asleep," he said, moving close enough for her to feel the shape of him. She didn't reply. "Fine, have it your way," he muttered, turning his back on her. Helle stared unseeing into the dark.

He couldn't sleep. Beside him, he heard her breathing deepen, and he rolled over on his side, propping himself up on an elbow to look at her. She'd gone to bed with her hair damp, and the resulting tangle of curls stood like a haystack around her head. She'd gone to bed alone and hurt, because of him. Jason sighed, fingers hovering over the ugly bruises on her arm. Rationally, he realised he was reacting like a numbskull, punishing her for things that might or might not have happened in a distant past. Emotionally, it was driving red hot knives through him to imagine her in the throes of passion with Samion, while he hung helpless in his chains.

After a futile hour or two attempting to sleep, he got up. Moonlight streamed in through the uncovered window that faced the overgrown garden, and he moved over to rest his forehead against the cool glass. Behind him, she began to toss, mumbling something. A sharp inhalation, a soft whimper and she sat bolt upright, clutching the sheet. She turned towards his side, her hand running over the indentation left by his body, and the tenderness of the gesture made him swallow.

"Come here." He kept his voice low. Helle threw back the sheets and came towards him, her naked body shimmering in the bright moonlight. His fingers encircled her wrist, pulling her towards him.

"You're mine, Helle," he said roughly. "Never forget that you're mine." He increased the pressure on her wrist, but she didn't flinch, eyes never leaving his face. He knew he was hurting her, the heat in his hand searing her skin. There was a defiant set to her face as she held her ground, refusing to show any discomfort.

With a curse, he let her go, shoving her back against the wall. His hands cupped her face, holding her still as he brought his mouth down on hers. Her lips parted, and he plunged his tongue into her mouth, claiming it as his, only his. The way she softened under his mouth, the way she pressed her breasts against him—it had his cock hardening, demanding that he bury himself in her. Fuck her until she screamed his name out loud.

"Tell me," he said, tearing his lips away from hers, "did he ever make you feel like this?" He kissed her again, hard. "Did you want him, Helle? Did you ask him to please come inside as you do me?" He held her against the wall, wedging one thigh between hers to nail her into place. His hand slipped in between her legs.

"No," she answered unsteadily, "how can you even think that?" She moaned out loud, her hips grinding against his probing fingers.

"Then how?" He bit her ear—a tad too hard. "How come

he remembers you moaning in his arms? Willingly submitting to him?" She tried to slap him, but he easily caught her wrist. He sank his eyes into hers, requiring an answer, and all the while his fingers slid through her moist folds, rubbed her clit.

"It was never him that made me moan, you idiot!" She wrenched her hand free and shoved at him, eyes narrowed with rage while her mouth was plump and wet after their recent kisses.

"That's not what he said, was it? He seemed to remember you enjoying yourself." Why did this matter so much? Damn it, he knew Samion was a liar, so why did it eviscerate him, leave him with far too tangible images of his Helle, legs tangled with Samion's, head thrown back? He pulled out his fingers from inside of her, trailing her wetness up her flank to her breasts.

"Son of a bitch!" She aimed for his cheek with her nails, he deflected. "When I moaned, I did so because I pretended it was you, not him!" She punched at him, he grabbed both her hands and pinned her wrists to the wall high over her head, his mouth coming down on hers again. Rough—yes, most definitely—but also needy, his lips softening against hers. She tore herself free, gasping for air. "I did it for you. I had no choice, damn you." Helle wriggled, tugging at her trapped hands. He just tightened his hold, pressing his throbbing erection against the soft skin of her belly.

"But you liked it at times, didn't you?"

"Liked it? You have no fucking idea. You have no idea what he did to me. Every night, Jason. Every single night during all those months." She leaned her head back against the wall and closed her eyes. "And yes, there were times when my body betrayed me, when I responded to his touch. It made me hate myself, but when he ordered me to kiss him, to love him, I did it knowing that if I didn't, you'd be maimed and I couldn't bear the thought of that." Yet another tug at her hands, and this time he released her wrists. She massaged the reddened skin, scowling at him.

"Maybe that would have been better," he said, cupping her arse to pull her close. "Maybe it would have been easier for me to lose my hand than to know you slept in his arms."

He flexed his hips, his cock hard and hot where it was trapped between them. God, he wanted her, torn between wanting to fuck her into submission, and loving her until she was reduced to a trembling wreck in his arms.

"Asshole. Don't you see? It would have killed me."

"It would?" he asked, kissing her hungrily.

"Yes." She emitted a muffled squeal when he bit her lip. "It would have destroyed me. You know that. And so did he, damn him, so did he."

"Helle," he groaned, wrapping his arms around her. "Oh, my brave, beautiful lioness!"

They were down on the floor, and he buried his face in her groin, inhaling the scent of her—his woman. He licked her, tasted her, and her heels scrabbled on the carpet, her hips lifting off the floor. He moved upwards. A flicker of his tongue along the lower edge of her ribcage, and she drew in her breath sharply. Round breasts in his hands, a hard nipple in his mouth, and she gripped his hair, moaning his name. Her neck. Her jawline, the contour of her ear, her beautiful, beautiful eyes—he kissed them all. Her lips parted, he lunged, devouring her mouth.

She undulated below him, hands as light as angel wings brushed over his head, his back, all the while with her mouth soldered to his. At his touch, her legs widened. Without releasing her lips, he positioned himself between her thighs, the head of his cock nudging at her opening.

Lips and tongues, legs that twisted together, her hands in his hair. Skin gliding against skin, a foot caressing his calf, her nails sinking demandingly into his back. Jason found purchase with his knees, gripped her by the shoulders and sank himself to the root, swallowing down her responding groan. Again. Again, again, again—he hammered into her, fast and forceful, and at some point he had to let go of her mouth, had to gulp down air.

"Mine," he said hoarsely. "Only mine."

"Only yours," she agreed breathlessly. "Forever and ever."

Forever, he thought fuzzily. Forever is a long, long time. And then he didn't think anymore, as every single atom in his body was jolted out of orbit when he came.

He lay back exhausted, his breath coming in long heaving gulps. His heart still thundered in his chest and he could taste her blood on his lips from where he had bitten her. It was an effort to open his eyes, an even bigger effort to grope for her hand and clasp it. They just looked at each other, lying close enough that her breaths tickled his face.

At long last he managed to pick her up, carrying her over to the bed. She wound her arms around his neck and kissed him, hiding her face against his skin. He cradled her to him and stroked her hair until she fell asleep, her head pillowed on his chest, her hand curled firmly round his thumb.

She woke him in the early morning. She woke him with kisses and tenderness, her eyes half closed as she smiled down at him. She woke him with the sinuous movements of her hips, the words she whispered in his ear. And he knew then that he owned her—body, soul and heart—just as she owned him.

Chapter 33

After the upheaval of the last few days, some long boring stints at the office were just what Helle needed. With the holiday season done and dusted, business was beginning to take off, and Helle installed herself behind her new desk and submerged herself in detailed analysis of one company after the other, churning out complicated Excel sheets summarising her findings.

She was uncomfortable working for Jason, had even made a half-hearted attempt to contact a recruitment agency, but Jason was adamant: he wanted her close. He also, apparently, wanted her to be empowered, which led to an embarrassing Wednesday meeting with Curtis, who eyed Helle as if she were a potential gold-digger while presenting her with one document after the other to sign.

"Congratulations," he said when he'd finished. "You now have as much access to company funds as he does."

"Not at my request," she told him.

Curtis' gaze raked her from head to toe. "No. Just don't try anything. I'll crucify you if you do."

"Maybe I should start flexing my new powers by finding a new solicitor," she snapped. Curtis glowered. She glowered right back at him. Finally, he did an exaggerated eye-roll and held out his hand.

"My bad," he said simply. "If Jason trusts you, so should I."

"Too right." She threw a look at Jason, who was sitting in his leather chair, feet propped up on his desk. He grinned and winked, no more. He looked hot in his dark blue shirt and matching suit, and he also looked happy, no doubt a residual effect of that morning's activity. She licked her lips, having the satisfaction of seeing him adjust his pants.

Curtis left after having booked a padel tennis date with Jason. Clearly, this combo tennis-squash sport was the hot thing among Jason's friends. Helle sauntered over to Jason.

"You sure about doing this?" She sat down on the desk, swinging her legs. Jason ran a finger over her jeans-clad thigh, leaving a trail of warmth behind.

"More than sure. Everything that's mine is yours." His hand slid up her leg. "And everything that's yours is mine," he added in that dark hoarse voice of his. "Like this." He cupped her crotch.

"You're being very single-minded of late," she teased.

"Takes two to tango, lioness. It wasn't me going down on my knees in the shower this morning, was it?" He smiled, a dazzling smile that had her leaning towards him, eager to taste those lips, kiss that mouth.

There was a knock on the door and it swung open, revealing Steve. His floppy hair covered half his face, his bespoke jacket and elegant dress shirt hugged a trim narrow frame, the effect somewhat ruined by the gym pants he was wearing to accommodate the cast on his leg. He was holding an iPad.

"I think you should look at this." He sounded grim. "Woolf & Partners has just announced that they've acquired a minority interest in Morris & Son."

"What?" Jason was on his feet. Steve handed him the tablet. "Fucking hell!" Jason cursed. "That damned Spencer, I swear, I'm going to strangle him! I have to call him."

Spencer? Who was he? Oh, right, the cousin in New Zealand. "What, now?" It had to be close to midnight in New Zealand.

"Now," Jason said, already making for his phone. He cut Helle a look. "Get hold of Nigel."

Helle nodded and hurried out of the room, Steve hot on her heels.

"So you're a director now," Steve said to her back.

"What? I am?" Helle dug through the mess on her desk, trying to locate her phone.

"That's what Angela tells me. Sleeping your way to the top, hey?"

Helle rounded on him. "Repeat that, and I'll kick you in the balls. And I dare you to say that to Jason."

Steve looked quite stricken. "I…" He cleared his throat. "I was just ragging."

"Whatever." She didn't have time for him. With shaking fingers she texted Nigel and seconds later he replied, saying he was coming over.

Jason's former good mood had been replaced by simmering rage. He paced his office, alternating between cursing Spencer to hell for not having contacted him first, and swearing revenge on Woolf for having threatened Spencer with all sorts of nasty surprises if he didn't sell his stake. Halfway through his ranting he froze.

"Uncle Everett!" he said.

"Everett?" Helle didn't quite follow.

"Everett is a damned lot closer than Spencer," Jason replied, already dialling. A rapid exchange of words, and he was put through to his great-uncle. From what Helle could gather, Woolf had been there as well—with little success, to judge from Jason's laughter. "You did what?" he asked. "Everett, this man is dangerous, you shouldn't…yes, yes, I know that, but trust me, he's worse than the Gestapo… A gun?" He lowered his voice. "You're not allowed to have guns there!" He hung up some minutes later.

"He was mostly angry," Jason said to Helle, nodding a greeting at Nigel as he came in through the door. "Told me undercover agents don't intimidate that easily."

"Undercover?" Helle asked.

"In the war," Nigel filled in. He grinned. "I like Everett. So, what's the matter?"

"It's a bloody mess, is what's the matter," Jason said, throwing himself down in his chair. Quickly, he brought Nigel up to date.

"Woolf trying to distract you the same way you're distracting him?" Helle suggested once he was done.

They'd spent recent evenings inventorying the documents Nigel had pilfered from the shadier side of Woolf's various businesses. Short messages specifying date and time for auctions, accompanying pictures of scantily clad girls staring at the camera like deer caught in the headlights. Men sold as labour, whisked off to God knows where; boys not yet in their teens delivered all over the world, women obliged to swallow bags of drugs and sent as couriers—it was a sickening and huge operation, run entirely through the darker side of the internet.

"That would suppose he knows I'm trying to distract him." Jason doodled something on his blotter.

"Not exactly a quantum leap," Helle muttered, making Nigel smile—if briefly. "That security breach up in his warehouse in Hull must have made him suspect you're onto him." The warehouse figured prominently as the delivery address for all those special 'packages' destined for UK customers—including Woolf's legit club business.

"Not so sure about that," Nigel replied. "In Woolf's line of business, enemies are easy to come by."

It had been a successful manoeuvre. By hacking the security system, Nigel had been able to set off a number of alarms, dispatching everything from the police to the fire brigade to Woolf's premises. As a consequence, Woolf had taken off for Hull, allowing Jason and Helle to relax their constant surveillance.

"He suspects something, though." Nigel tugged at the tassels of his Peruvian hat, sucking in his lower lip so that he could worry at his piercing with his teeth. "He's ordered a major clean up, and stuff is being deleted all over the place."

"Damn!" Jason slammed his hand against his desk.

"Relax." Nigel rummaged in his backpack and produced two hard drives and a couple of USBs. "There's enough there to make things very uncomfortable for him. Plus I have camera footage of containers arriving at his Hull base, full of human merchandise."

"Human merchandise?" Helle made a face. "And how did you get hold of that?"

Nigel tapped at Jason's laptop. "Embedded webcams can be hijacked." In response, Jason closed the laptop. "Anyway," Nigel continued, "there's enough there to keep Woolf very busy and very much on the defensive. But is there enough to put him away for good?" He shook his head. "A good brief will argue someone else has been using Woolf's buildings and logistics network. Nothing in his official IT systems, on his laptop, on his phone, will in any way tie him to the darker side of his business. Except of course…" Nigel waved a USB stick. "If I manage to upload this on his office network, an investigator will find remnants of deleted documents. Enough to have them throw the book at him—for a while."

"Good." Jason pulled one of the hard drives towards him. "I will make sure Curtis puts this in the right hands. You will upload the content onto Woolf's computer system—"

"…and keep this baby safe." Nigel took the last of the hard drives. "I've also closed down the server I've been using—one of Woolf's IT experts managed to trace one of my invasive actions back to it."

"Can it be connected to us? To you?" Jason asked.

"Nope." Nigel gave him a condescending look. "I'm not daft." He yawned. "We need to decide on timing. It will take me some time to work my way through Woolf's personal security systems—he's a tad paranoid at present, changing passwords and login IDs every day or so. So how about you tell Curtis to get this to his contact by Monday?"

Jason gave him a distracted nod, staring down at his beeping phone.

"What?" Helle asked.

"Nothing."

Helle raised her brows—she knew him far too well by now.

"Juliet," he said curtly. "She's wondering why I haven't called her."

"Really?" Nigel snorted softly. "That's rich, coming from her."

Jason's face clouded. "And what does that mean?"

Nigel scratched at his patchy beard. "Didn't you see the pictures?"

"What pictures?" Helle asked.

"I left you a USB—just before Christmas," Nigel said.

"And?" Jason sounded defensive.

"Have you looked at them?" Nigel asked.

"No."

"Well then do so—before calling her." He stood. Today's outfit consisted of nudie jeans that hung far too low on his narrow hips, a woollen jumper depicting several happy sheep leaping over a gate, and the ubiquitous necklaces and bracelets. Since last time, he'd added a Celtic cross in heavy silver, adorned with what looked like amethysts. With a little wave, he jangled his way out of the room.

"So, Monday is D-day," Helle said—instead of yelling at him to find the damned USB and show her the pictures.

"Yes." He upended his laptop bag on his desk. A couple of USB sticks fell out, but it was obvious which one came from Nigel, its bright purple hue drawing the eye. Jason's phone rang. He palmed the USB, stuffing it in his pocket at the same time as he answered the phone. A long conversation in Turkish followed.

"Selim," he said needlessly once he'd hung up. He grinned. "They've just received a breakthrough order from Samsung."

"That's good." She remained where she was, pointedly looking at his pocket. With an exasperated sound he sat down by his laptop and beckoned her over. There were five pictures, all of them of Juliet—and Woolf.

"They're friends?"

"No." Jason frowned, studying a picture in which Juliet was smiling at Woolf.

"Sure looks as if they are." Woolf's powerful arm round her waist, Juliet's face obscured by her swirling hair. It could be an embrace, it could also be a show of force, him propelling her along.

"They've met before. Not under amicable terms, I might add." But he sounded hesitant, eyes glued to the last picture, the one where Woolf was holding Juliet's car door open and bending over, as if talking with her.

"So what were they talking about here, do you think?"

"I don't know." His brows pulled together. "But I intend to find out."

"I've never been to Southampton," Helle said some hours later, breaking a tense silence. Jason kept his eyes on the road, still in two minds about having Helle accompany him on this trip. Not that she'd given him much choice.

"You'll not be seeing much of it at this time of the day." It was already dark, the January day having morphed seamlessly into night. He drummed his fingers against the steering wheel. Juliet had sounded pleased to hear from him and had readily agreed to meeting up. It remained to be seen how happy she would be to see Helle again.

"In how many lives have you run into Juliet?"

Jason smiled. She was trying to sound casual, but failed rather spectacularly, jealousy leaking through every syllable.

"I don't know. Seven, eight perhaps?" Jason shifted in his seat.

"Have you had sex with her every time?"

"Is that really any of your business?" He floored the accelerator, overtaking three cars in a row.

"Wouldn't you want to know, if it were me, hooking up with Mr Gorgeous life after life?"

He risked a glance in her direction. She was leaning her head against the window, her hands clasped tightly in her lap.

"Yes," he replied. "I would." He drove in silence for a while, considering just how much to say. He suspected Juliet would be more than happy to embellish things should she get the opportunity. "Yes, she and I have been lovers whenever we've met."

"Oh." A small sound, conveying uncharted depths of uncertainty. "As if you were in a relationship?"

"Yes," he answered reluctantly. "In our second to last life together we lived together for several years."

"Wow. Just goes to prove you know her much better than you know me—and that she knows you a hell of a lot more than I do."

"Juliet is irrelevant," he snapped.

"What a terrible thing to say," she said. "How can a woman you've slept with, not only repeatedly in this life, but repeatedly over several lives, be irrelevant?"

He shook his head, exasperated, and the car swerved too much. "What I mean is that she's irrelevant to us." He wove through the traffic, slid into the inner lane and lowered his speed. He placed a hand on her leg and squeezed lightly. "I love you. Admittedly, I love her as well, but it's not the same."

"You love her?" It came out with an edge. "And how is that supposed to make me feel?" She shoved his hand away.

"Oh, for God's sake, how many times do I need to tell you this?" He managed to grab hold of her hand, squeezing hard enough for her to breathe in sharply. "You sit alone in my heart, Helle." He interlaced his fingers with hers. "You're the only reason I'm still around." That, he noted with satisfaction, shut her up.

Juliet lived in Chilworth, a village on the outskirts of Southampton. Picturesque thatched houses mingled with modern bungalows, traffic was light, hedges were high, and all in all this was a quiet pleasant area. Jason parked in front of the low wrought iron gate he'd helped Juliet fix some years back, just as he'd helped her with the stone path that meandered to the front door of the Tudor-style cottage, flanked by huge rosebushes that were quite impressive in the summer, but at present were mostly a collection of nasty thorns.

Juliet threw the door wide open, a huge smile on her face. At the sight of Helle, her radiance dimmed somewhat.

"You brought her?"

"As you can see." Jason set a hand on the small of Helle's back, a protective gesture that had Juliet's mouth thinning.

"Well, you'd best come in." Juliet preceded them into the house. Lit candles on every table and every window sill, a crackling fire in the living room, and on the coffee table a chilled bottle of Bollinger and two flutes. On a large silver tray was an assortment of canapés, and in the background John Legend was crooning. Helle didn't say anything; she didn't need to, her shoulders stiffening perceptibly. She stepped out of reach of Jason's hand, blue eyes surveying Juliet.

The dark hair had been brushed to a lustrous shine. Juliet's mouth glistened invitingly, and in a short wraparound dress with a plunging neckline, she looked dangerously attractive, the impression further highlighted by her smoky eyes and the fuck-me heels. Jason berated himself silently for not having been sufficiently clear when he called her. Juliet was expecting an erotic rendezvous, and instead he was here to question her about Woolf.

Juliet recovered swiftly from her surprise. A third flute appeared miraculously, and soon they were toasting each other and the New Year.

"You're still wearing it." Juliet smiled as she refilled his glass. "The ear-stud," she clarified, brushing at his hair. He leaned away from her hand, throwing her an angry look, which she ignored. "I gave it to him for his eighteenth birthday," Juliet explained to Helle. "A memento of all our special moments."

"How sweet," Helle muttered, filleting Juliet with her eyes.

"I know, it is, isn't it? A little diamond to remind him that some things are forever."

Jason choked on his champagne.

"I even held his hand when they pierced his ear," Juliet continued.

"No you didn't," he protested, giving Helle a wary look. Juliet laughed and swung her head so that her dark hair more or less bounced in his face.

"Yes I did. The least I could do after that time in the tattoo parlour."

"The tattoo parlour?" Helle asked.

"Oh, you don't really want to know." Juliet painted a huge smile on her face. "You see, Jason and I have so much history."

"I can imagine." Helle seated herself as far away as possible from both of them. The glass in her hand trembled slightly as she lifted it to her mouth, trembled just as much when she set it back, empty, on the table. During the ensuing minutes, she retreated into silence, her face a neutral mask. Jason wished she had been close enough to take her hand.

Helle decided she didn't dislike Juliet: she hated her, all the way from those ridiculous high heels to the generous swell of her breasts—tits that at least twice so far had brushed against Jason's arm. Mr Greeny totally agreed, offering various alternative approaches. Helle could scratch her eyes out, or yank down that indecent neckline so her boobs spilled out. She rather liked the sound of the last one, but thankfully Juliet excused herself before she could act on it.

"I didn't know you liked tattoos." She wiped her hands on her jeans, regretting not having worn clothes as sexy and clingy as Juliet's.

"I don't. She does, and the only tattoo she has is of a rose on her left ankle."

"How would you know? Unless, of course, you've seen all of her recently." Like all those weeks ago, when she'd come round to Jason's only to find Juliet there.

"I haven't—not since I realised you were in London."

"And when was that?"

"September?" He shrugged. "It started as a premonition, no more, and grew into a certainty."

"Ah." She crossed her legs. "When are you going to ask her about Woolf?"

"Leave that to me."

"Right. And will you be the one to tell her we're engaged, or should I? I'm having a hard time watching her almost press her tits in your face."

"Helle," he sighed. What? She folded her arms over her chest, feeling admonished and small.

Her dislike of Juliet increased exponentially over the coming hour as she watched her flirt blatantly with Jason. She was all over him, her arm brushing his in passing, a slight stumble making her lean against him for support. She kept on throwing Helle quick glances, probably assessing how far she could go before Helle blew a fuse, but Helle worked hard on the impervious look, smiling sweetly whenever their eyes met. And she hated Jason for not moving out of range, for not telling her to keep her damned hands to herself.

Finally, Helle had had enough. She stood up and glared at Jason. "I'm leaving."

"At last," Juliet mumbled, making Helle whip round to face her.

"Yeah, I'm leaving because I'm sick and tired of seeing you throw yourself at my man—my fiancé, if we're going to be quite correct." Ostentatiously, Helle held up her third finger to display her ring. "And I'm just as sick and tired of watching my goddamn fiancé do nothing at all to stop you."

"Fiancé?" Juliet said, looking at Jason. "You're getting married?"

"At present, the jury is out on that one," Helle retorted before Jason could reply. "In actual fact, maybe he should give you his ring instead." She yanked at the thick band.

"Stop it." Jason's hand closed over hers.

"Is it true? You're marrying her?" Juliet's dark eyes inked into a deeper shade of brown.

"I am. If she will have me, that is." His thumb caressed Helle's hand. "I should have told you already on the phone."

"Yes," Juliet agreed, "that would have been better." She sat back, folded her legs beneath her and looked at him. "So why are you here, then?"

Jason sat down, pulling Helle down to sit beside him in the sofa.

"Because of this." He pulled out a folded paper from his pocket and handed it to her. "I'd really like to know why you're meeting with Sam Woolf."

Juliet's face tightened, eyes flying to Helle. The moment they did, Helle knew. She felt nauseous.

"A case of mutual interests, I believe," she said. "Woolf gets me, she gets you."

"No. Juliet would never do that to me."

"Really?" Helle directed herself to Juliet. "Is he right?"

Even Jason couldn't miss the way Juliet's face crumpled.

"I told him no," she said. "I swear, Jason, I said I wouldn't take part in his little scheme." Jason made a disgusted sound and Juliet lunged, gripping his sleeve. "You should be with me. It's been you and me before, and it's been good, hasn't it?"

"Juliet," Jason interrupted, but she raised her voice.

"All these years, these lives, in which you've been moaning about your precious Helle, well, I was expecting something truly special, a gorgeous amazon or something, but instead…"

she waved her hand at Helle. "She's just so ordinary!"

Helle was tempted to punch her, but Jason had his arm round her shoulders, holding her still.

"How can you choose her over me?" Juliet asked. "I'm the woman you need, not her. I know every inch of your body, I—"

"Enough!" Jason's voice dropped an octave or two. "There is no point in continuing this discussion. You and I have always been on borrowed time, and I've never lied to you about it, have I?"

"No." Juliet looked deflated. For a nanosecond Helle almost fell sorry for her—almost. Then Juliet tossed her head, giving Helle a challenging look. "I'm glad you found her. Once it sinks in that the reality of her is nowhere close to the idealised picture you've been carrying about for the last three thousand years, I'll be here for you, waiting."

Bitch! "In which case you'll spend the rest of your life waiting!" Helle curled her fingers, pretending they were talons and the sofa cushion Juliet's perfect complexion.

"Really?" Juliet laughed. "Look at me, then look at yourself. This is a contest that's over before it begins. He's mine. He's just too besotted to realise that—yet."

Jason rose, pulling Helle to her feet with him. "You're deluding yourself. Now that I've found her, I will never leave her. Never."

"Unless Woolf kills you," Juliet said cruelly. "Or her." Her beautiful face set in a scowl. "She should be with him—she was supposed to be his."

Jason tightened his hold on Helle. "Not true. I saw her first." He propelled Helle towards the door.

"Don't leave!" Juliet beat them to the hall, standing herself in front of the coat rack. "Jason, you can't just walk out like this."

"There's nothing left to say, is there?" Jason sounded tense. "You hope for more than you will ever get."

"So now you've found her you'll just toss me on the garbage heap?" Juliet made a grab for him. "I can make you happy, Jason. You know I can."

Jason disengaged her hands from his shirt. "Stop this," he

said in a low voice. "Don't ruin things completely."

"Ruin things? She's the one ruining things, not me!" Juliet's eyes filled with tears. "I deserve more than this. Life after life, I've stood by you, comforted you when needed it. Life after life, you've left me to face old age alone, always so eager to go on to a new life, a new existence with her, not me."

Put like that, it did make him sound like a major asshole. Helle slid him a look, all of her churning with guilt for his stunted lives, his constant wandering through time. Like Ahasverus, she thought, recalling her mother's story about the Wandering Jew, condemned to walk this earth until the Second Coming. And Juliet had become trapped in his wake, pulled along from life to life, just as stunted and as unfulfilled, because she wanted his heart when he could only offer affection.

When Jason made as if to take his coat, Juliet threw her arms around his neck, wailing his name. Helle ducked behind them, got hold of her leather jacket and escaped outside. She didn't want to witness this. She stood in the darkness of Juliet's little garden, hearing her plead with Jason not to leave. His voice was lower, more controlled.

"If you leave now don't bother to come back!" Juliet shrieked just as Jason stepped outside. "You walk out on me now, Jason Morris, and you'll never see me again."

The light from the lamp above the door illuminated his haggard expression. It made Helle want to scratch his eyes out—and Juliet's.

Chapter 34

It was too late to drive back to London, so Jason called ahead and found them a hotel in Winchester on the quaintly named Paternoster Row. The bored receptionist perked up at the sight of Jason's Platinum card, and ten minutes later they were ushered into one of the suites.

"Hungry?" Jason asked, flipping through the room service menu.

"Tired." She shrugged out of her clothes and wrapped herself in the complimentary bathrobe.

"You have to eat something." He picked up the phone and ordered salads and steaks. "Twenty minutes," he said when he hung up. "Enough time for a shower." He held out his hand to her.

Helle switched on the TV. "I'll just sit here."

Jason joined her on the bed. "Are you mad?"

"Mad? I'm emotionally drained. After all, your girlfriend through time has apparently been conspiring with Woolf—"

"She said she hadn't, that she refused."

"What else could she say?" Helle scowled. "And then there's all the crap about her being much better for you than I am, and how quickly you'll tire of me. Putting it mildly, that's not stuff that's fun to hear, but I guess I should be grateful she didn't give us a blow-by-blow account of your hot and oh, so satisfactory sex life." This is when he should have said something along the lines of nothing being comparable to what he had with her, but instead Jason remained silent, leaning against the headboard with a distant look on his face.

"You're such a goose at times," he said after a while. He leaned over to ruffle her hair, and she was stung by the gesture, reduced to a small child rather than a desirable woman.

"Sorry to be a disappointment," she replied, pulling away

from his touch. "Weren't you going to take a shower?"

"Helle," he sighed. She kept her eyes on the TV. With a muttered comment about stubborn women, Jason disappeared into the bathroom.

They ate in silence. Helle made a point of stacking all the spinach leaves to the side, wishing there'd been fries to go with the steak instead. Jason drank steadily of the wine, now and then regarding her over the rim of his glass. She toyed with her discarded salad.

"Eat it, it's good for you." He sounded stern. She made a face, and he leaned over the table, forked up a sizeable amount of spinach and held it to her mouth. "You need your strength, lioness."

"Huh." But she opened her mouth.

"And just so you know, nothing Juliet and I had together compares to what we have. It's like comparing a guttering candle to a lightning-storm." He smiled at her. "Which is why you must eat your spinach." He presented her with another forkful. "And as to what Juliet said, she's entitled to be bitter. She hoped that one day I'd outgrow you, instead..." He shrugged. "I suppose I'm genetically programmed to love you—only you."

"Sounds pretty awful," Helle said.

"Not anymore." He cleared away their plates, returning them to the trolley, and fiddled for some time with his laptop. Pink's distinctive voice flooded the room.

"Dance?" he asked. They danced close together, the music changed, they danced some more, but at some point they stopped moving. He tilted her chin up and kissed her. There was no urgency, none of his normal heated passion. This was an innocent kiss, sweet and soft.

"The first time I kissed you was in an orchard." His lips brushed over her brow, her nose. "You tasted of apples and almonds." This time, his mouth covered hers, a flicker of tongue teasing her lower lip. "Now you taste of spinach and wine." His hands closed on hers, fingers insisting until she linked hers with his. "The first time we made love, you undressed yourself and I didn't know what to do." He took a couple of steps backwards, until their arms were stretched between them.

"Now why do I find that hard to believe?" she asked, basking in the look he gave her. Jason laughed.

"Not like that, I was no stranger to the pleasures of the flesh. But with you..." He leaned forward, placing a tender kiss on her cheek. "With you it was love, and I was as innocent as you when it came to that, had no idea what to do with the fire that was burning through my loins, searing my heart."

He took hold of the lapels of her terry cloth robe, sliding it off her shoulders to land with a soft sigh on the floor.

"You, on the other hand, acted on instinct alone. And it was perfect." He cupped one of her breasts. "You smelled of olive oil and rosemary, and when I undid your hair, it stood like a halo round your head, backlit by the setting sun." Soft lips on her nipple, and Helle strained towards him. The back of his hand brushed her pubic mound.

"Sometimes, the simple ways are the best," he murmured, and she couldn't agree more. Not when he lifted her onto the bed and lay down beside her. Not when he kissed each of her fingers, not when she tasted his lips. Side by side, her leg hooked over his hip, he loved her slowly, gently. He rolled them over, so that he was on top, and he came and went, came and went, his eyes never leaving hers.

This was no earth-shattering climax, this was a joyful but quiet joining, a coming together that ended with a suppressed gasp as heat flooded her womb. He enfolded her in his presence, and she never wanted to leave the cocoon of love and warmth he spun around them both.

Helle woke to a day that was bathed in foggy sunshine. Jason was already at his laptop, but he'd pulled back the curtains, allowing her a fantastic view of Winchester Cathedral. The old stone construction was a pleasing muted grey, and looked as if it had permanently rooted itself where it stood. To some extent, she supposed it had—according to Jason, there'd been a church here for well over a thousand years.

She turned her attention to the inside view instead. Jason

had worked out, his hair still damp from his shower, his skin glowing. His gym bag was thrown in a corner, he'd toed off his sneakers halfway to the bathroom, and now he was sitting in only his underwear, long legs extended before him. To her biased eyes he looked edible, all the way from his broad shoulders through his tight abs to his muscled thighs.

"…right. No, on Monday. Keep it in your safe until then." Jason listened, fingers flying over his keyboard. Helle went over to stand behind him, slipping her arms round his neck while resting her cheek against his hair. He covered her hands with his and craned his head back, lips puckered. She kissed them, making him smile. "Absolutely. Yes… I know, not exactly choir boy material, is he?" He frowned. "No, you're right, it's not funny… Yes, she's here… Of course… yes, you too. Talk to you on Monday." He disconnected. "It's set in motion. Curtis will deliver the hard drive to his mate on Monday."

"Great." She didn't want to talk about Woolf. Helle slid onto his lap. "How about some sightseeing before we drive back?"

"Here?" Jason sounded hesitant.

"You don't like Winchester?"

He glanced in the direction of the cathedral. "I lived here once. One of the unhappy lives."

"Oh?"

He deposited her on the floor. "Get dressed. I'll tell you the whole story once we're outside."

Jason put his arm round her shoulders, and she encircled his waist as they walked slowly along the old streets of central Winchester. The city was empty: it was too early to draw the tourist crowds, too late for those who had regular jobs to go to. They wandered onto the green that surrounded the cathedral, and Jason drew them to a stop, gazing upwards.

"In 1290, Edward I issued the edict expelling all Jews from England," he began. "No longer content with taxing them to death, he wanted them out of the country, gone. I turned six that year, and as my father had recently died, there was only me and my mother." He gestured to the south of the cathedral. "We lived over there. My mother was a seamstress. The summer of 1290, she fell ill, and accordingly, our taxes went unpaid. When the edict was proclaimed in July, she was being held in prison for unpaid debts. Me she had entrusted to an old priest, but when they came to fetch me to take me and her down to Southampton and a waiting ship, he denied I was her son, insisting the Jewess was lying, so eager was she to get her hands on a Christian boy."

"Didn't you protest?"

"I tried. He beat me senseless for doing so." Jason rubbed at his shoulder, eyes lost in the pale sky above. "He insisted he was doing it for my own good, a child as young as I could still be saved by embracing Christianity." Jason kicked at the ground. "Some months later, I was baptised, the obstinate Jew forever driven from my soul by his repeated beatings."

"And your mother?"

Jason threw out his hands. "I have no idea. Anyway," he continued, "the priest then turned me over to a Cistercian monk, and by All Hallows I was living in Netley Abbey— down near Southampton Water." He gestured to the southwest.

Helle had never heard of Cistercian monks. Jason gave her a brief description of a life devoted to hard manual work and regular services, of monks swishing down the stairs from the dormitory in the middle of the night for matins, their distinctive white robes visible in the dark.

"Were they mean to you?" she asked.

"For being Jewish? No. They were kinder than the priest and raised me with love and care. Their own little convert." His face darkened. "They had more problems when I started recalling my other lives, when I started screaming for you in a foreign language."

Poor, vulnerable boy, Helle thought, filled with sadness for him.

"So what happened?"

Jason took her hand, playing with her fingers. "The abbot was a wise man. He had me moved into a cell away from the others, and he sat with me through the nights as my dreams hardened into memories, as I understood the purpose of my existence. To find you again." He kissed her ring finger and dropped her hand, wrapping his arm around her shoulder instead. He stood staring up at the huge window that decorated the cathedral's western facade, a weak sun gilding his pale skin.

"Father Adrian listened in horror to my story. If I was speaking the truth, the whole foundation of the Church was false."

Helle had to think about that. Of course, she nodded, understanding dawning: if you could travel on, Heaven and Hell were not quite as final as destinations.

"He should have turned me over to his superiors, but he was a man of compassion, and he pitied me, this orphaned confused boy, burdened by memories from too many lives. So instead, we spent hours alone, he and I, talking about God's greatness, and how this one certainty could be reconciled with what I remembered." He pulled them down onto a bench, his eyes still on the church. Helle nestled into him, cold in her short leather jacket when the sun disappeared in a cloud bank.

"After much debate, we agreed there was no conflict between my story and believing in the one God. It was just that in some cases, God gave us more lives to muddle through before calling us home." He fell silent, and she pillowed her head on his chest, lulled by the sound of his steady heartbeat.

"We didn't tell anyone," he said after a while. "We both knew our compromise wouldn't be respected elsewhere. And Father Adrian swore me to silence, describing in detail how I would die should I ever be unwise enough to tell anyone else my memories." His voice was harsh, the hand on his thigh tightening into a fist.

"How old were you?" she asked.

"Thirteen."

A child, a child with no roots and no home.

"I was sixteen when I discovered my fire gift. I didn't tell anyone about that."

Very smart choice, in Helle's opinion. "So," she said, more to change the subject than anything else, "you believe in God."

"Of course," Jason sounded astounded. "Don't you?"

366

"I'm not sure," she hedged. "I don't really buy into the idea of a white-bearded benign god."

"I don't either," Jason assured her, laughing. In a more serious tone, he continued, "God gives us the two things that define us as humans: our sense of right and wrong and our free choice. After that it is up to us to listen to or ignore the voice of our conscience. He is there to help if we should need it, and He very often does." He fell silent, staring off into space. "And some of us, as I said before, just get some more lives to work it all out."

She liked that. She could believe in that.

Chapter 35

They were in the car when Nigel rang. His voice echoed over the car's loudspeaker system and it didn't take a genius to gather Nigel was upset.

"Where are you?" he demanded, with no greeting whatsoever. Jason raised his brows: he knew for a fact Nigel had GPS tracking on the Aston Martin.

"Making our way out of Winchester."

"So's he," Nigel said. "That Sam Woolf, he's just outside Winchester."

"He is?" Jason strove to sound calm, but tightened his hands on the steering wheel.

"It's her," Nigel continued. "Juliet has been in contact with him."

"What?" Helle exclaimed.

"How do you know?" Jason asked

"How? I monitor his phone, remember? She's setting you up, Jason, I'm telling you—"

"Don't be ridiculous," Jason cut him off. "She doesn't even know we're here."

"No? So what did you text her about this morning?"

Jason cursed silently, all too aware of Helle's eyes on his face.

"I was just checking up on her," he said. "She was pretty torn up last night."

Nigel emitted a sound that resembled a honk. "For your information, Juliet just told Woolf you're in Hampshire—and that she will lead him to you."

There was a sharp inbreath to his left. He slid Helle a look. She was clutching her seatbelt, staring straight ahead.

"Seeing as she doesn't know where we are, that will be difficult for her to do," Jason replied calmly. Would Juliet do this to him? No, he couldn't get his head round it. No matter how jealous, she'd know he would never forgive her if she helped Woolf abduct his Helle.

"Keep it that way." Nigel rang off. An uncomfortable silence settled in the car. Jason shifted in his seat, pretending great concentration on the road.

"I was only making sure she was all right," he said at long last, hearing how defensive he sounded. No response. Jason sighed—loudly. It was something of a relief when the phone rang again, even if Helle scowled at the displayed name.

Jason would have preferred to disconnect the hands-free, but wisely decided not to.

"Jason? Is that you Jason?" Juliet's voice came over loud and sharp, making Helle wince.

"Hi, Juliet." He lowered the volume a tad.

"Listen, Jason, I'm going to take care of things." Juliet hiccupped. "Oh, yes, I'm taking care of them." She giggled. "I have my shotgun with me. He won't know what hit him."

"What exactly are you talking about?" Jason asked, sharing a quick look with Helle.

"Samion. Or Sam Woolf, as he calls himself these days." Yet another giggle. "I've baited the trap with something he can't resist. You."

"Is she drunk?" Helle asked in an undertone. Juliet kept on talking, rambling incoherently about Woolf and how she'd told him Jason was taking Helle down memory lane.

"I told him you were going to Netley Abbey." She laughed out loud. "Guess we'll see how well those protective spells work, right?"

"Damn!" Jason banged his hand against the steering wheel. Helle looked confused, but there was no time to explain. "Juliet, stop this." Jason injected his voice with as much authority as he could muster. "You will not go down to Netley Abbey, you hear?"

"For you, J'son, for you." She slurred her words. "Bang, bang, he's dead." A high-pitched giggle, and the line went dead.

Jason did a U-turn, throwing Helle back into her seat.

"What are you doing?"

"I have to stop her!" He pressed the accelerator to the

floor, and the engine roared in response. "She can't take Woolf on by herself—not even at Netley Abbey."

"What if it's all a ruse?" Helle demanded, gripping her seat. "Maybe she knew this was exactly how you would react."

"Not a chance I'm willing to take," he retorted, ignoring the hurt look on her face. He swung up onto the M3, heading due south.

"Maybe I am," she muttered.

She broke the silence first. "Why Netley Abbey? Does it have some significance to Woolf?"

"No." He sped past a number of cars. "But I told Juliet about the protective measures Father Adrian took."

"What measures?"

"Father Adrian was a man who believed in hedging his bets." He smiled at the memory of the monk, bright blue eyes and hair as white as cotton wool—well, what little he had left, what with the tonsure and old age. "When I told him chances were Samion could be around, he consulted some ancient tomes about rituals to keep evil at bay and attempted to create a protective circle round the cloisters." He glanced at her. "He might have wanted to keep you out as well, should you pop up. Father Adrian was a firm believer in women being temptresses."

"I'll not hold it against him," she said. "So do you think his magical stuff works?"

"To a point." Jason increased the speed. "But not enough to protect Juliet should Woolf go after her."

They were just turning into the last stretch off the A27, following the road leading to Netley, when Nigel called again.

"Juliet's phone just went dead," he said.

"Dead?" Jason kept his eyes on the approaching ruins, visible beyond the screen of trees. A sharp turn to the right, and he parked the car alongside two others. No red BMW in sight.

"The signal stopped." There was the sound of fingers on a keyboard. "Either she switched it off, or—"

"Her car isn't here." Jason said. "I'll go have a look." He

disconnected and scrambled out of the car. Helle followed suit. They jogged in the directions of the ruins, a sad collection of stones that bore little resemblance to the monastery Jason remembered. The once thriving religious community reduced to rubble and masonry, he reflected, hastening towards what remained of the central church. No Juliet. No distinctive red car in the other parking lot. Only an elderly couple contemplating the reredorter, and further away a lady with a camera.

"She isn't here." Jason did a half-turn, scanning the rocks, the trees, for anything resembling Juliet's willowy shape.

"Maybe she ran out of battery." Helle stuck her hands into her pockets. "Charging her phone was probably not top of her priority-list last night."

"No," he agreed, feeling a wave of relief sweep through him. Perhaps she'd come to her senses and pulled over somewhere, was sleeping off the drink with her shotgun cradled to her chest. It made him smile; knowing Juliet, she was probably dressed to match, in a waxed jacket and tight trousers.

Helle took hold of his arm. "We should get going, before Woolf gets here."

He nodded distractedly. There were three cars in the parking lot—and one motorbike, standing well to the side. The elderly couple probably belonged with the Audi, the camera lady with the Toyota, and the motorbike? Jason scanned the ruins yet again. He put a protective arm round Helle's shoulders, hastening them back towards the Aston Martin.

Jason's phone buzzed.

"Yes?" he barked.

"There's been an accident," Nigel said. "A mile or so from where you are." He swallowed audibly. "It's a red BMW and it's on fire."

Helle did not need to hear the conversation to understand the news was bad. Jason swayed, his face drained of blood.

"What?" she asked, jogging to keep up as he made for the car.

"Juliet," he said, "she's—" Whatever else he'd been about to say was drowned in his exclamation. There, standing just in front of the copse of trees was Sam Woolf. He straightened up, all black clothes, black hair. Menace rippled from him, wisps of dark smoke swirling around him. An apparition, she thought, a vibrating collection of evil and darkness, out of place in a spot so filled with peace and quiet. The ruins glowed golden in the January sun, there were even a couple of snowdrops peeping out of the ground. White, fragile blooms that were brutally trampled by Woolf's heavy boots.

Up closer, she realised he was covered in soot. A distinctive stench of singed leather and hair made her want to hold her breath. He came towards them in unhurried strides. Beside her, Jason stiffened.

"Let's go," Helle suggested, trying to move Jason in the direction of his Aston Martin. He didn't budge, eyes never leaving Woolf.

"Greetings from your dark-haired bitch," Woolf said. "She didn't quite expect me to be waiting for her where I was."

"What have you done to her?" Jason demanded, his voice hoarse.

"Done?" Woolf wiped his gloved hands down his dirty motorcycle leathers. "Death by fire, Wanderer—something you're more than acquainted with, aren't you?"

What? Helle's knees sagged. Juliet was dead? Jason reeled, bumping into Helle who staggered under his weight.

"May you rot in hell!" Jason regained his balance, planting himself slightly in front of Helle.

"Tit for tat," Woolf snarled. "She had it coming, after what she did to me last time we met—even more when she tried to set me up, the stupid bitch." Woolf advanced. Jason grabbed Helle's arm and pulled her with him, towards the ruins. Woolf sneered and raised his arm. It was like being struck full in the chest by a battering ram. Helle wheezed and staggered, clutching at Jason's hand. Woolf laughed, a sound that sent icy fingers down Helle's spine. Power and smoke leaked from Woolf's every pore, and when he raised his arm again, Jason doubled over, clutching at his stomach, while Helle was flung to the ground. She scrambled back to her feet, digging in her pocket for her phone. They needed help.

Jason retreated, with Woolf following, arms slightly spread. Waves of smoke drifted round him, shrouding him in fog. Jason extended his hand, and a sudden burst of heat had Woolf's hair bursting into flames. He grunted and clapped a hand to his head. The men circled each other, primitive alpha-males preparing to fight to the death. Jason bared his teeth, his eyes glowing like pools of fire. Woolf's hands curled, fingers like claws. The ground between them shook, and way up high, the sun scurried away to hide in a bank of clouds.

Helle found her phone. Woolf's voice was back in her head, snarling at her not to touch it. She tried all the same, and Woolf wheeled in her direction, flinging out his arm. Helle was hurled backwards, landing on her back, all air knocked out of her. She heard Jason call her name, wanted to tell him she was okay, but she had problems moving, problems thinking, her entire brain fogged by thick black smoke.

Somehow, she got to her knees, shaking her head free of dark cobwebs. She needed a weapon, and her fingers closed on a largish stone. Several yards away, Jason was standing in a weak ray of reappearing sun. Woolf had stopped, arms extended as he touched an invisible barrier of sorts.

"Evil may not enter," Jason said, holding up his hands. His fingers dripped fire, miniature sparks that hissed when they hit the damp grass.

"What, you think the protective spells of an old monk will help you?" Woolf laughed. "Oh, yes, Juliet told me about that fool of a monk." He leaned towards Jason. "One of those lives when you ended up at the stake, wasn't it?" He took a decisive step towards Jason, but it was as if he'd slammed into a wall. Yes! Helle rose, ignoring the resulting dizziness. If only she could get to Jason's side, they'd be safe. She edged towards him, just as Woolf slammed into the invisible wall a second time, this time with such force he was propelled backwards a couple of steps.

Jason closed his eyes and extended his hands, the tendons in his neck straining. His nostrils dilated and when he opened his eyes, they blazed with fire—as did the grass at Woolf's feet. A ring of flames, and Jason's face was rigid, eyes never leaving

373

the dark shape that was Woolf. Helle tried to close her mouth. She'd ended up in a crouch, still clutching her ridiculous piece of rock, transfixed by the horrifying beauty of Jason's gift, by how Woolf twisted inside the shrinking ring of fire.

Woolf laughed. "Oh no. Not this time. This time I am not a bleeding wreck, incapable of fleeing your fires." With the grace of a buck, he leapt, all but his boots clearing the imprisoning flames. He landed a couple of yards from Helle. "Evil may not enter, you say?" He pulled something out of his jacket. "But will it stop a bullet, I wonder?"

It took her a moment to register what was happening. Woolf's gloved hand closed round the butt of his pistol, his arm moved in slow motion, lifting the gun until it aimed straight at Jason. Woolf widened his stance. His finger closed on the trigger.

"No!" Helle launched herself, screaming Jason's name. A soft pop. Jason's arms flew wide, the fires instantaneously quenched. Helle crashed into Woolf. Yet another pop, and Jason crumpled to the ground. Helle brought the stone down on Woolf's head. He staggered, tried to push her away, but she screamed, smashing the rock into his face.

He fell, she landed on top. Red invaded her brain. Kill, kill, kill…Something crunched, Woolf's voice rose in pain. Blood spattered her hand. Kill, kill, kill…Up went the rock, down it crashed, and the body beneath her jerked. She clawed his face and bared her teeth. She was going to rip his windpipe out. She howled, raised the bloodied stone to the sky, and Woolf slumped, a deadweight that didn't move, did not even seem to breathe.

"Helle."

It was no more than a whisper, but the sound of his voice was sufficient to tear through the veils of red ire.

"Jason?" She crawled towards him. Why was he still lying on the ground, and what was that wet stain on his front? Oh, God! Helle gulped. She could hear his breath whistle its way in and out, and his chest shuddered with each rasping lungful of air. There was too much blood; red tendrils snaking from his nose, dark as it soaked through his sweater, sticky in his hair.

She crawled towards her dropped phone, her fingers clumsy and fat on the display. Three numbers, no more, and then there was someone on the other side, a calm voice that reassured her help was on its way, someone else had already called in.

Helle put her hand on his forehead, and the skin was cold and clammy. At a remove, she heard the sound of other people, but she couldn't tear her eyes away from his face. His eyes flew open, pools of gold that tried to focus.

"Helle," his voice was barely audible. "My Helle." He tried to smile, his hand moving erratically, and she took it, raising it to her mouth. "I found you," he whispered. "I found you and held you one more time."

No, no, no! She wanted to yell at him not to say things like that. He closed his eyes, a small bubble of bloody saliva appearing on his lips. The bubble grew and contracted with every breath, and she watched it, mesmerised. A hand on her shoulder, and the elderly lady she'd seen in the distance lowered herself carefully to her knees beside her.

"He's still alive," she said, giving Helle an encouraging pat. "Let's make sure he stays that way." She took off her coat, gestured for Helle to do the same. Helle tucked Jason in, her hand caressing his wan face. The warmth of his breath tickled her palm. He was still alive, still struggling.

Once she had dreamed of a man, waking up with tears on her cheeks because he was dead and so was she and she would never, ever see him again. One day that man walked into her life, and he was warm and alive and her heart leaped with joy. And now he lay bleeding in front of her, already slipping out of her grasp, and she knew that she would never, ever see him again if she let him go.

Helle took a determined breath. "What do I do?" she asked the woman kneeling beside her.

"You breathe for him," she said. "It's oxygen he needs."

So Helle did, filling her lung with air and covering his bloodied lips with hers as she blew precious air into his lungs. Live, she told him silently, live for me, for us. His chest rose and fell, the woman beside her had her hand on his wrist, assuring her she could still feel a pulse, but his eyes narrowed into slivers of gold, his broken body lying still and pale on the wintry grass.

She heard the sirens but did not stop what she was doing. Not until a young paramedic fell to her knees beside her.

"We'll take over now," she said. Helle blinked and shook her head. She had to… His bloodied lips, his lungs, he needed air, goddamn it!

"Miss?" Someone disengaged her hands from Jason, and she choked back a sob as she was helped to stand. She licked her lips. They tasted of him, of his blood. Someone wrapped her in a blanket, while on the ground two people busied themselves with Jason. His arms lay wide open, hands inert and still. Dark lashes shadowed cheeks so pale it looked as if someone had chalked them. Oh God: Helle stuffed a fist in her mouth. If he died…

"Where's the other bloke?" someone asked. "They said two men down, not one."

Helle's undivided focus on Jason wavered and she glanced in the direction of Woolf. Except he wasn't there. The grass was flattened, as if the bastard had dragged himself away, leaving nothing but the gun behind. How he had managed to move was a mystery: the damned man had been lifeless. Helle studied her hand, staring down at the blood that caked it, rimmed the nails. Some of it was Woolf's, most of it was Jason's. If he dies, she vowed silently, if my Jason doesn't survive, neither will Sam Woolf.

A policeman was asking her questions, and she answered as well as she could, her gaze never shifting from where the paramedic was leaning over Jason.

"Look, I have to," she interrupted the policeman, gesturing at Jason. "I…"

"By all means," the policeman said, standing aside to allow her to kneel beside Jason. She carefully smoothed the hair that was stuck to his forehead off his face, she traced his ear, ran a trembling finger over his mouth. Would she ever see it smile again? Feel it move against her lips? She set the back of her hand against his cheek, and it was still warm. He was still alive.

They loaded Jason into the ambulance. Helle scrambled in behind him, wedging herself into the narrow space by his side. She took his hand. The female paramedic gave her an encouraging smile.

"A bullet through the lung is not fatal—not when you're young and strong." Her face fell somewhat. "Let's hope the shot to his head has not done any permanent damage."

"He has a bullet in his head?" She hiccupped. People died with bullets in their head.

"It doesn't seem so. But he's badly wounded all the same."

Helle chose to ignore her last remark. Instead, she kneaded his warm if unresponsive hand between hers, silently repeating 'He is strong, he will live,' like a mantra. When they arrived at the hospital, she squeezed his hand. He squeezed back, and for a moment she imagined she saw a glimmer of his eyes underneath his lashes—a moment, no more.

And then he was gone, rushed inside by the medical team, and Helle wanted to go with them, but the door swung shut in her face. She clutched at herself. Keep it together, Helle. Don't give in to the desire to scream and cry, because if you do, you'll not be able to stop.

They'd taken her Jason, they'd carried him away, immobile and pale. Helle staggered away from the door. A weak sun in a wintry sky, tufts of white clouds adorning an endless, chilly blue. She raised her eyes to the sky and shook her dirty, sore fist at it.

"Not fair," she yelled, not caring that there were people in the car park. He couldn't die, not now, when she'd found him, after years and years without him. No. Please, no. Her legs gave way, she sank down, and it was cold and wet, but she didn't care. Sun caught her ring, set the ruby on fire. His ring, his fire. "He will live," she mumbled. He had to. A shadow fell over her.

"Are you all right?"

All right? Helle strangled a guffaw. She squinted up at the person. With an effort she got to her feet.

"He will live," she told the stranger, before squaring her shoulders and making for the hospital entrance. Jason needed her—and she needed Jason.

"Jason," she said, her voice hollow. "Will we never see each other again if we die?" He looked down at her with all his fourteen-year-old

wisdom and tweaked her cheek.

"Of course we will. People like us never die, we just go on."
He pointed at the evening star, barely visible over the horizon. "She
reappears every night, and so will you and I. We will wander through
each other's lives forever and ever."

"But we won't die yet," she stated, smiling up at him.

"No," he replied, a teasing tone to his voice. "We have to marry,
have many babies and grow very old first. Then we die." She nodded,
satisfied. He smiled at her and took her hand, waiting patiently while
she undid first one sandal, then the other, with her other hand. She
started to run and they flew through the darkening evening, their
laughter bouncing off the surrounding cliffs. The lions came, closing
in around them, and they ran, their bodies golden and alive, into the
setting sun.

Want to find out what happens next?

Keep an eye out for **SMOKE IN HER EYES**

Chapter 1

She'd nearly killed him. Bitch! Sam Woolf took the opportunity offered by all the hubbub around the accursed Wanderer to drag himself out of sight behind a tangle of brambles. She'd clawed at him, bit him, bashed him over the head with that fucking rock she'd been holding, as ferocious as a lioness in the protection of what was hers. Admirable, he supposed, but his insides twisted with corroding jealousy. He should be the one she defended. He should be the one she hastened to please and serve, not that damned Jason. Sam breathed through his mouth, running a careful hand over his limbs, his head. His healing powers were impressive, but these wounds required more than his touch, and damn it, he suspected his left arm was broken. He found his phone, scrolled down and made one call.

"Pick me up," he said, giving brief directions to the ruined abbey visible through the screen of branches. "Make it fast."

Using what little he had left of his powers to wipe away any evidence of his presence left him so drained it required a huge effort of will just to breathe. Some moments of rest and he'd recovered sufficiently to half-crawl, half-drag himself deeper into the trees. Only when he reached the empty car park did he discover he had dropped the gun.

Helle Madsen was dirty, covered in blood and couldn't give a shit. All she could think about was Jason, a silent prayer that he would live echoing in her head. She glanced at a clock, noting with some surprise it was two o'clock. Five hours since she'd sat snuggled in his lap, only two hours since they'd left Winchester. Now they were here, at Southampton General Hospital, and Jason was in surgery, while she could do nothing but wait. And wait.

Two bullets, one to the side of his head, the other lodged somewhere in his ribcage. Helle pulled the blanket she'd been given closer round her shoulders. Not that it helped. The seeping chill invading her limbs came from within, her mind's eye frozen on the image of Jason, so pale and still as they transferred him from the stretcher to the bed.

"Relative of Jason Morris?" A nurse stood in the door to the waiting room. Helle got to her feet and nodded. The nurse's eyes widened. "Well, love, you look a bit of a mess, don't you?"

"I guess." She followed the nurse to the station, filled out the forms she was handed, fumbled as she pulled out Jason's driver's licence from his wallet. His face, staring up at him from the license…A sob tore her throat. Oh, God—if she started to cry, she wouldn't be able to stop. Helle took a breath, sank her nails into her palms and willed back the tears.

"Here." The nurse set down a mug of steaming tea. "Always helps, I find." She squinted down at the forms. "So you're the fiancée. No other relatives?"

"He has an uncle up in Warwick—but he's infirm. And then there's an aunt…" Helle didn't finish, ashamed of the jealousy the thought of Juliet woke in her. After all, Juliet was much more than an aunt; she'd been Jason's companion through multiple lives. "Her name is Juliet Morris, but I think she's dead."

"Think?"

"There was an accident earlier. A car fire." An image of Juliet, all dark glossy hair and impeccable clothing, rose before her. To imagine that sleek beauty burned to death…Helle shivered. Damn Sam Woolf! Just thinking his name made her hands close into fists. The man who'd set Juliet's car alight, who'd shot Jason, and no matter that the police had searched the area, they hadn't found as much as a trace of him. She rubbed at her face. The scent of blood on her hands made her stomach heave. His blood—Woolf's blood. She'd thought she'd killed him, so how come he'd got away—again?

"…here," the nurse said.

"What?" Helle blinked. "I'm sorry, I was thinking about…"

"No need to apologise." A warm hand covered her own. "I was just saying, that aunt of his is here. Juliet Morris came in an hour ago. Awful coincidence, two accidents in the same family." The nurse gave her a kindly smile. "I suppose that leaves you to look in on them both, right?"

"Umm…" Helle decided to go for vague. She had no intention of sitting at Juliet's bedside—and she was quite certain Juliet would hate to have her there.

She shuffled back to the waiting room, feeling cold, hungry and scared—not necessarily in that order. She took a seat in a corner, far enough from the other three people there to be left alone. Tears stung her eyes, clogged her throat, but she had promised herself she wouldn't cry, not until Jason was out of danger.

Her phone buzzed. Nigel.

WTF is happening?

Well, no one could accuse him of not being to the point. Helle replied just as tersely.

J shot, in S-hampton hosp. SW gone missing.

It took him exactly three seconds to reply.

Coming.

She couldn't exactly tell him not to—Jason's best friend loved her man almost as much as she did. Besides, the thought of having Nigel here was comforting.

Helle closed her eyes and her mind swam with images of Jason. Of him laughing, sleeping, running on a treadmill, unbuttoning his shirt. Jason cooking, leaning over his laptop. Jason with his mane of hair, wearing a linen tunic, his cloak fastened at his shoulder by a large bronze pin. Jason, as he was now—images that were crisp and clear. Jason, as he'd been then, in their first life over three thousand years ago. These images were fuzzy round the edges, sometimes nothing more than an outline of a young man with glorious dark-red hair and eyes the colour of amber.

She buried her face in her arms. Five months ago, she'd been normal—well, relatively—Helle Madsen, an up-and-coming financial professional. Since then she'd been redefined as a reincarnated soul, a woman with very, very many lives in her past—lives she could not remember, thankfully. Even that first life was no more than fragments of memory, little shards of an entire life that now and then blinked through her brain, brought to life by Jason's reappearance in her world.

Jason. She muffled a sigh. Her eternal torch-bearer, the man who had been driven by guilt to go after her in life after life, hoping for one opportunity for redemption. And now, when she and Jason had finally ended up in the same timeframe, that damned Sam Woolf, former Prince of Kolchis, had to show up as well. God had a very odd sense of humour. Or maybe it was the Fates, fickle spinners of destiny, who had decided that it would be good to throw all three of them together again. And look how great that had turned out... Curse Woolf to hell and back!

The sound of someone clearing their throat had her looking up to find a policeman standing in front of her.

"Miss Madsen?" The policeman gave her a hesitant smile. "I'm sorry, miss, but I need a statement."

"Now?"

He held out his arms in an apologetic gesture before firing off his questions. Yes, she'd recognised the assailant, no, she had no idea why he'd shot Jason—she had to break off here, take a couple of deep breaths. No, she hadn't known Woolf had a gun. Yes, she was sure he was injured.

"How?" the policeman asked.

"I hit him." She studied her bruised and bloodied hands. "I had to."

The policeman tucked away his notepad, told her that was all for now, and left. Helle closed her eyes and rested her head against the wall.

She was still sitting in her corner, huddled under her blanket, when Nigel entered the room three hours later. So far, the only news she'd had was that the doctors were still working on

Jason, and that she should just sit down and wait, they'd let her know if anything happened.

"Hey, Lion-tamer," Nigel said, bumping her lightly on the arm. Helle lifted her head from her arms. He crouched, his face on level with hers. "You all right?"

Helle shook her head but bit her lip. Don't cry, don't cry. He pulled her into an embrace—surprisingly strong, given just how spindly his arms were, how narrow his torso. Her cheek ended up pressed to all his necklaces, an assortment of amulets and religious symbols that had Jason calling him an ecumenical Christmas tree.

"I brought your mum," Nigel said, releasing her. He rubbed his thumb over something on her cheek, causing the multiple bracelets on his arm to jangle. "And you need to wash." He gave her a little smile, his dark eyes soft with concern.

"I can't leave. What if they come in and—"

"I'll fetch you." He lifted her to her feet. "Go on, there's your mother. She'll help you."

Mum was standing in the doorway, her brown hair swept off her face and twisted into a messy bun. She opened her arms and Helle fell into them. This time she did cry, if only a little.

In clean clothes, with newly scrubbed hands and face, she returned to the waiting room just as the doctor came looking for her.

"He's out of surgery." The doctor undid his gown as he spoke. "The injury to his chest is minor and will heal—the lung was punctured, but we have that under control." He fell silent.

"But…" Helle prompted, glad to have Mum on one side, Nigel on the other.

"The shot to his head is another matter. While the bullet did not penetrate, there's been substantial bleeding and there's a largish bone splinter we daren't extract." He gave her a helpless look. "There may be damage, but we won't know until he wakes up. For now, we've performed a craniotomy…" he paused. "We've sawed a small hole in his skull," he explained.

"What?" Helle gasped.

"Normal procedure," Nigel assured her. "To relieve pressure when the brain swells."

"Precisely." The doctor gave him a grateful look and directed the rest of his little speech to Nigel, man to man. All Helle understood was that they didn't know what the permanent injuries might be.

About the Author

Had Anna been allowed to choose, she'd have become a time-traveller. As this was impossible, she became a financial professional with three absorbing interests: history, love stories and writing.

Anna has authored the acclaimed time travelling series The Graham Saga, set in 17th century Scotland and Maryland, as well as the equally acclaimed medieval series The King's Greatest Enemy which is set in 14th century England. (Medieval knight was also high on Anna's list of potential professions. Yet another disappointment…)

With Jason and Helle, Anna has stepped out of her historical comfort zone and has loved doing so. She hopes her readers will love it too.

Find out more about Anna by visiting her website,
www.annabelfrage.com

or her Amazon page,
http://Author.to/ABG